CROSSING
THE COLOR LINE

CROSSING
THE COLOR LINE

Readings in Black and White

EDITED BY

Suzanne W. Jones

UNIVERSITY OF SOUTH CAROLINA PRESS

© 2000 University of South Carolina

Published in Columbia, South Carolina, by the
University of South Carolina Press

Manufactured in the United States of America

04   03   02   01   00   5   4   3   2   1

Library of Congress Cataloging-in-Publication Data
Crossing the color line : readings in Black and white / edited by Suzanne W. Jones.
     p.   cm.
     ISBN 1-57003-376-5 (alk. paper)
     1. Afro-Americans—Fiction.   2. Short stories, American—Afro-American
authors.   3. Race relations—Fiction.   4. Short stories, American.   I. Jones,
Suzanne Whitmore.
PS647.A35 C76   2000
813'.0108355—dc21   00-009501

Source and credit information for previously copyrighted material appears at the
end of the book.

for my children and my students,
the next generation

we seek beyond history
for a new and more possible meaning

Audre Lorde

Contents

Acknowledgments

I have been on the lookout for short fiction about race relations since I conceived this project almost a decade ago, and in that time many readers have helped point me toward many interesting stories. First, I must thank my student assistants at the University of Richmond—Marti Ackerman, Kenneth Broyles, Catherine Costantino, Lisa Green, Patricia Higgins, Amy Terdiman Lovett, Michelle Roberts, and Kim Turner—who combed through story collections and magazines and journals and bibliographies to locate the hundreds of stories I read, checked out stacks of books for me, filled out numerous interlibrary loan requests, and read stories with as much interest as I did. Their library searches were always fruitful, thanks to the guidance of Nancy Vick and Marcia Whitehead. Students in my classes have enthusiastically let me know which stories they have found powerful and poignant, mind-bending and eye-opening. I am especially indebted to Judy McLeod, Alice Walker, and Tony Grooms for their generosity; to professors Bert Ashe, Daryl Dance, Vanessa Dickerson, Mary Ellis Gibson, Tony Grooms, Barbara Ladd, Debbie McDowell, Sharon Monteith, Peggy Prenshaw, and Jerry Ward for their helpful suggestions; and to Rob Mawyer and Mark Bell for their assistance in the final stages of this project.

Wendy Levy and Kathy Zacher in the English Department of the University of Richmond magically managed to make the sixty-five miles between my home office and my university office disappear by assisting me no matter where I was working. When I turned the project over to the University of South Carolina Press (thanks to a tip from historian Walter Edgar), my editor Barry Blose and press director Catherine Fry and her hardworking staff made me very happy that I had chanced to meet Walter at a conference in Aero, Denmark.

My husband, Frank Papovich, took precious time from his own projects to support me and mine. As always, I am very grateful for his concern and his advice.

Introduction

At the turn of the last century, W. E. B. Du Bois predicted that "the problem of the twentieth century is the problem of the color line." Since the hopeful years of the civil rights movement, the United States has made uneven progress toward solving this problem. In 1968, at the end of a turbulent decade, the National Advisory Commission on Civil Disorders concluded, "Our nation is moving toward two societies, one black, one white, separate and unequal." Although we have since passed laws to foster racial equality, real economic, social, and emotional gulfs still exist. Strains between blacks and whites, which were partially hidden for a couple of decades, have become painfully evident in the last few years. The highly publicized and legally complex cases of Rodney King and O. J. Simpson and the divergent public reactions their trials generated suggest just how vexing the problem of the color line remains.

In an increasingly multiethnic nation, a focus on relationships between blacks and whites may seem incomplete, but our history of slavery and legal segregation creates a unique difference between minority groups that continues to confront us despite our current, and certainly important, attempts to address the problems of all minority groups in the United States. It seems especially appropriate at the turn of a new century to reflect on what Du Bois so accurately predicted would be America's gravest and most frustrating twentieth-century problem by examining fiction written since the movement that marked our country's concerted efforts to rectify the problem.

With such frequent calls for dialogue across racial lines, so many pleas for cross-racial understanding, and so much desire for a more inclusive American culture, the time seems right for a new collection of stories about relationships that cross the color line. Because of our country's painful racial history and the complexity of our current economic and social problems, these relationships are difficult to think about and to discuss, but the representation of race relations and racial identity in *Crossing the Color Line* will, I hope, help to provoke both thought and discussion. In *Loose Canons: Notes on the Culture Wars*, Henry Louis Gates Jr. states that we live in a world divided by race, class, nationality, and gender, but he goes on to argue that "the only way to transcend these divisions—to forge for once a civic culture that respects both differences and commonalities—is through education that seeks to comprehend the diversity of human culture." The stories in this collection not only illuminate both differences and commonalities, but also have the potential to alter perceptions of our world and to reshape values.

After the Civil War, Walt Whitman said that laws were not enough to make America a democracy; he believed the country needed a national literature that would build bridges between diverse peoples. While Whitman's faith in the written word may seem somewhat idealistic today, no other medium is more effective than literature in allowing us to enter the minds and hearts of people who are different from ourselves. When I was a student in a segregated high school in the 1960s, I discovered that reading about race relations can be transforming, both intellectually and emotionally. Today, as a teacher, I know that teaching stories about race relations can foster cross-racial understanding. The stories in *Crossing the Color Line* will give readers encounters with others that may not be part of their daily lives.

I have divided *Crossing the Color Line* into three parts: "Misreadings," "Rereadings," and "New Readings." These headings highlight the way characters in the stories perceive members of other races, and the divisions are roughly chronological in the evolution of representing black–white relationships since the civil rights movement. While most selections in "Misreadings" were published in the 1960s and 1970s, most selections in "New Readings" were published in the 1990s. The stories in "Misreadings" concern relationships between lower-class and working-class blacks and the white people who employ them or otherwise have authority over them, while the stories in "New Readings" involve relationships between blacks and whites of the middle and professional classes. A comparison reveals that the likelihood of meaningful relationships between blacks and whites increases as the equations between race and class, race and power, change.

The stories in "Misreadings" focus on white characters' misreadings of black people and their experiences. Because white skin has afforded economic power and social privilege for many, the white characters rarely look beyond racial stereotypes. Yet while these stories involve cross-racial misunderstandings that the white characters fail to perceive, the authors make such misreadings plain for their readers through narrative point of view or narrative irony. Alice Adams and Reynolds Price employ multiple perspectives so that readers can understand the thoughts and emotions of both black and white characters, even when they do not talk about their feelings with each other. Although the other writers in this section relate their stories from a single point of view, they employ unrelenting irony to highlight the injustices of prejudice and discrimination, proving simultaneously that people on both sides of the color line are harmed by white racism. In all of these stories readers witness the misunderstandings that occur across the color line when people mislabel social and cultural differences as biological, or when they equate race and class.

The protagonists of the stories in "Rereadings" eventually realize their misperceptions about race and difference. Stories by Alice Walker, Anthony Grooms, and Randall Kenan involve black characters who initially misread white characters. Stories by James Alan McPherson, Joan Williams, and Frances Sherwood take white characters beyond misperceptions that are caused by objectifying black people, viewing them either as inferior or exotic. The stories in this section examine situations that promote understanding across racial lines. Their endings are cautiously optimistic, although the conflicts are far from simplistically resolved. Race relations in these stories are always complicated by issues such as politics, religion, class, gender, and sexual orientation, to say nothing of a variety of individual concerns involving love and money. These stories give readers the opportunity to witness the misunderstandings that occur when complex experiences are simplified and when unfamiliar life stories are misinterpreted. They also model ways for readers to understand the life stories of those who are different from themselves and to redefine difference so as to understand it, not fear it. In "Recitatif" Toni Morrison provokes readers to read without foregrounding race, by undermining attempts to racially identify her characters and by making their class differences starkly obvious. When reading the stories in this section, readers actually dwell in the possibility of cross-racial understanding.

In "New Readings" the stories turn on personal similarities as often as on racial differences. For example, Clifford Thompson focuses on changing gender role expectations in dating relationships and Alyce Miller concentrates on marital troubles. But even here the legacy of racism lingers and tests the emerging friendship of Alyce Miller's female characters, the professional relationship of David Means's male characters, the love relationship of Reginald McKnight's black man and white woman, and the strictly business venture of Elizabeth Spencer's white woman and black man. Strains occur across the color line both because characters try so hard to relate to each other (whites wary of saying anything that might be construed as offensive, blacks on guard for offenses) and because family, friends, and colleagues continue to harbor misunderstandings about race and stereotypes about cross-racial relationships. However, a large measure of the power and the promise of these recent stories comes from the possibility that equal and amiable relationships can exist across the color line.

SUZANNE W. JONES

Misreadings

Verlie I Say Unto You

Alice Adams

Every morning of all the years of the Thirties, at around seven, Verlie Jones begins her long and laborious walk to the Todds' house, two miles uphill. She works for the Todds—their maid. Her own house, where she lives with her four children, is a slatted floorless cabin, in a grove of enormous sheltering oaks. It is just down a gravelly road from the bending highway, and that steep small road is the first thing she has to climb, starting out early in the morning. Arrived at the highway she stops and sighs, and looks around and then starts out. Walking steadily but not in any hurry, beside the winding white concrete.

First there are fields of broomstraw on either side of the road, stretching back to the woods, thick, clustered dark pines and cedars, trees whose lower limbs are cluttered with underbrush. Then the land gradually rises until on one side there is a steep red clay bank, going up to the woods; on the other side a wide cornfield, rich furrows dotted over in spring with tiny wild flowers, all colors—in the winter dry and rutted, sometimes frosted over, frost as shiny as splintered glass.

Then the creek. Before she comes to the small concrete bridge, she can see the heavier growth at the edge of the fields, green, edging the water. On the creek's steep banks, below the bridge, are huge peeling poplars, ghostly, old. She stands there looking down at the water (the bridge is halfway to the Todds'). The water is thick and swollen, rushing, full of twigs and leaf trash and swirling logs in the spring. Trickling and almost dried out when summer is over, in the early fall.

Past the bridge is the filling station, where they sell loaves of bread and cookies and soap, along with the gas and things for cars. Always there are men sitting around at the station, white men in overalls, dusty and dried out. Sometimes they nod to Verlie. "Morning, Verlie. Going to be any hot day?"

Occasionally, maybe a couple of times a year, a chain gang will be along there, working on the road. The colored men chained together, in their dirty, wide-striped uniforms, working with their picks. And the thin, mean guard (a white man) with his rifle, watching them. Looking quickly, briefly at Verlie as she passes. She looks everywhere but there, as her heart falls down to her stomach and turns upside down. All kinds of fears grab at her, all together: she is afraid of the guard and of those men (their heavy eyes) and also a chain gang is one of the places where her deserting husband, Horace, might well be, and she never wants to see Horace again. Not anywhere.

After the filling station some houses start. Small box houses, sitting up high on brick stilts. On the other side of the highway red clay roads lead back into the hills, to the woods. To the fields of country with no roads at all, where sometimes Mr. Todd goes to hunt rabbits, and where at other times, in summer, the children, Avery and Devlin Todd, take lunches and stay all day.

From a certain bend in the highway Verlie can see the Todds' house, but she rarely bothers to look anymore. She sighs and shifts her weight before starting up the steep, white, graveled road, and then the road to the right that swings around to the back of the house, to the back door that leads into the kitchen.

There on the back porch she has her own small bathroom that Mr. Todd put in for her. There is a mirror and some nails to hang her things on, and a flush toilet, ordered from Montgomery Ward, that still works. No washbasin, but she can wash her hands in the kitchen sink.

She hangs up her cardigan sweater in her bathroom and takes an apron off a nail. She goes into the kitchen to start everyone's breakfast.

They all eat separate. First Avery, who likes oatmeal and then soft-boiled eggs; then Mr. Todd (oatmeal and scrambled eggs and bacon and coffee); Devlin (toast and peanut butter and jam); and Mrs. Todd (tea and toast).

Verlie sighs, and puts the water on.

Verlie has always been with the Todds; that is how they put it to their friends. "Verlie has always been with us." Of course, that is not true. Actually she came to them about ten years before, when Avery was a baby. What they meant was that they did not know much about her life before them, and also (a more important meaning) they cannot imagine their life without her. They say, "We couldn't get along without Verlie," but it is unlikely that any of them (except possibly Jessica, with her mournful, exacerbated and extreme intelligence) realizes the full truth of the remark. And, laughingly, one of them will add, "No one else could put up with us." Another truth, or perhaps only a partial truth: in those days, there and then, most maids put up with a lot, and possibly Verlie suffers no more than most.

She does get more money than most maids, thirteen dollars a week (most get along on ten or eleven). And she gets to go home before dinner, around six (she first leaves the meal all fixed for them), since they—since Mr. Todd likes to have a lot of drinks and then eat late.

Every third Sunday she gets off to go to church.

None of them is stupid enough to say that she is like a member of the family.

Tom Todd, that handsome, guiltily faithless husband, troubled professor (the 10 percent salary cuts of the Depression; his history of abandoned projects—the book on Shelley, the innumerable articles)—Tom was the one who asked Verlie about her name.

"You know, it's like in the Bible. Verlie I say unto you."

Tom felt that he successfully concealed his amusement at that, and later, makes a marvelous story, especially in academic circles, in those days when funny-maid stories are standard social fare. In fact people (white people) are somewhat competitive as to who has heard or known the most comical colored person, comical meaning outrageously childishly ignorant. Tom's story always goes over well.

In her summer sneakers, shorts and little shirt, Avery comes into the dining room, a small, dark-haired girl carrying a big book. Since she has learned to read (her mother taught her, when she was no bigger than a minute) she reads all the time, curled up in big chairs in the living room or in her own room, in the bed. At the breakfast table.

"Good morning, Verlie."

"Morning. How you?"

"Fine, thank you. Going to be hot today?"

"Well, I reckon so."

Avery drinks her orange juice, and then Verlie takes out the glass and brings in her bowl of hot oatmeal. Avery reads the thick book while she eats. Verlie takes out the oatmeal bowl and brings in the soft-boiled eggs and a glass of milk.

"You drink your milk, now, hear?"

Verlie is about four times the size of Avery and more times than that her age. (But Verlie can't read.)

Verlie is an exceptionally handsome woman, big and tall and strong, with big bright eyes and smooth yellow skin over high cheekbones. A wide curving mouth, and strong white teeth.

Once there was a bad time between Avery and Verlie: Avery was playing with some children down the road, and it got to be suppertime. Jessica sent Verlie down to get Avery, who didn't want to come home. "Blah blah blah blah!" she yelled at Verlie—who, unaccountably, turned and walked away.

The next person Avery saw was furious Jessica, arms akimbo. "How are you, how *could* you? Verlie, who's loved you all your life? How could you be so cruel, calling her black?"

"I didn't—I said blah. I never said black. Where is she?"

"Gone home. Very hurt."

Jessica remained stiff and unforgiving (she had problems of her own); but the next morning Avery ran down into the kitchen at the first sound of Verlie. "Verlie, I said blah blah—I didn't say black."

And Verlie smiled, and it was all over. For good.

Tom Todd comes into the dining room, carrying the newspaper. "Good morning, Avery. Morning, Verlie. Well, it doesn't look like a day for getting out our umbrellas, does it now?"

That is the way he talks.

"Avery, please put your book away. Who knows, we might have an absolutely fascinating conversation."

She gives him a small sad smile and closes her book. "Pass the cream?"

"With the greatest of pleasure."

"Thanks."

But despite the intense and often painful complications of his character, Tom's relationship with Verlie is perhaps the simplest in that family. Within their rigidly defined roles they are even fond of each other. Verlie thinks he talks funny, but not much more so than most men—white men. He runs around with women (she knows that from his handkerchiefs, the lipstick stains that he couldn't have bothered to hide from her) but not as much as Horace did. He bosses his wife and children but he doesn't hit them. He acts as Verlie expects a man to act, and perhaps a little better.

And from Tom's point of view Verlie behaves like a Negro maid. She is somewhat lazy; she does as little cleaning as she can. She laughs at his jokes. She sometimes sneaks drinks from his liquor closet. He does not, of course, think of Verlie as a woman—a woman in the sense of sexual possibility; in fact he once sincerely (astoundingly) remarked that he could not imagine a sexual impulse toward a colored person.

• • •

Devlin comes in next. A small and frightened boy, afraid of Verlie. Once as he stood up in his bath she touched his tiny penis and laughed and said, "This here's going to grow to something nice and big." He was terrified: what would he do with something big, down there?

He mutters good morning to his father and sister and to Verlie.

Then Jessica. Mrs. Todd. "Good morning, everyone. Morning, Verlie. My, doesn't it look like a lovely spring day?"

She sighs, as no one answers.

The end of breakfast. Verlie clears the table, washes up, as those four people separate.

There is a Negro man who also (sometimes) works for the Todds, named Clifton. Yard work: raking leaves in the fall, building a fence around the garbage cans, and then a dog kennel, then a playhouse for the children.

When Verlie saw Clifton the first time he came into the yard (a man who had walked a long way, looking for work), what she thought was: Lord, I never saw no man so beautiful. Her second thought was: He sick.

Clifton is bronze-colored. Reddish. Shining. Not brown like most colored (or yellow, as Verlie is). His eyes are big and brown, but dragged downward with his inside sickness. And his sadness: he is a lonesome man, almost out of luck.

"Whatever do you suppose they talk about?" Tom Todd says to Jessica, who has come into his study to help him with the index of his book, an hour or so after breakfast. They can hear the slow, quiet sounds of Verlie's voice, with Clifton's, from the kitchen.

"Us, maybe?" Jessica makes this light, attempting a joke, but she really wonders if in fact she and Tom are their subject. Her own communication with Verlie is so mystifyingly nonverbal that she sometimes suspects Verlie of secret (and accurate) appraisals, as though Verlie knows her in ways that no one else does, herself included. At other times she thinks that Verlie is just plain stubborn.

From the window come spring breaths of blossom and grasses and leaves. Of spring earth. Aging plump Jessica deeply sighs.

Tom says, "I very much doubt that, my dear. Incredibly fascinating though we be."

In near total despair Jessica says, "Sometimes I think I just don't have the feeling for an index."

The telephone rings. Tom and Jessica look at each other, and then Verlie's face comes to the study door. "It's for you, Mr. Todd. A long distance."

Clifton has had a bad life; it almost seems cursed. The same sickness one spring down in Mississippi carried off his wife and three poor little children, and after that everything got even worse: every job that he got came apart like a bunch of sticks in his hands. Folks all said that they had no money to pay. He even made deliveries for a bootlegger, knocking on back doors at night, but the man got arrested and sent to jail before Clifton got any money.

He likes working for the Todds, and at the few other jobs around town that Mrs. Todd finds for him. But he doesn't feel good. Sometimes he thinks he has some kind of sickness.

He looks anxiously at Verlie as he says this last, as though he, like Jessica, believes that she can see inside him.

"You nervous," Verlie says. "You be all right, come summertime." But she can't look at him as she says this.

They are standing in the small apple orchard where Verlie's clotheslines are. She has been hanging out the sheets. They billow, shuddering in the lively restive air of early spring.

Clifton suddenly takes hold of her face, and turns it around to his. He presses his mouth and his body to hers, standing there. Something deep inside Verlie heats up and makes her almost melt.

"Verlie!"

It is Avery, suddenly coming up on them, so that they cumbersomely step apart.

"Verlie, my father wants you." Avery runs away almost before she has stopped speaking.

Clifton asks, "You reckon we ought to tell her not to tell?"

"No, she's not going to tell."

Verlie is right, but it is a scene that Avery thinks about. Of course, she has seen other grown-ups kissing: her father and Irene McGinnis or someone after a party. But Verlie and Clifton looked different; for one thing they were more absorbed. It took them a long time to hear her voice.

• • •

Tom is desperately questioning Jessica. "How in God's name will I tell her?" he asks.

Verlie's husband, Horace, is dead. He died in a Memphis hospital, after a knife fight, having first told a doctor the name of the people and the town where his wife worked.

"I could tell her," Jessica forces herself to say, and for a few minutes they look at each other, with this suggestion lying between them. But they both know, with some dark and intimate Southern knowledge, that Tom will have to be the one to tell her. And alone: it would not even "do" for Jessica to stay on in the room, although neither of them could have explained these certainties.

Having been clearly (and kindly) told by Tom what has happened in Memphis, Verlie then asks, "You sure? You sure it's Horace, not any other man?"

Why couldn't he have let Jessica tell her, or at least have let her stay in the room? Tom is uncomfortable; it wildly occurs to him to offer Verlie a drink (to offer Verlie a drink?). He mumbles, "Yes, I'm afraid there's no doubt at all." He adds, in his more reasonable, professorial voice, "You see, another man wouldn't have said Verlie Jones, who works for the Todd family, in Hilton."

Incredibly, a smile breaks out on Verlie's face. ("For a minute I actually thought she was going to *laugh*," Tom later says to Jessica.)

Verlie says, "I reckon that's right. Couldn't be no other man." And then she says, "Lunch about ready now," and she goes back into the kitchen.

Jessica has been hovering in the dining room, pushing at the arrangement of violets and cowslips in a silver bowl. She follows Verlie into the kitchen; she says, "Verlie, I'm terribly sorry. Verlie, wouldn't you like to go on home? Take the afternoon off. I could drive you . . ."

"No'm. No, thank you. I'd liefer get on with the ironing."

And so, with a stiff and unreadable face, opaque dark-brown eyes, Verlie serves their lunch.

What could they know, what could any of them know about a man like Horace? Had any of them seen her scars? Knife scars and beating scars, and worse things he had done without leaving any scars. All the times he forced her, when he was so hurting and quick, and she was sick or just plain exhausted. The girls she always knew he had. The mean tricks he played on little kids, his kids. The dollars of hers that he stole to get drunk on.

She had always thought Horace was too mean to die, and as she cleans up the lunch dishes and starts to sprinkle the dry sheets for ironing, she still wonders: *Is* Horace dead?

She tries to imagine an open casket, full of Horace, dead. His finicky little moustache and his long, strong fingers folded together on his chest. But the casket floats off into the recesses of her mind and what she sees is Horace, alive and terrifying.

A familiar dry smell tells her that she has scorched a sheet, and tears begin to roll slowly down her face.

"When I went into the kitchen to see how she was, she was standing there with tears rolling down her face," Jessica reports to Tom—and then is appalled at what she hears as satisfaction in her own voice.

"I find that hardly surprising," Tom says, with a questioning raise of his eyebrows.

Aware that she has lost his attention, Jessica goes on. (Where *is* he—with whom?) "I just meant, it seems awful to feel a sort of relief when she cries. As though I thought that's what she ought to do. Maybe she didn't really care for Horace. He hasn't been around for years, after all." (As usual she is making things worse: it is apparent that Tom can barely listen.)

She says, "I think I'll take the index cards back to my desk," and she manages not to cry.

Picking up the sheets to take upstairs to the linen closet, Verlie decides that she won't tell Clifton about Horace; dimly she thinks that if she tells anyone, especially Clifton, it won't be true: Horace, alive, will be waiting for her at her house, as almost every night she is afraid that he will be.

Sitting at her desk, unseeingly Jessica looks out across the deep valley, where the creek winds down toward the sea, to the further hills that are bright green with spring. Despair slowly fills her blood so that it seems heavy in her veins, and thick, and there is a heavy pressure in her head.

And she dreams for a moment, as she has sometimes before, of a friend to whom she could say, "I can't stand anything about my life. My husband either is untrue to me or would like to be—constantly. It comes to the same thing, didn't St. Paul say that? My daughter's eyes are beginning to go cold against me, and my son is terrified of everyone. Of me." But there is no one to whom she could say a word of this; she is known among her friends for dignity and restraint. (Only sometimes her mind explodes, and she breaks out screaming—at Tom, at one of her children, once at Verlie—leaving them all sick and shocked, especially herself sick and shocked, and further apart than ever.)

Now Verlie comes through the room with an armful of fresh, folded sheets, and for an instant, looking at her, Jessica has the thought that Verlie could be that friend, that listener. That Verlie could understand.

She dismisses the impulse almost as quickly as it came.

Lately she has spent a lot of time remembering college, those distant happy years, among friends. Her successes of that time. The two years when she directed the Greek play, on May Day weekend (really better than being in the May Court). Her senior year, elected president of the secret honor society. (And the springs of wisteria, heavily flowering, scented, lavender and white, the heavy vines everywhere.)

From those college days she still has two friends, to whom she writes, and visits at rarer intervals. Elizabeth, who is visibly happily married to handsome and successful Jackson Stuart (although he is, to Jessica, a shocking racial bigot). And Mary John James, who teaches Latin in a girls' school, in Richmond—who has never married. Neither of them could be her imagined friend (any more than Verlie could).

Not wanting to see Jessica's sad eyes again (the sorrow in that woman's face, the mourning!), Verlie puts the sheets in the linen closet and goes down the back stairs. She is halfway down, walking slow, when she feels a sudden coolness in her blood, as though from a breeze. She stops, she listens to nothing and then she is flooded with the certain knowledge that Horace is dead, is at that very moment laid away in Memphis (wherever Memphis is). Standing there alone, by the halfway window that looks out to the giant rhododendron, she begins to smile, peacefully and slowly—an interior, pervasive smile.

Then she goes on down the stairs, through the dining room and into the kitchen.

Clifton is there.

Her smile changes; her face becomes brighter and more animated, although she doesn't say anything—not quite trusting herself not to say everything, as she has promised herself.

"You looking perky," Clifton says, by way of a question. He is standing at the sink with a drink of water.

Her smile broadens, and she lies. "Thinking about the social at the church. Just studying if or not I ought to go."

"You do right to go," he says. And then, "You be surprise, you find me there?"

(They have never arranged any meeting before, much less in another place, at night; they have always pretended that they were in the same place in the yard or orchard by accident.)

She laughs. "You never find the way."

He grins at her, his face brighter than any face that she has ever seen. "I be there," he says to her.

A long, hot summer, extending into fall. A hot October, and then there is sudden cold. Splinters of frost on the red clay erosions in the fields. Ice in the shallow edges of the creek.

For Verlie it has been the happiest summer of her life, but no one of the Todds has remarked on this, nor been consciously aware of unusual feelings, near at hand. They all have preoccupations of their own.

Clifton has been working for the Macombers, friends and neighbors of the Todds, and it is Irene Macomber who telephones to tell Jessica the sad news that he had a kind of seizure (a hemorrhage) and that when they finally got him to the Negro hospital (twelve miles away) it was too late, and he died.

Depressing news, on that dark November day. Jessica supposes that the first thing is to tell Verlie. (After all, she and Clifton were friends, and Verlie might know of relatives.)

She is not prepared for Verlie's reaction.

A wail— "Aieeeee"—that goes on and on, from Verlie's wide mouth, and her wide, wild eyes. "Aieee—"

Then it stops abruptly, as Verlie claps her hands over her mouth, and bends over and blindly reaches for a chair, her rocker. She pulls herself toward the chair, she falls into it, she bends over double and begins to cough, deep and wrackingly.

Poor shocked Jessica has no notion what to do. To go over to Verlie and embrace her, to press her own sorrowing face to Verlie's face? To creep shyly and sadly from the room?

This last is what she does—is all, perhaps, that she is able to do.

"You know," says Tom Todd (seriously) to Irene McGinnis, in one of their rare lapses from the steady demands of unconsummated love, "I believe those two people had a real affection for each other."

. . .

Verlie is sick for a week and more after that, with what is called "misery in the chest." (No one mentions her heart.)

Thinking to amuse her children (she is clearly at a loss without Verlie, and she knows this), Jessica takes them for a long walk, on the hard, narrow, white roads that lead up into the hills, the heavy, thick, dark woods of fall, smelling of leaves and earth and woodsmoke. But a melancholy mood settles over them all; it is cold and the children are tired, and Jessica finds that she is thinking of Verlie and Clifton. (Is it possible that they were lovers? She uncomfortably shrugs off this possibility.)

Dark comes early, and there is a raw, red sunset at the black edge of the horizon, as finally they reach home.

Verlie comes back the next day, to everyone's relief. But there is a grayish tinge to the color of her skin that does not go away.

But on that rare spring day months earlier (the day Horace is dead and laid away in Memphis) Verlie walks the miles home with an exceptional lightness of heart, smiling to herself at all the colors of the bright new flowers, and at the smells of spring, the promises.

1974

Son in the Afternoon

John A. Williams

It was hot. I tend to be a bitch when it's hot. I goosed the little Ford over Sepulveda Boulevard toward Santa Monica until I got stuck in the traffic that pours from L.A. into the surrounding towns. I'd had a very lousy day at the studio.

I was—still am—a writer and this studio had hired me to check scripts and films with Negroes in them to make sure the Negro moviegoer wouldn't be offended. The signs were already clear one day the whole of American industry would be racing pell-mell to get a Negro, showcase a spade. I was kind of a pioneer. I'm a *Negro* writer, you see. The day had been tough because of a couple of verbs—slink and walk. One of those Hollywood hippies had done a script calling for a Negro waiter to slink away from the table where a dinner party was glaring at him. I said the waiter should walk, not slink, because later on he becomes a hero. The Hollywood hippie, who understood it all because he had some colored friends, said that it was essential to the plot that the waiter slink. I said you don't slink one minute and become a hero the next; there has to be some consistency. The Negro actor I was standing up for said nothing either way. He had played Uncle Tom roles so long that he had become Uncle Tom. But the director agreed with me.

Anyway . . . hear me out now. I was on my way to Santa Monica to pick up my mother, Nora. It was a long haul for such a hot day. I had planned a quiet evening: a nice shower, fresh clothes, and then I would have dinner at the Watkins and talk with some of the musicians on the scene for a quick taste before they cut to their gigs. After, I was going to the Pigalle down on Figueroa and catch Earl Grant at the organ, and still later, if nothing exciting happened, I'd pick up Scottie and make it to the Lighthouse on the Beach or to the Strollers and listen to some of the white boys play. I liked the long drive, especially while listening to Sleepy Stein's show on the radio. Later, much later of course, it would be home, back to Watts.

So you see, this picking up Nora was a little inconvenient. My mother was a maid for the Couchmans. Ronald Couchman was an architect, a good one I understood from Nora who has a fine sense for this sort of thing; you don't work in some hundred-odd houses during your life without getting some idea of the way a house should be laid out. Couchman's wife, Kay, was a playgirl who drove a white Jaguar from one party to another. My mother didn't like her too much; she didn't seem to care much for her son, Ronald, junior. There's something wrong with a parent who can't really love her own child, Nora thought. The Couchmans lived in a real fine residential section, of course. A number of actors lived nearby, character actors, not really big stars.

Somehow it is very funny. I mean that the maids and butlers knew everything about these people, and these people knew nothing at all about the help. Through Nora and her friends I knew who was laying whose wife; who had money and who *really* had money; I knew about the wild parties hours before the police, and who smoked marijuana, when, and where they got it.

To get to Couchman's driveway I had to go three blocks up one side of a palm-planted center strip and back down the other. The driveway bent gently, then swept back out of sight of the main road. The house, sheltered by slim palms, looked like a transplanted New England Colonial. I parked and walked to the kitchen door, skirting the growling Great Dane who was tied to a tree. That was the route to the kitchen door.

I don't like kitchen doors. Entering people's houses by them, I mean. I'd done this thing most of my life when I called at places where Nora worked to pick up the patched or worn sheets or the half-eaten roasts, the battered, tarnished silver—the fringe benefits of a housemaid. As a teen-ager I'd told Nora I was through with that crap; I was not going through anyone's kitchen door. She only laughed and said I'd learn. One day soon after, I called for her and without knocking walked right through the front door of this house and right on through the living room. I was almost out of the room when I saw feet behind the couch. I leaned over and there was Mr. Jorgensen and his wife making out like crazy. I guess they thought Nora had gone and it must have hit them sort of suddenly and they went at it like the hell-bomb was due to drop any minute. I've been that way too, mostly in the spring. Of course, when Mr. Jorgensen looked over his shoulder and saw me, you know what happened. I was thrown out and Nora right behind me. It was the middle of winter, the old man was sick and the coal bill three months overdue. Nora was right about those kitchen doors: I learned.

My mother saw me before I could ring the bell. She opened the door. "Hello," she said. She was breathing hard, like she'd been running or something. "Come in and sit down. I don't know *where* that Kay is. Little Ronald is sick and she's probably out gettin' drunk again." She left me then and trotted back through the house, I guess to be with Ronnie. I hated the combination of her white nylon uniform, her dark brown face and the wide streaks of gray in her hair. Nora had married this guy from Texas a few years after the old man had died. He was all right. He made out okay. Nora didn't have to work, but she just couldn't be still; she always had to be doing something. I suggested she quit work, but I had as much luck as her husband. I used to tease her about liking to be around those white folks. It would have been good for her to take an extended trip around the country visiting my brothers and sisters. Once she got to Philadelphia, she could go right out to the cemetery and sit awhile with the old man.

I walked through the Couchman home. I liked the library. I thought if I knew Couchman I'd like him. The room made me feel like that. I left it and went into the big living room. You could tell that Couchman had let his wife do that. Everything in it was fast, dart-like, with no sense of ease. But on the walls were several of Couchman's conceptions of buildings and homes. I guess he was a disciple of Wright. My mother walked rapidly through the room without looking at me and said, "Just be patient, Wendell. She should be here real soon."

"Yeah," I said, "with a snootful." I had turned back to the drawings when Ronnie scampered into the room, his face twisted with rage.

"Nora!" he tried to roar, perhaps the way he'd seen the parents of some of his friends roar at their maids. I'm quite sure Kay didn't shout at Nora, and I don't think Couchman would. But then no one shouts at Nora. "Nora, you come right back here this minute!" the little bastard shouted and stamped and pointed to a spot on the floor where Nora was supposed to come to roost. I have a nasty temper. Sometimes it lies dormant for ages and at other times, like when the weather is hot and nothing seems to be going right, it's bubbling and ready to explode. "Don't talk to *my* mother like that, you little—!" I said sharply, breaking off just before I cursed. I wanted him to be large enough for me to strike. "How'd you like me to talk to *your* mother like that?"

The nine-year-old looked up at me in surprise and confusion. He hadn't expected me to say anything. I was just another piece of furniture. Tears rose in his eyes and spilled out onto his pale cheeks. He put his hands behind him, twisted them. He moved backwards, away from me. He looked at my mother with a "Nora, come help me" look. And sure enough, there was Nora, speeding back across the room, gathering the kid in her arms, tucking his robe together. I was too angry to feel hatred for myself.

Ronnie was the Couchman's only kid. Nora loved him. I suppose that was the trouble. Couchman was gone ten, twelve hours a day. Kay didn't stay around the house any longer than she had to. So Ronnie had only my mother. I think kids should have someone to love, and Nora wasn't a bad sort. But somehow when the six of us, her own children, were growing up we never had her. She was gone, out scuffling to get those crumbs to put into our mouths and shoes for our feet and praying for something to happen so that all the space in between would be taken care of. Nora's affection for us took the form of rushing out into the morning's five o'clock blackness to wake some silly bitch and get her coffee; took form in her trudging five miles home every night instead of taking the streetcar to save money to buy tablets for us, to use at school, we said. But the truth was that all of us liked to draw and we went through a writing tablet in a couple of hours every day. Can you imagine? There's not a goddamn artist among us. We never had the physical affection, the pat on the head, the quick, smiling kiss, the "gimmee a hug" routine. All of this Ronnie was getting.

Now he buried his little blond head in Nora's breast and sobbed.

"There, there now," Nora said. "Don't you cry, Ronnie. Ol' Wendell is just jealous, and he hasn't much sense either. He didn't mean nuthin'."

I left the room. Nora had hit it of course, hit it and passed on. I looked back. It didn't look so incongruous, the white and black together, I mean. Ronnie was still sobbing. His head bobbed gently on Nora's shoulder. The only time I ever got that close to her was when she trapped me with a bearhug so she could whale the daylights out of me after I put a snowball through Mrs. Grant's window. I walked outside and lit a cigarette. When Ronnie was in the hospital the month before, Nora got me to run her way over to Hollywood every night to see him. I didn't like that worth a damn. All right, I'll admit it: it did upset me. All that affection I didn't get nor my brothers and sisters going to that little white boy who, without a doubt, when away from her called her the names he'd learned from adults. Can you imagine a nine-year-old kid calling Nora a "girl," "our girl"? I spat at the Great Dane. He snarled and then I bounced a rock off his fanny. "Lay down, you bastard," I muttered. It was a good thing he was tied up.

I heard the low cough of the Jaguar slapping against the road. The car was throttled down, and with a muted roar it swung into the driveway. The woman aimed for me. I was evil enough not to move. I was tired of playing with these people. At the last moment, grinning, she swung the wheel over and braked. She bounded out of the car like a tennis player vaulting over a net.

"Hi," she said, tugging at her shorts.

"Hello."

"You're Nora's boy?"

"I'm Nora's son." Hell, I was as old as she was; besides, I can't stand "boy."

"Nora tells us you're working in Hollywood. Like it?"

"It's all right."

"You must be pretty talented."

We stood looking at each other while the dog whined for her attention. Kay had a nice body and it was well tanned. She was high, boy, was she high. Looking at her, I could feel myself going into my sexy bastard routine; sometimes I can swing it great. Maybe it all had to do with the business inside. Kay took off her sunglasses and took a good look at me. "Do you have a cigarette?"

I gave her one and lit it. "Nice tan," I said. Most white people I know think it's a great big deal if a Negro compliments them on their tans. It's a large laugh. You have all this volleyball about color and come summer you can't hold the white folks back from the beaches, anyplace where you can get some sun. And of course the blacker they get, the more pleased they are. Crazy. If there is ever a Negro revolt, it will come during the summer and Negroes will descend upon the beaches around the nation and paralyze the country. You can't conceal cattle prods and bombs and pistols and police dogs when you're showing your birthday suit to the sun.

"You like it?" she asked. She was pleased. She placed her arm next to mine. "Almost the same color," she said.

"Ronnie isn't feeling well," I said.

"Oh, the poor kid. I'm so glad we have Nora. She's such a charm. I'll run right in and look at him. Do have a drink in the bar. Fix me one too, will you?" Kay skipped inside and I went to the bar and poured out two strong drinks. I made hers stronger than mine. She was back soon. "Nora was trying to put him to sleep and she made me stay out." She giggled. She quickly tossed off her drink. "Another, please?" While I was fixing her drink she was saying how amazing it was for Nora to have such a talented son. What she was really saying was that it was amazing for a servant to have a son who was not also a servant. "Anything can happen in a democracy," I said. "Servants' sons drink with madames and so on."

"Oh, Nora isn't a servant," Kay said. "She's part of the family."

Yeah, I thought. Where and how many times had I heard *that* before?

In the ensuing silence, she started to admire her tan again. "You think it's pretty good, do you? You don't know how hard I worked to get it." I moved close to her and held her arm. I placed my other arm around her. She pretended not to see or feel it, but she wasn't trying to get away either. In fact she was pressing closer and the register in my brain that tells me at the precise moment when I'm in, went off. Kay was very high. I put both arms around her and she put both hers around me. When I kissed her, she responded completely.

"Mom!"

"Ronnie, come back to bed," I heard Nora shout from the other room. We could hear Ronnie running over the rug in the outer room. Kay tried to get away from me, push me to one side, because we could tell that Ronnie knew where to look for his Mom: he was running right for the bar, where we were. "Oh, please," she said, "don't let him see us." I wouldn't let her push me away. "Stop!" she hissed. "He'll *see* us!" We stopped struggling just for an instant, and we listened to the echoes of the word *see*. She gritted her teeth and renewed her efforts to get away.

Me? I had the scene laid right out. The kid breaks into the room, see, and sees his mother in this real wriggly clinch with this colored guy who's just shouted at him, see, and no matter how his mother explains it away, the kid has the image—the colored guy and his mother—for the rest of his life, see?

That's the way it happened. The kid's mother hissed under her breath. "You're *crazy*!" and she looked at me as though she were seeing me or something about me for the very first time. I'd released her as soon as Ronnie, romping into the bar, saw us and came to a full, open-mouthed halt. Kay went to him. He looked first at me, then at his mother. Kay turned to me, but she couldn't speak.

Outside in the living room my mother called, "Wendell, where are you? We can go now."

I started to move past Kay and Ronnie. I felt many things, but I made myself think mostly, *There you little bastard, there.*

My mother thrust her face inside the door and said, "Good-bye, Mrs. Couchman. See you tomorrow. 'Bye, Ronnie."

"Yes," Kay said, sort of stunned. "Tomorrow." She was reaching for Ronnie's hand as we left, but the kid was slapping her hand away. I hurried quickly after Nora, hating the long drive back to Watts.

1962

I Just Love Carrie Lee
(*Homochitto*)

Ellen Douglas

All the time we were away from here, living in Atlanta, I paid Carrie Lee's wages—seven dollars a week for eight years. Of course, part of the time, after Billy married and came back to Homochitto, she was working for him in the country. She rides the bus to Wildwood, seven miles over the river, every day. I don't know why she doesn't move back over there, but she likes to live in town. She owns her own house and she likes to visit around. The truth of the matter is, she thinks she might miss something if she moved over the river; and besides, she never has had any use for "field niggers." (That's Carrie Lee talking, not me.) Anyway, as I was saying, I did pay her wages all those years we were away from here. I knew Mama would have wanted me to, and besides, I feel the same responsibility toward her that Mama did. You understand that, don't you? She was our responsibility. So few people think that way nowadays. Nobody has the feeling for Negroes they used to have. People look at me as if they think I'm crazy when I say I paid Carrie Lee all that time.

I remember when I first had an inkling how things were changing. It was during the Depression when the Edwardses moved next door to us. They were Chicago people, and they'd never had any dealings with Negroes. Old Mrs. Edwards expected the baseboards to be scrubbed every week. I suppose she scrubbed them herself in Chicago. Oh, I don't mean there was anything wrong with her. She was a good, hard-working Christian soul; and *he* was a cut above *her*. I've heard he came from an old St. Louis family. But a woman sets the tone of a household, and her tone was middle-western to the marrow. All her children said "come" for "came," and "I want in," and I had a time keeping mine from picking it up.

To make a long story short, she came to me one day in the late fall and asked me what the yardmen in Homochitto did in the winter.

"What do you mean?" I said.

"I mean where do they work?"

"Well," I said, "mine sits around the kitchen and shells pecans and polishes silver all winter."

"You mean you keep him on when there's actually nothing for him to do?" she said.

"He *works* for us," I said. "He's been working for us for years."

"I haven't got that kind of money," she said. "I had to let mine go yesterday, and I was wondering where he would get a job."

I tried to explain to her how things were down here, how you couldn't let a man go in the winter, but she didn't understand. She got huffy as could be.

"I suppose that's what you call *noblesse oblige*," she said.

"You could, if you wanted to be fancy," I said.

And do you know what she said to me? She said, "They're not going to catch me in that trap, the *Nee*-grows. I can do all my own work and like it, if it comes to that. I'm going to stand on my rights."

They didn't stay in Homochitto long.

Wasn't that odd? Everyone is like that nowadays. Maybe not for such a queer reason, but no one feels any responsibility any more. No one cares, white or black.

That's the reason Carrie Lee is so precious to us. She cares about us. She knows from experience what kind of people we are. It's a boon in this day and age just to be recognized.

The truth of the matter is I couldn't tell you what Carrie Lee has meant to us. She's been like a member of the family for almost fifty years. She raised me and she's raised my children. Ask Sarah and Billy, Carrie Lee was more of a mother to them than I was. I was too young when I first married to be saddled with children, and too full of life to stay at home with them. Bill was always on the go, and I wouldn't have let him go without me for anything. It was fortunate I could leave the children with Carrie Lee and never have a moment's worry. She loved them like they were her own, and she could control them without ever laying a hand on them. She has her own philosophy, and while *I* don't always understand it, children do.

Carrie Lee is a bright Negro—both ways, I mean, and both for the same reason, I reckon. I don't know exactly where the white blood came from (it's not the kind of thing they told young ladies in my day), but I can guess. Probably an overseer. Her mama was lighter than she, and married a dark man. The old mammy, Carrie Lee's grandmother, was black as the ace of spades, so Mama said. I judge some overseer on Grandfather's place must have been Carrie Lee's grandfather. She has always said she has Indian blood, too, said her mama told her so. But how much truth there is in that I don't know. The hawk nose and high cheekbones look Indian, all right, and there is something about her—maybe that she won't make a fool of herself to entertain you. You know she's different. And she could put the fear of God into the children, like a Cherokee chief out after their scalps.

Billy says Carrie Lee taught him his first lesson in getting along with people. He was the youngest boy in the neighborhood, and of course the other children made him run all their errands; they teased and bullied him unmercifully until he was big enough to stand up for himself. This is the kind of thing they'd do. One day in the middle of my mah-jongg club meeting, he came running in the house crying. Some of the children had mixed up a mess of coffee grounds and blackberry jam and tried to make him eat it. It was an initiation. They formed a new club every week or two and Billy was the one they always initiated.

"Mama's busy, honey," I said. "Tell it to Carrie Lee. She'll tend to 'em for you."

Carrie Lee took him on her lap like a baby and rocked him and loved him until he stopped crying, and then he sat up and said, "But Carrie Lee, who am I going to play with? Everybody's in the club but me."

And she said, "Honey, they bigger than you. If you wants to play, you gits on out there and eats they pudding. If you don't like it, you holds it in your mouth and spits it out when they ain't looking."

"But s'pose they feed me more than I can hold in my mouth?" he said.

"Honey, if they does, you got to make your mouth stretch," she said.

Billy has never forgotten that.

Carrie Lee came to work for Mama when she was fourteen years old. She was only a child, it's true, but even then she had more sense than most grown Negroes. Mama had seen her on their place outside Atlanta and taken a fancy to her. *Her* mother (Carrie Lee's, I mean) cooked for the manager's family there, and Carrie Lee was already taking care of five or six younger brothers and sisters while the mother was at work. You can imagine what it meant to her to come to town. Mama clothed her and fed her and made a finished servant of her. Why, she even saw to it that Carrie Lee went to school through the fifth grade; she'd never been able to go more than a couple of terms in the country. Fifty years ago, practically none of the Negroes went more than a year or two, if that long. When they were seven or eight, they either went to the field or stayed at home to nurse the younger ones.

By the time we moved to Homochitto, Mama couldn't have gotten along without Carrie Lee, and so she came with us. At first Mama was miserable here—homesick for Georgia and her own family and the social life of Atlanta. Compared to Atlanta, Homochitto then was nothing but a village. And the weather! We had never been through a Mississippi summer before, or, for that matter, a Georgia summer; we'd always gone to the mountains—Monteagle, or White Sulphur Springs, or some place like that. But that first year in Homochitto Papa couldn't leave, and Mama got in one of her stubborn spells and wouldn't go without him. To tell you the truth, I think she wanted him to see her suffer, so he'd take her back to Atlanta. She used to say then that no one understood how she felt except Carrie Lee. And I suppose it's true that Carrie Lee missed her family too, in spite of the hard life she'd had with them. In the mornings she and Mama would sit in the kitchen peeling figs or pears or peaches, or washing berries, preserving together, and Carrie Lee would tell stories to entertain Mama. I'd hang around and listen. I remember one day Carrie Lee had said something 'specially outrageous, and Mama said, "Carrie Lee, I don't believe half you say. Why do you make up those awful tales?"

Carrie Lee stopped peeling pears and began to eat the peelings. She always did eat the peelings when they were preserving, everything except figs—a hangover from hungry days, I reckon. She hushed talking a minute, eating and thinking, and then she looked at Mama and said:

"To keep us from the lonely hours,
And being sad so far from home."

It was just like a poem. I had to get up and run out of the house to keep them from seeing me cry. Do you suppose she understood what she'd said and how beautifully she'd said it? Or is it something about language that comes to them as naturally as sleeping—and music?

When Mama died, I felt as if she had more or less left Carrie Lee to me, and I've been taking care of her ever since. Oh, she's no burden. There's no telling *how* much money she has in the bank. There she is, drawing wages from Billy and from me, owns her own house and rents out a room, nobody to spend it on but herself and one step-daughter, and she never has to spend a dime on herself. Between us, Sarah and I give her everything she wears; and as for her house, every stick she has came out of our old house.

When we sold the house, after Mama died, Carrie Lee took her pick of what was left. Of course, I had gotten all the good pieces—the things that were bought before the war—but she wouldn't have wanted them anyway; nothing I chose would have suited her taste. She has a genius for the hideous. She took the wicker porch chairs—you know, the kind with fan backs and magazine racks in the arms and trays hooked onto the sides for glasses—and painted them blue and put them in her living room; and she took a set of crocheted table mats that Mama made years ago. (They were beautiful things, but if you've ever had a set, you know what a nuisance they are. Not a washwoman in Homochitto does fine laundering any more, and *I* certainly wouldn't wash and starch and stretch them *myself*. And besides, where would anyone in a small apartment like this keep those devilish boards with nails in them, that you have to stretch them on?) Anyway, Carrie Lee took those place mats and put them on the wicker chairs like antimacassars, if you can believe it. But that's just the beginning. All the junk collected by a houseful of pack rats like Bill's family—the monstrosities they acquired between 1890 and 1930 would be something to read about. And Bill and Mama had stored everything in Mama's attic when Bill sold his father's house in 1933. Why, I couldn't say, except that Bill always hated to throw anything away. That's a trait that runs in his family: they hang on to what they have. And if his father hadn't hung on to Wildwood during hard times and good, where would we be now?

Fortunately, he did hang on to it, and to everything else his father left him. You know, Bill's family didn't have the hard time most people had after the Civil War. His grandfather started the little railroad line from Homochitto to Jackson that was eventually bought by the Southern. He was a practical businessman and he didn't sit back like so many people, after we were defeated, and let his property get away from him out of sheer outrage. And so, the family was able to travel and to buy whatever was stylish at the time. Carrie Lee loved everything they bought, and she has as much of it as she can squeeze into her house: heavy golden oak sideboard and table, a fine brass bed polished up fit to blind you, a player piano that doesn't work, with a Spanish shawl draped over it, and on the walls souvenir plates from Niagara Falls and the St. Louis Exposition, and pictures of Mama and me and the children, sandwiched in between pictures of all her sisters and brothers and their families. It's too fine.

Actually, there are some people around here who disapprove of Carrie Lee and me; but as far as I'm concerned they can say what they like. I just love Carrie Lee and that's all there is to it. When she comes to call, she sits in the parlor with the white folks. She has good sense about it. If she's in the house on Sunday afternoon visiting with me, and guests come, she goes to the door and lets them in as if she were working that day, and then she goes back to the kitchen and fixes coffee and finds an apron and serves us. Everything goes smoothly. She knows how to make things comfortable for everybody. But half the time, whoever it is, I wish they hadn't come. I'd rather visit with Carrie Lee.

And people who talk about it don't know what they're saying. They don't know how I feel. When Bill died (that was only a year after Mama died, and there I was, left alone with a houseful of *babies* to raise and all that property to manage), who do you think walked down the aisle with me and sat with me at the funeral? Carrie Lee. If I hadn't been half crazy with grief, I suppose I might have thought twice before I did a thing like that. But I did it, and I wouldn't have let anyone prevent me.

Weddings are a different matter, of course. If you have them at home, it's no problem; the colored folks are all in the kitchen anyhow, and it's easy enough for them to slip in and see the ceremony. I know Winston and Jimmy and the ones we've known for years who turn up at weddings and big parties would *rather* stay in the kitchen. Jimmy takes charge of the punch bowl and sees that all the help stay sober enough to serve, at least until the rector goes home.

But it's not customary in Homochitto to include the servants at a church wedding. There's no balcony in the Episcopal church like the slave gallery in the Presbyterian church, and so there's no place to seat them. I couldn't do anything about that at Sarah's wedding; I just had to leave the rest of the servants out, but we did take Carrie Lee to the church.

I'll never forget how she behaved; if she'd been the mama, she couldn't have been more upset.

Sarah was only nineteen, too young, way too young to marry. To tell you the truth I was crushed at the time. I never, *never* thought any good would come of it. Oh, I realize I was even younger when I married. But in my day young ladies were brought up for marriage, and marriages were made on other terms, terms I understood. Bill was nearly thirty when we married, and he had exactly the same ideas Papa had. He simply finished my education. Which proves my contention—that a woman is old enough to marry when she has sense enough to pick the right man. If she doesn't, she isn't ready. That's the way it was with Sarah.

Wesley was just a boy—a selfish, unpredictable boy. He never understood how sheltered Sarah had been, how little she knew of the world, how indulgent we had been with her as a child, how totally unprepared she was for—for him. And afterwards she said it was all my fault. That's children for you. But I hadn't meant to prepare her for *Wesley*. I wouldn't have had him!

To go back to the wedding, Carrie Lee rode to the church with Sarah, and put the finishing touches on her hair and arranged her train. I didn't see this because of course I was sitting in the front of the church, but the people in the back said when Sarah and Brother George started down the aisle, Carrie Lee ran after them, straightening Sarah's train, the tears streaming down her face. I believe she would have followed them to the altar, but Edwin Ware slipped out of his pew and got her to go back. She was crying like a child, saying, "My baby. She's *my baby*."

You'd never have known she had children of her own the way she worshiped mine—still does.

But she had a married interlude. She was too old to carry a child; she had two miscarriages and lost one shortly after it was born. But she raised two or three of her husband's children. Negroes are so funny. Even Carrie Lee, as well as I know her, surprises me sometimes. She turned up at work one morning just as usual. (She never came until ten-thirty, and then stayed to serve supper and wash the dishes at night.) Bertie, who was cooking for me then, had been muttering and snickering to herself in the kitchen all morning, and, when I came in to plan dinner, she acted like she had a cricket down her bosom.

"What in the world are you giggling and wiggling about, Bertie?" I said. Bertie *fell* out.

Carrie Lee, forty if she was a day, stood there glowering. "You know Bertie, Miss Emma," she said. "Bertie's crazy as a road lizard."

Bertie pointed her finger at Carrie Lee and then she sort of hollered out, "She *ma'ied*, Miss Emma! She ma'ied."

You could have knocked me over with a feather. I didn't even know she was thinking about it. "Are you really, Carrie Lee?" I said.

"Yes'm."

"Well, Carrie Lee!" I said. "My feelings are hurt. Why didn't you tell us ahead of time. We could have had a fine wedding—something special."

I *was* disappointed, too. I've always wanted to put on a colored wedding, and *there*, I'd missed my chance.

Carrie Lee didn't say a word. I never *have* been able to figure out why she didn't tell us beforehand.

And then that nitwit, Bertie, began to laugh and holler again. "She don't need no special wedding, Miss Emma," Bertie said. "Ain't nothing special about getting ma'ied to Carrie Lee."

I was tickled at that, but I was surprised, too. Oh, I'm not so stupid that I don't understand how different Negro morals are from ours. Most of them simply don't have any. And I understand that it all comes from the way things were in slavery times. But our family was different. Grandmother told me many a time that they always went to a lot of trouble with the slave weddings and, after the war, with the tenants'. She kept a wedding dress and veil for the girls to wear, and she made sure everything was done right—license, preacher, reception, and all the trimmings. There was no jumping the broomstick in our family. And Carrie Lee's people had been on our place for generations. I never would have thought she'd carry on with a man.

She seemed devoted to her husband. If she had carried on with one, she must have carried on with others, but I reckon she'd had her fling and was ready to retire. The husband, Henry, was a "settled man," as they say, fifteen years older than Carrie Lee, and had a half-grown son and daughter and two or three younger children. He farmed about thirty acres of Wildwood. I had known the family ever since we moved to Homochitto. (Can you imagine that— my own place, and I didn't know about him and Carrie Lee!)

Later on, shortly before he died, he managed with Carrie Lee's help to buy a little place of his own.

I always let Carrie Lee off at noon on Saturday and gave her all day Sunday, although I hated running after the children. When they got old enough to amuse themselves, it wasn't so bad, but when they were little . . . ! Usually I got Bertie to take over for me. But I never believed in working a servant seven days a week, even when everybody did it, when they were lucky to get Emancipation Day and the Fourth of July. I never treated a servant like that. Bertie had her day off, too.

Henry would be waiting for Carrie Lee in his buggy when she got off on Saturday, and they'd catch the ferry across the river and drive out to Wildwood; and early Monday morning he'd send his son to drive her in to town—it was a couple of hours ride in the buggy. She didn't want to sell her house and move to the country (thank God!) and Henry wouldn't move to town. As Carrie Lee said, he didn't know nothing but farming, and he wasn't fixing to change his ways.

Once in a while she'd take the children to the country with her on Saturday afternoon, and I'd drive over after supper to get them. Every Saturday they begged to go; it was the greatest treat in the world to them to ride to Wildwood in the buggy, and they were crazy about the old man. For a while I kept their horses there, and when Billy was older he used to go over there to hunt. Henry taught him everything he knows about hunting. That was before cotton-dusting killed all the quail in this part of the country.

Well, Carrie Lee lived like that until we moved back to Atlanta, riding to the country every Saturday afternoon and coming in at daybreak on Monday morning. It's hard to understand how anyone could be satisfied with such a life, but Carrie Lee has a happy nature, and of course the fact that she was so much better off financially than most Negroes made a difference. Besides, I wouldn't be surprised if she wasn't glad to have the peace and quiet of a single life during the week. You might say she had her cake and ate it too.

Then I left Homochitto for several years. It's the only time Carrie Lee and I have ever been separated for more than a month or two.

I'd always heard Mama talk about Atlanta; she kept after Papa to go back, right up to his dying day. I'd been too young when we moved to care, but later, after Mama and Bill died, I got the notion that someday I'd go back. So finally, I went. The children were away at school, Billy at Episcopal High and Sarah at Ardsley Hall, and there was no reason for me to stay in Homochitto.

I thought of course Carrie Lee would go with me, but she didn't. For all her talk in Mama's day about how she missed Georgia, she didn't go back. She stayed with Henry. And, as I told you, I paid her wages all the time I was gone. We wrote to each other, and we saw each other when I brought the children to Homochitto for a visit. They never got used to Atlanta and never wanted to stay there in the summer. Then Billy settled in Homochitto and began to farm Wildwood himself, and I came home.

I wish I had kept some of Carrie Lee's letters. She has a beautiful hand. She used to practice copying Mama's script, and finally got so you could hardly tell them apart. It always gives me a turn to get a letter from her, addressed in Mama's hand, and then, inside, what a difference! When she writes something she thinks will amuse me, she puts "smile" after it in parentheses. Did you know that practically all Negroes do that, even the educated ones? I sometimes see pictures of all the ones that are so much in the news nowadays—diplomats and martyrs and so forth, and I wonder if they put (smile) in their letters.

Carrie Lee used to advise me in her letters, where she would never do such a thing face to face. Like one time, I remember, she wrote me, "All the babies is gone, yours and mine. I writes Miss Sarah and Mr. Billy and they don't answer me. True, I got the old man's kids, but you haven't got none. When will you get married again, Miss Emma? Find you a good man to warm your bed." And then she wrote (smile)—to make sure I understood she wasn't being impudent, I reckon.

It was while I was living in Atlanta that Carrie Lee got her picture in the magazine. I never quite understood how it happened, unless through ignorance on all sides—ignorance on the part of the photographer about Carrie Lee's real circumstances, and ignorance on her part about what the photographer wanted. We all laughed about it afterwards, although, of course, I never mentioned it to Carrie Lee.

When we left Homochitto, she had moved over to Wildwood and rented her house in town. That's how they saved enough money for the old man to buy a place of his own. I think she gave him every cent she made. But they had their pictures taken the winter before they bought the place, the last winter they were on Wildwood.

I'll never forget how shocked I was. I had gone out for dinner and bridge one night, and was quietly enjoying a drink when one of the men at the party picked up a copy of *Life* or *Fortune* or one of those magazines.

"By the way," he said to me, "I was reading about your old stamping ground today."

I might have known he was teasing me. None of those magazines ever has anything good to say about Mississippi. But I was interested in news of Homochitto, and never thought of that; and of course *he* didn't know it was Carrie Lee. I sat there while he found the article, and there she was—there they all were, Carrie Lee, Henry, and all the children, staring at me practically life-sized from a full-page picture.

The article was on sharecropping, and *they* were the examples of the downtrodden sharecropper. I must admit they looked seedy. I recognized my dress on Carrie Lee and one of Sarah's on the little girl. They were standing in a row outside the old man's house, grinning as if they knew what it was all about. At least, all of them except Carrie Lee were grinning. She's not much of a grinner.

A November day in the South—the trees bare and black, the stubble still standing in the cotton fields, an unpainted Negro cabin with the porch roof sagging, half a dozen dirty, ragged Negro children, and a bedraggled hound. What more could a Northern editor have asked?

What will these children get for Christmas?

I could have told him what they'd get for Christmas, and who had bought the presents and sent them off just the day before. And I could have told him whose money was accumulating in the teapot on the mantelpiece.

To do them justice, I'll say I don't believe Carrie Lee or Henry had the faintest idea why he'd taken their pictures. They just liked to have their pictures taken. But the very idea of them as poverty-stricken, downtrodden tenants! I couldn't have run them off Wildwood with a posse and a pack of bloodhounds.

We got a big kick out of it. I cut the picture out and sent it to Sarah.

The old man died the year after they began to buy their farm, and then Carrie Lee moved to town, and shortly after that I came back to Homochitto for good. Henry, Jr., took over the payments on the farm and lives on it. He's a sullen Negro—not like his father—but he's good to Carrie Lee. In the summer he keeps her supplied with fresh vegetables; he comes in and makes repairs on her house to save her the price of a carpenter; things like that. But he's sullen. I never have liked these Negroes who're always kowtowing and grinning like idiots—"white folks' niggers," some people down here call them—but it wouldn't hurt that boy to learn some manners. I told Carrie Lee as much one time.

I had gone into the kitchen to see about dinner, and he was sitting at the table with his hat on—this was after we moved back here, and old Henry was dead—eating his breakfast—*my* food, need I add. He didn't even look at me, much less get up.

"Good morning, Henry," I said.

He mumbled something and still didn't get up.

"*Good morning, Henry,*" I said again.

"Morning," he said, just as sullen as he could be.

I went to Carrie Lee later and told her that any man, black, white, blue, or green, could get up and take off his hat when a lady came into the room. That's not prejudice. That's good manners.

"He ain't *bad,* Miss Emma," she said. "Just seems like he always got one misery or another. Born to trouble, as the sparks fly upward, like the Good Book says."

"Well, he'd feel a lot better, if he'd get a smile on that sullen face of his," I said. "Sometimes people bring trouble on themselves just by their dispositions."

"Ah, Miss Emma," she said, "ever since he married, it's been *root, hog, or die* for Henry, Jr. He ain't settled into it yet."

Of course, I didn't know then about the boy's sister, Carrie Lee's stepdaughter. Didn't know she had left Homochitto, much less that she had come back. She apparently married and moved to "*Dee*-troit" while we were living in Atlanta. I didn't see her until some time after she came to live in town with Carrie Lee, just a few years ago. Henry, Jr., finally had to turn her over to Carrie Lee. I can't blame him for *that*, I don't suppose. By then he had five children of his own, and there was scarcely room for them in the house, much less the sister.

I found out about the sister because Sarah left Wesley. That was a hard year. Sarah packed up the children and everything she owned and came home from Cleveland, inconsolable. I suppose I could have said, "I told you so," but I didn't have the heart. She'd married too young, there's no getting around it, and by the time she was old enough to know her own mind, there she was with two children. I tell you, people say to me: "You don't know how lucky you are that Bill left you so well-fixed. Never any money problems." They don't know how wrong they are. Money's a preoccupying worry. It keeps your mind off worse things. If you don't have to work or to worry about money, you're free to worry more about yourself and your children. Believe me, *nobody's* exempt from disappointment. I'm *proud* of the way I've raised my children. I've taught them everything I know about good manners and responsibility and honor, and I've kept their property safe for them. I've tried to give them everything that my family and Bill gave me. But when love fails you, none of it is any use. Your bed is soft and warm, but one dark night you find that sleep won't come.

I was half crazy over Sarah. She slept until noon every day and moped around the house all afternoon. Then she'd start drinking and keep me up till all hours crying and carrying on. "What am I going to do? What am I going to do?"

She still loved that good-for-nothing man.

I borrowed Carrie Lee from Billy to take care of Sarah's babies while she was here. I'm too old to chase a two-year-old child, and Sarah hardly looked at the children. She was too busy grieving over Wesley. So Carrie Lee was a boon; she took over, and we never had a minute's concern for them. Like all children, they adored her.

Billy's wife was furious with me for taking her, but I simply had to. And Carrie Lee was in seventh heaven, back with Sarah and me; she never has gotten along too well with Billy's wife. Oh, she goes out there faithfully, on account of Billy and the children. But Billy's wife is different from us—a different breed of cat, altogether, there's no getting around it. I get along fine with her because I mind my own business, but Carrie Lee considers our business her business. And then too, as I said, Carrie Lee is a *finished* servant. She has run my house for months at a time without a word of direction from me. She can plan and put on a formal dinner for twelve without batting an eye. Billy's wife doesn't know anything about good servants. She tells Carrie Lee every day what she wants done that day; and she insulted her, the first time she had a party, by showing her how to set the table.

No doubt there are two sides to the story. I'm sure Billy's wife gets sick of hearing Carrie Lee say, "But Miss Emma don't do it that way." It must be like having an extra mother-in-law. I won't go into that. I know it's the style nowadays not to get along with your mother-in-law, although I don't see why. I never had a breath of trouble with mine.

But I'm wandering again. I want to tell you the wonderful thing Carrie Lee said when she was telling us about her stepdaughter.

The children were taking their naps one afternoon, and Sarah and I were lying down in my room and Carrie Lee was sitting in there talking to us. Sarah was still thrashing around about Wesley. The truth is she wanted to go back to him. She was hollering to Carrie Lee about how he'd betrayed her and how she could never forgive him—just asking somebody please to find her a good reason why she should forgive him, if the truth be known. But I wasn't going to help her; I knew it would never work.

Carrie Lee listened a while and thought about it a while and then she said, "Miss Sarah, honey, you know I got a crazy child?"

That took the wind out of Sarah's sails, and she sat up and stopped crying and said, "What?"

I was surprised, too. I didn't know a thing about that crazy girl. When I thought about it, I remembered that Carrie Lee had mentioned her to me once or twice, but at the time I hadn't paid any attention.

"I got a crazy child," Carrie Lee says. "Least, she ain't exactly my child, she old Henry's. But she *sho* crazy."

"I didn't know that, Carrie Lee," I said. "Where does she stay?"

"She stay with me," Carrie Lee says. "Right there in the house with me. Neighbors tend to her in the daytime. I ain't had her with me long—no more than a year or two."

"Well, what do I care? What's it got to do with me?" Sarah said, and she began to cry again. She wasn't herself, or she wouldn't have been so mean.

"This what," Carrie Lee says. "You know why she crazy? A man driv her crazy, that's why. You don't watch out, a man gonna drive you crazy."

Sarah lay back on the bed and kicked her feet like a baby.

"Honey, you want me to tell you how to keep a man from driving you crazy? And not only a man. Howsomever it happens, the day comes when one of God's creatures, young or old, is bound to break your heart. I'll tell you how to bear it."

Sarah shook her head.

"I'm gonna tell you anyhow. Look at me. I'm sixty years old. I looks forty-five. No man never driv me crazy, nor nobody else. I tell you how I keep him from it."

Sarah couldn't help it. She sat up and listened.

"See everything, see nothing," says Carrie Lee. "Hear everything, hear nothing. Know everything, know nothing. Trust in the Lord and love little children. That's how to ease your heart."

Did you ever? Well sir, maybe Sarah would have gone anyway, or maybe she heeded Carrie Lee's advice. Anyway, she took the two children soon afterwards and went back to Wesley, and it wasn't until three years later that they got a divorce.

So here we are, Carrie Lee and I, getting old. You might say we've spent our lives together. I reckon I know her better than I would have known my own sister, if I had had one. As Carrie Lee would say, "We've seen some wonderful distressing times."

On Sundays, when she's off, lots of times she bakes me a cake and brings it around and we sit and talk of the old days when Mama and Bill were alive and when the children were little. We talk about the days of the flood, about this year's crop, about the rains in April, and in August the dry weather, about Billy's wife, and Sarah and Billy's grown-up troubles, about the grandchildren, and "all the days we've seen."

If she comes to see me on Sunday, Carrie Lee will tell me something that amuses me the whole week long. Like a couple of weeks ago we were talking about the crop. I'd been worrying all summer about the drought. It looked for a while as if Billy wouldn't make a bale to the acre. And every time I mentioned it to Carrie Lee, she'd say, "Trust in the Lord, Miss Emma." She's still a great one for leaving things to the Almighty.

Then, bless John, the cotton popped open, and, in spite of everything, it's a good year.

"Well, Carrie Lee," I said, "it looks like you were right and I was wrong. Billy's got a fine crop."

And Carrie Lee says (just listen to this), she says, "Miss Emma, if I say a chicken dips snuff, you look under his bill."

Isn't that killing? When I got by myself, I just hollered.

Looking at it another way, though, it isn't so funny. Billy's a man, and a son is never the companion to his mother that a daughter is. You know the old saying, "A son is a son till he gets him a wife, but a daughter's a daughter all of her life." I think if his father had lived, if there were a man in the house, Billy would come to see me more often. If Sarah were here, we would enjoy each other, I know; but she's married again and lives so far away, they seldom come home, and when they do, it's only for a few days.

I've never been a reader, either. I like to visit, to *talk*. I'm an articulate person. And nowadays, instead of visiting, people sit and stare at a television set. Oh, I still play cards and mah-jongg. I have friends here, but we drifted apart during the years I was in Atlanta, and things have never been quite the same since I came back.

So I'm often alone on Sunday afternoon when Carrie Lee comes to see

me. That's how it happens we sit so long together, drinking coffee and talking. Late in the afternoon, Billy sometimes comes and brings the children to
call, but they never stay for long. They go home to Wildwood because Billy's
wife doesn't like to be there alone after dark. Carrie Lee stays on, and we go
in the kitchen and she fixes my supper. As I've told you, I'd rather visit with
her than with most white folks. She understands me. When I think about it,
it sometimes seems to me, with Bill and Mama dead and the children grown
and gone, that Carrie Lee is all I have left of my own.

1963

The Hammer Man

Toni Cade Bambara

I was glad to hear that Manny had fallen off the roof. I had put out the tale that I was down with yellow fever, but nobody paid me no mind, least of all Dirty Red who stomped right in to announce that Manny had fallen off the roof and that I could come out of hiding now. My mother dropped what she was doing, which was the laundry, and got the whole story out of Red. "Bad enough you gots to hang around with boys," she said. "But fight with them too. And you would pick the craziest one at that."

Manny was supposed to be crazy. That was his story. To say you were bad put some people off. But to say you were crazy, well, you were officially not to be messed with. So that was his story. On the other hand, after I called him what I called him and said a few choice things about his mother, his face did go through some piercing changes. And I did kind of wonder if maybe he sure was nuts. I didn't wait to find out. I got in the wind. And then he waited for me on my stoop all day and all night, not hardly speaking to the people going in and out. And he was there all day Saturday, with his sister bringing him peanut-butter sandwiches and cream sodas. He must've gone to the bathroom right there cause every time I looked out the kitchen window, there he was. And Sunday, too. I got to thinking the boy was mad.

"You got no sense of humor, that's your trouble," I told him. He looked up, but he didn't say nothing. All at once I was real sorry about the whole thing. I should've settled for hitting off the little girls in the school yard, or waiting for Frankie to come in so we could raise some kind of hell. This way I had to play sick when my mother was around cause my father had already taken away my BB gun and hid it.

I don't know how they got Manny on the roof finally. Maybe the Wakefield kids, the ones who keep the pigeons, called him up. Manny was a sucker for sick animals and things like that. Or maybe Frankie got some nasty girls to go up on the roof with him and got Manny to join him. I don't know. Anyway, the catwalk had lost all its cement and the roof always did kind of slant downward. So Manny fell off the roof. I got over my yellow fever right quick, needless to say, and ventured outside. But by this time I had already told Miss Rose that Crazy Manny was after me. And Miss Rose, being who she was, quite naturally went over to Manny's house and said a few harsh words to his mother, who, being who she was, chased Miss Rose out into the street and they commenced to get with it, snatching bottles out of the garbage cans and breaking them on the johnny pumps and stuff like that.

Dirty Red didn't have to tell us about this. Everybody could see and hear all. I never figured the garbage cans for an arsenal, but Miss Rose came up with sticks and table legs and things, and Manny's mother had her share of scissor blades and bicycle chains. They got to rolling in the streets and all you could see was pink drawers and fat legs. It was something else. Miss Rose is nutty but Manny's mother's crazier than Manny. They were at it a couple of times during my sick spell. Everyone would congregate on the window sills or the fire escape, commenting that it was still much too cold for this kind of nonsense. But they watched anyway. And then Manny fell off the roof. And that was that. Miss Rose went back to her dream books and Manny's mother went back to her tumbled-down kitchen of dirty clothes and bundles and bundles of rags and children.

My father got in on it too, cause he happened to ask Manny one night why he was sitting on the stoop like that every night. Manny told him right off that he was going to kill me first chance he got. Quite naturally this made my father a little warm, me being his only daughter and planning to become a doctor and take care of him in his old age. So he had a few words with Manny first, and then he got hold of the older brother, Bernard, who was more his size. Bernard didn't see how any of it was his business or my father's business, so my father got mad and jammed Bernard's head into the mailbox. Then my father started getting messages from Bernard's uncle about where to meet him for a showdown and all. My father didn't say a word to my mother all this time; just sat around mumbling and picking up the phone and putting it down, or grabbing my stickball bat and putting it back. He carried on like this for days till I thought I would scream if the yellow fever didn't have me so weak. And then Manny fell off the roof, and my father went back to his beer-drinking buddies.

I was in the school yard, pitching pennies with the little boys from the elementary school, when my friend Violet hits my brand-new Spaudeen over the wall. She came running back to tell me that Manny was coming down the block. I peeked beyond the fence and there he was all right. He had his head all wound up like a mummy and his arm in a sling and his leg in a cast. It looked phony to me, especially that walking cane. I figured Dirty Red had told me a tale just to get me out there so Manny could stomp me, and Manny was playing it up with costume and all till he could get me.

"What happened to him?" Violet's sisters whispered. But I was too busy trying to figure out how this act was supposed to work. Then Manny passed real close to the fence and gave me a look.

"You had enough, Hammer Head," I yelled. "Just bring your crummy self in this yard and I'll pick up where I left off." Violet was knocked out and the other kids went into a huddle. I didn't have to say anything else. And when they all pressed me later, I just said, "You know that hammer he always carries in his fatigues?" And they'd all nod waiting for the rest of a long story. "Well, I took it away from him." And I walked off nonchalantly.

Manny stayed indoors for a long time. I almost forgot about him. New kids moved into the block and I got all caught up with that. And then Miss Rose finally hit the numbers and started ordering a whole lot of stuff through the mail and we would sit on the curb and watch these weird-looking packages being carried in, trying to figure out what simple-minded thing she had thrown her money away on when she might just as well wait for the warm weather and throw a block party for all her godchildren.

After a while a center opened up and my mother said she'd increase my allowance if I went and joined because I'd have to get out of my pants and stay in skirts, on account of that's the way things were at the center. So I joined and got to thinking about everything else but old Hammer Head. It was a rough place to get along in, the center, but my mother said that I needed to be be'd with and she needed to not be with me, so I went. And that time I sneaked into the office, that's when I really got turned on. I looked into one of those not-quite-white folders and saw that I was from a deviant family in a deviant neighborhood. I showed my mother the word in the dictionary, but she didn't pay me no mind. It was my favorite word after that. I ran it in the ground till one day my father got the strap just to show how deviant he could get. So I gave up trying to improve my vocabulary. And I almost gave up my dungarees.

Then one night I'm walking past the Douglas Street park cause I got thrown out of the center for playing pool when I should've been sewing, even though I had already decided that this was going to be my last fling with boy things, and starting tomorrow I was going to fix my hair right and wear skirts all the time just so my mother would stop talking about her gray hairs, and Miss Rose would stop calling me by my brother's name by mistake. So I'm walking past the park and there's ole Manny on the basketball court, perfecting his lay-ups and talking with himself. Being me, I quite naturally walk right up and ask what the hell he's doing playing in the dark, and he looks up and all around like the dark had crept up on him when he wasn't looking. So I knew right away that he'd been out there for a long time with his eyes just going along with the program.

"There was two seconds to go and we were one point behind," he said, shaking his head and staring at his sneakers like they was somebody. "And I was in the clear. I'd left the men in the backcourt and there I was, smiling, you dig, cause it was in the bag. They passed the ball and I slid the ball up nice and easy cause there was nothing to worry about. And . . ." He shook his head. "I muffed the goddamn shot. Ball bounced off the rim. . ." He stared at his hands. "The game of the season. Last game." And then he ignored me altogether, though he wasn't talking to me in the first place. He went back to the lay-ups, always from the same spot with his arms crooked in the same way, over and over. I must've gotten hypnotized cause I probably stood there for at least an hour watching like a fool till I couldn't even see the damn ball, much less the basket. But I stood there anyway for no reason I know of. He never missed. But he cursed himself away. It was torture. And then a squad car pulled up and a short cop with hair like one of the Marx Brothers came out hitching up his pants. He looked real hard at me and then at Manny.

"What are you two doing?"

"He's doing a lay-up. I'm watching," I said with my smart self.

Then the cop just stood there and finally turned to the other one who was just getting out of the car.

"Who unlocked the gate?" the big one said.

"It's always unlocked," I said. Then we three just stood there like a bunch of penguins watching Manny go at it.

"This on the level?" the big guy asked, tilting his hat back with the thumb the way big guys do in hot weather. "Hey you," he said, walking over to Manny. "I'm talking to you." He finally grabbed the ball to get Manny's attention. But that didn't work. Manny just stood there with his arms out waiting for the pass so he could save the game. He wasn't paying no mind to the cop. So, quite naturally, when the cop slapped him upside his head it was a surprise. And when the cop started counting three to go, Manny had already recovered from the slap and was just ticking off the seconds before the buzzer sounded and all was lost.

"Gimme the ball, man." Manny's face was all tightened up and ready to pop.

"Did you hear what I said, black boy?"

Now, when somebody says that word like that, I gets warm. And crazy or no crazy, Manny was my brother at that moment and the cop was the enemy.

"You better give him back his ball," I said. "Manny don't take no mess from no cops. He ain't bothering nobody. He's gonna be Mister Basketball when he grows up. Just trying to get a little practice in before the softball season starts."

"Look here, sister, we'll run you in too," Harpo said.

"I damn sure can't be your sister seeing how I'm a black girl. Boy, I sure will be glad when you run me in so I can tell everybody about that. You must think you're in the South, mister."

The big guy screwed his mouth up and let one of them hard-day sighs. "The park's closed, little girl, so why don't you and your boyfriend go on home."

That really got me. The "little girl" was bad enough but that "boy friend" was too much. But I kept cool, mostly because Manny looked so piti-ful waiting there with his hands in a time-out and there being no one to stop the clock. But I kept my cool mostly cause of that hammer in Manny's pocket and no telling how frantic things can get what with a big-mouth like me, a couple of wise cops, and a crazy boy too.

"The gates are open," I said real quiet-like, "and this here's a free coun-try. So why don't you give him back his ball?"

The big cop did another one of those sighs, his specialty I guess, and then he bounced the ball to Manny who went right into his gliding thing clear up to the backboard, damn near like he was some kind of very beauti-ful bird. And then he swooshed that ball in, even if there was no net, and you couldn't really hear the swoosh. Something happened to the bones in my chest. It was something.

"Crazy kids anyhow," the one with the wig said and turned to go. But the big guy watched Manny for a while and I guess something must've snapped in his head, cause all of a sudden he was hot for taking Manny to jail or court or somewhere and started yelling at him and everything, which is a bad thing to do to Manny, I can tell you. And I'm standing there thinking that none of my teachers, from kindergarten right on up, none of them knew what they were talking about. I'll be damned if I ever knew one of them rosy-cheeked cops that smiled and helped you get to school without neither you or your little raggedy dog getting hit by a truck that had a smile on its face, too. Not that I ever believed it. I knew Dick and Jane was full of crap from the get-go, especially them cops. Like this dude, for example, pulling on Manny's clothes like that when obviously he had just done about the most beautiful thing a man can do and not be a fag. No cop could swoosh without a net.

"Look out, man," was all Manny said, but it was the way he pushed the cop that started the real yelling and threats. And I thought to myself, Oh God here I am trying to change my ways, and not talk back in school, and do like my mother wants, but just have this last fling, and now this—getting shot in the stomach and bleeding to death in Douglas Street park and poor Manny getting pistol-whipped by those bastards and whatnot. I could see it all, practically crying too. And it just wasn't no kind of thing to happen to a small child like me with my confirmation picture in the paper next to my weeping parents and schoolmates. I could feel the blood sticking to my shirt and my eyeballs slipping away, and then that confirmation picture again; and my mother and her gray hair; and Miss Rose heading for the precinct with a shotgun; and my father getting old and feeble with no one to doctor him up and all.

And I wished Manny had fallen off the damn roof and died right then and there and saved me all this aggravation of being killed with him by these cops who surely didn't come out of no fifth-grade reader. But it didn't happen. They just took the ball and Manny followed them real quiet-like right out of the park into the dark, then into the squad car with his head drooping and his arms in a crook. And I went on home cause what the hell am I going to do on a basketball court, and it getting to be nearly midnight?

I didn't see Manny no more after he got into that squad car. But they didn't kill him after all cause Miss Rose heard he was in some kind of big house for people who lose their marbles. And then it was spring finally, and me and Violet was in this very boss fashion show at the center. And Miss Rose bought me my first corsage—yellow roses to match my shoes.

1966

Community of Victims

Ekwueme Michael Thelwell

Mitch came out of the cool dimness of the bar and started down the block to the bus stop. The city heat, which seemed sticky and grimy, was reflected off the pavements, scarcely tempered by a slight breeze, which was itself hot and dusty.

Beer always relaxed him and he walked loosely, jauntily, with an athlete's grace, full of confidence in his own youth and power. He came up to the bus stop with a casual arrogance, hardly noticing the people loosely grouped around. He thought of the letter in his pocket: "The committee has voted to make available to you—" a year in Europe—Goddamn, the "spook" halfback isn't doing so bad! All you had to do was to learn to maneuver in their world, speak their language—. His hand went automatically to the back pocket of his jeans for the book, which he had found as necessary a part of the use of the transit system as the token.

The book was by some white psychologist who had probed into the psyche of an old tribal chief in South Africa and seemed to have been shocked at the levels of conscious, disguised, and subliminal hate that his probings had disclosed.

And him a psychologist, too, Mitch thought sourly; the white man's innocence syndrome again. Such outrageous naïveté. Serves him right—what in hell else did he expect? He found the book a trifle obvious, unless of course, you were "Ofay," in which case you could be discomfited by the African's image of yourself and your world. Mitch knew that he wasn't really reading the book, that while his eyes leaped over the words his mind was detached. He became aware that he was, in fact, brandishing the book. It made a symbol because of the angry bold words of the title and the corrugated black face, at once barbaric and pathetic, which adorned the jacket. The picture of the chief with his collapsed, untidy, old mouth, which even bitterness couldn't firm up, and his ancient and murderous eyes, was startling. Strange how fidgety people could become when confronted with anything real like hate and death, or any symbol of these things. It's like white Americans when confronted with anything Negro that won't fit the accepted justifications and myths—

Maybe it is just because they have been too insulated, too well-fed, have been made to feel too fraudulently secure, entombed and comforted in the pink-and-white pastel blandness of their society for too long, that a thing like a snarling black face can disturb them. Mitch closed the book.

The knowledge that he himself was compensating, projecting, being smug, feeling superior, was amusing. Hell, he had every right to his own prejudices and resentments, like everyone else. He let his glance, overtly challenging, rove over the faces of the people around him at the bus stop. The usual city group—the same gray armored-up faces and the same shabby, perpetually soiled look that the nonaffluent members of the "affluent society" seemed to wear like a badge in some secret organization that existed for the perverse pleasure of giving the lie to the society's assumptions.

Mitch noticed with some disappointment that nobody appeared affected by his defiant glance. Such arrogance in the gesture, too, like a Flamenco dancer or a matador, and no one noticed. So remote and tired they seemed, so damned remote and tired, each one turned in on himself, completely caught up in the closed back-reaches of his own concern. The community of the city. Hah! How mechanical, somehow listless, and enervated they were.

Mitch found himself changing position quickly and impatiently, as though by doing so he could assure himself that *he* was as yet undefeated and vital, and that there was a force, an energy in him, that would not let him be still. He recognized his posturing for what it was and grinned sardonically at himself. "You shouldn't have to prove it, Baby, you don't have to prove a thing. What's it Bouf said in *The Blacks*, 'They aren't really white but shades of pink and yellow and gray?' "

He began to amuse himself by staring openly at his companions to see how accurate that pronouncement was. That little man, Christ, he's bright yellow. Probably "takes the sun" at Coney Island with a fat, shapeless wife and a horde of kids on Sundays. And two little boys discussing "da movies" in adenoidal Brooklynese: they were colorless, their faces marked by an urban pallor. A girl in her early teens, standing slightly knock-kneed, her braced teeth chomping on a wad of gum, her hair in curlers, stood gazing vacantly at nothing; she was whitish and pink in streaks and patches, Mitch noted. And in a few years she will probably be beautiful or at least *chic*—from nine to five anyway, until she gets married, then back to baggy shorts and daytime curlers.

Then he saw the woman. She was tall and well-fleshed, with a strong, well-formed face. Mitch looked into her frank gray eyes and looked away surprised. She had actually seen him, actually looked at him! This sudden and totally unexpected contact surprised him. He retained the image of rounded womanly arms, a simple, sleeveless cotton dress, belted at the waist like an ancient Greek tunic, and light, sun-streaked blond hair. Preparing himself, he allowed, his eyes to move methodically across the group until he was looking directly at her. The sunlight shone off her hair and dress, and she appeared strangely clean, her face untouched by makeup. She returned his gaze from eyes that upset him by their unexpected serenity. He realized grudgingly that she was not to be easily reduced to self-consciousness and he returned to looking at his book.

She is, he thought, a wholesome-looking woman. But it isn't the neuter kind of sterile wholesomeness that Madison Avenue uses to sell its beer and cigarettes. No—it's something more personal, a fully sexed, carnal cleanness that is altogether out of place among such soiled-looking city people.

He tried to engross himself in his book, but he could not forget the alert liveliness of the woman's eyes. Oh, well, I guess some of us manage to retain some humanity, he thought.

Yet for some reason the woman's tranquillity jarred him; she defied the neat compartments into which it was his habit, and his defense, to fit and, thereby, dispose of all white people. Hell, they were either smug, deluded, and completely out of touch with their own existence, or hyperanxious and neurotic. This woman clearly did not fit into such categories.

His reflections were broken by a new sound introducing itself into the steady drone of the street noises. A little Negro man, very drunk, who might have been 40 years old, was babbling at the girl.

"You're a nish girl—Ah like you. Don't you like me? Have a drink, now!" He was leaning on a signpost precariously close to the woman, offering her his flat bottle half full of a yellow wine.

"Here, baby, have a drink," he insisted, dribbling saliva. "You're a nish girl. Let's have a drink, uh?"

A tense silence held the crowd for a minute. Nobody seemed to want to look at the drunk, except for the two little boys who were grinning. Two middle-aged women were now a part of the crowd. Mitch hadn't seen them join the group, but somehow they had become conspicuous, backs stiff, stringy necks bristling with a suppressed, yet communicated outrage. They stared up the street with their lips moving silently. Yeah, Mitch thought, disgraceful, disgraceful, what is the world coming to? I agree with you, you old hags.

The drunk's voice was growing louder, its initial wheedling intimacy beginning to harden into anger. Mitch's first impulse was to laugh. The woman was so much taller, appeared so much stronger, than the wasted little drunk that his approving, almost condescending, "You're a nish girl" was funny. But it wasn't really funny.

Oh, well, maybe she *is* his girl, Mitch thought, snickering at the absurdity of the idea, and if she isn't, it's like the man said, *'Tis a consummation devoutly to be wished!* It wasn't working. The mental wisecracks did not relieve the embarrassment he felt growing, and his anger at himself for feeling vulnerable and compromised by the actions of some drunken Negro he didn't know fed his discomfort.

The woman was behaving rather well, he observed, with a twinge of resentment. She had pulled herself erect, stepped away from the drunk's breath, but she had not lost her composure. She caught Mitch's glance and her eyebrows arched in a tolerant what-can-I-do? expression, which, whatever it was supposed to do, only succeeded in crystallizing Mitch's anger. He jerked his eyes away furiously, "Don't look at me, bitch, I'm not involved," he wanted to say. The other people at the bus stop were stubbornly maintaining their detachment. Nothing was their business!

Yeah, but what are they thinking, the slobs. Here's food for all the prejudices you want and need so badly to cling to, Mitch thought, something to go home and tell your friends about, and cluck over, and to remember on the day I come into the neighborhood.

The drunken monotone continued, ranging in a pathetic burlesque between courtship and rape, at once threatening and cajoling. "You're a nish girl. Don't you like me?"

The drunk's mind seemed finally to register the snickers of the two boys, a humiliating testimony to his own presumptuousness and ineffectuality. His voice grew louder, his stance mock-menacing, and he tried to introduce a note of toughness into his voice. He appeared to want to walk away, but now that the incident had become public, he seemed unable to do this or to accept the rejection that only his drunkenness could have disguised as less than inevitable. He tried to threaten.

"Not gonna ask you again. Gawddam, have a drink." He waved his bottle belligerently. "Ish good stuff, I tol' you, we kin have fun. Don't you like me?"

Stop it, you stupid son-of-a-bitch, Mitch thought, stop it. You are giving *them* excuses. Still he felt an unreasonable compassion for the little man. If only the bitch seemed threatened! How Goddamn composed she is! He found himself wishing that it was night, that the area was secluded, that the drunk was nigger-big, razor-scarred and evil-looking. What would happen to her Goddamned "Miss Ann" composure then, he thought. And yet she *was* reacting with unusual patience.

Leave her alone, man. Don't do this to yourself, to her. Hit her, rape her, anything, but stop that Goddamned whining, stop begging. Not like that, man, not like that. And you, white woman, be disgusted, or uncomfortable, or best of all, afraid. But not so damned unreachable. At least recognize his existence some other way: Call a cop, even. Another headwhipping in the basement of some precinct wouldn't scar the poor drunk as deeply as this public evidence of his own futility. Then he'd be a threat, or even a pest—something to be stamped on; but he would have broken in. He would be *something*.

The drunk was trying to be mean now. His voice grew louder, and he caught the woman by the arm, desperately trying to be tough, to evoke some reaction. But in his bleary eyes were tears, maybe from the dust and glare, maybe from shame at the absurdity of his role; watching him, Mitch knew sickly that this was no new role for the little man. The woman gently disengaged her arm from the drunk's grip and walked to the other side of the bus stop, nearer to Mitch. She managed, as she did this, to give the impression that she was acting more for the drunk's protection than for herself.

The drunk stood gaping at his empty hand, then removing the cap from the bottle, took a long drink, letting the wine run down his stringy neck. He stood in the middle of the sidewalk shaking his head and noisily clearing his throat. There was a look of foolish, drunken bewilderment on his face as he stood there blinking, and now Mitch saw that his late victim was looking at him with concern.

Disgust, he thought angrily, or anger. That's what you are supposed to feel, not pity. It's way too late for your pity, way too late for that. Oh, hell, if he starts again I should stop him. She doesn't deserve to be molested and embarrassed. Still he knew and was confused by the knowledge, that had the drunk struck her, he'd have been outraged. He would have stopped him and been truly sorry, and maybe even felt a little guilty. But he would not have been sickened in quite the same way.

Oh Goddamn this stupid, screwed-up accumulation of inherited guilt and hate and endless retribution that created this poor ineffectual drunk, incapable of being lover or defiler, and not even malignant enough to evoke disgust. What is left him? And the woman, why did she have to be embarrassed, and why do I have to be caught in the middle between them?

Mitch looked at the drunk, a shabby, forlorn figure now, as he stood outlined in the glare ten yards away, isolated. When the drunk passed his hand over his face, his eyes cleared for a moment, and Mitch felt the physical presence of vulnerability and sadness that somehow shone from his eyes in a sudden moment of clarity. It passed and he was coming over to the group again, mumbling and slobbering, his face set in lines of drunken stubbornness.

The sun-yellowed little man saw him coming, and a look of hesitance flickered across his face. Then, apparently reaching a decision, he started toward the drunken Negro.

"Oh, a defender of white womanhood, too," Mitch muttered, "now where does this little schmuck think he's going—to set things in their proper perspective?"

Aloud he said, "Easy, pal, just stay where you are, OK?" And he caught the would-be knight reassuringly by the arm, his grip as strong as he could make it, and he noticed the man wince as he checked his movement. Mitch wasn't sure why he stopped the man, except that it was action, a way of declaring himself, but he felt certain that the man was grateful at being spared any involvement. Above all, Mitch did not want the drunk to swallow another defeat, and at the hands of such a seedy-looking little white man. He stepped deliberately in front of the blond woman then, his back almost touching her, making it impossible for the drunk to reach her, he folded his arms and pretended to read.

"'Scush me, man, gotta see someone."

Mitch pretended not to hear. The drunk's voice grew angry as he became aware of what Mitch was doing,

"Ah said, Outta ma way, man. What's the matter anyway?"

"Oh? Oh, I'm sorry, sir, excuse me." Mitch had not moved.

"Whaddya tryin' to do, man? Who do you think you are anyway?"

The drunk sounded really indignant now. He suspected that Mitch's action was telling him that he was making a fool of himself and this triggered the first anger that Mitch had noticed in him. Mitch realized that he was glad to see this change. It was a hell of a lot better than the shamed half servility, half anger of a few moments before. He felt a fierce compassion for the little man, yet he knew that he would hit him if it became necessary.

Now who's defending white womanhood, he thought bitterly, and something close to hatred rose in him for this woman who had done nothing but be white and desirable.

"Man, don't do it, please don't do it. I don't want to have to—" Mitch's voice was low, insistent, almost a whisper. For some reason he did not want the woman, standing just behind him, to hear. It was very important that she did not.

"Don't do what? What are you talking about?" the drunk demanded with drunken truculence. "Outta mah way. Jes who the fugg do ya think ya are?" He was obviously finding in Mitch a more legitimate object for his wrath.

Mitch wanted to throw his arm across the thin shoulders, to lead him away, and to say, "Be cool, man. I'm with you. Don't do this to yourself. Don't do it to me. Like we stand together, man, let's forget it." Instead he stood in front of the little drunk, feet spread, arms folded, feeling his face harden and his eyes growing hostile. The bus was stopping behind him. He heard the doors open and people entering. The drunk looked past him and something much like relief reflected in his eyes, to be immediately replaced with blustering anger. He started to speak and Mitch cut him off.

"Mister," he said, "I am not sure what I did to you, but I'm sorry. I really am." He tried to make his voice and manner convey diffidence. If I can only give this cat back something, he thought. The drunk contemplated the sudden capitulation blankly for a few seconds, scarcely able to hide his surprise and confusion. Mitch wondered how long it had been since anyone had thought enough of the derelict to be scared of him.

"You're lucky," the drunk growled. "Jus' never try to be so lucky again."

You're one real lucky young punk. Messing wid me, hah." He punctuated the last phrase with a jabbing finger.

"Thanks, thanks, sir," Mitch said as he stepped into the bus. Through the window he saw the drunk point a final warning finger in his direction before turning away.

Poor screwed-up little guy. Probably feels real tough now. Mitch found a seat and immediately riveted his eyes to the book. He couldn't shake the engulfing sense of personal loss and of being somehow diminished himself.

"Excuse me." Her voice was clear but hesitant. "I just wanted to thank you for—" She broke off when Mitch shook her hand from his wrist and leveled into her eyes a steady, hostile stare.

"I hope you don't think that I did you any service, miss." Their eyes locked for a short time and Mitch wondered, does this broad think I'm going to apologize for the drunk? Does she think I did it for her? Can't she understand that it might have been for the drunk, or for me, or even for the Goddamned race, but not for her.

He felt like the betrayer of some vaguely understood bond. His mind groped frantically for the word, the gesture, some way to establish clearly to her and himself that he had acted only out of a desire to save something of the drunk's pride—to keep him from another encounter with the white man's jail. But he could only glare into her earnest gray eyes.

Under the seething, inarticulate fury of the glare she flushed slightly and lowered her eyes. Somewhat appeased, Mitch continued the pretense of reading, scowling down at the book.

"Mister? I think you might not have understood."

"And what might I not have understood, miss?" He stared at her again.

"That," and her voice faltered again before his mute hostility, "that I— I think I understand. I don't blame him."

Oho, she understands, he thought. What the hell does she understand? A generous, compassionate, tolerant white woman. Well, she's either too late or too early. Who in hell needs her compassion or understanding? Hope she chokes on it.

"Don't you think you *should* blame him, miss? No man has the right, drunk or otherwise, to molest a woman. Or is his case special?"

The woman looked astonished.

"No, no," she said. "I just mean that, well, that it wasn't his fault. It wasn't mine either."

"Oh, lady, how could *anything* be your fault? I don't know what you are talking about."

Mitch rudely changed his seat, asking himself as he got up, Now what the hell are you mad about now?

1964

The Fare to the Moon

Reynolds Price

One

As ever, she woke sometime before light. In the fall of the year, and with war savings-time, that meant it was just before five o'clock. The nearest time-piece in the house was his watch; and that was under his pillow still, still on his wrist. His brother would be here in half an hour; his overnight satchel was already packed—a clean pair of drawers, his toothbrush and razor, a Hershey bar she hid in a pair of his mended socks. There was nothing for her to do here now but make the coffee and watch him walk through the door, down the slope to his brother's car and then away.

She had halfway dreaded the news all summer; but when the letter came three weeks ago and he said "Well" and left it open on the table to read, she knew this morning would be the last. No way the Army would turn down a man as strong as him—not scarce as men were, this late in the war. When he had seen her pick up the letter, he stood at the screen door, watching the woods, and told her the ways you could beat the draft—all the foolish dodges he'd heard from scared boys. His favorite seemed to be vinegar and prune pits. The night before your physical exam, you drank a tall glass of white cider vinegar and swallowed three prune pits. Then you told the Army you had stomach ulcers; they X-rayed your belly, saw the dark shadows and the shriveled lining and sent you home with a sympathetic wave.

Without a word, she had bought the prunes and left them out on the shelf by the stove; the vinegar was always there in plain view. But he never mentioned the plan again, and last night she knew not to bring it up. Every bone in her body guessed he meant to leave. It made good sense, though it hurt like barbed wire raked down her face. She even guessed it hurt him as bad, but he never said it. And she wouldn't force it from him, not that last night. That was up to him.

After she brushed her teeth on the stoop and peed in the bushes, she came back in, damped the woodstove down, then shucked her sweater and dungarees, put on the flannel night shirt and crawled in beside him. She had lain there flat, saying her few prayers quick before he touched her. But he never did, not with his hands. Their hipbones touched and parts of their legs; but somehow the warm space built up between them till she felt gone already, that near him.

After five minutes he said "Remember, I set the alarm." He knew how much she hated the bell; it was one more way to say *You do it. You wake up and spare us.*

She had said "All right" and then "I'm thinking you'll live through it, Kayes." He had said many times that he knew, if they took him, he'd die overseas; and most of the times, he would laugh or sing a few lines of some hymn. But she knew he meant it; she said it to help him face the night, not because she was sure. And as far as she could tell, he had slept like a baby. She thought *I slept like a baby too, a mighty sick child;* but she also knew she had not dreamed once. That froze her as much as the cold dawn air—*If I didn't dream last night, I'm the corpse*—and she calculated they had the minutes to hitch up, one more farewell time. Her hand went toward him under the cover.

For the only time in the months he had known her, he stopped the hand with his own and held it. In another minute he said "Much obliged," then threw back his side of the cover and sat up.

It was still too dark to see him move; so before he could strike a match to the lamp, she thought *Except for this war, we'd stay right here. He don't give a goddamn for nothing but me.* Even without the sight of his face, she almost half-believed it was true. And early as it was in a chilly week, she was more than half right. It had been nearly true for six quick months. He had never admitted as much by day; but he proved it at dusk by turning back up at this door here, living her life beside her in private and sometimes in town and telling her things with his body by dark that, she almost knew, were meant to last.

When he finished the coffee, he poured hot water in the big tin pan, lit the lamp by the mirror and slowly shaved.

She sat at the table and watched every move. All her life, she envied men those minutes each morning, staring at a face they seemed not to notice, not trying to make it thinner or lighter, just taking it in.

Then he put on the first necktie he had worn since moving here; it had waited on a nail in the old pie safe. He took his change and knife from the shelf and portioned them out into several pockets. He took up the long narrow wallet and searched it.

She thought "Oh Jesus, now here it comes. Like every other white man God ever made, he thinks we can cross this out with money."

But he managed it altogether differently. He came the whole way to the table and sat again, in a fresh cold chair. He said "Please look right here at my eyes." When she looked, he said "You have been too good to me, every day. I will know that fact from here to my grave, wherever I find it. If I don't come back alive in time, remember I said I loved you *true*. I was sober when I said it, and I meant every word." He had still not smiled, but he leaned well forward. "Now give me both hands."

She had no choice but to spread both palms between them on the table, though she watched him still.

He laid two fifty-dollar bills down first; then he took off his watch and laid it on them. He had sometimes let her wear it on days when she doubted his promise to be here by dark.

She said "The money will help me a lot; thank you kindly. But you're going to need that watch overseas."

He understood she didn't mean that; she meant she thought it belonged to his wife, had been his wife's gift to him years ago. So he closed both her hands now, money and watch, and said "I bought that watch myself. It's yours till the day I walk back in here, claiming it again."

She had to nod, dry-eyed as a boy.

He stood up and, before he got both arms in his coat, a car horn blew way down by the road. He stepped to the door.

She stood where she was.

With a hand in the air, he kept her in place. "Don't let me see you in the cold," he said. Then someway he melted, silent, and was gone.

It was then that she knew the room was hot and dry as a kiln. She thought she was free to howl like a dog, and she sat there and waited for a moan to rise. But the car door slammed; and she heard it leave and fade completely away toward Raleigh with still no tears in her eyes, no moan. She said his name *Kayes* and waited again. But no, nothing came. So she stood and rinsed out both their cups and set them upside down on the shelf where they sat before he ever came here. Beyond her even, they had been her grandmother's and had sat unbroken in this same room long before she was born to meet this man that hurt her like this.

Two

You could call me anything—I used to answer. But from way before I remember good, every soul I knew but my mother called me Blackie. That was because my skin wasn't black. Mama was medium dark, a good walnut. And Red, Mama's aunt that mostly raised me, said my gone daddy was what they called blue gum that long ago, with skin so black his gums were blue. Most Negro babies are born real pale; but even with the kin I had behind me, everybody said I was born nearly white and stayed that way when most children shade on off, tan or dark. So somebody called me Blackie early, the way they called my fat friend Skinny Minnie; and Blackie hung onto my life like a burr—Blackster, Black, Blackheart. I answered.

Even Kayes sometimes called me Black but just if he got mad or hungry— "Black, get your butt to the stove and start frying." Mostly he called me Leah or Lee, Leeana, since Leah is my given name. Mama always said it came from the Bible.

But when I got old enough to read for myself, the Bible said Leah was what Jacob got for his first wife when what he worked so long for was Rachel. It even said he hated Leah; and that set me back—I was meeting stiff winds from a good many sides, without adding that. So I waited till Mama was gone one night, and then I asked Red. She said "Your mama can't read a soap box, much less the Good Book. What you think she know about some dead Leah? She just heard a preacher calling that name and liked the sound. Your mama would crawl to the moon for a sound—music in her bones; her daddy could sing."

There have been many people that took me for white. And they didn't think my name was a joke, or maybe it came from my straight hair. Red said I come here *a nappy-haired baby; but it straightened out natural when my bosoms came. Half the men I know—any color you name—have tried to touch my hair, just for luck if no more, in serious fun. I been a clean person; I mean my* skin. *Even before I could hardly talk, in this cold house,* Red said I *would scrub in icy well-water before she had time to boil the first kettle—said* "Black, you would flat-out polish *your hide."*

I would. And it paid. I don't mean I've yet took one penny for it. I'm way too proud and, till this spring, I never saw a man I wanted to have it. I mean my skin is the finest I've seen; and I've been up and down the land since 1919, when Mama lit out of here with me by the hand. First stop was Wilmington, Delaware. She stayed a few years; then came on back, too sick to take that winter they have. Watching her cough blood, I began to see I'd die some day. So I traveled a lot while I had strength.

Harlem, Springfield, Pittsburgh—you name it. And nobody, white or green, can match me, nobody I've seen; and I've seen a heap of shows. It's made me good friends, all up the line. Friends, *I'm saying, not tomcats prowling—they'll eat any* meat. *Monied ladies in Packard cars, old men at clubs where I served meals, they told me time and again* "You're splendid. Can I touch you for luck?" *I tell em I'll touch* them *and then touch their hand or the back of their wrist. That does the trick.*

It puts them at ease, almost every time, and I pass on. I've met little meanness, wherever I went; and the little I meet, I dodge in the road or slap up side the head bad, *then run. So I was up North from eighteen to thirty, from the year Mama died down here with T.B. till fifteen months ago when Red broke her hip and sent for me. I hauled my precious skin on home, this ramshackle room, and kept watch with her till she passed on.*

If I do say so, I did more than watch. Red got far more worse off than a baby, *couldn't hold her water nor none of her mess. She thought I was my own mama most nights. She would lay me out for bringing men close as her Cape jasmine bush, under that window facing the road, and humping on the* ground *where Red could hear, when I hadn't even left the room.*

I heard more of Mama than anybody knew. And God's my witness, till I got Red laid out in a casket in white satin pleats and deep in the grave, no man nor boy— not to mention hot women, and several have tried—ever laid more skin on me than a finger. I was one brown girl that had heard enough from two tails pumping. I'd take any music on Earth to that, any wreck or scream.

All through Red's last weeks alive, men would walk in here with hot fish dinners, chicken salad, peach pie. I'd thank them "profusely," as Red used to say, and ask had they heard any war news today? That *would throw em for a loop!* They were all 4–Fers with pus in their blood or, worse, they were hiding out from the Army. *Till this war's over, I won't take that; I feel right patriotic someway.* Back at first, I even had dreams of being an Army nurse and going to England when they were so bad off, bombs every night. I was still fool enough to think they could train you fast and ship you out. Every Negro I told said "Get your head tested, child. It ain't your fight. They don't want you." So I stopped telling my hopes and dreams. But my mind never changed, which is why I couldn't tell Kayes to shirk, even with that box of prunes I bought.

He came to Red's funeral with Riley his brother. When Kayes walks in, nobody sees Riley; but he's all right or used to be. Red had been their grandmother's cook many years; and they were so welcome that one of my cousins, the big head-usher, set Kayes on the front row next to the aisle. When they led me in behind the casket, the only pew vacant was that same pew. So I nodded to Kayes, that was next to me, and sat two or three yards' distance down from him.

Make a long story short—he came on with us to the grave out back and saw Red covered. It near killed me and, swear to God, I thought he filled up. See, he had loved his grandmother much as I loved Red. She had raised him when his own mother left, run off with her own first cousin—a drunk—and left Kayes' daddy, Kayes himself who had just started talking good and Riley, an even younger baby. She left *them,* clean as a bat leaves Hell every evening at dusk. And Kayes' old grandmother, Miss Marianne, she took the whole crowd in and raised him right. Or at least the best she knew how to do, with my Red cooking every crumb they ate and washing and pressing every thread they wore. So sure, he ought to have cried at her grave.

What he did after that was walk halfway through the grove to his Chevy with Riley beside him. Then he stopped in his tracks like my eyes had shot him. I hadn't been watching him all that close—I was bent with the hardest grief I'd known, till this week now—but he spoke to Riley, who kept on going; and then he came back. When I saw him turn, I said in my heart "He's coming to me." I was dead-out wrong. It was still too early in the spring for flowers. But somehow, somewhere Kayes found a bloom—a white carnation that had seen better days. It was in his left hand. No other carnations were anywhere near, no wreath he could have stolen it from. I know I told myself "Black, he's grown it." I must have thought it bloomed that minute in his fist—big fist that had already bruised it some.

Anyhow not looking to me one time, he came right back to the edge of the grave, where Red's coffin sat with clods on the lid—two boys were standing there, waiting for me to move out of sight so they could finish——and he reached far down as his arm would go and let that one bloom fall on the dirt, where I knew Red's face was still

*looking up. I've never been partial to grown white people. Red and Mama both said
you could trust them if you'd known them long.*

*I'd known Kayes Paschal since I was maybe four years old—Red bringing me to
work some days when Mama was too sick to watch me and then was dead. I never
had paid him that much notice. There at the grave though, I thought he looked good.
Everybody but Kayes thought that and still thinks it. But sad as I was, he got no
deeper into my mind or bosom than any tan man, not to mention the dark. I knew
he married the banker's daughter that Red once said "could frost the sun," and she
didn't mean with sugar.*

*But once I heard that flower hit Red's dirt, something snapped inside me in the
midst of my chest. It takes a lot more than a white carnation to catch my eye. I did-
n't forget we were separate people, Kayes and me. I never once thought he'd speak to
me, and I didn't dream I'd want it. But for some strange reason, I had held up good,
right to that moment. You'd have thought I was some neat-dressed great-niece of
Red's. But with Kayes coming back, giving Red that much, I said in my heart "Live
through this, Leah, and you're guaranteed." I don't know what my fool mind meant.*

*It sure didn't think how hard his family had worked poor Red and for what slim
pay, or how they'd drive her out every night to this piece of a shed, saying "See you
tomorrow," when for all they knew she'd die in the night of cold or snakebite. All I
understand, even today, is I took the first step forward to meet him. Kayes saw me
moving and stepped on toward me. It wasn't till he put out his big hand that I saw
the wide gold ring on his left; he was still married to her. But it meant no more to
me that day than a callus or a mole on his finger would.*

*Four days later though, as I was thinking I might better get my butt back
North, I had stepped out into Red's yard to wash my hair in the sun. It was almost
dry when something made me look toward the road. And here come Kayes again,
walking the way he had to Red's grave, with his chin tucked down and leaning a little forward on the air, like a wind was trying to send him home. I said to myself "It's
nothing but Kayes."*

*But once he got through the blackberry vines and spoke to the dog—they were
friends, way back—I felt my eyes go straight to his hands. Big as they were that day
by the grave, they had grown again. The right hand carried a brown paper sack
(turned out it was three of the Hershey bars that Red used to want); the left hand
that day was naked as mine. My mind said "Blackster, here it comes. Say no. You're
too good for this." Even if no two people alive would believe a woman named Blackie
was a virgin at thirty-one, I meant not to change, not for this white man I'd known
all my life—gold ring or no. Turned out I was wrong.*

Three

Kayes's only brother was driving—Riley, three years younger but badly near-
sighted and safe from the draft. He had married young, a plain girl tall as
Riley and patient with all his shyness and fears. And they had two daughters,
both smart and so lovely you might have looked at their pleasant parents and

thought each girl was bought or adopted from a line of beauties or personally sent as a gift by God. As Kayes sat quiet in the car beside him, he thought
You're plain as boiled potatoes, but you sure got the luck.

It was not self-pity, just the visible truth—look at Riley's wife, their
girls, his money. Kayes and Riley had split their father's land with an ami-
cable coin toss. Kayes got the better half and a hard-working tenant but lost
money most years. Riley coined gold on sandy soil with a string of tenants
no better than thieves. Look at his homely wife, not a penny to call her own
and from poor country stock but a certified saint. Kayes's wife Daphne had
money to spare from her banker daddy and blood so blue it could pass for
ink; but her mind had shut when the son was born, named Curtis after her
dead father.

Good as Curtis was, the boy drew all her care onto him. Kayes had
guessed that things would balance out as the boy got older. But now he was
fourteen, and still Daphne watched him like the first angel landed. So for that
many years, except on unpredictable nights when her gate swung open with
no complaint, Kayes was lonesome as the last tree standing on the moon
itself. And full though he was of love and need, until he saw Leah that day at
Red's funeral, he had touched no more than three other women. And all were
white, all big young country girls that laughed at the end and went back to
work with barely a word to prove he'd known them.

The Negro part had concerned him at once. When he turned away
from Red's graveside, and Leah there behind him, he told himself "Forget
her *now*." And he nearly succeeded. Despite the fresh sight of Leah's good
face and his older memory of tales his friends told, long years back about
colored girls, Kayes's mind soon turned to the things he must order for his
tenant at the Feed and Seed—a load of cottonseed meal, one of lime, a case
of formula powder for the baby (the tenant had four, none old enough to
work).

It wasn't until he climbed the steps of his house an hour later and heard
Daphne calling to Curtis—"Baby, *run*"—that Leah rose again in his mind,
exactly as fine a face and bones as anybody left in the county, any woman.
And before his hand touched the front-door knob, Kayes thought "I've
known her since before she could talk." It was simply true but it meant a
great deal, much more than he planned, from that week on till now today.

Riley cleared his throat to break the long silence. "You think they'll want
you?"

Kayes was so far off, it came at him strangely. "Want me? The Army?
They'd want *you*, Bud, if you weren't blind."

Riley took both hands off the wheel and bent to the windshield to search
out the road, a blind driver. Dawn was in progress, a dull tin color, and the
windows were still transmitting cold. "You used to have your old heart mur-
mur. What happened to that?"

Kayes said "My heart ain't spoke for years." He did not mean anything deep or sad; but once it was out, he thought it through. It was wrong; he had spoke out to Leah, just now, in the room. Knowing they had less chance in the world than a baby left all night in the snow, Kayes had finally told her the weight she had in his mind and heart. He turned to the side of his brother's thin face. They had not shared secrets for twenty-odd years; but they'd never broke faith, never lied when pressed or failed one another's unending trust. So Kayes said something he had planned for days, "Riley, if I get killed over—"

Riley didn't look but his right hand came out accurately and brushed Kayes's mouth.

"No, old Bud, this has to be. If I come back in less than top shape, you'll be my executor; so you need to know. Daphne has got her own money, aplenty. Anyhow the law gives her a widow's share. Most of the rest goes to Curtis of course, but I put down five thousand dollars for you. Please give half of that to Leah."

"Leah?"

"Lee—Blackie—you know. Don't fail me, Bud."

Riley said "Absolutely." And when Kayes stayed quiet, he said "You really want to leave, don't you, Kay?"

Kayes nodded. "Yes, God—*leave* now awhile but not *die*, I guess." Then he chuckled.

Riley said "I'll be here to meet you, be sure. But where will you live?"

Kayes looked to his right. The sun, in climbing, had turned the pines from a near-black green to a color that made him think *Emerald*. As a boy Kayes collected the *most*, the *best*, the *scarcest* things; and somewhere he read that perfect emeralds were rarer than diamonds and cost more money. Though he was the least poetic of souls and cared less for money than a year-old infant, he looked at the pines now and thought "Countless billions." Then he wondered what in the world he meant. Well, surely he was trying to dodge Riley's question. So he kept on looking, counting pine trunks now.

Riley said "You understand Blackie will need to leave, if the Army takes you?"

Kayes said "Why's that?" He still faced outward.

"Assuming some white trash doesn't burn her house down, what will she eat? Nobody that knows about you and Daphne will give Black a job."

Kayes saw that was right. But he played the words again in his mind—was Riley hateful at all, out to hurt him? Did he mean to harm Leah? But in memory, the words played back straight and true. As ever, Riley had no grain of spite. So Kayes felt safe to look around—Riley met his eyes for as long as was safe—and said "O.K., I'll authorize you to pay her a wage to stay at old Red's house and fix it up. Paint the walls, mend the windows—Lee's smart with a hammer; she says she's worked, painting rooms up North."

Riley said "I don't doubt it. But Kay, that's not your house to fix. Nor mine, don't forget. Grandmother gave it to Red, long since, and the half acre round it."

It was news to Kayes; he thought the house was on Riley's half of the family land. All through his time out there with Leah, when his mind backslid, he told himself "My family's owned this house forever. Let any fool tell me to leave." He gave a little shake and tried to laugh. But Riley's profile was solemn again. So Kayes said "You might have told me that, months ago."

Riley said "You're a grown man. You chose your path."

Kayes waited a good while. "How lost did I get?"

"Beg your pardon?"

Kayes saw Riley now as he was in childhood, a serious boy who would answer you true—anything you asked. "How much have I broke?"

Riley knew they were in deep water now; he gave the question the thought it required. Then again he looked over, for the time he could spare. "Maybe nothing. Daphne's strong as an iron stake." He tried to end there.

Kayes pushed him on. "I've got a son—"

Riley nodded. "I'm his godfather. You forget that?"

"Have you talked to Curtis in all these months?"

Riley said "Every Sunday but Easter—he was busy."

"How much does he hate me?"

Riley said "A good deal. He's protecting his mother. You know how that is."

"Any chance he could ever feel better about me?"

To both their surprise, Riley suddenly laughed. "If you died a big hero, scaling the breastworks, shot in the brow, Curt might recover."

Kayes managed to smile. "I may oblige him."

"They don't have breastworks these days, Kay."

By now they had passed all the good things to see, the useful sights—trees and fields and low white houses in bare oak groves, the big hollow rock where a family was buried upright in a shaft, a mother and father and three young boys. Now they were coming to the fringe of Raleigh, where the town swelled out and killed the land from bedrock upward. Even the vacant ground was blighted, unwilling to yield. Kayes told himself "They are all better off, with me out of sight." He meant all the people who thought they needed to lean on him; he hoped they knew better.

Riley spoke as if each word cost thousands. "I guess this here is your best bet, a piece of the war. But I want you to know—I'll miss you terrible. You're a lot to me, Kayes; and nothing's changed that."

Kayes knew not to look; it would break them both. But he said "I guarantee I feel the same." And from there till they parked in front of the place where he and assorted men and boys would be examined for nothing but strength and the sense—if called upon—to die decent, Kayes thought about Leah.

Forget about Hitler and the wide Pacific, I could die this minute in full posses-
sion of all I hoped to find in life, whoever I hurt—and I stand ready to pay for them,
two of the faces (I can't help Leah). One smart grown woman wanted *me. Just me*
in a room, no money, no stunts, no lifetime deal. No mention of what any blind man
could see—we were different animals, her and me, not meant to plow in a double
yoke, not here nor now.

But we made it last for six whole months. Any hour on the clock, I could slide
my car in off that road, below Red's pitiful piece of a home, and set my foot to the
ground to climb those last hundred yards; and Lee would know *it. Some piece of her*
mind would know I was back and would raise her whole fine shape to meet me. Not
a time, no single time I recall, did I climb all the way to the house without her walk-
ing to meet me or waiting in the yard with a cup of water or, if it was cold, in the
window at least with oil light behind her and both eyes ready to smile me in.

My skin. She evermore used my skin. She was like a sensible squaw in the win-
ter, kids starving around her; and then her man kills one last deer—Leah took my
body and used every part *to save us both, not a particle wasted. It was all food and*
easement. That's a word I'd never used but in farming, giving somebody an ease-
ment on land, to haul his crop across some corner of your woods or fields. But toward
the end of the first whole week I stayed at Red's, I woke in the night and could hear
Leah breathing like she was awake. She didn't speak though. The few other women
I've known, deep in, would need to speak at a time like that, just to prove it was real.
Lee was calm as ever. So a word just came to my lips, and I said it—"Easement"—
and Lee said "True." I still think she understood all I meant, though we never dis-
cussed it by daylight. Never.

Have I wrecked her too? Bud's right; some trash boys might try to scare her—
the Cagles or some of the moron Coggins. But once I finally told her, last night, the
possible mess I might leave her in, didn't she say "Where you think I been? I didn't
turn nigger this afternoon. All my life I lived for trouble—and child, trouble came—
so I take my chances, like I took on you. Look what that got me." When I asked her
what?, she said "Some time, a piece of time to think about in my old age, if I live to
keep thinking and figuring out." Then she broke out smiling in the dim oil light, the
smile that could give me all I lacked. And when I tried to say what to do tonight, if
the Army kept me, she put both hands to her ears and frowned—a grown woman's
frown, knowing all she knows. And speaking of pain, she out-knows me.

Riley found a parking place in sight of the warehouse and killed the
engine. He looked to Kayes and said "Can I come in?"

Kayes said "Thank you, no. They'd ship you straight to Japan by noon."
It didn't mean anything but "Clear out please; let me do this right."

"But what if they fail your stiff old joints?—you've got to ride home."

The fact had really not dawned on Kayes; he was so sure of leaving. He
thought it out, chose to skip the word *home* (where on Earth was that?) and
then said "The bus'll stop right by Red's, if I ask it to. I won't need it though."

He leaned over slowly and amazed his brother with a silent hug. When Kayes sat back, he looked to the panel clock; it was almost seven; he was in good time. He opened his door and said the last thing. "If you don't hear from me by dusk, please drive out to Red's and tell Lee I'm gone. If she needs to go on somewhere safe—maybe one of her cousins—I'll pay for your gas." He handed Riley the keys to his car.

Riley took them and nodded.

And Kayes loped away. Within three yards he told himself "I will never see that boy's face again." The boy was Riley, as ever in his mind. Sad as he knew he ought to feel, Kayes was light on his feet; and when a kid stood back to let him enter the building first, Kayes said "We're in the same rowboat, son. You first. After you."

The boy said "Yes sir" and took the lead with all the joy of a Judas goat at the slaughter pen.

For an instant as the boy moved, the side of his face looked like young Curtis—young as Curt anyhow, smart and distrustful. But still Kayes could laugh.

Four

Since it was Saturday, Curtis had planned to sleep till ten, maybe closer to noon. Then he meant to find Cally, his friend with the rifle, and go squirrel hunting. But at eight o'clock, Daphne came to the shut door, waited a minute, creaked it open and said "Please, Curt. I need you today."

He could always wake on a dime, that fast; but he lay on and thought "You need somebody but I'm not the man." Beneath him, his dick was hard as a spike; he thought "I'll never get it down in time." But he said "What for?"

"What time did your father say he was leaving?"

Kayes had been at the west-side door of school yesterday afternoon as Curtis came out. The boy had seen the car, first thing, and was split between a taste for running straight to it with pleasure and the colder sense of his mother's pride—what she was still bearing and would need from him. He had seen his father only four short times in the past six months, and each time was worse than the one before. So Curtis walked over slowly now, opened the door and leaned in gravely. Kayes asked him to sit for a minute and talk. The boy obeyed but the talk came mostly from Kayes—he had already given Riley instructions to pay for anything Curt really needed. If the Army took him, he'd write letters weekly; please write to him.

All Curtis could do was nod "Yes sir" and wish it would stop. He loved this man so much and so deeply, so faraway back in the fourteen years that felt long to him. Bitterness poured up into his mouth now and nearly choked him. Curtis kept saying, time and again to himself, "If he just won't say that woman's name"—the only name Curtis knew was Blackie; and he heard that at school, not once from his mother. She'd die before speaking it.

When Kayes let up, the boy looked at him for the first full time and said "I've thought this through a lot. I hope they take you, I hope you come back, I hope it's *you* when you get here though." Kayes waited awhile, looking ahead, and then said "I thank you. And I'll work on it, son. But this may *be* me, right here and now." Then he gave Curt an envelope that, back home, turned out to be two fifties—new as if printed that morning. At the supper table when the boy's mother asked if Kayes had seen him, Curtis told her all of the truth he could risk, "Yes ma'm. He looked ready." She started the growling edge of a sneer; but Curt faced her down—no word, wide-eyed.

Now as he lay still, praying she would vanish, she held her ground and repeated "What time?"

"Ask Riley," Curtis said.

"*Uncle* Riley—"

"You know who I mean; he's got a phone."

"Don't be impudent, son—I slept at least two minutes last night. Anyhow I know Riley's driving him to Raleigh."

"Then you know more than me. I was sleeping fine."

"Curt, where is his car?"

"In Raleigh, I guess."

Daphne said "Surely not; he'd ride with Riley."

Curtis sat up suddenly and faced his mother. Her face, the face he served every day, was strung tight now and scarily pale. Still he said "Then I guess the damned car is at Blackie's place. He gave it to her." Curtis had never seen Blackie, not close at hand. But once her name was loose in the room, it threatened to stand her between them now, tall and stern and smelling like Kayes.

Daphne swallowed hard but concealed the shock. Finally she said "Is that a known fact, or are you just dealing in meanness today?"

Curtis said to himself "One more bull's-eye," and his face flushed red. He turned to the wall, but he said "What now?"

She said "I've thought all night. By decent rights, that car is ours—"

"He's not dead, Mother."

"*Hush.* But you know full well the Army will take him."

"I don't, no ma'm."

Daphne waited. "Not a blemish on him, not to the eye."

Curtis said "His ear, that strawberry mark."

Before she thought, Daphne said "*No*, that used to be lovely." Then she heard herself and took a step to leave.

But Curtis said "We could drive out and get it."

"You and me? But who would drive it back? Baby, you aren't legal at the wheel, not yet."

"You got your key? I can drive as good as any two men; nobody'll stop us."

Daphne said "What if she's there? And what if Riley brings him back?"

Curtis's dick was calm for the moment. He knew he must take that chance to dress. As he threw back the cover, he said "I'll tell my father it was my idea; he still likes me. You can let me out on the road and head back. I'll handle the rest." As his mother turned to get herself ready, Curtis made his voice easy; but what he said was "My father's name is *Kayes*—remember?—not just *he*."

Daphne said "I can't say it." It was only a fact, not a plea for pity.

But all the way into deeper country, with Curtis sullen on the seat beside her, she gripped the wheel and thought little else. *Kayes, Kayes. I want it all back, those short first years we were good to each other. You can't want this; surely you're crazy. But none of your people have lost their minds; God knows, none of mine. And I can't blame liquor, which both of my sisters can blame in good faith—I doubt you've had three drinks in ten years—so here I've stood with no explanation to give the world, except to say you've lost your mind.*

All the women I know say that much already, when I'm not present—though ten days ago in this same car, Roe Boyd said, out of the absolute blue, "Daph, the fact that the girl's light-skinned as you makes it all the worse." I pretended I missed it and Roe shut up. But I understood her—Kayes, if you'd gone to a coal-black girl, we'd have had this over long months ago and be back together, on the old right rails. Tell that to any three doctors south of Baltimore, and they'd sign an order in a New-York minute to strait-jacket you and cool you off till reason prevails.

But you picked a woman no darker than I am, after two or three clear days at the beach. And stayed beside her in a house the wind can walk right through. I've been there with you, far more than once, to see old Red at Christmas and Easter. Remember I told you her roof was bad and you sent a man out with brand-new tin, and Red sent me two big dressed chickens, ready to fry? Red would die all over again, if she knew—you preying on a child she raised, a Negro that naturally thinks you're God or, if she doesn't, can't help herself; can't make you leave; may even die for knowing you, if you leave today and the trash get at her.

I'd pray to die, if Curtis didn't need me. I've asked the Lord if I can pray for you to die in battle soon, in some brave act that cancels this and lets us lift our heads and move on. But I get no more from God than from you—not a word, not a look. I go to church and sit there waiting. It might as well be one dim coffin with me nailed down, alive and stifling and beating the lid; but nobody hears and no help comes.

The nights I've lain awake and watched your pistol on the table, begging me to pick it up and drive the six miles out to Red's and blow you and her to deepest Hell, some days at least before God does it. I've cursed the marksman lesson you gave me. Remember that? Remember anything we liked to do or pledged to keep on doing for-ever—like trusting, honoring, serving each other, come sun or storm?

We were not back from the honeymoon for more than a month when you took me out that bright cold Sunday. I thought we were riding around, just looking. We passed the farm and waved at the tenants. I thought you'd stop and give the children the Tootsie Rolls we bought in town. But you pushed on, not saying a word, and finally took a sandy trail that sloped so steep downhill I thought we'd be in water any minute, deep in. I remember quoting St. Paul to myself, "Love hopes all things, endures all things."

I thought I was joking, whistling in the dark. And the sand did deepen till we nearly got trapped and you stopped cold in a thick bank of briars. I said "You want me to try to push?" You met my eyes like some rank stranger. And that was the time I first had to think I'd married a boy I'd never met, much less really knew.

Finally you said "I want you to learn something useful for once." You always laughed at my fund of knowledge. Remember telling my father that Christmas "Daph knows everything but how to breathe"? You reached down under your edge of the seat and pulled out the pistol in a clean white rag. It looked as big as a cannon to me. Till then I hadn't seen it—you'd bought it that week. Strange as you looked, I didn't feel scared, just puzzled as always. You got out then and beckoned me on. And what did I do but follow behind you in two-inch heels for what seemed a mile of ruts and briars? Then the brush stopped dead, we were in a wide clearing, the light was murky.

But you stood still, not looking at me, and fired six shots at a helpless pine. Then you reloaded and—still not meeting my eyes or speaking—you held it my way.

No choice but to take it. Well, I learned to shoot, at the same old tree. We must have killed it—maybe sixty rounds, most of them mine. Not a single miss. I could find the pine right now, if it's there.

Were we on Mars? Has any of this, these fifteen years, really happened, Kayes, or am I asleep? I thought I'd love you till both of us died. I thought it meant—the one weird day you taught me to shoot—that you had to love me. You wanted me, above all, to be protected in a world you already claimed was wild, though I didn't believe you yet awhile.

Even now, this close to Blackie's face, I beg you to live and come on in. I can say your name. I can even say hers; but here and now, in my private mind, I can barely say home. Come back to where you promised to stay. Everybody will know it was nothing but a nightmare. Wake on up, Kayes. There may be time.

Five

The car was there, parked just off the road in a patch of young cedars. The path to Red's ran uphill from it; and by the time Daphne pulled to the shoulder, smoke was pouring from the chimney up there. For an instant she thought "They've burnt it." Then she thought "She's burning up things of his." But she knew both were wrong. And Curtis was reaching to open his door. So she said "I'll drive on down to that sycamore, turn and then follow you on home. Drive slow and easy; and if a patrolman stops you, I'll explain you're helping your mother."

Curtis had got his door wide open, and one leg was out. "Mother, I'm a lot better driver than you. You better hope I'm near if you get stopped." He finally looked back and halfway grinned.

But Daphne had seen a flash of green. The door of Red's house had swung back silently; and somebody wearing a bright green coat was standing there, at the top of the steps. A long brown skirt, tall, a lot of black hair. That moment, for some entirely strange reason, Daphne wanted to wave, to lean out the window and say "Step here please." The idea scared her but still, to her wonderment, she felt no shock. She had not seen Blackie for twenty years maybe; but now the memory of her face in childhood came to Daphne—such a pale child, more than normally serious with lovely hair, coarse and strong as an Indian's.

By then Black had come down two of her steps. Two more and she'd be in the yard, by the path.

Daphne said "Curt, don't say a word. She'll know who you are. Just unlock the car and be ready when I turn. You take the lead."

Curtis shut the door gently and moved to the car. As he bent to unlock the door, Blackie gave a wide slow wave, took the last two steps and started toward him.

Then Daphne was scared but also angry. Curt must get out of this, with no more hurt or shame on his head. So she opened her door to meet what came. Blackie was no more than twenty yards off, looking down but still moving.

Curtis looked back with a heavy scowl. "I'm serious, Mother. Go turn around and wait down there." He pointed to the white sycamore. And when his mother paused, he said again "*Go!* Go straight home now. If anything's wrong, I'll hitchhike in."

His power was so new that Daphne obeyed it. She went to the huge tree, backed around slowly; and though the woman had got down to Curtis and they were standing as still as horses, Daphne passed on by.

When the sound of her car had vanished, Leah said "You got to be Curtis."

"Yes ma'm, I—" He felt his face burn and pointed to where his mother had gone. "I guess I'm supposed to drive this home."

Leah said "Was it his idea, your father's?"

"No ma'm, she—" He pointed toward Daphne again.

Leah smiled a little and raised a hushing finger to her lips. "No need to call me *ma'm* now, Curtis. I may be pale but I live with the niggers."

He laughed, then flushed again—this was all wrong; he was falling all over himself like a child. Finally he said "If this car's yours, or anything in it, I'll hitch right back. It don't really matter." Not thinking, he had switched to the voice he used with Negroes.

Leah corrected him—"*Doesn't* matter"—but renewed her smile. "I been to school, Curtis; I did right well." She leaned to see inside the car. The back seat was littered with Kayes's farm papers, old catalogs, a pair of gray socks. "Not a thing of mine, nowhere in *sight*." Her smile hung on. "You might be standing there, two or three days. This road is lonesome."

Curtis nodded. "I know it. My father and I, we hunt out here." They had not hunted for nearly two years.

Leah said "You know how much you look like him?" Her hand came up and touched her own face.

Curtis said "Exactly, before he changed."

"How much has he changed?" She asked sincerely, truly not knowing.

Somehow the boy felt stronger now, older and honest. He said "I didn't mean you and—all this." He pointed to the house. "I mean all the years I've known him, fourteen."

Leah said "I knew him longer. My grandmother cooked for your great-grandmother. I was in her kitchen when he was a boy."

Curtis said "I didn't know that." It was only the truth, though even as he said it, he knew he could barely hear himself think. Nobody had dealt with him like this, in his whole life till now—this clean dead-level eye-to-eye truth. He knew he was being rammed forward through time. Any second now, he would be a grown man, tall enough to do what was right. But though they both stood waiting for a long time, nothing, right or wrong, came to his mind.

At last Leah said "What if they say no and he comes back?"

"Fine by me—"

"The car, I mean. What'll he have to drive, if you take the car?"

Curtis said "He can hitch into town and get it. You don't have a car?"

Leah looked around as though she might. The only other machine in view was a dead old cookstove, flung in a ditch. She turned back to Curtis. "I don't have good sense, much less a car." She wanted to laugh but a hoarse bark came. She wiped her lips slowly with the back of her hand.

So Curtis said "Did he live here?" He pointed uphill.

"Who?"

"Mr. Kayes Paschal, the man we mentioned."

Leah also looked behind, to the house, as if she had waked in another life and sought landmarks. And she spoke uphill, away from the boy. "He spent most nights for the past six months, ate a good many suppers, drank a whole world of coffee—"

"Hope the Army has coffee or he'll desert."

She said "They got it."

Curtis said "Don't think I came out here to be mean, but tell me one thing please—what was this *for*?"

At first Leah thought "He can't be a child." Then she knew nobody but a child could have aimed it, that dead-eye straight. She said "You trying to kill me, fast?"

"No, I'm hoping to find my father. See, I'm the one missed him all this time."

Leah's hand went out again—stop please now. Thank Jesus she'd spent no time around children. "I wish I could answer, son. Did we hurt you bad?"

"Bad. Yes. And I'm *his* son." He tried to ease it with a partial smile.

She took it full-face but had to wait. "Did me being colored make it worse on you?"

Curtis knew at once and shook his head firmly. "It was you being in this world, out here."

As calmly as if she asked for the time, Leah said "You want me to die right now?"

He said "No. Not now—years ago, before I was born."

"What about your mother?"

He said "What about her?" He had already noticed they hadn't mentioned her.

"You don't fault her for any of this?"

Curtis said "Not more than fifty percent."

Calm as she looked, this meeting had struck Leah harder than anything yet, anything her mind had bothered to store. She said "How would you be different now, if this hadn't been?" She also pointed back at Red's house.

He tried to think. But all he could find was "At least I wouldn't be praying my father would head out to war and be shot dead."

Her hand went up to her open mouth.

Curtis nodded.

"Say no." She took the steps forward and reached for his wrist. Then she shook it between them in the strong new light—the sky had cleared all through their talk. "Tell God right now you don't mean that."

Curtis said "I don't. I meant to hurt you."

Leah said "You did, man. Don't worry, you did." But he looked so much like her memory of Kayes—Kayes way back when—that she had to say "You hate me this much?"

Curtis had heard her call him *man*. He all but smiled. "I'd probably like you. I'm an outgoing fellow."

"But the way things happened put bad blood between us—" She read it as if it was printed plain on the hood of the car.

Curtis said "I guess." He did not know yet, but his face was sliding back in time. He looked like a child again, tired and hungry.

Leah said "You eat your breakfast yet?"

"No, I came out here too fast."

"I'll cook you some eggs."

He meant to say yes; he could learn so much. But now he was young, he said "My mother is waiting for me."

Leah said "If Kayes comes back, I'll tell him you drove it." She looked at him closely, the first time since they grappled so close. He looked even younger than he had at the start. "You sure you got a driver's license?"

Curtis said "No but that won't matter. All the young patrolmen are off killing Japs. These poor old fellows won't even see me."

Leah nodded and walked a long five steps on the uphill path. Then she turned and said "*I* see you, Curtis. I wish I'd seen you sooner than this."

He said "No you don't. I'd have ruined your time." He didn't know everything he meant. He did know he wanted to smile once more but his mouth refused.

Back in the house, Leah went to the mirror and faced herself. No change, same eyes, same clean tight skin. She thought "I'm going to pack my duds and walk out of here, *whoever* comes back. I didn't set up to be this harmful." But the thought alone hurt as much as any words said this whole long day, that had only just started. In the glass she could also see behind her the neat-made bed where her grandmother died and Red (gone crazy) and where she and Kayes had spent their nights.

In that empty space, above those pillows, they said things neither one had said elsewhere—Kayes promised her that. And where were they now? The words anyhow were gone past hearing, they had hurt as many people as they helped, she must get them out of her mind right now. Before she could turn away to pack, Leah faced herself a final moment."Leave it all here, Black. Leave it and go."

And all through his peaceful ride back home, Curtis knew he had learned some large true thing that would lead him into a better life than he'd known till now—less mess, less meanness, fewer people draining his life for blood. He tried to name his hard new knowledge; he wanted to say it out loud in the car so he'd never forget it. And he dug to find it but got no further than the words "I must—"

He pounded the wheel with both clenched hands and rode for more than a mile, feeling bad. But then he noticed how the sky had opened. The sun was strong as he eased into town; and when he paused at the first stoplight, two country girls from his grade in school crossed the street before him—Willie and Flay. They were both already grown up front and had known, for months, things that still baffled him. So he knocked on the windshield and leaned his face well forward in the sun, with eyes half shut.

Both of them saw him, shrieked; then waved and skipped faster, though they looked back, time and again, and talked a clear blue streak till he turned left and moved away—*Curt Paschal's driving, like he's got good sense when we know he* ain't.

Six

Kayes walked through the morning like a man still dreaming. When he entered the draft induction center, he found exactly the room he expected—a dim tall space, two-tone gray walls with benches and maybe a hundred men. Mostly boys, as he'd imagined, all smoking like chimneys and nervous as squirrels. The obvious cause for worry was a sergeant, built like a concrete bunker and seated on a low platform in a kind of pulpit. Everybody tried not to notice him, Kayes included. So Kayes stopped inside the door, leaned on the wall and searched all the faces. Some of the boys looked younger than Curtis and were digging at their crotches, trying to laugh. Only when he hunted a place to sit did he find a friend.

A deep voice called his first two names, "Wilton Kayes." An arm went up, a man half-stood; and Lord, it was Brutus Bickford from grade school.

Kayes stepped over to him. "Brutus, they caught us."

Brutus had grinned but now his face sobered. When Kayes was safely down beside him, Brutus said "They ain't catching *me*, I tell you." He fumbled in his watch pocket, drew out a capsule not much bigger than a grain of rice, revealed it to Kayes, checked to see that the sergeant was turned away and then gulped it.

Kayes said "What will that do?"

"You remember I had high blood pressure, don't you?"

High blood pressure in the third damned grade? Still Kayes said "Sure, I forgot for a minute." Wide as Brutus was, and dazed in the eyes, he looked like a calm rock bathed in the sun.

"I've already had what they call strokettes. A friend of mine claims this pill *guarantees* me freedom today."

Kayes thought *Well, death may amount to freedom—good luck, old son.* But he said "We'll know in an hour, I guess."

Brutus said "Kayes, Christ, when have I seen you?"

To his surprise, Kayes knew, to the day. "The morning your mama pulled you out of Miss Allen's class and left. The sixth grade, right after Easter Monday. Y'all moved up here, if memory serves."

Brutus took it for granted that his past was remembered. He merely nodded and said "That bastard, Calvin Pepper—Mama said they were married, her third or fourth husband; I still think they were just shacked up. Anyhow some scoundrel meaner than Cal took umbrage one Saturday night that summer and drilled Cal's pea-brain with one clean shot, smack-dab right *here*." Brutus tapped a huge finger between his blue eyes, then broke up laughing. "Her and me bought a case of Pepsis with his cash and two bus tickets to Carolina Beach."

"You still live there?"

"Oh no. She may; I come on back up here and been working. I got a young wife, and she's got kids of her own to feed, so I'm a plasterer and good at it too—let me lay you some walls." Then he locked an unblinking stare on Kayes. "Where you been, Bo?"

Kayes suddenly knew he would tell the truth, and it felt like a fruitful island discovered after months at sea. "I been living in the country with a Negro woman named Leah Birch, Red Birch's niece. You remember old Red, mean as a snake?"

Brutus said "I've known very few niggers, Kayes. We couldn't afford em and now I don't care."

Kayes took it peacefully, telling himself *That's a novel approach. In a million years, I'd have never guessed that.* There was nothing to say.

But after a wait, Brutus said "You love her?"

Here was a whole new level of surprise. It seemed as unlikely as an angel visit. And a need to tell the truth was still strong. So Kayes said "I doubt I know what love amounts to."

Brutus laughed. "Sure you do. You used to be smart."

Kayes suddenly saw a new piece of the afternoon when Brutus's mother took him away. It was right after lunch; and they were into rest time, hearing Miss Allen read *Penrod and Sam.* No warning at all, the hall door opened. And there stood a tall woman, dark purple dress, like a country girl with a big open face but confused in the eyes and with caked-on rouge. She didn't even speak to Miss Allen but looked round wildly and said "Where you *at?*" Brutus sat two seats from Kayes; and at that, he stood like a child agreeing to die at dawn. She said "Hey, boy. We're leaving *out.*" By then Miss Allen had summoned her wits and was asking questions. But all the woman would say was "No, he's mine and we're going."

When Brutus had got his jacket from the cloak room—his books were still inside his desk—he went to his mother but looked back at Kayes. And when Kayes half-waved, Brutus had to pretend he couldn't see. His eyes flinched hard but then firmed up and never blinked, from then till the time she turned him and vanished. Kayes had thought before that the worst thing would be to have your father come to school drunk and call your name. But to have your mother come like this, a raucous gypsy—it shocked Kayes, even now, to see it. So he said to this big man beside him, "I hope I do." In the midst of the words, Kayes wondered what in the world they meant.

"You still married to the Mitchell girl?"

How would Brutus know that? "Legally, yes."

Brutus laughed again, not mocking but in sympathy. "That's what matters, ain't it?—that thin piece of paper. They can slice you with that worse than any bullwhip."

Kayes tried to smile and skate on through it. "They've got you over miles of barrels, all right." He wondered how many wives Brutus had left, but he knew not to ask. The sergeant had picked up a clipboard and was standing.

Brutus said "You're praying he takes *you*, I bet." By then his face was a new shade of red; the pill was working.

The sergeant said "Alphabetize yourselves." The alphabet was strung round the walls on dingy cards. A lot of the boys were baffled by the order, and Kayes was trying to smile at that.

Brutus spotted the B and pointed to it, but he said to Kayes "I never saw much wrong with niggers that money wouldn't fix. How dark is she, Bo?"

Kayes said "Light as me."

Brutus said "Then you're waist-deep in cow pies, ain't you?" But he didn't explain and before Kayes could ask, he whispered "Look, I'm not feeling so good. If I stroke out here, tell the doc what happened and send my regrets."

Kayes said "Be glad to."

Brutus laughed and went.

Half an hour later when Kayes got upstairs, naked as a newt in a line of men in similar trouble, huddled there in a corner was a ring of doctors around a cot. As Kayes worked through a set of chores for medics—kneeling, bending, exposing his ass and throat and coughing—he came near enough to see the cot. Brutus was laid out naked too, pink as a shrimp with a blood-pressure sleeve on and two doctors, each one holding a wrist. Brutus's eyes were shut and Kayes wondered if he had killed himself with that one pill. He figured the doctors didn't know names, so he said "Brutus" firmly.

Brutus looked up and found Kayes near. Hot as he was, for a long moment Brutus tried to look solemn. But then he checked on the doctors—they were busy—so he winked at Kayes.

Kayes lifted a finger and smiled. But through the rest of the next half hour, in other rooms, he went on seeing Brutus two ways—the boy leaving school and the clown on the cot, swollen with blood, gambling with death. And when he had done all the shameful stunts they forced on his body and another sergeant had looked down a list and said "So Paschal, you're found fit to serve," Kayes walked away with a stinging surge of raw grief in his eyes and mind. Over and over, he told himself what he thought was the truth. With all the pain he had on his own—the people he had crushed and a war to face—this sadness now was for no one or nothing but Brutus Bickford years ago, a twelve-year-old boy run like a wind-up doll by a whore.

Seven

Twenty minutes later, dressed and calm, Kayes got his turn in a dark phone booth. He paid for the first call, to Riley's house. Riley would hardly be home yet; and though his wife had let Kayes know she despised his face, he could tell her at least that now he was boarding a bus to Fort Jackson and basic training. That should satisfy her so much she might unbend enough to say his name, which had not crossed her lips since the night he left home.

But Riley answered on the second ring with a slow "Riley Paschal."

Kayes seized up again but cleared his throat. "Sir, this is Dog–Soldier Paschal, reporting."

Riley said "Oh God—"

"They're herding us onto a bus any minute now, for South Carolina. I passed, flying colors, which is all I know. I'll write you from down there, soon as I can."

Riley said "Kay, *call* me, night or day. And call collect; that'll make it go faster." He needed a long pause. "You bearing up?"

"I plan to live."

Riley said "Don't say it."

"Why?"

"Just don't make claims. This is one show run by others now."

Kayes chuckled. "I recently got that impression."

"What can I send you? You're bound to need something."

Kayes said "I've got my shaving kit. They throw in the clothes at camp, I guess."

"Sure, you'll have a full khaki wardrobe, down to the handkerchiefs. I just meant—what?—snacks, playing cards, writing paper, a Bible with one of those bulletproof covers."

Kayes said "Could you ship me a live new brain?"

"Beg your pardon?"

"A head, in good working order. I could bolt it right on."

Riley said "Got a headache?"

The joke had failed. Kayes paused to say it right. "You remember I asked for one more favor."

"I do indeed."

"Will you please do it soon?"

Riley said "You think she'll still be there?"

"I guarantee it."

"Then what do I say? I don't want to tell her too much, good or bad." Riley might have been contemplating trade with the stars; he was that far out of his element.

But Kayes stayed calm. "Just tell her the news—I'm gone; I've already told her the rest. Then see if she wants you to drive her somewhere, in reason, today. She'd never use my car; and you scared me a little there, mentioning trouble. I guess I was fool enough not to expect it. You know Red's got those peculiar nieces on the Alston farm, the ones with orange hair. They'd take Leah in, for a few days at least. She'll run it from there."

Riley said "Red's house is Black's now, don't forget. I can't make her leave. Far as we're concerned, she can stay on there till the roof falls in or she's dead—one."

Kayes said "That may be any day now." He knew he was suddenly past understanding himself.

"You want her to stay?" Riley spoke with the cool authority of a good secretary, taking dictation.

Kayes had never asked his brother's advice in this before. But the desolation of an airless phone booth forced him on. "What if I say yes, keep her there till I'm back; set her up in style?"

Riley knew at once. "I'd say you were cruel."

Kayes suddenly saw why he hadn't asked sooner—Riley would never volunteer a judgment; but ask him and you got it, full blast, both barrels in the mouth. "Bud, is *cruel* all I've been up to now?"

Riley said "I prize you too much, Kay, to answer that. I think you did what you wanted to. I know you watched where you put your feet. You saw who you crushed. And I doubt you pressed anybody too weak to bear your weight."

Kayes said "Curtis."

Riley said "Well, Curt—" and he paused too.

Kayes knew he could not take up the slack yet. And in that instant, the smell of boys' feet and the scurf of this old phone's mouthpiece hit his empty gut. He swallowed hard at a gob that rose to his tongue and teeth.

Riley said "You and Daphne have swamped that boy. You owe him and me a careful war, Kay. Get your ass back here in one piece soon, and make him a father for a few more years."

Perfect, Kayes thought. *Thank Jesus for Riley*. But all he said was "Bud, my ass comes in halves like yours."

Riley said "I wore my ass off years ago, dragging after you."

Kayes said "I love you."

Riley said "*Ditto*."

Kayes took ten seconds to crack the door, draw a deep breath and ask the next boy in line for two minutes. Then he dialed the operator and placed a call, collect to Curtis Paschal. The ring went on till he almost quit, though he couldn't imagine the maid at least wasn't home to answer.

Then it stopped, a long wait—Kayes thought it was dead—and Daphne spoke. When the operator asked for Curtis, she said "Curtis Paschal isn't here. I'll accept the charges if your party has a message."

Kayes had not heard Daphne speak in four months; and through that prologue, he could barely listen for the shock he felt in hearing a voice he had all but forgot, a voice he had once loved near to distraction—what?—two or three seconds ago in his life. Time felt that short; his whole sorry life felt five minutes long. So he said "Operator, I'll talk with the lady, if she accepts."

Daphne said "Surely" and the operator vanished.

"Daphne, it looks like I'm in the Army."

"I'm sorry, Kayes." She meant it, though she had not thought of the ways.

"Curt's gone, you say?"

"Right now," she said. "He's out at old Red's place, getting the car."

Blood flooded into Kayes's eyes and mind, but he knew to wait. Then he said "That can't have been Curt's idea."

"It was mine. Your son and I are your family, nobody else yet." Her voice was level, no glint of meanness, just the facts to-date.

Kayes said "But what if I'd got back tonight?"

"The car would have been yours the instant you asked."

He waited again.

So Daphne said "I'm sorry you're mad."

"Oh Jesus, I'm not. I'm standing here though, trying not to break."

Daphne said "I know. Think how I'd have felt if that girl drove your car up here and knocked on the door or left it in the yard."

Kayes said "She's a full-grown woman, Daph, with manners the equal of any I've known. Red raised her, remember, the same as me."

"Your manners—yes, well." Then she heard that they'd come, one more sad time, to the place where every speech was a blade they forced each other to walk, barefoot. "You want to leave some word for Curt?"

"Just the news—the government wants his dad for a while. I'll be in South Carolina by dark and will write him a letter as soon as they let me."

"I'll tell him, Kayes." She seemed to be writing the actual words. "Will you go overseas?"

"May well. This war is far from won."

"We'll both pray for you."

"Can you do that?"

Daphne thought, to be certain. "I haven't stopped yet. I married you—yesterday, it feels like now." Then she almost laughed. "It's hardly likely I'd cease to care."

"Can you say how much?" He amazed himself.

"No, not here, not down a phone wire."

Riley was right; he hadn't broke Daphne. So he honored her pride and said "I'll try to write to you, hear? I'm a rotten—no—I'm the youngest boy in this whole building, and that's a big claim. It's a poor damned excuse, but I swear it feels true." He knew nothing else.

She said "I'm so old, I knew *Elijah*." And she thought "Where in God's name did that come from?" She found herself laughing.

Kayes joined in, glad for the first time in days.

But before he could say a decent goodbye, she was gone, hung up.

He spoke her name twice to the dead receiver, then hung up also, clamped his eyes to flush the pain and opened the booth. To the tall young Negro patiently waiting, he said "I wish you better luck, friend."

The solemn black face nodded but said "If I get it, be the first time *I* smelled luck."

Kayes wanted to stand, like a steer in the road, and bellow, *bellow*. Very likely nobody here would notice. But he looked for the bus door and soon found a sign for *Loading Dock*. Those wide red double doors had to be it. Three boys that looked a bare fifteen were pushing through, grinning. For a long moment, Kayes saw their skulls and how they looked in the graves they would find, no time from now.

Eight

By four that afternoon, Curtis and Cally his only real friend had shot three squirrels and a rabbit between them. They would head on in by dark, skin the catch and take it to the freezer-locker plant where they were storing the fall and winter meat for a stew to serve their grade at school on an early-spring picnic. But while the light was as good as this, they sat on a broad flat rock by the creek and watched the creatures they had spared for now.

Cally watched anyway; he suspected Curt was not seeing much. Beyond the water was a chattering flock of starlings that a full cyclone could hardly scatter, much less a rifle. They flung their bodies through the woods like handfuls of fat black seed; then walked around like important Negroes, casing the leaves.

Cally knew that today was touchy for Curt, and Curt had not met his eyes for hours, so he finally took the risk and spoke. "You see your pa off?"

Curtis nodded. "Yesterday."

"Will he let you know if they draft his ass?"

"No, Cal. He'll just vanish off like a ghost. He don't give a shit."

The voice was so hard, and the fury behind it, that Cally thought Curt meant all he said—he hated his father for living with a nigger and was glad to lose him. They'd said very little about this, through these past six months; but with Curt not caring now, maybe he could ask. Cal said "You ever get a look at that girl?"

"What girl?"

"Blackie, I guess they call her—you know."

Curtis faced around with eyes blank as washes. And he waited about a month to speak—it felt that long anyhow to both boys. "I spent a good part of this morning with her."

"*No.*"

Curtis swore in silence, with his hand up between them.

Cally had known Curt all his life. Even with a rifle beneath their hands, he knew he was safe. "You feel like telling?"

Curtis looked off again, back toward the starlings but still blank–eyed. Then he passed his left hand over all he saw. "I feel like wiping out everything but me." His right hand dug in the dead rabbit's fur, as if for gold.

Cally said "You'd wipe out *everything*—the WACs and nurses and General MacArthur?" He had always served as Curt's private jokester.

But Curt nodded fiercely.

"Present company included?"

Curtis stood up suddenly; the starlings lifted, then settled again. Cal's rifle was still at his feet on the rock. Throughout what came, Curt kept on hurling rocks at the birds, who hardly noticed. "I flat-out liked her. I saw the damned point."

"In him living with her? Quitting you and your mother to live with a nigger in a one-room shack?"

"Your mother didn't tell you that word was trash?"

Cally said "Sure but I figure she's earned it—that Blackie girl."

"She's old enough to be your mother."

"Thank Christ she ain't." When Curt said nothing, Cal tried again. "You're bound to know what people are saying."

"People are what I'm wiping out, when my time comes."

Cally said "*Halt*, when's that going to be?"

"Me and God only know."

"You think any white girls will go with you now—down the road, I mean, you know, dates and screwing?"

Curtis said "I screw my own right hand. It's free and it's safe, never hurt *nobody*."

"How about your friend God? He claims it's a sin."

Curtis said "Friend God has said He loves my ass, right down to the ground. I bet He forgives me."

"I won't stand by you on Judgment Day though; I might get singed."

"Cally, you were jacking off four times a day, when I thought dicks were plumbing fixtures."

"You know better now."

Curtis said "I know they've caused more trouble than Adolf Hitler and the Japanese Navy."

Cally said "Not mine. Mine's good to me."

"You wait." Curtis put both hands to his mouth and threw a long shout to the trees beyond them. It was not a word; but it seemed to have meaning, though no one bird paid the slightest notice. He took the cool bodies of all they'd killed and, one by one, pitched them gently toward the deepest pool of the creek below them. Then he bent for Cal's rifle and stood a long moment. He thought "Pray Jesus don't let him speak. I might go wild."

But Cally sat calm as the rock beneath them, still watching the pool where the squirrels had sunk. For some weird reason the rabbit's head was floating still.

When it finally sank, Curtis started back to a home he'd rather have died, here now, than see again.

Cally spoke out strong enough to carry. "I'm still what I've always been to you, hear?"

Curtis never looked back.

"That's my damned rifle."

Curt said "Come get it." But he thought "*Die*, fool" and kept on going, hoping he would see, sometime between this minute and the grave, one narrow path in the thicket ahead that darkened now with every step.

Nine

Riley turned off the road just before five. He saw at once that the car was missing, and he naturally thought that Blackie was gone. But smoke was rising from the chimney still; and since the house might burn if the stove was lit, he got out and headed up the hill. Before he had gone six feet, up there the door opened; and Blackie was standing—it had to be her, right age and color, though Riley hadn't seen her since Red's funeral day and then just a glimpse, when her eyes were down.

She watched him come another three steps; then she put a hand to her mouth, turned back and shut the door.

Riley saw a good stick beside the path and leaned to get it, in case of dogs. Since childhood Riley had dreaded dogs; and Red kept a rough old mongrel that could be here. Dogs hated strange skin-color worse than people did. But he got to the front steps with no mishap and stood to wait. Surely she would come to the window at least. When a quiet minute passed, he called out "Hey?" No answer, nothing. So he climbed the rickety steps and knocked. Absolute silence, a far-off crow, cars on the highway two miles west. He tried the china doorknob—open. And he entered slowly.

The room was dark but he stood on the sill and let his eyes open. Then sitting there on Red's old bed was a woman, fine hair and skin, with eyes big as saucers. He said "Is it Blackie? It's been a long time."

"Leah Birch," she said. "You called me Blackie when we used to play."

Riley covered the distance and held out his hand.

She stood and met it—her own palm was cold. Then she went past him and stood by the stove. "I know they took him."

Riley could hear she was sealing a fact, not asking for news. But he gave her a fair account of the trip to Raleigh that morning and Kayes's phone call—no mention of the will of course.

She heard him out, with hardly a move, both her hands flat down on the stove as if it was cool or she was iron. But even when Riley said that Kayes had asked him to drive her to her cousins' for safety, she never budged, shed a tear or spoke. Even as the stillness grew in the room, she stayed there upright frozen inside.

Riley saw Kayes's watch on her wrist. What else? How much more of his brother would walk out of here, if she left now? He didn't mean theft, just sad curiosity. Like others, he noticed when Kayes stopped wearing his wedding ring. Where was that for instance—in his shaving kit? What chance did it have when this all ended, Blackie up North and the war truly won? He told himself he was wasting time. And at last he spoke to Blackie again, "I'm as sorry as you." He had not said what he was sorry for—that Kayes was gone with four people hurt, that this here was ended or that Black must scuttle in the cold dusk now like a wanted thing. That far, Riley was truthful with himself and her—he did not know what he meant and might never.

Still no move from Blackie; was she drunk or doped? So he said "Kayes is gone, to parts mysterious. That much we know. He and I talked about you as kind as we could. We think you may be in trouble here, if you try to stay on—all the mean old boys aren't dead yet, Leah. So I'll be glad to drive you on to your cousins' place or even the bus station now, while it's light. But listen, it's over. This time here at least."

Of all wild things, she broke out smiling; and her lips came open but still no words. She pointed to the left of Riley, toward the bed.

He looked behind him and there on the floor was a cardboard suitcase, a green umbrella, a bright green coat and a mannish hat. "Good. I'll take these down to the car. But first let's see if the stove is safe."

"Safe. I looked."

Why had that broke her loose? Whyever, Riley knew he must trust her. If the place burned down, and the brush all round it, he must not doubt her now. He saw into Leah's clenched mind that far. He took up the suitcase and said "I guess you'll wear that hat." Then he thought of the dog. "Red's old dog—is he still alive?"

"He was way too old, and nobody round here to take care of him. I killed him, this morning. Buried out back." She pointed through the wall.

"Killed him? How?"

"Red's pistol. One shot." She reached up and tapped the crown of her skull.

"Red never had a gun."

Leah nodded. "*Did.* Your grandmother gave it to her, week before your grandma died."

"Where is it now, Black?"

"In your hand. In that suitcase."

"Is it loaded still?"

She nodded. "Five shots."

"Can I open the bag and take out the bullets? You keep them on you, just not in the gun."

"I'll do it." She stayed there but held out her hand.

So Riley stepped over and gave her the suitcase.

She took it with both hands and looked hard at him. "Riley, please go on down and wait. I won't keep you."

At first he thought she wanted the privacy to open her things; so he stepped out and was halfway down before he thought "Oh God, this is it." He walked on slower, awaiting the shot. If it came, he knew the sheriff would believe him—no risk for him. But for everybody's sake, he hoped she'd live. The sight of her hair came now to his eyes, in beautiful waves. He actually spoke, "No, Black. Go easy."

By the time he reached the car, there had been no sound. So he stood on the far side there and waited. The light was leaking away fast now, and a chill was rising. By then he was thinking it might be fate—he believed more nearly in fate than God, some blind hand liable to thrust in the dark. And nothing behind him, in all his life, told Riley who to blame. He thought they had each done the natural thing, every soul involved. Nobody had set out to strew blood and pain. Nobody was wrong but he knew who lost—everybody in sight, Black and Curtis the most. What was taking so long? He thought "I'll call her name again." It would break whatever spell they were under, that barred them apart while each one waited for life or death. With both hands up to his mouth, Riley called out "Leah?" twice.

And at once she was there in the door, climbing down. Even this late, the green coat looked like spring on the way. The hat was far on the back of her head, and it made her look tall as the nearest pine. She had left the umbrella but clutched the suitcase.

Whatever he believed, Riley said "Thank *you*." Then he went to help her, the little he could.

When he met her halfway down the path, she held out the bag; and when he took it, his hand brushed hers. To himself Riley said "It was simple as that"—he meant the tie between her and Kayes. What else was it for but two human skins, together awhile? It was not a mean or scornful thought; it was really what he guessed had been here. Now it was over. In all his years, Riley had touched no woman but his homely wife. And though his mind, even now, could drift in warm spring weather, no one yet had drawn him toward her—God knew, none here. This pitiful soul with no home to take her and skin that was four strikes against her, wherever. Again he thought "Just let the pain fade." He mostly found that was all you could hope for.

They reached the car. Riley opened the trunk and put in her suitcase. It didn't weigh six pounds; was this all she owned? Surely she had things stored up North. He knew he had a twenty-dollar bill; he'd give her that much.

By the time he got to the driver's door, Leah had seated herself in back, the usual seat for Negro women bound home from work.

Riley almost asked her to sit up front, no harm in it now. But when he looked in the rearview mirror, he thought he could see that her eyes were closed. He cranked the engine and looked again. By then the eyes were open but fixed; so he said in the gentlest voice he could manage "Which is it—the bus or your cousins' place?"

She waited. "Riley, I just don't—" She stopped, dug into a pocket of her coat and brought out a quarter. She cupped both hands to make a tumbler and shook the coin for a long ten seconds, saying "Heads is the bus." Then she opened her hands and looked. "Heads it is."

"The bus station then?"

"That'll be a first step." She still looked down, talking to the coin.

Riley said "To Wilmington, Delaware?"

"Or North Hell, Arkansas. I'll know when I get there." She suddenly laughed.

He tried to join her. "You sure you got the fare for that distance? I could help you a little."

Leah said "I'm richer than you know, Riley. I could buy me a ticket from here to the moon, if the notion struck me."

"Let it *strike*. Shoot fire!—that's a fine idea." He turned back, grinning at the change of tone.

And Leah nodded to him but said "Easy, child. We're all too sad. Let's show some respect."

Riley also nodded, then backed out slowly. By the time they stopped at the first crossroads, it was pitch-black night, that soon and final, the dark of the moon.

Ten

At that same time a long way south, Kayes woke in a dim bus among boys, mostly asleep and dreaming. He checked the watch of the gaunt lad beside him and saw that somehow he had slept two hours. Then he checked his mind—no dreams he recalled, no blameful faces. But then the stifling pall of grief he had borne all day fell on him again. He shut his eyes and, for the first time, asked to know what he could do to heal some part of the lives he'd crushed—his wife and son and Leah Birch.

Curtis and Daphne at least stood together and shared the weight. But the sight in his mind of Leah alone hurt too bad to watch, even here far off. So he silently asked her face for pardon; no sound came. Why in God's name should it? He knew there was no least hope of pardon till Riley could write and say she was gone, was safe again working and fed somewhere up North where people, at worst, would just ignore her.

It could be a long wait. How could he last through it?—well, minute by minute like all the pain a grown man causes. How could *she?* Kayes tried to imagine her mind, a thing he had never attempted before. Even as a young boy, he thought he had understood his mother when she left them all. He knew he could read all Daphne's thoughts; it was part of why he had to leave—she ached too much every time he touched her.

But part of Leah had stayed shut to him, the part of the mind that planned for him. He was almost sure it had nothing to do with her color; he had known Old Red like an easy book. (Among what Kayes could not know here was that, trusting him with her actual life, Leah was forced against her will to hide and damp her hope and dread.) So now he cleared his mind, leaned back again and asked for strength to wait in patience, for the grace to recognize and make all due amends as time cooled down. He sat for a long dry spell in the dark. But no help landed, no word, no clue but the moaning breath of the boy beside him.

In the orange shine of the aisle light, Kayes reached to his own feet, found his shaving kit and felt through it slowly, a blind beggar. Finally, under a damp washrag, he found the ring that Daphne gave him, before God and man, the day they were married fifteen years ago. He knew it would be wrong to wear it now, wrong to all concerned, a sorry joke. But vain as all his prayers had been, this empty circle might hold inside it his only chance of coming back whole from this new danger and starting over in decency.

He knew the notion was maybe childish, maybe wild as Brutus risking his own life on a dynamite pill. Still he checked to see that no one watched. Then he brought the gold to his lips and slid it under his tongue. For all the last miles to this place, it stayed there, hard and bitter but hot. He hoped there would be a place at the camp, some vault or locker, to hide it.

But what Kayes knew—all he knew tonight—was a harder fact than a golden ring or even this night that hid the world (they might be parts of a riding dream). This much was true—he had spent from eight to twenty-four hours a day, these six months, beside a kind intelligent person who fit against his mind and body, and *chose* to fit, in every way a sane human being would pray to find this side of death. She was one real woman named Leah Birch—whatever her color or the size of her house—who had finally cared so deep and steady as to all but fill the gully cut in him by his beautiful mother when she heard his prayers one December night and kissed his cheek and then left him forever by morning. Now Lee was gone too. He had run them both off.

Who else on Earth will ever risk Kayes Paschal again?

Eleven

Five hours later, home from the picture show and asleep, Curtis told himself the night's first story, a dream to mend as much as he could in his own cut mind. *This boy and I are standing on a hill at the end of what looks like a big picnic—plates on all sides, chicken bones. All but us have gone on home, but we stand here and face the sunset. I tell him we ought to watch till it's gone, completely night. He says well no, then we'll never get down. But I can see he's not really scared; he just may not want to scramble in the dark. I think it's because he's older than me, more dignified. At least he's taller and his eyes blink less. I want his company so I fall in with him as he leaves too.*

He was right. Before we're halfway down, the light is too thin to see the rocks and gullies beneath us. I can't even see him clear ahead. Pretty soon I'm scared but I feel my way by listening to where he puts his feet. Before long though, even they fade off. I'm feeling my way with bleeding hands, from root to root on the steep dry ground. Finally I'm so deep gone in the dark, and losing blood, that I think "I'm going to yell. He's bound to come." But Lord, I can't remember his name; so I do stop there in the miserable dirt and call my own name, more than once.

Then something pulls my messed-up hands. I can't even see them, but I feel the tug. And then there seems to be a new light, way above me. I'm not even sure which way up is, but I take a chance. And yes, my friend—is he still my friend?—is flying there in a kind of fire that he seems to throw as he moves, like a falling star. But he rises. He rises in slow perfect circles—he knows the way or is climbing to find it— and after a while, I can barely see. I think he goes that far to catch the last daylight, and I try to wait.

That's when the line really hurts my hands. My friend is moving now like a kite, and I've got the string. It's a thick plaited line and is almost gone, so I grab at it while I still have time. And recalling kites and how not to lose them, I reel him toward me turn by turn till, sure, he's back on the ground in reach. But his back is turned. By now I'm guessing it's Kayes somehow. Once he moves though, he's dark again and I can't know. Still I feel the line draw tight once more, and I guess he's tugging me on back down. Without even knowing his face or voice, I try to bet he's taking me home.

Even as the dream threaded Curt's mind and drew him on, in a whole cool room of his understanding, he saw he was dreaming, saw he was easing himself ahead with childish hope. Yet in that same room, he had watched Kayes soar and wished him luck. From the ground Curt even shouted his thanks to the arms that worked in pure dark now—or so he trusted. At the least, that sight of a useful father let Curt sleep till Sunday daylight, clear and dry with slow church bells, the first whole day of his grown man's life.

1991

Rereadings

A Loaf of Bread

James Alan McPherson

It was one of those obscene situations, pedestrian to most people, but invested with meaning for a few poor folk whose lives are usually spent outside the imaginations of their fellow citizens. A grocer named Harold Green was caught red-handed selling to one group of people the very same goods he sold at lower prices at similar outlets in better neighborhoods. He had been doing this for many years, and at first he could not understand the outrage heaped upon him. He acted only from habit, he insisted, and had nothing personal against the people whom he served. They were his neighbors. Many of them he had carried on the cuff during hard times. Yet, through some mysterious access to a television station, the poor folk were now empowered to make grand denunciations of the grocer. Green's children now saw their father's business being picketed on the Monday evening news.

No one could question the fact that the grocer had been overcharging the people. On the news even the reporter grimaced distastefully while reading the statistics. His expression said, "It is my job to report the news, but sometimes even I must disassociate myself from it to protect my honor." This, at least, was the impression the grocer's children seemed to bring away from the television. Their father's name had not been mentioned, but there was a close-up of his store with angry black people, and a few outraged whites, marching in groups of three in front of it. There was also a close-up of his name. After seeing this, they were in no mood to watch cartoons. At the dinner table, disturbed by his children's silence, Harold Green felt compelled to say, "I am not a dishonest man." Then he felt ashamed. The children, a boy and his older sister, immediately left the table, leaving Green alone with his wife. "Ruth, I am not dishonest," he repeated to her.

Ruth Green did not say anything. She knew, and her husband did not, that the outraged people had also picketed the school attended by their children. They had threatened to return each day until Green lowered his prices. When they called her at home to report this, she had promised she would talk with him. Since she could not tell him this, she waited for an opening. She looked at her husband across the table.

"I did not make the world," Green began, recognizing at once the seriousness in her stare. "My father came to this country with nothing but his shirt. He was exploited for as long as he couldn't help himself. He did not protest or picket. He put himself in a position to play by the rules he had learned." He waited for his wife to answer, and when she did not, he tried again. "I did not make this world," he repeated. "I only make my way in it. Such people as these, they do not know enough to not be exploited. If not me, there would be a Greek, a Chinaman, maybe an Arab or a smart one of their own kind. Believe me, I deal with them. There is something in their style that lacks the patience to run a concern such as mine. If I closed down, take my word on it, someone else would do what has to be done."

But Ruth Green was not thinking of his leaving. Her mind was on other matters. Her children had cried when they came home early from school. She had no special feeling for the people who picketed, but she did not like to see her children cry. She had kissed them generously, then sworn them to silence. "One day this week," she told her husband, "you will give free, for eight hours, anything your customers come in to buy. There will be no publicity, except what they spread by word of mouth. No matter what they say to you, no matter what they take, you will remain silent." She stared deeply into him for what she knew was there. "If you refuse, you have seen the last of your children and myself."

Her husband grunted. Then he leaned toward her. "I will not knuckle under," he said. "I will *not* give!"

"We shall see," his wife told him.

The black pickets, for the most part, had at first been frightened by the audacity of their undertaking. They were peasants whose minds had long before become resigned to their fate as victims. None of them, before now, had thought to challenge this. But now, when they watched themselves on television, they hardly recognized the faces they saw beneath the hoisted banners and placards. Instead of reflecting the meekness they all felt, the faces looked angry. The close-ups looked especially intimidating. Several of the first pickets, maids who worked in the suburbs, reported that their employers, seeing the activity on the afternoon news, had begun treating them with new respect. One woman, midway through the weather report, called around the neighborhood to disclose that her employer had that very day given her a new china plate for her meals. The paper plates, on which all previous meals had been served, had been thrown into the wastebasket. One recipient of this call, a middle-aged woman known for her bashfulness and humility, rejoined that her husband, a sheet-metal worker, had only a few hours before been called "Mister" by his supervisor, a white man with a passionate hatred of color. She added the tale of a neighbor down the street, a widow-woman named Murphy, who had at first been reluctant to join the picket; this woman now was insisting it should be made a daily event. Such talk as this circulated among the people who had been instrumental in raising the issue. As news of their victory leaked into the ears of others who had not participated, they received all through the night calls from strangers requesting verification, offering advice, and vowing support. Such strangers listened, and then volunteered stories about indignities inflicted on them by city officials, policemen, other grocers. In this way, over a period of hours, the community became even more incensed and restless than it had been at the time of the initial picket.

Soon, the man who had set events in motion found himself a hero. His name was Nelson Reed, and all his adult life he had been employed as an assembly-line worker. He was a steady husband, the father of three children, and a deacon in the Baptist church. All his life he had trusted in God and gotten along. But now something in him capitulated to the reality that came suddenly into focus. "I was wrong," he told people who called him. "The onliest thing that matters in this world is *money*. And when was the last time you seen a picture of Jesus on a dollar bill?" This line, which he repeated over and over, caused a few callers to laugh nervously, but not without some affirmation that this was indeed the way things were. Many said they had known it all along. Others argued that although it was certainly true, it was one thing to live without money and quite another to live without faith. But still most callers laughed and said, "You right. You *know* I know you right. Ain't it the truth, though?" Only a few people, among them Nelson Reed's wife, said nothing and looked very sad.

Why they looked sad, however, they would not communicate. And anyone observing their troubled faces would have to trust his own intuition. It is known that Reed's wife, Betty, measured all events against the fullness of her own experience. She was skeptical of everything. Brought to the church after a number of years of living openly with a jazz musician, she had embraced religion when she married Nelson Reed. But though she no longer believed completely in the world, she nonetheless had not fully embraced God. There was something in the nature of Christ's swift rise that had always bothered her, and something in the blood and vengeance of the Old Testament that was mellowing and refreshing. But she had never communicated these thoughts to anyone, especially her husband. Instead, she smiled vacantly while others professed leaps of faith, remained silent when friends spoke fiercely of their convictions. The presence of this vacuum in her contributed to her personal mystery; people said she was beautiful, although she was not outwardly so. Perhaps it was because she wished to protect this inner beauty that she did not smile now, and looked extremely sad, listening to her husband on the telephone.

Nelson Reed had no reason to be sad. He seemed to grow more energized and talkative as the days passed. He was invited by an alderman, on the Tuesday after the initial picket, to tell his story on a local television talk show. He sweated heavily under the hot white lights and attempted to be philosophical. "I notice," the host said to him, "that you are not angry at this exploitative treatment. What, Mr. Reed, is the source of your calm?" The assembly-line worker looked unabashedly into the camera and said, "I have always believed in *Justice* with a capital *J*. I was raised up from a baby believin' that God ain't gonna let nobody go *too* far. See, in *my* mind God is in charge of *all* the capital letters in the alphabet of this world. It say in the Scripture He is Alpha and Omega, the first and the last. He is just about the *onliest* capitalizer they is." Both Reed and the alderman laughed. "Now, when *men* start to capitalize, they gets *greedy*. They put a little *j* in *joy* and a littler one in *justice*. They raise up a big *G* in *Greed* and a big *E* in *Evil*. Well, soon as they commence to put a little *g* in *god*, you can expect some kind of reaction. The Savior will just raise up the *H* in *Hell* and go on from there. And that's just what I'm doin', giving these sharpies *HELL* with a big *H*." The talk show host laughed along with Nelson Reed and the alderman. After the taping they drank coffee in the back room of the studio and talked about the sad shape of the world.

Three days before he was to comply with his wife's request, Green, the grocer, saw this talk show on television while at home. The words of Nelson Reed sent a chill through him. Though Reed had attempted to be philosophical, Green did not perceive the statement in this light. Instead, he saw a vindictive-looking black man seated between an ambitious alderman and a smug talk-show host. He saw them chatting comfortably about the nature of evil. The cameraman had shot mostly close-ups, and Green could see the set in Nelson Reed's jaw. The color of Reed's face was maddening. When his children came into the den, the grocer was in a sweat. Before he could think, he had shouted at them and struck the button turning off the set. The two children rushed from the room screaming. Ruth Green ran in from the kitchen. She knew why he was upset because she had received a call about the show; but she said nothing and pretended ignorance. Her children's school had been picketed that day, as it had the day before. But both children were still forbidden to speak of this to their father.

"Where do they get so much power?" Green said to his wife. "Two days ago, nobody would have cared. Now, everywhere, even in my home, I am condemned as a rascal. And what do I own? An airline? A multinational? Half of South America? *No!* I own three stores, one of which happens to be in a certain neighborhood inhabited by people who cost me money to run it." He sighed and sat upright on the sofa, his chubby legs spread wide. "A cab driver has a meter that clicks as he goes along. I pay extra for insurance, iron bars, pilfering by customers and employees. Nothing clicks. But when I add a little overhead to my prices, suddenly everything clicks. But for someone else. When was there last such a world?" He pressed the palms of both hands to his temples, suggesting a bombardment of brain-stinging sounds.

This gesture evoked no response from Ruth Green. She remained standing by the door, looking steadily at him. She said, "To protect yourself, I would not stock any more fresh cuts of meat in the store until after the giveaway on Saturday. Also, I would not tell it to the employees until after the first customer of the day has begun to check out. But I would urge you to hire several security guards to close the door promptly at seven-thirty, as is usual." She wanted to say much more than this, but did not. Instead she watched him. He was looking at the blank gray television screen, his palms still pressed against his ears. "In case you need to hear again," she continued in a weighty tone of voice, "I said two days ago, and I say again now, that if you fail to do this you will not see your children again for many years."

He twisted his head and looked up at her. "What is the color of these people?" he asked.

"Black," his wife said.

"And what is the name of my children?"

"Green."

The grocer smiled. "There is your answer," he told his wife. "Green is the only color I am interested in."

His wife did not smile. "Insufficient," she said.

"The world is mad!" he moaned. "But it is a point of sanity with me to not bend. I will not bend." He crossed his legs and pressed one hand firmly atop his knee. "*I will not bend,*" he said.

"We will see," his wife said.

Nelson Reed, after the television interview, became the acknowledged leader of the disgruntled neighbors. At first a number of them met in the kitchen at his house; then, as space was lacking for curious newcomers, a mass meeting was held on Thursday in an abandoned theater. His wife and three children sat in the front row. Behind them sat the widow Murphy, Lloyd Dukes, Tyrone Brown, Les Jones—those who had joined him on the first picket line. Behind these sat people who bought occasionally at the store, people who lived on the fringes of the neighborhood, people from other neighborhoods come to investigate the problem, and the merely curious. The middle rows were occupied by a few people from the suburbs, those who had seen the talk show and whose outrage at the grocer proved much more powerful than their fear of black people. In the rear of the theater crowded aging, old-style leftists, somber students, cynical young black men with angry grudges to explain with inarticulate gestures. Leaning against the walls, and huddled near the doors at the rear, tape-recorder-bearing social scientists looked as detached and serene as bookies at the track. Here and there, in this diverse crowd, a politician stationed himself, pumping hands vigorously and pressing his palms gently against the shoulders of elderly people. Other visitors passed out leaflets, buttons, glossy color prints of men who promoted causes, the familiar and obscure. There was a hubbub of voices, a blend of the strident and the playful, the outraged and the reverent, lending an undercurrent of ominous energy to the assembly.

Nelson Reed spoke from a platform on the stage, standing before a yellowed, shredded screen that had once reflected the images of matinee idols. "I don't mind sayin' that I have always been a sucker," he told the crowd. "All my life I have been a sucker for the words of Jesus. Being a natural-born fool, I just ain't never had the *sense* to learn no better. Even right today, while the whole world is sayin' wrong is right and up is down, I'm so dumb I'm *still* steady believin' what is wrote in the Good Book . . ."

From the audience, especially the front rows, came a chorus singing, "Preach!"

"I have no doubt," he continued in a low baritone, "that it's true what is writ in the Good Book: 'The last shall be first and the first shall be last.' I don't know about y'all, but I have *always* been the last. I never wanted to be the first, but sometimes it look like the world get so bad that them that's holdin' onto the tree of life is the onliest ones left when God commence to blowin' dead leafs off the branches."

"Now you preaching," someone called.

In the rear of the theater a white student shouted an awkward "Amen."

Nelson Reed began walking across the stage to occupy the major part of his nervous energy. But to those in the audience, who now hung on his every word, it looked as though he strutted. "All my life," he said, "I have claimed to be a man without earnin' the right to call myself that. You know, the *average* man ain't really a man. The average man is a *bootlicker.* In fact, the *average* man would run *away* if he found hisself standing alone facin' down a adversary. I have done that *too many a time* in my life. But *not no more.* Better to be *once* was than *never* was a man. I will tell you tonight, there is somethin' *wrong* in being average. *I intend to stand up!* Now, if your average man that ain't really a man stand up, two things gonna happen: *One,* he g'on bust through all the weights that been place on his head, and, *two,* he g'on feel a lot of pain. But that same hurt is what make things fall in place. That, and gettin' your hands on one of these slick four-flushers tight enough so's you can squeeze him and say, *'No more!'* You do that, you g'on hurt some, but *you won't be average no more* . . ."

"No more!" a few people in the front rows repeated.

"I say *no more!*" Nelson Reed shouted.

"No more! No more! No more!" The chant rustled through the crowd like the rhythm of an autumn wind against a shedding tree.

Then people laughed and chattered in celebration.

As for the grocer, from the evening of the television interview he had begun to make plans. Unknown to his wife, he cloistered himself several times with his brother-in-law, an insurance salesman, and plotted a course. He had no intention of tossing steaks to the crowd. "And why should I, Tommy?" he asked his wife's brother, a lean, bald-headed man named Thomas. "I don't cheat anyone. I have never cheated anyone. The businesses I run are always on the up-and-up. So why should I pay?"

"Quite so," the brother-in-law said, chewing an unlit cigarillo. "The world has gone crazy. Next they will say that people in my business are responsible for prolonging life. I have found that people who refuse to believe in death refuse also to believe in the harshness of life. I sell well by saying that death is a long happiness. I show people the realities of life and compare this to a funeral with dignity, *and* the promise of a bundle for every loved one salted away. When they look around hard at life, they usually buy."

"So?" asked Green. Thomas was a college graduate with a penchant for philosophy.

"So," Thomas answered. "You must fight to show these people the reality of both your situation and theirs. How would it be if you visited one of their meetings and chalked out, on a blackboard, the dollars and cents of your operation? Explain your overhead, your security fees, all the additional expenses. If you treat them with respect, they might understand."

Green frowned. "That I would never do," he said. "It would be admission of a certain guilt."

The brother-in-law smiled, but only with one corner of his mouth. "Then you have something to feel guilty about?" he asked.

The grocer frowned at him. *"Nothing!"* he said with great emphasis.

"So?" Thomas said.

This first meeting between the grocer and his brother-in-law took place on Thursday, in a crowded barroom.

At the second meeting, in a luncheonette, it was agreed that the grocer should speak privately with the leader of the group, Nelson Reed. The meeting at which this was agreed took place on Friday afternoon. After accepting this advice from Thomas, the grocer resigned himself to explain to Reed, in as finite detail as possible, the economic structure of his operation. He vowed to suppress no information. He would explain everything: inventories, markups, sale items, inflation, balance sheets, specialty items, overhead, and that mysterious item called profit. This last item, promising to be the most difficult to explain, Green and his brother-in-law debated over for several hours. They agreed first of all that a man should not work for free, then they agreed that it was unethical to ruthlessly exploit. From these parameters, they staked out an area between fifteen and forty percent, and agreed that someplace between these two borders lay an amount of return that could be called fair. This was easy, but then Thomas introduced the factor of circumstance. He questioned whether the fact that one serviced a risky area justified the earning of profits closer to the forty-percent edge of the scale. Green was unsure. Thomas smiled. "Here is a case that will point out an analogy," he said, licking a cigarillo. "I read in the papers that a family wants to sell an electric stove. I call the home and the man says fifty dollars. I ask to come out and inspect the merchandise. When I arrive I see they are poor, have already bought a new stove that is connected, and are selling the old one for fifty dollars because they want it out of the place. The electric stove is in good condition, worth much more than fifty. But because I see what I see I offer forty-five."

Green, for some reason, wrote down this figure on the back of the sales slip for the coffee they were drinking.

The brother-in-law smiled. He chewed his cigarillo. "The man agrees to take forty-five dollars, saying he has had no other calls. I look at the stove again and see a spot of rust. I say I will give him forty dollars. He agrees to this on condition that I myself haul it away. I say I will haul it away if he comes down to thirty. You, of course, see where I am going."

The grocer nodded. "The circumstances of his situation, his need to get rid of the stove quickly, placed him in a position where he has little room to bargain?"

"Yes," Thomas answered. "So? Is it ethical, Harry?"

Harold Green frowned. He had never liked his brother-in-law, and now he thought the insurance agent was being crafty. "But," he answered, "this man does not *have* to sell! It is his choice whether to wait for other calls. It is not the fault of the buyer that the seller is in a hurry. It is the right of the buyer to get what he wants at the lowest price possible. That is the rule. That has *always* been the rule. And the reverse of it applies to the seller as well."

"Yes," Thomas said, sipping coffee from the Styrofoam cup. "But suppose that in addition to his hurry to sell, the owner was also of a weak soul. There are, after all, many such people." He smiled. "Suppose he placed no value on the money?"

"Then," Green answered, "your example is academic. Here we are not talking about real life. One man lives by the code, one man does not. Who is there free enough to make a judgment?" He laughed. "Now you see," he told his brother-in-law. "Much more than a few dollars are at stake. If this one buyer is to be condemned, then so are most people in the history of the world. An examination of history provides the only answer to your question.

This code will be here tomorrow, long after the ones who do not honor it are not."

They argued fiercely late into the afternoon, the brother-in-law leaning heavily on his readings. When they parted, a little before 5:00 P.M., nothing had been resolved.

Neither was much resolved during the meeting between Green and Nelson Reed. Reached at home by the grocer in the early evening, the leader of the group spoke coldly at first, but consented finally to meet his adversary at a nearby drugstore for coffee and a talk. They met at the lunch counter, shook hands awkwardly, and sat for a few minutes discussing the weather. Then the grocer pulled two gray ledgers from his briefcase. "You have for years come into my place," he told the man. "In my memory I have always treated you well. Now our relationship has come to this." He slid the books along the counter until they touched Nelson Reed's arm.

Reed opened the top book and flipped the thick green pages with his thumb. He did not examine the figures. "All I know," he said, "is over at your place a can of soup cost me fifty-five cents, and two miles away at your other store for white folks you chargin' thirty-nine cents." He said this with the calm authority of an outraged soul. A quality of condescension tinged with pity crept into his gaze.

The grocer drummed his fingers on the counter top. He twisted his head and looked away, toward shelves containing cosmetics, laxatives, toothpaste. His eyes lingered on a poster of a woman's apple red lips and milk white teeth. The rest of the face was missing.

"Ain't no use to hide," Nelson Reed said, as to a child. "*I* know you wrong, *you* know you wrong, and before I finish, *everybody in this city* g'on know you wrong. God don't *like* ugly." He closed his eyes and gripped the cup of coffee. Then he swung his head suddenly and faced the grocer again. "Man, why you want to *do* people that way?" he asked. "We human, same as you."

"Before *God!*" Green exclaimed, looking squarely into the face of Nelson Reed. "Before God!" he said again. "*I am not an evil man!*" These last words sounded more like a moan as he tightened the muscles in his throat to lower the sound of his voice. He tossed his left shoulder as if adjusting the sleeve of his coat, or as if throwing off some unwanted weight. Then he peered along the countertop. No one was watching. At the end of the counter the waitress was scrubbing the coffee urn. "Look at these figures, please," he said to Reed.

The man did not drop his gaze. His eyes remained fixed on the grocer's face.

"All right," Green said. "Don't look. I'll tell you what is in these books, believe me if you want. I work twelve hours a day, one day off per week, running my business in three stores. I am not a wealthy person. In one place, in the area you call white, I get by barely by smiling lustily at old ladies, stocking gourmet stuff on the chance I will build a reputation as a quality store. The two clerks there cheat me; there is nothing I can do. In this business you must be friendly with everybody. The second place is on the other side of town, in a neighborhood as poor as this one. I get out there seldom. The profits are not worth the gas. I use the loss there as a write-off against some other properties." he paused. "Do you understand write-off?" he asked Nelson Reed.

"Naw," the man said.

Harold Green laughed. "What does it matter?" he said in a tone of voice intended for himself alone. "In this area I will admit I make a profit, but it is not so much as you think. But I do not make a profit here because the people are black. I make a profit because a profit is here to be made. I invest more here in window bars, theft losses, insurance, spoilage; I deserve to make more here than at the other places." He looked, almost imploringly, at the man seated next to him. "You don't accept this as the right of a man in business?"

Reed grunted. "Did the bear shit in the woods?" he said.

Again Green laughed. He gulped his coffee awkwardly, as if eager to go. Yet his motions slowed once he had set the coffee cup down on the blue plastic saucer. "Place yourself in *my* situation," he said, his voice high and tentative. "If *you* were running my store in this neighborhood, what would be your position? Say on a profit scale of fifteen to forty percent, at what point in between would you draw the line?"

Nelson Reed thought. He sipped his coffee and seemed to chew the liquid. "Fifteen to forty?" he repeated.

"Yes."

"I'm a churchgoin' man," he said. "Closer to fifteen than to forty."

"How close?"

Nelson Reed thought. "In church you tithe ten percent."

"In restaurants you tip fifteen," the grocer said quickly.

"All right," Reed said. "Over fifteen."

"How much over?"

Nelson Reed thought.

"Twenty, thirty, thirty-five?" Green chanted, leaning closer to Reed.

Still the man thought.

"Forty? Maybe even forty-five or fifty?" the grocer breathed in Reed's ear. "In the supermarkets, you know, they have more subtle ways of accomplishing such feats."

Reed slapped his coffee cup with the back of his right hand. The brown liquid swirled across the counter top, wetting the books. "*Damn this!*" he shouted.

Startled, Green rose from his stool.

Nelson Reed was trembling. "I ain't *you*," he said in a deep baritone. "I ain't the *supermarket* neither. All I is is a poor man that works *too* hard to see his pay slip through his fingers like rainwater. All I know is you done *cheat* me, you done *cheat* everybody in the neighborhood, and we organized now to get some of it *back!*" Then he stood and faced the grocer. "My daddy sharecropped down in Mississippi and bought in the company store. He owed them twenty-three years when he died. I paid off five of them years and then run away to up here. Now, I'm a deacon in the Baptist church. I raised my kids the way my daddy raise me and don't bother nobody. Now come to find out, after all my runnin', they done lift that *same company store* up out of Mississippi and slip it down on us here! Well, my daddy was a *fighter*, and if he hadn't owed all them years he would of raise him some hell. Me, I'm steady my daddy's child, plus I got seniority in my union. I'm a free man. Buddy, don't you know *I'm gonna raise me some hell!*"

Harold Green reached for a paper napkin to sop the coffee soaking into his books.

Nelson Reed threw a dollar on top of the books and walked away.

"I *will not* do it!" Harold Green said to his wife that same evening. They were in the bathroom of their home. Bending over the face bowl, she was washing her hair with a towel draped around her neck. The grocer stood by the door, looking in at her. "I will not bankrupt myself tomorrow," he said.

"I've been thinking about it, too," Ruth Green said, shaking her wet hair. "You'll do it, Harry."

"Why should I?" he asked. "You won't leave. You know it was a bluff. I've waited this long for you to calm down. Tomorrow is Saturday. This week has been a hard one. Tonight let's be realistic."

"Of course you'll do it," Ruth Green said. She said it the way she would say "Have some toast." She said, "You'll do it because you want to see your children grow up."

"And for what other reason?" he asked.

She pulled the towel tighter around her neck. "Because you are at heart a moral man."

He grinned painfully. "If I am, why should I have to prove it to *them?*"

"Not them," Ruth Green said, freezing her movements and looking in the mirror. "Certainly not them. By no means them. They have absolutely nothing to do with this."

"Who, then?" he asked, moving from the door into the room. "Who else should I prove something to?"

His wife was crying. But her entire face was wet. The tears moved secretly down her face.

"Who else?" Harold Green asked.

It was almost 11:00 P.M. and the children were in bed. They had also cried when they came home from school. Ruth Green said, "For yourself, Harry. For the love that lives inside your heart."

All night the grocer thought about this.

Nelson Reed also slept little that Friday night. When he returned home from the drugstore, he reported to his wife as much of the conversation as he could remember. At first he had joked about the exchange between himself and the grocer, but as more details returned to his conscious mind he grew solemn and then bitter. "He ask me to put myself in *his* place," Reed told his wife. "Can you imagine that kind of gumption? I never cheated nobody in my life. All my life I have lived on Bible principles. I am a deacon in the church. I have work all my life for other folks and I don't even own the house I live in." He paced up and down the kitchen, his big arms flapping loosely at his sides. Betty Reed sat at the table, watching. "This here's a low-down, ass-kicking world," he said. "I swear to God it is! All my life I have lived on principle and I ain't got a dime in the bank. Betty," he turned suddenly toward her, "don't you think I'm a fool?"

"Mr. Reed," she said. "Let's go on to bed."

But he would not go to bed. Instead, he took the fifth of bourbon from the cabinet under the sink and poured himself a shot. His wife refused to join him. Reed drained the glass of whiskey, and then another, while he resumed pacing the kitchen floor. He slapped his hands against his sides. "*I* think I'm a fool," he said. "Ain't got a dime in the bank, ain't got a pot to *pee* in or a wall to pitch it over, and that there *cheat* ask me to put myself inside *his* shoes. Hell, I can't even afford the kind of shoes he wears." He stopped pacing and looked at his wife.

"Mr. Reed," she whispered, "tomorrow ain't a work day. Let's go to bed."

Nelson Reed laughed, the bitterness in his voice rattling his wife. "The *hell* I will!" he said.

He strode to the yellow telephone on the wall beside the sink and began to dial. The first call was to Lloyd Dukes, a neighbor two blocks away and a lieutenant in the organization. Dukes was not at home. The second call was to McElroy's Bar on the corner of 65th and Carroll, where Stanley Harper, another of the lieutenants, worked as a bartender. It was Harper who spread the word, among those men at the bar, that the organization would picket the grocer's store the following morning. And all through the night, in the bedroom of their house, Betty Reed was awakened by telephone calls coming from Lester Jones, Nat Lucas, Mrs. Tyrone Brown, the widow-woman named Murphy, all coordinating the time when they would march in a group against the store owned by Harold Green. Betty Reed's heart beat loudly beneath the covers as she listened to the bitterness and rage in her husband's voice. On several occasions, hearing him declare himself a fool, she pressed the pillow against her eyes and cried.

The grocer opened later than usual this Saturday morning, but still it was early enough to make him one of the first walkers in the neighborhood. He parked his car one block from the store and strolled to work. There were no birds singing. The sky in this area was not blue. It was smog-smutted and gray, seeming on the verge of a light rain. The street, as always, was littered with cans, papers, bits of broken glass. As always the garbage cans over-flowed. The morning breeze plastered a sheet of newspaper playfully around the sides of a rusted garbage can. For some reason, using his right foot, he loosened the paper and stood watching it slide into the street and down the block. The movement made him feel good. He whistled while unlocking the bars shielding the windows and door of his store. When he had unlocked the main door he stepped in quickly and threw a switch to the right of the jamb, before the shrill sound of the alarm could shatter his mood. Then he switched on the lights. Everything was as it had been the night before. He had already telephoned his two employees and given them the day off. He busied himself doing the usual things—hauling milk and vegetables from the cooler, putting cash in the till—not thinking about the silence of his wife, or the look in her eyes, only an hour before when he left home. He had deter-mined, at some point while driving through the city, that today it would be business as usual. But he expected very few customers.

The first customer of the day was Mrs. Nelson Reed. She came in around 9:30 A.M. and wandered about the store. He watched her from the checkout counter. She seemed uncertain of what she wanted to buy. She kept glancing at him down the center aisle. His suspicions aroused, he said finally, "Yes, may I help you, Mrs. Reed?" His words caused her to jerk, as if some devious thought had been perceived going through her mind. She reached over quickly and lifted a loaf of whole wheat bread from the rack and walked with it to the counter. She looked at him and smiled. The smile was a broad, shy one, that rare kind of smile one sees on virgin girls when they first con-fess love to themselves. Betty Reed was a woman of about forty-five. For some reason he could not comprehend, this gesture touched him. When she pulled a dollar from her purse and laid it on the counter, an impulse, from no place he could locate with his mind, seized control of his tongue. "Free," he told Betty Reed. She paused, then pushed the dollar toward him with a firm and determined thrust of her arm. "Free," he heard himself saying strongly, his right palm spread and meeting her thrust with absolute force. She clutched the loaf of bread and walked out of his store.

The next customer, a little girl, arriving well after 10:30 A.M., selected a candy bar from the rack beside the counter. "Free," Green said cheerfully. The little girl left the candy on the counter and ran out of the store.

At 11:15 A.M. a wino came in looking desperate enough to sell his soul. The grocer watched him only for an instant. Then he went to the wine counter and selected a half-gallon of medium-grade red wine. He shoved the jug into the belly of the wino, the man's sour breath bathing his face. "Free," the grocer said. "But you must not drink it in here."

He felt good about the entire world, watching the wino through the window gulping the wine and looking guiltily around.

At 11:25 A.M. the pickets arrived.

Two dozen people, men and women, young and old, crowded the pavement in front of his store. Their signs, placards, and voices denounced him as a parasite. The grocer laughed inside himself. He felt lighthearted and wild, like a man drugged. He rushed to the meat counter and pulled a long roll of brown wrapping paper from the rack, tearing it neatly with a quick shift of his body resembling a dance step practiced fervently in his youth. He laid the paper on the chopping block and with the black-inked, felt-tipped marker scrawled, in giant letters, the word FREE. This he took to the window and pasted in place with many strands of Scotch tape. He was laughing wildly. "Free!" he shouted from behind the brown paper. "Free! Free! Free! Free! Free! Free!" He rushed to the door, pushed his head out, and screamed to the confused crowd, "*Free!*" Then he ran back to the counter and stood behind it, like a soldier at attention.

They came in slowly.

Nelson Reed entered first, working his right foot across the dirty tile as if tracking a squiggling worm. The others followed: Lloyd Dukes dragging a placard, Mr. and Mrs. Tyrone Brown, Stanley Harper walking with his fists clenched, Lester Jones with three of his children, Nat Lucas looking sheepish and detached, a clutch of winos, several bashful nuns, ironic smiling teenagers and a few students. Bringing up the rear was a bearded social scientist holding a tape recorder to his chest. "Free!" the grocer screamed. He threw up his arms in a gesture that embraced, or dismissed, the entire store. "*All free!*" he shouted. He was grinning with the grace of a madman.

The winos began grabbing first. They stripped the shelf of wine in a matter of seconds. Then they fled, dropping bottles on the tile in their wake. The others, stepping quickly through this liquid, soon congealed it into a sticky, blood-like consistency. The young men went for the cigarettes and luncheon meats and beer. One of them had the prescience to grab a sack from the counter, while the others loaded their arms swiftly, hugging cartons and packages of cold cuts like long-lost friends. The students joined them, less for greed than for the thrill of the experience. The two nuns backed toward the door. As for the older people, men and women, they stood at first as if stuck to the wine-smeared floor. Then Stanley Harper, the bartender, shouted, "The man said *free*, y'all heard him." He paused. "Didn't you say *free* now?" he called to the grocer.

"I said free," Harold Green answered, his temples pounding.

A cheer went up. The older people began grabbing, as if the secret lusts of a lifetime had suddenly seized command of their arms and eyes. They grabbed toilet tissue, cold cuts, pickles, sardines, boxes of raisins, boxes of starch, cans of soup, tins of tuna fish and salmon, bottles of spices, cans of boned chicken, slippery cans of olive oil. Here a man, Lester Jones, burdened himself with several heads of lettuce, while his wife, in another aisle, shouted for him to drop those small items and concentrate on the gourmet section. She herself took imported sardines, wheat crackers, bottles of candied pickles, herring, anchovies, imported olives, French wafers, an ancient, half rusted can of paté, stocked, by mistake, from the inventory of another store. Others packed their arms with detergents, hams, chocolate-coated cereal, whole chickens with hanging asses, wedges of bologna and salami like squashed footballs, chunks of cheeses, yellow and white, shriveled onions, and green peppers. Mrs. Tyrone Brown hung a curve of pepperoni around her neck and seemed to take on instant dignity, much like a person of noble birth in possession now of a long sought-after gem. Another woman, the widow Murphy, stuffed tomatoes into her bosom, holding a half-chewed lemon in her mouth. The more enterprising fought desperately over the three rusted shopping carts, and the victors wheeled these along the narrow aisles, sweeping into them bulk items—beer in six-packs, sacks of sugar, flour, glass bottles of syrup, toilet cleanser, sugar cookies, prune, apple and tomato juices—while others endeavored to snatch the carts from them. There were several fistfights and much cursing. The grocer, standing behind the counter, hummed and rang his cash register like a madman.

Nelson Reed, the first into the store, followed the nuns out, empty-handed.

In less than half an hour the others had stripped the store and vanished many directions up and down the block. But still more people came, those late in hearing the news. And when they saw the shelves were bare, they cursed soberly and chased those few stragglers still bearing away goods. Soon only the grocer and the social scientist remained, the latter stationed at the door with his tape recorder sucking in leftover sounds. Then he too slipped away up the block.

By 12:10 P.M. the grocer was leaning against the counter, trying to make his mind slow down. Not a man given to drink during work hours, he nonetheless took a swallow from a bottle of wine, a dusty bottle from beneath the wine shelf, somehow overlooked by the winos. Somewhat recovered, he was preparing to remember what he should do next when he glanced toward a figure at the door. Nelson Reed was standing there, watching him.

"All gone," Harold Green said. "My friend, Mr. Reed, there is no more." Still the man stood in the doorway, peering into the store.

The grocer waved his arms about the empty room. Not a display case had a single item standing. "All gone," he said again, as if addressing a stupid child. "There is nothing left to get. You, my friend, have come back too late for a second load. I am cleaned out."

Nelson Reed stepped into the store and strode toward the counter. He moved through wine-stained flour, lettuce leaves, red, green, and blue labels, bits and pieces of broken glass. He walked toward the counter.

"All day," the grocer laughed, not quite hysterically now, "all day long I have not made a single cent of profit. The entire day was a loss. This store, like the others, is *bleeding* me." He waved his arms about the room in a magnificent gesture of uncaring loss. "Now do you understand?" he said. "Now will you put yourself in my shoes? I have nothing here. Come, now, Mr. Reed, would it not be so bad a thing to walk in my shoes?"

"Mr. Green," Nelson Reed said coldly. "My wife bought a loaf of bread in here this mornin'. She forgot to pay you. I, myself, have come here to pay you your money."

"Oh," the grocer said.

"I think it was brown bread. Don't that cost more than white?"

The two men looked away from each other, but not at anything in the store.

"In my store, yes," Harold Green said. He rang the register with the most casual movement of his finger. The register read fifty-five cents.

Nelson Reed held out a dollar.

"And two cents tax," the grocer said.

The man held out the dollar.

"After all," Harold Green said. "We are all, after all, Mr. Reed, in debt to the government."

He rang the register again. It read fifty-seven cents.

Nelson Reed held out a dollar.

1977

Spring Is Now

Joan Williams

Sandra heard first in Miss Loma's store about the Negroes. She was buying cornstarch for her mother when Mr. Mal Walker rushed in, leaving his car at the gas pump, without filling it, to tell the news. His hair plastered to his forehead, he was as breathless and hot as if he had been running. "The school bus was loaded and the driver passed up some niggers in De Soto," he said. "They threw rocks at the bus and a brick that broke the driver's arm." That was all he knew about that. "But," he said, pausing until everyone in the store was paying attention. "There's some registered for your high school in Indian Hill."

At that moment Sandra found the cornstarch. The thought of going to school with Negroes leapt at her as confusedly as the box's yellow-and-blue design. Coming slowly around the bread rack, she saw Mal Walker, rapidly swallowing a Dr Pepper he had taken from the cold-drink case. She put the cornstarch on the counter. Miss Loma fitted a sack over the box and said, "Is that all?"

Sandra nodded and signed the credit pad Miss Loma shoved along the counter. In Miss Loma's pierced ears, small gold hoops shook as, turning back to Mal Walker, she said, "How many?"

"Three I heard." Almost smiling, he looked around and announced—as if the store were full of people, though there was only an apologetic-looking country woman, with a dime, waiting for the party line to clear—"If your kids haven't eat with niggers yet, they will have by Friday. I thank the Lord I live in Indian Hill. Mine will walk home to lunch. When it comes to eating with them, I draw the line."

"Sandra, you want something else?" Miss Loma said.

"No ma'am." Sandra went out and slowly up the hill toward her house opposite, thinking how many times she had eaten with Minnie, who worked for her mother, and how often her mother had eaten in the kitchen, while Minnie ironed. Even Grandmomma had said she would sit down with Minnie, Minnie was like one of the family, though Sandra could not remember that her grandmother ever had. For one reason, she was always in the living room looking at television. There now, she was shelling butter beans and Sandra passed behind her chair, saying nothing, because Grandmomma was hard of hearing. In the kitchen, Sandra put down the cornstarch and said, "Mother, Mister Mal Walker says there's Negroes coming to our high school."

"Are you sure?" Her mother, Flo, was frying chicken and stood suddenly motionless, a long-handled fork outstretched over the skillet full of popping meat and grease. She and Sandra had similar pale faces and placid gray-green eyes, which they widened now, in worry. "I guess we knew it was coming," Flo said.

"Three, he thinks."

In bifocals, Grandmomma's eyes looked enormous. She stood in the doorway saying, "Three what?" Having seen Flo motionless, she sensed something had happened and hearing what, she threw her hands to her throat and said, "Oh, you don't mean to tell me." With the fork, Flo stuck chicken pieces, lifting them onto paper toweling. "Now, Momma," she said, "we knew it was coming." Then Grandmomma, resigned to one more thing she had not expected to live to see, let her hands fall to her sides. "I sure do hate to hear it," she said. "Are they girls and boys?"

"I don't know," Sandra said.

"I just hope to goodness it's girls," Grandmomma said, looking at Flo, who said again, "Now, Momma."

At sundown, when her father came from the fields, Sandra was watching television with Grandmomma. The pickup stopped, a door slammed, but the motor continued to run. From the window she saw her father, a sturdy, graying man; he was talking to Willson, a field hand, who backed the truck from the drive as her father came inside. "Daddy," she said, "there's Negroes going to our school."

He stood a moment looking tired from more than work. Then he said, "I guess it had to happen." He frowned and his eyebrows drew together across his forehead. "The schools that don't take them don't get government money. I knew you'd be with them at the university. But I'm sorry you had to start a year earlier."

Grandmomma, looking up from her program, said, "I just hope they're girls."

"Oh, Grandmomma," Sandra said with irritation and followed her father across the hall. "Why'd Willson take the truck, Daddy?"

Having bent over the bathroom basin to wash, he lifted his head. "That boy of his sick in Memphis can come home tonight. I loaned him the truck to go get him," he said, and his splashed face seemed weighted by the drops of water falling away.

"The one that's had all that trouble with his leg swelling?" Flo said. She brought the platter of chicken to the table.

"He's on crutches but will be all right," the father said.

"I declare, that boy's had a time," Grandmomma said, joining them at the table. "When Willson brings the truck, give him some of my grape jelly to carry to the boy."

They bent their heads and Sandra's father said his usual long blessing. Afterward they looked at one another across the centerpiece of zinnias, as if words were left unsaid. But no one said anything and they began to eat. Then the father said, "Guess what happened? Willson and some of his friends asked if I'd run for road supervisor."

"Why, Tate," Flo said. "What'd you say?"

"I said, 'When would I find the time?'" he said.

"It shows the way they're thinking." Flo said.

"How?" Sandra said.

"They know they can't run one of them yet, but they want a man elected they choose," she said. "Still, Tate, it's a compliment."

"I guess it is," he said.

"The time's just going to come," Grandmomma said.

"Of course, it is," he said.

At six-fifteen the next morning, Sandra from her bed heard a repeated knock rattling the side door. There were the smells of coffee and sausage, and Flo, summoned, pushed her chair from the table to answer the door. Air-conditioning so early made the house too cold and Sandra, reaching for her thin blanket, kept her eyes closed.

"Morning, how're you?" It was Johnson, the Negro who cleaned the Methodist church. He had come to get his pay from Flo, the church's treasurer.

"Pretty good, Johnson, how're you?" Flo said.

"Good but not pretty." He and Flo laughed, then were quiet while she wrote the check. Sandra heard him walk off down the gravel drive and it seemed a long time before she fell back to sleep. Then Flo shook her, saying, "Louise wants to drive the car pool today. You have to be at school at ten to register. Hurry, it's after nine."

"Why'd Johnson come so early?" she said.

"Breakfast was the only time he knew he could catch me home," Flo said.

Drinking orange juice, Sandra stood by the refrigerator and Grandmomma called from the living room, "Are you going to school all winter with your hair streaming down your back like that? I wish you'd get it cut today."

"I don't want it cut," Sandra said.

"Well, I wish you'd wear it pretty like this girl on television then. Look, with it held back behind a band like that."

Sandra came into the living room to look. "Her hair's in a pageboy; it's shorter than mine," she said.

"At least comb it," her mother called from the kitchen.

"I combed it!" Sandra said.

"Well you need to comb it again," her mother said. "And eat something."

"I'm not hungry in the mornings," Sandra said and went out into the heat and down the steep driveway to wait for her friend Louise. There was no high school in their town and they went twenty miles away to a larger place. "Cold," Sandra said, getting in Louise's car.

"Turn that valve and the air conditioner won't blow straight on you," Louise said. She pushed back hair that fell, like a mane, over her glasses. "You heard?"

"About the Negroes?"

"Yes. I heard there were thirteen."

"Thirteen! I heard three."

Louise laughed. "Maybe there's none and everybody's excited about nothing."

There had been a drought all summer in northwest Mississippi. They rode looking out at cotton fields nowhere near bloom, corn limp and brown, and soybeans stunted, flat to the ground. Between the fields were stretches of crumbly dirt, enormous and empty, where crops failed from the drought had been plowed under. Nearby, a pickup raced along a gravel road and as far as they could see, dust trailed it, one cloud rising above the flatland. Once, workmen along the road turned to them faces yellowed by dust, with dark holes for eyes, and Sandra thought of the worry that had been on her father's face all summer, as farmers waited for rain. And all summer, wherever they went, her mother had said, "You don't remember what it was like before everybody had air-conditioned cars. All this dust blew in the windows. Whew! I don't know how we stood it."

And, not remembering she had said it before, Grandmomma would say, "You don't remember either what it was like trying to sleep. Sometimes we'd move our mattresses out into the yard and sleep under the trees. We'd wring out towels and put them on the bed wet to cool the sheets." That she had lived then, though she did not remember it, seemed strange to Sandra.

At school, she found out only that some Negroes had already registered. None were there and the teachers would answer no other questions. Standing in long lines all morning, Sandra found she watched for the Negroes anyway. Other students said they had done the same. She thought the Negroes had been paid more attention by being absent than if they had been present. On the way home, Louise said, "If it weren't such a mystery, I don't think I'd think much about them. If there's a few, I just feel I'm not going to bother them and they're not going to bother me, if they're not smart–alecky."

"I know," Sandra said. "What's the difference, three or thirteen, with the rest of us white?" They stopped on the highway at the Mug'n Cone for hot dogs and root beer. Nearing home, Sandra began to dread questions she would be asked, particularly since she knew little more than when she left. At Miss Loma's, she got out to buy shampoo. The old men were gathered on the store porch playing dominoes, and she said only, "Afternoon," though her mother always said they would be glad for conversation. She thought of when her grandfather had been among them and entered the store.

Miss Loma had already heard the news from the Indian Hill school. She and a Memphis salesman were talking about a family nearby, in the Delta, who passed as white, though people steered clear of them, believing they had Negro blood. "I'll tell you how you can always tell a Negro," the salesman said. "By the blue moons on their nails. They can't hide those."

"I've heard," Miss Loma said, her earrings shaking, "they have black streaks at the ends of their spinal cords. Now, that's what men who've been with them in the army say. Of course, I don't know if it's true. I doubt it." She and the salesman could not decide whether she ought to stock up on straight-lined or dotted-lined primary tablets. With a practical finger, Miss Loma twirled the wire school-supply rack. The salesman pushed back a sporty straw hat with a fishing-fly ornament and said, "Wait till school starts and see what the teacher wants. One thing I hate to see is, somebody stuck with primary tablets they can't sell."

An amber container decided Sandra on a shampoo. She brought the bottle to the counter. "I've heard," she said, "they wear makeup on TV that'll make them look whiter."

"Of course they do," Miss Loma said.

Also, Sandra had heard that Negroes never kissed one another. They made love without preliminaries, like animals, or did nothing. But she was afraid to offer that information. Sometimes, even her mother and father did not seem to know she knew people made love.

Miss Loma said, "Honey, take that shampoo on home as a present. Happy birthday."

"How'd you know it was my birthday?"

"A bird told me."

"Grandmomma," Sandra said.

"You heard about the little nigger baby up in Memphis that's two parts animal?" the salesman said.

"No!" Miss Loma said.

"It's got a little dear face and bare feet," the salesman said, and when Sandra went out, he and Miss Loma were laughing.

In his dusty, green pickup, Sandra's father drew up to the gas pump. Willson's wife, along with another Negro woman, stepped from the truck's cab and went into a grocery across the road. "I see you got your nigger women with you today, Tate," said one of the old men playing dominoes.

Lifting the hose, Sandra's father stood putting in gas, laughing. "Yeah, I carried them with me today," he said. "Sandra, I got to go on back to the field. There's a dressed chicken on the front seat Ida sent. Take it on to your Momma." Sandra opened the truck's door, thinking how many people made remarks about her father letting Negroes ride up front with him. He always answered that if somebody asked him for a ride, he gave it to them; why should they sit out in the open truck bed covered with dust and hit by gravel? She heard him call into the store, "Four-ninety for gas, Loma," and holding the chicken, Sandra waved as he drove off.

Ida's husband had been a field hand for Sandra's father and now was too old to work. Sandra's father let the old couple stay on, rent free, in the cabin on his land. Ida raised chickens and brought one to Flo whenever she killed them. When Flo went to the bakery in Indian Hill, she brought Ida something sweet. Sandra came into the kitchen now and put the chicken on the sink. "That's a nice plump one," Flo said. "If we hadn't had chicken last night, I'd put it on to cook. I hope your daddy let Ida know how much we appreciate it."

"He says he always thanks her," Sandra said.

"But I don't know whether he thanks her enough," her mother said.

The kitchen smelled of cake baking and Sandra pretended not to notice. "Aren't you going to ask about the Negroes at school?" she said.

"Honey, I couldn't wait for you to come wandering in. I called around till I found out."

"I don't see why they got to register at a special time. Why couldn't they register when we did?" Sandra said.

"I don't understand it myself," Flo said.

"I don't understand why they have to be there at all," Grandmomma said, on her way to the bathroom during a commercial. "I declare, I don't."

"Oh Grandmomma," Sandra said.

"I guess they didn't want to take chances on trouble during registration," Flo said. "If the Negroes are just there when school starts, no one can say anything."

"There's plenty of things folks could say if they just would," Grandmomma called.

"I thought she was hard of hearing," Sandra said.

"Not all of the time," Flo said. When Grandmomma came back through the kitchen, Flo said, "We haven't had anything to say about what's happened so far. Everything else has just been shoved down our throats, Mother. I don't know why you think we'd have a chance to say anything now." Sandra, going out and down the hall, wondered why her mother bothered trying to explain to Grandmomma. "What are you going to do?" Flo called.

"Wash my hair," Sandra said.

"Well, for heaven's sake, roll it up as tight as you can and try to keep it curled."

"I wish you'd put it behind a band like that girl on television," Grandmomma called, and Sandra closed the bathroom door.

The candles flickered, then burned, as Flo hesitated in the doorway, smiling, before bringing the decorated cake in to supper. The family sang "Happy Birthday" to Sandra. Her father rolled in a portable television atop brass legs and she jumped up with a squeal. Her hair, waved and tied with a ribbon to please them, loosened and fell toward her shoulders. Now she could see programs without arguing with Grandmomma.

Flo's face was in wrinkles, anxious, as though she feared Ida had not been thanked enough for a chicken, and Sandra knew she was to like her grandmomma's present more than ordinarily. On pink tissue paper, in a tiny box, lay a heavy gold pin twisted like rope into a circle. "Why, Grandmomma!" Sandra said in surprise. Her exclamation was taken for admiration and everyone looked pleased. When she had gone into Grandmomma's room as a small child, to poke among her things, she had been shown the pin. Grandmomma's only heirloom, it had been her own mother's. "I've been afraid I wouldn't live till you were sixteen," Grandmomma said. "But I wanted to give you the pin when you were old enough to appreciate it."

"She never would give it even to me," Flo said.

"No, it was to be for my first grandchild," Grandmomma said. "I decided that when Momma died and left it to me. It was all in the world she had to leave and it's all I've got. But I want you to enjoy it now, instead of when I'm gone."

Had she made enough fuss over the pin? Sandra asked later. Flo said she had, but to thank her grandmother occasionally again. "Mother, it's not really the kind of pin anyone wears," Sandra said. The pin hung limply, lopsided, on her striped turtleneck jersey.

Flo said, "It is kind of heavy and antique. Maybe you'll like it when you're grown. Wear it a few times anyway."

The morning that school started, Sandra hung the pin on her coat lapel and forgot it. She walked into her class and there sat a Negro boy. His simply sitting there was disappointing; she felt like a child who had waited so long for Christmas that when it came, it had to be a letdown. He was to be the only Negro in school. The others had changed their minds, the students heard. But by then everyone had heard so many rumors, no one knew what to believe. The Negro was tall and light-skinned. Louise said the officials always tried to send light-skinned ones first. He was noticeably quiet and the girls, at lunch, found he had spoken in none of his classes. Everyone wondered if he was smart enough to be in the school. From her table Sandra saw him eating by a window with several other boys. Still, he seemed alone and she felt sorry for him.

In the car pool with her and Louise were two boys, Don and Mark. Don, the younger, was an athlete. Going home that afternoon, he said the Negro was not the type for football but was so tall, maybe he would be good at basketball. Sandra thought how little she knew about the Negro and how many questions she would be asked. He had worn a blue shirt, she remembered, and he was thin. Certainly, he was clean. Grandmomma would ask that. She did not even know the Negro's name until Don said, "He lives off this road."

"Who?" she said.

"The colored boy, Jack Lawrence," he said.

"We could ask him to be in the car pool," Louise said, laughing.

Mark, sandy-haired and serious, said, "You all better watch your talk. I had my interview at the university this summer and ate lunch in the cafeteria. There were lots of Negroes and all kinds of people. Indians. Not with feathers, from India. Exchange students."

Dust drifted like clouds over fields, and kudzu vine, taking over the countryside, filling ditches and climbing trees, was yellowed by it. Young pines, set out along the road banks, shone beneath a sun that was strong, even going down. Sandra looked out at tiny pink flowers just appearing on the cotton and tried to imagine going as far away, to a place as strange, as India. That Indians had come all the way to Mississippi to school made her think about people's lives in a way she never had. She entered the house saying, before Grandmomma could ask questions, "Grandmomma, you know they got Indians from India going to Ole Miss?"

Grandmomma looked up through the lower half of her glasses. "You don't mean to tell me," she said, and it took away some of her curiosity about the Negro too. At supper, Sandra gave all the information she could. The Negro boy was clean, looked nice, and his name was Jack Lawrence. All the information she could give in the next month was that he went his way and she went hers. Finally even Grandmomma stopped asking questions about him. He and Sandra had no reason to speak until one morning, she was working the combination to her locker when a voice, quite deep, said, "Sandra, you left this under your desk."

Her dark hair fell forward. In the moment that she pushed it back, something in the voice's deep tone made her think unaccountably how soft her own hair felt. Jack Lawrence held out the book she had forgotten, his face expressionless. It would have been much more natural for him to smile. She saw for the first time how carefully impersonal he was. Other students had mentioned that he never spoke, even to teachers, unless spoken to first. She smiled and said, "Lord, math. I'm bad enough without losing the book too. Thanks."

"Okay. I just happened to notice you left it." He started down the hall and Sandra joined him, as she would have anyone going the way she was. She held her books against her, as if hugging herself in anticipation, but of what, she did not know. She had a curiously excited feeling to be walking beside anyone so tall. No, she thought, not anyone, a boy. They talked about the afternoon's football game, then Jack Lawrence continued down the hall and Sandra turned into her class. There was certainly nothing to that, she thought. But Louise, leaning from her desk, whispered, "What were you talking *about?*"

"Football," Sandra said, shrugging. She thought of all the Negroes she had talked to in her life, of those she talked to every day, and wondered why it was strange to talk to Jack Lawrence. Her mother complained that at every meal, Sandra's father had to leave the table, answer the door, and talk to some Negro who worked for him. They would stand together a long time, like any two men, her father propping his foot on the truck's bumper, smoking and talking. Now she wondered what they talked about.

Jack Lawrence's eyes, when she looked into them, had been brown. Were the eyes of all Negroes? From now on, she would notice. On her way to the stadium that afternoon, she wondered if her gaiety was over the football game or the possibility of seeing—not the Negro, she thought, but Jack Lawrence? Louise went ahead of her up the steps and turned into the bleachers. "I have to sit higher," Sandra said, "or I can't see," adding, "Lon's up there." Louise was crazy about Lon, the basketball coach's son, and rising obediently, she followed Sandra to a seat below him. Lon was sitting with Jack Lawrence. Looking up, Sandra smiled but Jack Lawrence turned his eyes to the game and his lips made no movement at all. When she stood to cheer, to buy a Coke, popcorn, a hot dog, Sandra wondered if he watched her. After the game, he and Lon leapt from the bleachers and went out a back way. That night, she slept with a sense of disappointment.

At school, she always nodded and spoke to him and he spoke back: but they did not walk together again. Most often, he was alone. Even to football games, he did not bring a friend. There was a Thanksgiving dance in the gym, festooned with balloons and crepe paper, but he did not come. On Wednesday before the holiday, driving the car pool, Sandra had seen Jack Lawrence walking along a stretch of country road, hunched into his coat. The motor throbbed loudly in the cold country stillness as she stopped the car and said, "You want a ride?"

He stood, looking as if he did not want any favors, but with eyes almost sore-looking from the cold, then climbed into the back seat with Don and Mark. The countryside's stillness came again as Sandra stopped at the side road he mentioned. With coat collar turned up, untangling long legs, he got out. She was aware of the way her hair hung, of her grandmother's pin too old and heavy for her coat, of the skirt that did not cover her knees, which Grandmomma said was indecent. And she was aware of him, standing in the road against the melancholy winter sunset, looking down to say, "Thank you."

"You're welcome," she said, looking up.

That night she asked her father whether she should have given Jack Lawrence a ride. Her father said she was not to give a ride to Negroes when she was alone. "Not even to women?" she said.

"Oh well, to women," he said.

"Not even to Willson?" she said.

Her father seemed to look inward to himself a long time, then he answered, "No, not even to Willson."

Thanksgiving gave Sandra an excuse to start a conversation. She saw Jack Lawrence in the hall the first day afterward and said, "Did you have a nice holiday?"

"Yes," he said. "Did you?"

Sandra mentioned, briefly, things she had done. "Listen," she said. "We go your way every day, if you'd like a ride."

"Thanks," he said, "but most of the time I have one." He turned to his locker and put away his books and Sandra, going on down the hall, had the strangest feeling that he knew something she did not. She remained friendly, smiling when she saw him, though he made no attempt to talk. He only nodded and smiled when they met and she thought he seemed hesitant about doing that. She asked the boys in the car pool questions about him. Why hadn't he gone out for basketball, how were his grades, what did he talk about at lunch, did anybody know exactly where he lived, besides down that side road?—until one day, Louise said, "Sandra, you talk about that Negro so much, I think you like him."

"Yes, I like him. I mean, I don't dislike him, do you? What reason would we have."

"No, I don't dislike him," Louise said. "He's not at all smart-alecky."

In winter when they came home from school, it was dark. Flo said, "If you didn't have those boys in your car pool, I'd drive you girls back and forth myself. I don't know what Don and Mark could do if anything happened, but I feel better they're there." Sandra's parents, everyone, lived in fear of something happening. South of them, in the Delta, there was demonstrating, and Negroes tried to integrate restaurants and movies in several larger towns. Friends of Sandra's mother began carrying tear gas and pistols in their pocketbooks. Repeatedly, at the dinner table, in Miss Loma's, Sandra heard grown-ups say, "It's going to get worse before it gets any better. We won't see the end of this in our lifetime." Grandmomma always added, "I just hate to think what Sandra and her children will live to see."

One day after Christmas vacation, those in the car pool again saw Jack Lawrence walking along the road. "Should we stop?" Louise said. She was driving, with Don beside her.

"Of course. Would you just drive past him?" Sandra said. She was sitting in the back seat with Mark, and when Jack Lawrence climbed into the car, she was sitting between them. They spoke of the cold, of the snow that had fallen after Christmas, the deepest they could ever remember, and of how you came across patches of it, still, in unexpected places. Side roads were full of frozen ruts. Jack Lawrence said he hated to think of the mud when a thaw came. There could be one at any time. That was the way their weather was. In the midst of winter, you could suddenly have a stretch of bright, warm, almost spring days. There was a silence and Jack Lawrence, looking down at Sandra, said, "Did you lose that pin you always wear?"

"Oh Lord," Sandra said, her hand going quickly, flat, against her lapel.

"Sandra, your Grandmomma's pin!" Louise said, looking into the rearview mirror.

"Maybe it fell off in the car," Mark said. The three in back put their hands down the cracks around the seat. Sandra felt in her pockets, shook out her skirt. They held their feet up and looked under them. Don, turning, said, "Look up under the front seat."

Bending forward at the same instant, Sandra and Jack Lawrence knocked their heads together sharply. "Ow!" Mark cried out for them, while tears came to Sandra's eyes. They clutched their heads. Their faces were close, and though Sandra saw yellow, dancing dots, she thought, Of course Negroes kiss each other when they make love. She and Jack Lawrence fell back against the seat laughing, and seemed to laugh for miles, until she clutched her stomach in pain.

"Didn't it hurt? How can you laugh so?" Louise said.

"I got a hard head," Jack Lawrence said.

When he stood again in the road thanking them, his eyes, glancing into the car, held no message for Sandra. Tomorrow, he said silently, by ignoring her, they would smile and nod. That they had been for a time two people laughing together was enough. As they rode on, Sandra held tightly the pin he had found, remembering how she had looked at it one moment lying in his dark hand, with the lighter palm, and the next moment, she had touched the hand lightly, taking the pin. Opening her purse, she dropped the pin inside.

"Is the clasp broken?" Mark said.

"No, I guess I didn't have it fastened good," she said.

"Aren't you going to wear it anymore?" Louise said, looking back.

"No," she said.

"What will your grandmomma say?" Louise said.

"Nothing I can worry about," Sandra said.

1968

History

Frances Sherwood

When I think of our brief marriage twenty-six years ago, before freedom rides and busing, it is like recalling pages out of a history book. In photographs Marcus, with his scalp-short hair, the part properly shaved, his shoes shined to a mirrory sheen, looks like a member of the Southern Christian Leadership Conference. I, with my open, white-girl smile, long bundle of blond hair, and dirty toes in California sandals, am a caricature hippie.

In 1960 all the newspapers in the nation's capital listed housing under White or Colored. Wherever I called, the landlords' first question always was: White? Both, I'd answer. We are both. Immediately, on the other end, there would be a sudden intake of breath as if I were a crank call or obscene or had let loose a big, bad snake into the wire which was inching forward, making its way up the wire to bite off an ear, pinch a nerve. They would let down the phone that carefully.

"My husband is white," Mrs. Trakled had explained over the phone, and she brought it up again when she was showing us the upstairs apartment she had available. She and the Reverend lived downstairs. It was an immaculate rowhouse in a nice Negro neighborhood with clipped lawns, rosebushes, and green and white awnings unfurled over freshly painted porches.

"The thing is," Mrs. Trakled said, "is that I am picky about my tenants." She looked at Marcus approvingly. "I understand you are studying to be a doctor at Howard University. My, my, a medical man." Marcus had worn a three-piece suit for our interview, carried an umbrella and looked quite the Englishman—from the colonies. Mrs. Trakled was in purple. It was a plum dress for the Grand Tour, with pleated handkerchiefs springing clusters of violets pinned to her shoulders. She looked like Mercury on errand, wings at ready-alert. "And you, my dear," she said turning her motherly gaze on me, "working for the *Post*? I'm a professional woman, too."

Mrs. Trakled's sign hung in the front yard:

> The Reverend Mrs. Trakled
> Lessons in the Piano for Young Ladies

"Actually," she continued, "my husband is white-white. A man of the cloth."

I imagined ghost. Marcus gave me a look like Ku Klux Klan, but rabbit was more like it. The Reverend, who mysteriously materialized when we signed the lease across the grand piano, was albino and just about as old as Methuselah, with blinking, pink eyes and an embarrassed, bashful smile.

"The Reverend, once one of God's chosen orators, is now a man of few words," Mrs. Trakled explained. "We are from Mississippi, you see, and, would you believe it, we couldn't get married down there, had to ride separate cars up to D.C. and here we are."

"It sounds like the Underground Railway," I said.

"What say?" The Reverend shuffled forth, leaning in toward me. "They are newlyweds, Rev.," Mrs. Trakled giggled.

"Underground Railway, really Joanna." We were packing like mad to make the move to the Trakleds'. I could hardly wait.

"Can I help it that I was a history major?"

"Yes indeedy."

"Can you hug me, Marcus, in Virginia, where you come from?"

"Are you crazy?"

I was. It gave me leeway. But Marcus was Mr. Rational. In Control. It took me five minutes to stuff my meager belongings in my straw suitcase. We were staying at his ex-roommate's. Marcus folded all of his stuff neatly, arranging it in piles before putting it in his trunk. I noticed the letter from his mother. Back in Virginia, half a step out of Washington, she did not approve of me. Her letter had left enough space between the lines for me to evoke the whole scene, one Marcus had once described—the rickety front porch of the P.O. boasting a bevy of overalled, tobacco-chewing Guardians of Justice. On the side of her house hung an iron washtub, and under the one tree in the yard was an old carseat with a spring sticking out like a corkscrew. Marcus said his mother made him wear a clothespin on his nose every Saturday and that he was scrubbed Saturday night hard enough to bleed (read bleach). Yet she didn't like me, I, who was a natural.

My mother, at home in California amid her cats and dusty pottery, dashed off a quick note (more later) stating that she knew I would always marry somebody interesting. What she had in mind, I knew, was somebody larger than life—a Paul Robeson–John Henry type, a Byron or a Browning. Somebody dark and dangerous, and definitely *très beau*.

Marcus and I had met at Howard University, E. Franklin Frazier's course, "Negro in the United States." It was a history course and I felt pretty historic myself, for I was the only white person in the class and, from what I could see, on campus, save one exchange student from Oberlin who assiduously avoided me.

"How do you like Howard?" Marcus and I were upstairs in the library, late spring, fans already set up on long, lacquered tables. Outside the open windows, the air was still and dense even though it was eight o'clock at night.

"Fine," I answered, moving my long hair out of my eyes, giving the man a good look. He wore wire-frame glasses. Nobody did then, and he had an old-fashioned, professorial look about him.

"Be honest." His wrists were thinner than mine and his fingers were long. You could play the harp in heaven, I thought.

"I'm always honest," I lied. Downstairs in the lobby there was a portrait of General Howard, blue eyes, no left arm. The old Union general had gone from freeing slaves to killing Indians. The first students at Howard were not freemen, but Chinese. It was a place full of contradictions. Yet, familiar.

"It's like a white school," I said. Every afternoon, light-skinned sorority girls linked arms and sang on the quad. It was like *my* college.

"So we're disappointed, are we?" He had a condescending, slightly humorous way of looking at me over the top of his glasses. He made me feel amusing.

"Surprised," I said.

"We," and he gently put one of his long, brown fingers on my wrist as if feeling for the pulse, "are human just like everybody else. Not morally superior, particularly wise. Just people. Suffering is not a good teacher, all publicity to the contrary."

I should have listened to those words, for they would have provided a key to the language of our marriage. Instead, at that time, I didn't see how prim he was and only noted how different he was from my counterparts at the bookstore where I worked, those pale and pasty male versions of myself. Marcus was older, a hundred times more interesting and, of course, mysterious as Egypt. My heart did a fast flutter-butter, and I knew I was done for. Once before I had been in love, during college, and that had been pure disaster. He was Oriental.

"I'm going to New York next week." Strains of the A.K.A. song wafted up. A sorority sister was passing by. The fans moved left and right on their stiff necks like sunflowers following the sun. I knew it was presumptuous to tell him I was going away, that is, as if he were interested, but I took the risk.

"I'll visit you," he answered. "I mean it." And we exchanged names and addresses. His handwriting was small, elegant, a stylized code.

"Joanna Kandel," he read. "And where is this in New York?"

"The Village."

"Ah, of course."

"No, really, it's just a cheap sublet, I can't let the opportunity. . ."

"Of course not."

"Are you laughing at me again?"

"Good gracious no." He raised his hands in surrender. "Why would I do that?"

The job I found in New York was worse than the one I left in Washington. Not a bookstore, which is all a B.A. in History from Mills College netted me in Washington, but at a Discount China store. I would say discounted discount china and narrow as a ship's galley with place settings, each one an extraordinary bargain, rising to the ceiling like the Leaning Tower of Pisa. A stroll to the back of the store provided seasickness, and the bathroom was always at high tide.

"*Qué pasa?*" Some cute Puerto Rican guys worked as packers in the storeroom. I had to go by them all on the way to the bathroom.

"Degeneration of values in the western world, *hombres*," I'd answer, picking out a handy strip of Japanese newspaper from the packing crate. I read: " 'Likewise the eastern world.' Nobody committing harikari anymore, what *is* this world coming to, yen for life reported on all fronts."

They'd stare at my hairy legs and armpits as if they had never seen such before and give me the old thumbs-up. Yes, we understood each other. Ditto the other salesperson, with whom I had a deep rapport. She was an Argentinian, refugee from the Peronistas, and had hopes of meeting a dentist in America, moving to Queens. I told her a little about Marcus. Not all, of course.

Friday nights and the city still baking a good 92°, I would do the rounds of the air-conditioned bars, few and far between in 1960. I especially like the ones with aquariums, green bubbling, sea divers, startled sea horses. But no sooner would I get comfy on my stool than some lech would hunker up from the shadows, rest his chin on my shoulder. Oh yes, lust was the sawdust under our feet in those good old days. And I knew for sure somebody had to save me, for here I was in New York, New York, and I wasn't even having fun, couldn't even go for a decent drink. Sunday afternoons I spent in Washington Square Park watching city kids in scuba masks and flippers explore the briny depths of the three-foot fountain while I ate my Good Humor bar. Sometimes I went swimming at the Carmine Street swimming pool, where all the sleek lovelies stretched out on the rough concrete like numbers on some celestial clock.

One Friday night I was sitting on my chipped kitchen chair in my living-dining-kitchen wondering what to eat next when I heard a knock at my door. Only one person in the whole world knew where I lived.

That weekend we only went out for food and air. That was the time he told me about the P.O., Saturday baths, and the statue of the Confederate colonel in the town square. I told him that as kids my sister and I jumped on our bed until it broke and then we slept in a heap at a slant until one of my mother's boyfriends tied it up again with twine.

"Those chaotic days are over," he said. I wasn't sure what he meant, what new regime was in store for me, and I had never thought of my childhood as particularly chaotic, just fun. But I did think better of telling him about the time my mother, my sister and I drove through Mexico, the time we picked up a hitchhiker who dropped dead in the back seat of our car. When we drove back to the little seaside town near Ensenada where we had picked him up nobody knew him, wanted to claim him, so we buried him ourselves on a promontory overlooking the beach. We made a cross, since we figured everybody in Mexico was a Catholic, and my sister said a few words just as she had when Stravinsky, our pet beagle, died.

Coming home from work on Monday after our weekend, knowing that Marcus was waiting for me in the apartment, and watching the other working people in the subway with their bags of groceries, tired feet, I felt that at long last I had joined the human race, the real people. I was also going home, had my own bag of groceries and a bouquet of daisies for Marcus, who after all was from the country. Climbing the stairs to the apartment, I expected the door to be open but, from down the hallway, could see that not only was it closed but that somebody had pasted something to the door. At a distance, it looked like the Declaration of Independence, with lots of fancy signatures on it. Up close, I could see that it was a petition and eviction notice. All the mothers of the building, not the Ritz by any stretch of the imagination, alleged that I was a prostitute. Quietly, I unglued the document, stuffed it in my purse, and went inside. Marcus was packing, not because of the sign, which apparently he hadn't seen, but because he had to go back to Virginia, return to his job as a janitor.

At the train station, Marcus said, "I've been accepted at Howard Medical School." People were looking at us standing together, and this was New York.

"I love you, Marcus." I thought I should set the record straight. It was true. I had all the symptoms. Dry throat, clammy hands, etc.

"Do you think we should get married?" he said.

"I don't know." But I wasn't shocked at the idea. Love in my book did not necessarily mean marriage, but I was vaguely aware, even then, that Marcus's book was different. And I also knew, given the world, we had to be serious, all or nothing.

"I have GI benefits," he said. "Also, I've saved. It's been proven that married men do better in medical school than single ones."

"I would work, too."

"Until I finish," he added.

Marriage *was* a thought. After a rather haphazard upbringing, I had gone to a girl's college where everybody on my floor was engaged by senior year. Alumnae notes were full of tidbits about illustrious husbands and accomplished children. Marriage with Marcus would not be tame and ordinary. It might very well be the grandest adventure of all. I could see myself plucking burning crosses from our front yard with my bare hands. Insults from ignoramuses would bounce off my strong chest. I would be a moral Paul Bunyan, showing them all, showing myself. It would certainly be better than living alone in New York, or whatever else I could think of at the moment.

A Baptist preacher married us in Washington. Miscegenation was illegal in Virginia, and we didn't have the money for California. Marcus's former roommate stood up for us, looking zonked out of his mind. I laughed through the ceremony—cosmic joy, I told Marcus, who was miffed. I wore a paisley dress my mother had done up in a hurry, sent off. It was from an Indian bedspread, a pattern on the bottom of orange elephants trekking East. On my long yellow hair, I wore a wreath of laurels. Marcus was in his three-piecer, the one he wore for interviews and on Sundays for church.

Our bedroom overlooked a wonderful tree, and toward November the yellow leaves plastered themselves to the window like large, yellow hands, splayed fingers. They made me think of children's drawings of fall you see in school windows, and yes, I wanted children, a whole slew of them. They would be beautiful, brown Gauguins and I would be the Pied Piper leading them along the beach. Not Virginia Beach, natch. But some beach, somewhere. Marcus wanted two children, a boy and a girl, after he had finished medical school, his internship and residency.

November and the afternoons turned very dark. I'd come home from my job at the *Post* to find a hallway of little girls waiting for their piano lessons in Mary Janes and braids so tight their eyes would slant up. On Saturdays, when Marcus was studying in the library, I swept the leaves off the front porch, helped the Trakleds put in storm windows, learned how to make sweet potato pie and Mississippi mud cake. I took the Reverend's damp tobacco wads, lined up on the porch banister, inside. They looked like frozen bonbons. When Marcus came home he'd shower for hours it seemed, eat quickly, and then fall into bed, tucking up into a tight ball like small armored bugs who curl closed at a touch. My job in the newspaper morgue, where I clipped and filed stories all day, was more tedious than the china shop. At least there I had the Puerto Ricans, the homesick Argentinean. In the morgue, we were all disgruntled history majors, English majors. It was the bookstore all over again.

Around Christmas, Marcus and I were invited to a party. Finally, I was going to meet his study group, talk to some folks. Remembering my mother's parties featuring wine, good talk, I dressed in comfortable slacks, a bulky sweater and my long scarf of many colors. I was prepared to spend the evening on the floor arguing about Marxism, music, Richard Nixon. Marcus wore his suit, as always. Marcus was Marcus. Cuddling up to him on the streetcar going down Georgia Avenue, I thought of when we would be coming home that night. We'd be a little tipsy. It would be like New York again, that weekend, our courtship. But he inched over ever so slightly.

"Anymore and you'll be out the window," I said.

"Joanna."

"I know." He hated public displays of affection, considered them in bad taste. I moved back to my side. The trolley jiggled and jangled, careened around corners. (The tracks are all dug up now. And the trolleys are in museums.) I looked ahead. Washington at night was empty. You could not tell what part of the city was segregated except in terms of buildings. There were good buildings and bad buildings, those with doormen, those without.

"I'm thinking of taking some courses again," I said. "At night, when you're not home."

He didn't catch the hint.

"More history?"

"I won't make that mistake again. Maybe psychology." I knew what he thought of psychology. Not much.

"I'm going to have a lot of papers next semester," he said.

"Meaning?"

"I was hoping you could help type them."

"Ah." But we had arrived. We got off the trolley, crossed the street, entered a dingy, unkept building.

When the apartment door was opened, though, I could see that I was way out of my depth. All the furniture was creamy white, soft and modern. Huge baskets of ferns hung from the ceiling. The lighting was subdued, the music jazz—cool, subtle jazz. The drinks were not jug wine, paper cups, that sort of thing, but a full bar, J&B, a real bartender in uniform, obviously hired for the occasion. People were drinking martinis. The hors d'oeuvres, while not plentiful, were hot, complicated, on silver trays. But the very worst part was that everybody except me was dressed to the teeth in clothes with style and cut, the kind of thing you see in fashion magazines. Marcus should have warned me. I wished I could have just fainted right there on the spot so that I could be removed, on a stretcher, with a blanket thrown over my body. My only claim to class at the moment was my hair, which was the color of gold, and Marcus, but when I turned he was not there. He had vanished into the crowd.

"Scotch on the rocks," I requested of the bartender.

"Hello there," a voice said behind me. I turned around. The woman was in a sarong-like dress, pleated at the hips. The drape was perfect and the color was shades of green.

"My name is Casey," she said.

"Joanna." Her hair was in a Billie Holiday upsweep, but, instead of a gardenia, she wore a spray of mistletoe over her ear.

"I'm Marcus's wife." She would know Marcus, surely.

"I know." Her complexion and smile were reminiscent of Lena Horne. I couldn't believe this glamorous lady deemed me worthy of a conversation.

"What I've been wondering," and she arched her penciled eyebrows, "is don't they have men where you come from?"

I looked about in a panic searching for rescue, comfort, something, realized I was very much on my own.

"Excuse me, Casey." I was trying hard to hold the tears, keep some semblance of dignity. "I feel sick," I said.

"Then I ducked into the bathroom," I told Mrs. Trakled the next day over tea, candied violets. "I wanted to stay in there forever."

"Oh," Mrs. Trakled huffed. "Those high-brown Louisiana girls think they are something. Just jealous is all. Just jealous."

Mrs. Trakled's relatives looked down on us from their oval frames. They lined the dining room wall, daguerreotypes, in high-collared dresses, watch chains, struck poses. There was nothing of the Reverend, no trace to the past. Sometimes I thought of him spawned spontaneously in some backwoods swamps, a Mississippi grub, pale and translucent, turning in a single lifetime from worm to man, cell to angel. Actually, Mrs. Trakled told me, he had been a preacher doing revivals when she met him. She was called in when the white pianist failed to appear.

"Do you think I should tell Marcus?" I hadn't. Not a word.

"Good heavens, no. Don't tell him a thing."

That night Marcus and I were seated across from each, a late dinner, eight o'clock. I had the oven on and open for added warmth. The wind was whistling outside, and our bedroom windows were freezing up on the inside.

"Sometimes I wish I was in California, Marcus. Both of us."

"You act like it's my fault you're not." He folded his napkin.

"No I don't."

"Yes you do."

"Like hell I do." It slipped out.

"I hate vulgarity in a woman." I knew he did.

"I hate cruelty in a man," I replied.

"Oh, you people." He sighed, stood up.

"What people are you referring to, Marcus? California people? Other people? White people? For your information, I am *your* people."

"Joanna, what are you talking about?" He sat down again.

"Attitude. Yours."

"You are the one with an attitude."

"I am the one with a sense of family, the only one. Marcus, we are kin. You can't say, 'Oh, you people' to me. It makes you sound like that woman at the party."

"What woman?" He got up, leaned against the sink.

"The one who asked me if there weren't any men where I came from."

"Who said that?"

"Casey."

"She didn't mean anything."

"She meant plenty. Don't defend her. It was a mean thing to say."

"It didn't kill you, did it?"

"That's even meaner. Whose side are you on?"

He sat down, looked absolutely disgusted with me. "I take you to a party," he said wearily. "I thought you would like it."

"I hated it."

"Great, that's just great."

I picked up his dish, took it to the sink.

"You know, Joanna, those are my friends, the people who help me, the people who would help you. If anything happened . . ."

"Marcus," I turned around from the sink. "Those people would not help me off the sidewalk if I was dying and you know it."

"So what about your friends? Tell me, what they would do for me?"

"My friends don't live in Washington," I said meekly.

"Where *do* they live, Joanna? Anywhere on earth?"

I couldn't tell him what people at work said when I showed them pictures of my husband. I hadn't even told him about my experiences in looking for an apartment. He didn't know what had happened to my world, that it was more than divided, that it had simply fallen away.

"I didn't see your mother sending us any wedding presents," he continued, "or your sister."

"My mother made my wedding dress."

"That Halloween costume?"

I had to sit down at that. "At least my mother congratulated me," I offered. "Congratulated *us*, which is more much more than your mother did. Remember your mother's letter, Marcus? And I quote: Are you doing the right thing, Marcus? Unquote. She thought I was pregnant or something."

"You could have been. Easily."

"I'll let that go. The point is that you side with the woman at the party."

"There is a serious shortage of Negro men, so that when a white woman . . ."

"Has one of their own . . ."

"Do you know what people think of you, of me, Joanna?"

"Do *you* know? Anyway, I don't care what people think."

"I do."

"You care too much, that's your problem."

"We have to live in society."

"We are society, Marcus." I felt strong enough to get up again, start the dishes. Usually I let them soak, but Marcus recently had explained to me how unsanitary that was.

"The world out there, Marcus, is full of hypocrites and chickenshits."

"It doesn't solve anything to say that."

"It puts it in perspective, Marcus, lets us know what is important, that we are more important." I looked over at him, remembering how I had felt that first time in New York when I opened my door to him. It was instant recognition, as if my door was really a mirror I was looking into. I had felt that close. Now, looking at Marcus, I felt a chill go through me, and it was like being confronted with a blank wall.

"When I become a doctor, Joanna . . ."

"The world will stop."

"You can make fun of it if you want. But do you know what one of my professors told me? He said that when he was doing his internship in a big-city hospital, a northern city hospital, a woman came into the emergency room bleeding to death, but she would not let him stick a needle for a transfusion into her. She would rather bleed to death."

"Did she?"

"No, of course not. He got a nurse to do it."

I sat back down in the chair, put my head in my hands. I knew what was coming. "Tell me about Charles Drew, Marcus, isn't he the one, the one who discovered blood types and then bled to death on some southern road because the nearest hospital was white? Tell me all the stories, tell me all about it."

"You act like those things don't matter."

"I know they do, but *I* am not your enemy. And you can't play it both ways." The wind rattled the windows. "You seem to *be* like the woman at the party, like your mother, people who are outside but want to be inside, yet you hate the inside."

"And you?"

"I am an outsider, too, can't you see that?"

"No. If so, by choice."

"It's not just color, race." I felt outside of everything at that moment. But from my distance I could see that to Marcus I was an insider and that maybe it had been part of my attraction, and that I had taken him for an outsider, but that really in his heart he wasn't. "I'm on the fringe of things, Marcus, of all things, of your things, too; you should be proud of me. I need some company, can't you tell?"

The bare limbs of the tree were scratching against the window like skeleton hands trying to gain entrance. I looked down at Marcus's elegant hand, the one that would cut and snip, sew back up. Formaldehyde from anatomy lab had pinched up the little pads at the end of the fingertips. His knuckles were wrinkled. With a surge of affection, I reached for it. But Marcus drew his hand back.

"For God's sake, Marcus, I don't want to cut it off."

Yet I felt like it suddenly. I could have. Instead, I ran into the bathroom and with two big swipes, using the scissors brought all the way from California, I cut off two feet of my hair, which had taken me since junior high to grow. Then I marched back into the kitchen.

"See," I shouted, putting a fistful of hair before him. "A hair sandwich, how do you like them apples? See what you made me do? Happy now?"

"Joanna." He shook his head as if I was beyond all hope.

"I present you my hair." I tried to make it sound victorious, but my voice began to wobble and my whole body was shaking. Lying there on the table, my hair looked like a prone animal, like a complete supplicant, a totally defeated, dead beast.

"You are so crazy, Joanna. You make everything so damned hard."

"You make it impossible." I was feeling light-headed as if, like Samson, my strength resided in my hair. My neck felt cold, naked; my face was exposed. I was out there, stripped. Like a collaborator.

"You don't care," I wailed. "You don't even care."

"Shh," he said, putting a finger to his lips, but not rising from his chair to hug and soothe me. "You'll wake the Trakleds."

I wailed all the louder. A line of roaches sneaked out from the crack by the side of the table, took note, waved their antennae.

"Shut up, Joanna."

Then I really let loose, and in a few seconds there was a light tapping at the door.

"Joanna, honey, it is I, Matilda Trakled, are you all right?"

I went to the door, opened it a little.

"Mrs. Trakled."

"Oh child, you've gone and cut your beautiful hair, your crowning glory."

"No, it's all right," I said, sniffing. "Your hair is short, Mrs. Trakled."

"That's different. I'm an old woman."

"No you're not." I noticed that her bathrobe, like all her clothes, was a variation on violet.

"Do you want to come down and watch wrestling on TV? Gorgeous George is on."

Gorgeous George was our mutual favorite. Nights when Marcus was not home and the Reverend retired early, Mrs. Trakled and I stayed up for wrestling and mint juleps.

"Maybe some other time." I closed the door gently.

"Toodle-oo," she called, descending the stairs.

"You woke them up," Marcus accused.

"They were up." I looked at the African violet on top of the fridge. It was a gift from Mrs. Trakled, part of her collection, which she kept on a white teacart. Music was her vocation, she explained to me, and horticulture her avocation.

"You've wakened them," Marcus persisted. "Two innocent people."

"They are not that innocent, Marcus." In fact, Mrs. Trakled told me that the Reverend liked to put a pillow under her hips, hike her up. And during the train trip north, he bribed the porter and he and Mrs. Trakled, then Miss Gibson, got together on one of the top bunks in the Pullman. It was a metaphysical experience, I said to myself, their double-decker coupling, a preacher and his accompanist.

"You know, Joanna, I sometimes wonder," Marcus said.

"Me too. I wonder too, Marcus. Tell me." He had never said it, not once, not on our wedding night, never. "Tell me, honestly, do you love me?"

There was a moment of silence between us, a long moment, too long. I could hear the tree scraping and skittling along the baseboards, the roaches, lots of them, or mice. Another moment passed. I thought I could hear the plants on top of the fridge growing or at least straining towards us, its petals attuned to nuance, all hairs standing straight up. Then Marcus cleared his throat.

"Well?" I was waiting. That was it.

"I married you, didn't I?" he said.

He looked up at me, for I was still standing, and I read such fear in his eyes that I wanted to comfort him, tell him it was all right. Because I knew then that there was no point, that it was all over.

1987

Advancing Luna—and Ida B. Wells

Alice Walker

I met Luna the summer of 1965 in Atlanta where we both attended a political conference and rally. It was designed to give us the courage, as temporary
civil rights workers, to penetrate the small hamlets farther south. I had taken
a bus from Sarah Lawrence in New York and gone back to Georgia, my
home state, to try my hand at registering voters. It had become obvious from
the high spirits and sense of almost divine purpose exhibited by black people
that a revolution was going on, and I did not intend to miss it. Especially not
this summery, student-studded version of it. And I thought it would be fun
to spend some time on my own in the South.

Luna was sitting on the back of a pickup truck, waiting for someone
to take her from Faith Baptist, where the rally was held, to whatever gracious black Negro home awaited her. I remember because someone who
assumed I would also be traveling by pickup introduced us. I remember
her face when I said, "No, no more back of pickup trucks for me. I know
Atlanta well enough, I'll walk." She assumed of course (I guess) that I did
not wish to ride beside her because she was white, and I was not curious
enough about what she might have thought to explain it to her. And yet I
was struck by her passivity, her *patience* as she sat on the truck alone and
ignored, because someone had told her to wait there quietly until it was
time to go.

This look of passively waiting for something changed very little over the
years I knew her. It was only four or five years in all that I did. It seems
longer, perhaps because we met at such an optimistic time in our lives. John
Kennedy and Malcolm X had already been assassinated, but King had not
been and Bobby Kennedy had not been. Then too, the lethal, bizarre elimi-
nation by death of this militant or that, exiles, flights to Cuba, shoot-outs
between former Movement friends sundered forever by lies planted by the
FBI, the gunning down of Mrs. Martin Luther King, Sr., as she played the
Lord's Prayer on the piano in her church (was her name Alberta?), were still
in the happily unfathomable future.

We believed we could change America because we were young and
bright and held ourselves *responsible* for changing it. We did not believe we

would fail. That is what lent fervor (revivalist fervor, in fact; we would *revive* America!) to our songs, and lent sweetness to our friendships (in the beginning almost all interracial), and gave a wonderful fillip to our sex (which, too, in the beginning, was almost always interracial).

What first struck me about Luna when we later lived together was that she did not own a bra. This was curious to me, I suppose, because she also did not need one. Her chest was practically flat, her breasts like those of a child. Her face was round, and she suffered from acne. She carried with her always a tube of that "skin-colored" (if one's skin is pink or eggshell) medication designed to dry up pimples. At the oddest times—waiting for a light to change, listening to voter registration instructions, talking about her father's new girlfriend, she would apply the stuff, holding in her other hand a small brass mirror the size of her thumb, which she also carried for just this purpose.

We were assigned to work together in a small, rigidly segregated South Georgia town that the city fathers, incongruously and years ago, had named Freehold. Luna was slightly asthmatic and when overheated or nervous she breathed through her mouth. She wore her shoulder-length black hair with bangs to her eyebrows and the rest brushed behind her ears. Her eyes were brown and rather small. She was attractive, but just barely and with effort. Had she been the slightest bit overweight, for instance, she would have gone completely unnoticed, and would have faded into the background where, even in a revolution, fat people seem destined to go. I have a photograph of her sitting on the steps of a house in South Georgia. She is wearing tiny pearl earrings, a dark sleeveless shirt with Peter Pan collar, Bermuda shorts, and a pair of those East Indian sandals that seem to adhere to nothing but a big toe.

The summer of '65 was as hot as any other in that part of the South. There was an abundance of flies and mosquitoes. Everyone complained about the heat and the flies and the hard work, but Luna complained less than the rest of us. She walked ten miles a day with me up and down those straight Georgia highways, stopping at every house that looked black (one could always tell in 1965) and asking whether anyone needed help with learning how to vote. The simple mechanics: writing one's name, or making one's "X" in the proper column. And then, though we were required to walk, everywhere, we were empowered to offer prospective registrants a car in which they might safely ride down to the county courthouse. And later to the polling places. Luna, almost overcome by the heat, breathing through her mouth like a dog, her hair plastered with sweat to her head, kept looking straight ahead, and walking as if the walking itself was her reward.

I don't know if we accomplished much that summer. In retrospect, it seems not only minor, but irrelevant. A bunch of us, black and white, lived together. The black people who took us in were unfailingly hospitable and kind. I took them for granted in a way that now amazes me. I realize that at each and every house we visited I *assumed* hospitality, I *assumed* kindness. Luna was often startled by my "boldness." If we walked up to a secluded farmhouse and half a dozen dogs ran up barking around our heels and a large black man with a shotgun could be seen whistling to himself under a tree, she would become nervous. I, on the other hand, felt free to yell at this stranger's dogs, slap a couple of them on the nose, and call over to him about his hunting.

That month with Luna of approaching new black people every day taught me something about myself I had always suspected: I thought black people superior people. Not simply superior to white people, because even without thinking about it much, I assumed almost everyone was superior to them; but to everyone. Only white people, after all, would blow up a Sunday-school class and grin for television over their "victory," *i.e.*, the death of four small black girls. Any atrocity, at any time, was expected from them. On the other hand, it never occurred to me that black people *could* treat Luna and me with anything but warmth and concern. Even their curiosity about the sudden influx into their midst of rather ignorant white and black Northerners was restrained and courteous. I was treated as a relative, Luna as a much welcomed guest.

Luna and I were taken in by a middle-aged couple and their young school-age daughter. The mother worked outside the house in a local canning factory, the father worked in the paper plant in nearby Augusta. Never did they speak of the danger they were in of losing their jobs over keeping us, and never did their small daughter show any fear that her house might be attacked by racists because we were there. Again, I did not expect this family to complain, no matter what happened to them because of us. Having understood the danger, they had assumed the risk. I did not think them particularly brave, merely typical.

I think Luna liked the smallness—only four rooms—of the house. It was in this house that she ridiculed her mother's lack of taste. Her yellow-and-mauve house in Cleveland, the eleven rooms, the heated garage, the new car every year, her father's inability to remain faithful to her mother, their divorce, the fight over the property, even more bitter than over the children. Her mother kept the house and the children. Her father kept the car and his new girlfriend, whom he wanted Luna to meet and "approve." I could hardly imagine anyone disliking her mother so much. Everything Luna hated in her she summed up in three words: *"yellow and mauve."*

I have a second photograph of Luna and a group of us being bullied by a Georgia state trooper. This member of Georgia's finest had followed us out into the deserted countryside to lecture us on how misplaced—in the South— was our energy, when "the Lord knew" the North (where he thought all of us lived, expressing disbelief that most of us were Georgians) was just as bad. (He had a point that I recognized even then, but it did not seem the point where we were.) Luna is looking up at him, her mouth slightly open as always, a somewhat dazed look on her face. I cannot detect fear on any of our faces, though we were all afraid. After all, 1965 was only a year after 1964 when three civil rights workers had been taken deep into a Mississippi forest by local officials and sadistically tortured and murdered. Luna almost always carried a flat black shoulder bag. She is standing with it against her side, her thumb in the strap.

At night we slept in the same bed. We talked about our schools, lovers, girlfriends we didn't understand or missed. She dreamed, she said, of going to Goa. I dreamed of going to Africa. My dream came true earlier than hers: an offer of a grant from an unsuspected source reached me one day as I was writing poems under a tree. I left Freehold, Georgia, in the middle of summer, without regrets, and flew from New York to London, to Cairo, to Kenya, and, finally, to Uganda, where I settled among black people with the same assumptions of welcome and kindness I had taken for granted in Georgia. I was taken on rides down the Nile as a matter of course, and accepted all invitations to dinner, where the best local dishes were superbly prepared in my honor. I became, in fact, a lost relative of the people, whose ancestors had foolishly strayed, long ago, to America.

I wrote to Luna at once.

But I did not see her again for almost a year. I had graduated from college, moved into a borrowed apartment in Brooklyn Heights, and was being evicted after a month. Luna, living then in a tenement on East 9th Street, invited me to share her two-bedroom apartment. If I had seen the apartment before the day I moved in I might never have agreed to do so. Her building was between Avenues B and C and did not have a front door. Junkies, winos, and others often wandered in during the night (and occasionally during the day) to sleep underneath the stairs or to relieve themselves at the back of the first-floor hall.

Luna's apartment was on the third floor. Everything in it was painted white. The contrast between her three rooms and kitchen (with its red bathtub) and the grungy stairway was stunning. Her furniture consisted of two large brass beds inherited from a previous tenant and stripped of paint by Luna, and a long, high-backed church pew which she had managed somehow to bring up from the South. There was a simplicity about the small apartment that I liked. I also liked the notion of extreme contrast, and I do to this day. Outside our front window was the decaying neighborhood, as ugly and ill-lit as a battleground. (And allegedly as hostile, though somehow we were never threatened with bodily harm by the Hispanics who were our neighbors, and who seemed, more than anything, *bewildered* by the darkness and filth of their surroundings.) Inside was the church pew, as straight and spare as Abe Lincoln lying down, the white walls as spotless as a monastery's, and a small, unutterably pure patch of blue sky through the window of the back bedroom. (Luna did not believe in curtains, or couldn't afford them, and so we always undressed and bathed with the lights off and the rooms lit with candles, causing rather nun-shaped shadows to be cast on the walls by the long-sleeved high-necked nightgowns we both wore to bed.)

Over a period of weeks, our relationship, always marked by mutual respect, evolved into a warm and comfortable friendship which provided a stability and comfort we both needed at that time. I had taken a job at the Welfare Department during the day, and set up my typewriter permanently in the tiny living room for work after I got home. Luna worked in a kindergarten, and in the evenings taught herself Portuguese.

It was while we lived on East 9th Street that she told me she had been raped during her summer in the South. It is hard for me, even now, to relate my feeling of horror and incredulity. This was some time before Eldridge Cleaver wrote of being a rapist / revolutionary; of "practicing" on black women before moving on to white. It was also, unless I'm mistaken, before LeRoi Jones (as he was then known; now of course Imamu Baraka, which has an even more presumptuous meaning than "the King") wrote his advice to young black male insurrectionaries (women were not told what to do with *their* rebelliousness): "Rape the white girls. Rape their fathers." It was clear that he meant this literally and also as: to rape a white girl *is* to rape her father. It was the misogynous cruelty of this latter meaning that was habitually lost on black men (on men in general, actually), but nearly always perceived and rejected by women of whatever color.

"Details?" I asked.

She shrugged. Gave his name. A name recently in the news, though in very small print.

He was not a Movement star or anyone you would know. We had met once, briefly. I had not liked him because he was coarse and spoke of black women as "our" women. (In the early Movement, it was pleasant to think of black men wanting to own us as a group; later it became clear that owning us meant exactly *that* to them.) He was physically unattractive, I had thought, with something of the hoodlum about him: a swaggering, unnecessarily mobile walk, small eyes, rough skin, a mouthful of wandering or absent teeth. He was, ironically, among the first persons to shout the slogan everyone later attributed solely to Stokeley Carmichael—Black Power! Stokeley was chosen as the originator of this idea by the media, because he was physically beautiful and photogenic and articulate. Even the name—Freddie Pye—was diminutive, I thought, in an age of giants.

"What did you do?"

"Nothing that required making a noise."

"Why didn't you scream?" I felt I would have screamed my head off.

"You know why."

I did. I had seen a photograph of Emmett Till's body just after it was pulled from the river. I had seen photographs of white folks standing in a circle roasting something that had talked to them in their own language before they tore out its tongue. I knew why, all right.

"What was he trying to prove?"

"I don't know. Do you?"

"Maybe you filled him with unendurable lust," I said.

"I don't think so," she said.

Suddenly I was embarrassed. Then angry. Very, very angry. *How dare she tell me this!* I thought.

Who knows what the black woman thinks of rape? Who has asked her? Who *cares*? Who has even properly acknowledged that *she* and not the white woman in this story is the most likely victim of rape? Whenever interracial rape is mentioned, a black woman's first thought is to protect the lives of her brothers, her father, her sons, her lover. A history of lynching has bred this reflex in her. I feel it as strongly as anyone. While writing a fictional account of such a rape in a novel, I read Ida B. Wells's autobiography three times, as a means of praying to her spirit to forgive me.

My prayer, as I turned the pages, went like this: *"Please forgive me. I am a writer."* (This self-revealing statement alone often seems to me sufficient reason to require perpetual forgiveness; since the writer is guilty not only of always wanting to know—like Eve—but also of trying—again like Eve—to find out.) *"I cannot write contrary to what life reveals to me. I wish to malign no one. But I must struggle to understand at least my own tangled emotions about interracial rape. I know, Ida B. Wells, you spent your whole life protecting, and trying to protect, black men accused of raping white women, who were lynched by white mobs, or threatened with it. You know, better than I ever will, what it means for a whole people to live under the terror of lynching. Under the slander that their men, where white women are concerned, are creatures of uncontrollable sexual lust. You made it so clear that the black men accused of rape in the past were innocent victims of white criminals that I grew up believing black men literally did not rape white women. At all. Ever. Now it would appear that some of them, the very twisted, the terribly ill, do. What would you have me write about them?"*

Her answer was: *"Write nothing. Nothing at all. It will be used against black men and therefore against all of us. Eldridge Cleaver and LeRoi Jones don't know who they're dealing with. But you remember. You are dealing with people who brought their children to witness the murder of black human beings, falsely accused of rape. People who handed out, as trophies, black fingers and toes. Deny! Deny! Deny!"*

And yet, I have pursued it: *"Some black men themselves do not seem to know what the meaning of raping someone is. Some have admitted rape in order to denounce it, but others have accepted rape as a part of rebellion, of 'paying whitey back.' They have gloried in it."*

"They know nothing of America," she says. *"And neither, apparently, do you. No matter what you think you know, no matter what you feel about it, say nothing. And to your dying breath!"*

Which, to my mind, is virtually useless advice to give to a writer.

Freddie Pye was the kind of man I would not have looked at then, not even once. (Throughout that year I was more or less into exotica: white ethnics who knew languages were a peculiar weakness; a half-white hippie singer; also a large Chinese mathematician who was a marvelous dancer and who taught me to waltz.) There was no question of belief.

But, in retrospect, there was a momentary *suspension* of belief, a kind of *hope* that perhaps it had not really happened; that Luna had made up the rape, "as white women have been wont to do." I soon realized this was unlikely. I was the only person she had told.

She looked at me as if to say: "I'm glad *that* part of my life is over." We continued our usual routine. We saw every interminable, foreign, depressing, and poorly illuminated film ever made. We learned to eat brown rice and yogurt and to tolerate kasha and odd-tasting teas. My half-black hippie singer friend (now a well-known reggae singer who says he is from "de I-lands" and not Sheepshead Bay) was "into" tea and kasha and Chinese vegetables.

And yet the rape, the knowledge of the rape, out in the open, admitted, pondered over, was now between us. (And I began to think that perhaps— whether Luna had been raped or not—it had always been so; that her power over my life was exactly the power *her word on rape* had over the lives of black men, over *all* black men, whether they were guilty or not, and therefore over my whole people.)

Before she told me about the rape, I think we had assumed a lifelong friendship. The kind of friendship one dreams of having with a person one has known in adversity; under heat and mosquitoes and immaturity and the threat of death. We would each travel, we would write to each other from the three edges of the world.

We would continue to have an "international list" of lovers whose amorous talents or lack of talents we would continue (giggling into our dotage) to compare. Our friendship would survive everything, be truer than everything, endure even our respective marriages, children, husbands— assuming we *did*, out of desperation and boredom someday, marry, which did not seem a probability, exactly, but more in the area of an amusing idea.

But now there was a cooling off of our affection for each other. Luna was becoming mildly interested in drugs, because everyone we knew was. I was envious of the open-endedness of her life. The financial backing to it. When she left her job at the kindergarten because she was tired of working, her errant father immediately materialized. He took her to dine on scampi at an expensive restaurant, scolded her for living on East 9th Street, and looked at me as if to say: "Living in a slum of this magnitude must surely have been your idea." As a cullud, of course.

For me there was the welfare department every day, attempting to get the necessary food and shelter to people who would always live amid the dirty streets I knew I must soon leave. I was, after all, a Sarah Lawrence girl "with talent." It would be absurd to rot away in a building that had no front door.

I slept late one Sunday morning with a painter I had met at the Welfare Department. A man who looked for all the world like Gene Autry, the singing cowboy, but who painted wonderful surrealist pictures of birds and ghouls and fruit with *teeth*. The night before, three of us—me, the painter, and "an old Navy buddy" who looked like his twin and who had just arrived in town—had got high on wine and grass.

That morning the Navy buddy snored outside the bedrooms like a puppy waiting for its master. Luna got up early, made an immense racket getting breakfast, scowled at me as I emerged from my room, and left the apartment, slamming the door so hard she damaged the lock. (Luna had made it a rule to date black men almost exclusively. My insistence on dating, as she termed it, "anyone" was incomprehensible to her, since in a politically diseased society to "sleep with the enemy" was to become "infected" with the enemy's "political germs." There is more than a grain of truth in this, of course, but I was having too much fun to stare at it for long. Still, coming from Luna it was amusing, since she never took into account the risk her own black lovers ran by sleeping with "the white woman," and she had apparently been convinced that a summer of relatively innocuous political work in the South had cured her of any racial, economic, or sexual political disease.)

Luna never told me what irked her so that Sunday morning, yet I remember it as the end of our relationship. It was not, as I at first feared, that she thought my bringing the two men to the apartment was inconsiderate. The way we lived allowed us to *be* inconsiderate from time to time. Our friends were varied, vital, and often strange. Her friends especially were deeper than they should have been into drugs.

The distance between us continued to grow. She talked more of going to Goa. My guilt over my dissolute if pleasurable existence coupled with my mounting hatred of welfare work, propelled me in two directions: south and to West Africa. When the time came to choose, I discovered that *my* summer in the South had infected me with the need to return, to try to understand, and write about, the people I'd merely lived with before.

We never discussed the rape again. We never discussed, really, Freddie Pye or Luna's remaining feelings about what had happened. One night, the last month we lived together, I noticed a man's blue denim jacket thrown across the church pew. The next morning, out of Luna's bedroom walked Freddie Pye. He barely spoke to me—possibly because as a black woman I was expected to be hostile toward his presence in a white woman's bedroom. I was too surprised to exhibit hostility, however, which was only a part of what I felt, after all. He left.

Luna and I did not discuss this. It is odd, I think now, that we didn't. It was as if he was never there, as if he and Luna had not shared the bedroom that night. A month later, Luna went alone to Goa, in her solitary way. She lived on an island and slept, she wrote, on the beach. She mentioned she'd found a lover there who protected her from the local beachcombers and pests.

Several years later, she came to visit me in the South and brought a lovely piece of pottery which my daughter much later dropped and broke, but which I glued back together in such a way that the flaw improves the beauty and fragility of the design.

Afterwords, Afterwards
Second Thoughts

That is the "story." It has an "unresolved" ending. That is because Freddie Pye and Luna are still alive, as am I. However, one evening while talking to a friend, I heard myself say that I had, in fact, written *two* endings. One, which follows, I considered appropriate for such a story published in a country truly committed to justice, and the one above, which is the best I can afford to offer a society in which lynching is still reserved, at least subconsciously, as a means of racial control.

I said that if we in fact lived in a society committed to the establishment of justice for everyone ("justice" in this case encompassing equal housing, education, access to work, adequate dental care, et cetera), thereby placing Luna and Freddie Pye in their correct relationship to each other, *i.e.*, that of brother and sister, *compañeros*, then the two of them would be required to struggle together over what his rape of her had meant.

Since my friend is a black man whom I love and who loves me, we spent a considerable amount of time discussing what this particular rape meant to us. Morally wrong, we said, and not to be excused. Shameful; politically corrupt. Yet, as we thought of what might have happened to an indiscriminate number of innocent young black men in Freehold, Georgia, had Luna screamed, it became clear that more than a little of Ida B.

Wells's fear of probing the rape issue was running through us, too. The implications of this fear would not let me rest, so that months and years went by with most of the story written but with me incapable, or at least unwilling, to finish or to publish it.

In thinking about it over a period of years, there occurred a number of small changes, refinements, puzzles, in angle. Would these shed a wider light on the continuing subject? I do not know. In any case, I returned to my notes, hereto appended for the use of the reader.

Luna: Ida B. Wells—Discarded Notes

Additional characteristics of Luna: At a time when many in and out of the Movement considered "nigger" and "black" synonymous, and indulged in a sincere attempt to fake Southern "hip" speech, Luna resisted. She was the kind of WASP who could not easily imitate another's ethnic style, nor could she even exaggerate her own. She was what she was. A very straight, clear-eyed, coolly observant young woman with no talent for existing outside her own skin.

Imaginary Knowledge

Luna explained the visit from Freddie Pye in this way:

"He called that evening, said he was in town, and did I know the Movement was coming north? I replied that I did know that."

When could he see her? he wanted to know.

"Never," she replied.

He had burst into tears, or something that sounded like tears, over the phone. He was stranded at wherever the evening's fund-raising event had been held. Not in the place itself, but outside, in the street. The "stars" had left, everyone had left. He was alone. He knew no one else in the city. Had found her number in the phone book. And had no money, no place to stay.

Could he, he asked, crash? He was tired, hungry, broke—and even in the South had had no job, other than the Movement, for months. Et cetera.

When he arrived, she had placed our only steak knife in the waistband of her jeans.

He had asked for a drink of water. She gave him orange juice, some cheese, and a couple of slices of bread. She had told him he might sleep on the church pew and he had lain down with his head on his rolled-up denim jacket. She had retired to her room, locked the door, and tried to sleep. She was amazed to discover herself worrying that the church pew was both too narrow and too hard.

At first he muttered, groaned, and cursed in his sleep. Then he fell off the narrow church pew. He kept rolling off. At two in the morning she unlocked her door, showed him her knife, and invited him to share her bed.

Nothing whatever happened except they talked. At first, only he talked. Not about the rape, but about his life.

"He was a small person physically, remember?" Luna asked me. (She was right.

Over the years he had grown big and, yes, burly, in my imagination, and I'm sure in hers.) "That night he seemed tiny. A child. He was still fully dressed, except for the jacket and he, literally, hugged his side of the bed. I hugged mine. The whole bed, in fact, was between us. We were merely hanging to its edges."

At the fund-raiser—on Fifth Avenue and 71st Street, as it turned out—his leaders had introduced him as the unskilled, barely literate, former Southern field-worker that he was. They had pushed him at the rich people gathered there as an example of what "the system" did to "the little people" in the South. They asked him to tell about the thirty-seven times he had been jailed. The thirty-five times he had been beaten. The one time he had lost consciousness in the "hot" box. They told him not to worry about his grammar. "Which, as you may recall," said Luna, "was horrible." Even so, he had tried to censor his "ain'ts" and his "us'es." He had been painfully aware that he was on exhibit, like Frederick Douglass had been for the Abolitionists. But unlike Douglass he had no oratorical gift, no passionate language, no silver tongue. He knew the rich people and his own leaders perceived he was nothing: a broken man, unschooled, unskilled at anything . . . .

Yet he had spoken, trembling before so large a crowd of rich, white Northerners—who clearly thought their section of the country would never have the South's racial problems—begging, with the painful stories of his wretched life, for their money.

At the end, all of them—the black leaders, too—had gone. They left him watching the taillights of their cars, recalling the faces of the friends come to pick them up: the women dressed in African print that shone, with elaborately arranged hair, their jewelry sparkling, their perfume exotic. They were so beautiful, yet so strange. He could not imagine that one of them could comprehend his life. He did not ask for a ride, because of that, but also because he had no place to go. Then he had remembered Luna.

Soon Luna would be required to talk. She would mention her confusion over whether, in a black community surrounded by whites with a history of lynching blacks, she had a right to scream as Freddie Pye was raping her. For her, this was the crux of the matter.

And so they would continue talking through the night.

This is another ending, created from whole cloth. If I believed Luna's story about the rape, and I did (had she told anyone else I might have dismissed it), then this reconstruction of what might have happened is as probable an accounting as any is liable to be. Two people have now become "characters."

I have forced them to talk until they reached the stumbling block of the rape, *which they must remove themselves*, before proceeding to a place from which it will be possible to insist on a society in which Luna's word alone on rape can never be used to intimidate an entire people, and in which an innocent black man's protestation of innocence of rape is unprejudicially heard.

Until such a society is created, relationships of affection between black men and white women will always be poisoned—from within as from without— by historical fear and the threat of violence, and solidarity among black and white women is only rarely likely to exist.

Postscript: Havana, Cuba, November 1976

I am in Havana with a group of other black American artists. We have spent the morning apart from our Cuban hosts bringing each other up to date on the kind of work (there are no apolitical artists among us) we are doing in the United States. I have read "Luna."

High above the beautiful city of Havana I sit in the Havana Libre pavilion with the muralist / photographer in our group. He is in his mid-thirties, a handsome, brown, erect individual whom I have known casually for a number of years. During the sixties he designed and painted street murals for both SNCC and the Black Panthers, and in an earlier discussion with Cuban artists he showed impatience with their explanation of why we had seen no murals covering some of the city's rather dingy walls: Cuba, they had said, unlike Mexico, has no mural tradition. "But the point of a revolution," insisted Our Muralist, "is to make new traditions!" And he had pressed his argument with such passion for the *usefulness*, for revolutionary communication, of his craft, that the Cubans were both exasperated and impressed. They drove us around the city for a tour of their huge billboards, all advancing socialist thought and the heroism of men like Lenin, Camilo, and Che Guevara, and said, "These, *these* are our 'murals'!"

While we ate lunch, I asked Our Muralist what he'd thought of "Luna." Especially the appended section.

"Not much," was his reply. "Your view of human weakness is too biblical," he said. "You are unable to conceive of the man without conscience. The man who cares nothing about the state of his soul because he's long since sold it. In short," he said, "you do not understand that some people are simply evil, a disease on the lives of other people, and that to remove the disease altogether is preferable to trying to interpret, contain, or forgive it. Your 'Freddie Pye,'" and he laughed, "was probably raping white women on the instructions of his government."

Oh ho, I thought. Because, of course, for a second, during which I stalled my verbal reply, this comment made both very little and very much sense.

"I *am* sometimes naive and sentimental," I offered. I am sometimes both, though frequently by design. Admission in this way is tactical, a stimulant to conversation.

"And shocked at what I've said," he said, and laughed again. "Even though," he continued, "you know by now that blacks could be hired to blow up other blacks, and could be hired *by someone* to shoot down Brother Malcolm, and hired *by someone* to provide a diagram of Fred Hampton's bedroom so the pigs could shoot him easily while he slept, you find it hard to believe a black man could be hired *by someone* to rape white women. But think a minute, and you will see why it is the perfect disruptive act. Enough blacks raping or accused of raping enough white women and any political movement that cuts across racial lines is doomed.

"Larger forces are at work than your story would indicate," he continued. "You're still thinking of lust and rage, moving slowly into aggression and purely racial hatred. But you should be considering money—which the rapist would get, probably from your very own tax dollars, in fact—and a maintaining of the status quo; which those hiring the rapist would achieve. I know all this," he said, "because when I was broke and hungry and selling my blood to buy the food and the paint that allowed me to work, I was offered such 'other work.'"

"But you did not take it."

He frowned. "There you go again. How do you know I didn't take it? It paid, and I was starving."

"You didn't take it," I repeated.

"No," he said. "A black and white 'team' made the offer. I had enough energy left to threaten to throw them out of the room."

"But even if Freddie Pye *had been* hired *by someone* to rape Luna, that still would not explain his second visit."

"Probably nothing will explain that," said Our Muralist. "But assuming Freddie Pye was paid to disrupt—by raping a white woman—the black struggle in the South, he may have wised up enough later to comprehend the significance of Luna's decision not to scream."

"So you are saying he *did have* a conscience?" I asked.

"Maybe," he said, but his look clearly implied I would never understand anything about evil, power, or corrupted human beings in the modern world.

But of course he is wrong.

1977

Food That Pleases, Food to Take Home

Anthony Grooms

Annie McPhee wasn't sure about what Mary Taliferro was telling her. Mary said that colored people in Louisa should stand up for their rights. They were doing it in the cities. Mary said that Channel Six from Richmond had shown pictures of Negroes sitting in at lunch counters. She laughed that "colored people" were becoming "Negroes." Walter Cronkite had shown pictures from Albany and Birmingham. Negroes were on the move.

On the church lawn one bright Sunday, Mary caught hold of Annie's arm and whispered, "What choo think of Reverend Green's sermon?" She knew Annie had eyes for Reverend Green.

"It was nice," Annie said. She pushed the pillbox back onto her head and patted her flip curl.

"But don't you think he was right about doing something?"

"'Course he right," Annie said with a smack of her lips, "but ain't nobody gone do nothing." Then she saw a glint in Mary's eye. "What you gone do and where?"

"We could march."

"Who gone march?" Mary held her hat against the wind that rustled through the fallen oak leaves.

"We could organize a march downtown. We could march down Main Street and tell them white folks that we want our rights."

"And that'll be the end of it, girl. Who gone march with you? Everybody around here is scared to march."

Mary pulled on Annie's elbow and guided her away from the folks gathering in front of the clapboard church to the pebbly space next to the cemetery. "I know what you thinking, girl. But I'm too tired of it to be scared. I wish something would happen around here and I figure we just the ones to start it."

"*You* the one." Annie put on her dark glasses. "Tell me who I look like?"

"Hummph." Mary turned up her lips for a second. "I don't know, girl. Elizabeth Taylor?"

"Nurrrh, child. You know I don't look like no 'Lizabeth Taylor. Somebody else. Somebody even more famous than that."

"Richard Burton."

"I'm gone kill you. Do I look like a man?" Annie gave Mary one more chance: she stepped back, her heel sinking into the soft hill of a grave, and put her hands on her hips. The wind folded her dress against her thighs. "Look at the hair and the glasses."

Mary frowned as she examined Annie and finally she gave up.

"Jackie Kennedy! Don't I look just like Jackie Kennedy?"

"Yeah, with the sunglasses, I guess you do," Mary said. "Anybody would, even me, if I had them sunglasses on."

"It'll take more than a pair of sunglasses . . ."

"But for real," Mary continued and started toward the parking lot, "we could start something. We could make the news if we did something in Louisa. I can just see myself sittin' up there on Walter Cronkite."

"Sittin' in the Louisa jail be more like it. Them white folks don't want no trouble."

"It don't matter what *they* want. Just like Reverend Green said, it matter what's right."

"Then how come *he* ain't doing it?"

"I bet he will if somebody started it. You know he's a preacher and he just can't run out and start no stuff." Mary placed her palms on the hood of the used Fairlane she had bought in Richmond with a down payment she had saved from factory work. She leaned up on her toes as Reverend Green was known to do and deepened her voice. "The Lord helps them that helps themselves. Amen. Say, the Lord provides!"

Annie swatted at her and giggled. "Somebody gone hear you."

"The Lord will part the Red Sea of injustice and send down the manna of equal rights."

"Bill Green don't sound like that." Annie folded her arms.

"Since when you call him 'Bill'?"

"Since when I want to."

Mary's round cheeks dimpled and her teeth contrasted with her purplish black face. "Just think how *Bill* Green would like it if we did something."

"How do you know what *Reverend* Green would like?" Annie whispered pointedly.

"I just bet he would."

They dressed to kill. They put on Sunday suits, high heels, and pillboxes. Mary wore her good wig. They put on lipstick and rouge and false eyelashes and drove to town in Mary's Fairlane. They had decided to sit in at May's Drugstore. They parked at the far end of the one-stoplight street, deserted in the cool midmorning. People were at work in the factory, or in the fields, or at the schools. The few people they passed stared at them, but no one knew them.

"Don't you just hate it?" Mary said, seeming to bolster her anger as they walked down toward the store. "If you go in there, the minute you step in the door, ole lady May will break her neck running over to you—'Can I he'p you'—you know, in that syrupy sweet way. She won't let you look around for a second."

" 'Fraid you gone steal something." Annie looked straight ahead down the street of wooden and brick shops. The perspective was broken by the courthouse square and the little brick jailhouse beside it. Annie forced herself to match Mary's determined stride lest her legs tremble so badly she fell.

"Or just *touch* something. And a white person—they can put their hands on anything they want. Pick up stuff and put it back. Like they own everything."

"Lord, you know we better not touch nothing unless we ready to pay for it. Better have the money in your hand." Annie's voice trailed and stopped abruptly when she caught a glimpse of the sheriff's car parked behind the courthouse. What would Bill Green think if she got arrested? she wondered. She thought about the stories she had heard from her uncles, her mother's younger brothers, about spending time in the jailhouse for speeding or drinking. They told about the sheetless cots, the stench of the pee pot, but said that the sheriff's wife's biscuits were good. Annie did not want to try the sheriff's wife's biscuits. She did not want to be dragged out of May's by the sheriff, to be touched by his big hands with the hairy knuckles she had once seen up close when he had come to give a talk at her high school. The thought of being close to him, his chewed cigar and the big leather lump of holster and gun sent shivers through her. But Bill Green had said they should stand up. Bill Green had said that God would send the manna of justice if they would only stand up.

Mary grimaced and balled up her fists as if to force her anger to a boiling point. "White people make me sick. Every last one of them. Sick. What I'd really like to do is to take ole lady May by her scrawny little neck and choke her."

Annie tried to laugh, but her voice was too jittery. "We're suppose to be *peace* demonstrators."

"I'd like to kick a piece of her butt."

"I don't like her either," Annie said, thinking what Reverend Green might say, "but let's do this the right way. Let's just go in and ask to be served and . . ." Annie stopped under May's green awning.

"And when she don't?" Mary whispered. "What then?"

Except for the awning, May's was a flat-faced, white clapboard building with a flat roof and a stepped crest. Only one of its double doors opened to admit customers. A bell jingled when they entered. Annie stood with Mary by the door, her eyes adjusting to the dimness, and breathed in a mixture of smells dominated by dust and wood polish. To her right was the cashier's stand with a display of pocket combs, and crowded on long narrow shelves in the middle of the store were goods: bolts of cloth, children's dolls, sewing kits, toiletries, firecrackers, shotgun shells, fashion magazines, and among everything, *The Central*, the town's weekly newspaper. In the back, the RX sign hung from the ceiling above the druggist's counter, hidden behind the clutter of inventory. Along the left wall was a linoleum-topped lunch counter with five backless stools anchored in front of it. It was junked with jars of pickles, loaves of sandwich bread, buns and cake plates bearing doughnuts and pies. The spigots of a broken soda fountain were partially hidden in the clutter. Behind the counter was a grand mirror with ornate framing. It was placarded with menus and handwritten signs announcing "specials." The mirror was grease-spattered on one side from a small electric grill that sat on a shelf. On the other side, two huge coolers stood bubbling lemonade and orangeade. A broken neon sign above the mirror announced, "FOOD THAT PLEASES, FOOD TO TAKE HOME." High above were shelves on which rested plastic wreaths of cemetery flowers.

"She must be in the back," Mary whispered, "else she would've said something by now." Mary stepped quietly to the lunch counter and shot Annie an impatient frown. The scents of bath soaps and powders had attracted Annie as she passed the display, but she dared not touch them. "Maybe we should just buy something."

"What for? You scared?"

Annie straightened. "Do I look scared?"

"Like you gone pass a watermelon. Just do like I do. She gone be scareder than us."

The storage room door behind the lunch counter was open. A low voice came from the room, and suddenly they heard a long moan, as if someone, or some animal, were grieving.

"Jesus," whispered Annie. She pulled on Mary's elbow.

Mary pushed closer to the counter, took a deep breath, and pulled herself up onto the first stool. She sat for a moment, her eyes as excited as a child's on a fairground ride. "You ever sit on one of these?" She caught herself for being too loud. She put on a serious face, her lips folded under so as not to look too big, placed her feet on the shiny circular footrest, and adjusted her skirt.

Annie looked over her shoulder, expecting to see Mrs. May's sticklike figure marching hurriedly toward them, but all was still except for the putt-putting of the ceiling fans.

Mary beckoned to Annie to sit on the stool beside her, and gingerly as a child testing hot bathwater, Annie sat. She pulled herself up on the stool, forgetting to smooth her skirt as Mary had done. She sat ready to jump down at any moment; when the moan came again, she jumped.

"Be there in a minute," drawled a woman from the storage room. It was not Mrs. May's voice, which was thin and whiny. A heavy woman, dressed in a blue calico shift with a lace collar safety-pinned at the neck, stepped from the storage room. Her gray curls were pulled back. Her face looked soft, and her eyes were large and round. When she saw the girls, the woman looked confused for a moment, then she looked frightened and wrung her hands. "May I help ya?" she asked.

Annie looked at Mary, and Mary at Annie. They had never seen this woman before. After a moment, Mary drew a breath and said, "We would like to order." The woman pointed to the menu and stood back as if ready to retreat into the storage room. The moan came again from the room.

"We don't want no takeout," Mary said, growing bolder. "We want to eat at the counter like white folks. We want you to write it down on your little pad and bring us silverware wrapped in a napkin."

"But . . ." the woman said, and then she blanched. "But . . ."

The moan came again, loudly. She returned to the storage room.

When the woman came back she was shaking. "I . . . I can't serve colored."

"Why can't choo?" Mary said. She tried to sound sophisticated. "You have the food. You have the stove. All we want is a hamburger and some fries." She pointed to the orangeade. "And some of that orange drink."

The woman came slowly to Annie. Nervously, she put her hand out to the edge of the counter like she wanted to touch Annie. "I don't want trouble, miss," she said. "I'm just helping out my sister-in-law, Ella May. She's very sick, you know. She's got a gall bladder. I'm not even from here. I'm from West Virginia. I don't want any trouble."

"Yes, ma'am," Annie said, then cleared her throat, took a deep breath, and fought to control her jittery voice. "We just want our rights."

"Listen," the woman said, "I will give you some food if you'll just take it on home." Then she added in a whisper, "Mr. May will be back from the hospital soon and . . . please. . ."

"No," Mary said firmly, crisping her endings the way their English teacher Miss Bullock had told them was proper. "We done come all the way from Washington, D.C. We are part of President Johnson's civil rights committee. And we gone report you to the Doctor Martin Luther King."

The woman stepped back from the counter. She bumped against the ice cream box. She seemed not to believe Mary but was too afraid to say otherwise. "Mr. May will return soon," she said, too uncertain to be threatening. She strained to see out the front door. Annie knew she was looking to see if somebody white was out there, and spun in a sudden fright. Two black boys were brushing hayseed from their hair in front of the window.

"If it were up to me . . ." the woman said. "If it were up to me, I would be glad to serve you. I don't mind colored. Honest. I'm from West Virginia."

"It *is* up to you," Mary said, a crooked, dimpled smile on her face. "Who else is here? How come you don't want us Negroes to have our rights?"

"Please," the woman said, clasping her hands together, "I don't want to have to call the police. Don't make me call nobody." She strained again to see the street.

The moan came again. No one moved. They let the moan and the putt-putt of the fans bathe them. Annie felt the moan in the pit of her stomach. She held onto the seat of the stool. Maybe Mrs. May was dead, she thought, and someone was crying. They shouldn't be causing this trouble if Mrs. May was dead. "Well, maybe we should come back when Mrs. May is here," Annie said vacantly, all the time moving a little ways down the counter, focused on the crack in the doorway to the storage room. She could only see a bare lightbulb and switch cord and cans on the shelves.

"I'm not taking a step until I get served," Mary said. "I don't care if Miss May—if the owner—ain't here. You in charge and I want my rights."

The woman put her hand out to Annie. "What if I made you a nice sandwich and you can take it with you? I'll let you have it free of charge."

"Ain't that some mess?" Mary said, putting her hands on her hips. "You even give us food, but you don't want us to sit and eat it like people. You rather see us go out back and eat it like a dog. I know how you white people is. I done seen it. You have your damn dog eat at the table with you, but you won't let a colored person. Do I look like a dog to you?"

"I don't own a dog," the woman said. She no longer wrung her hands but gripped one inside the other. "I don't own this place. I'm just helping my sister-in-law like I told you. And besides, it is the law. Like I told you, I got nothing against you. Not in the least. But what would Mrs. May or Mr. May say if they walked in here and I was letting you eat? They wouldn't like it."

"I don't care what they like. The customer is always right."

The moan came again, this time discernible as a word: "Maaahhma."

"What's that?" Mary asked, her eyes wide.

"It's nothing to you," the woman said.

Annie saw a movement, a shadow, behind the door. It was a slow, awkward swaying. The door squeaked and moved slightly. Annie looked first at Mary and then at the woman.

"I'll tell you what *is* my business," Mary said. "This here piece of pie is. And I got a good mind to help myself to it right now." She reached out for the lid of the pie plate.

"Don't let me have to call somebody."

"Call who you like. I ain't scared. I'll go to jail if I have to."

"Don't be ugly," the woman said and waved her hand. She might have been snatching a fly out of orbit. "Just take it and go."

The moan came again, deep and pathetic. It reminded Annie of the mourning doves that she could hear from her bedroom window just after sunrise, only it was not so melodic as doves.

"Go!" the woman shouted. "You're upsetting him."

The shadow swayed again, and the door, squeaking, was pulled open farther. Annie moved closer to the door, directly in front of it, separated from it only by the counter gate. She knew there was someone there, some "him" the woman had said, but something monstrously sorrowful and she couldn't imagine what it was.

Mary hopped down from the stool. "I told you I wanted it here." She jabbed her finger on the countertop. "Why don't you admit it? You just like every white person I ever seen. Just as prejudice' as the day is long."

"I'm not!" the woman said. "You don't understand the position I'm in . . ."

"Maaaaahhhmmaaa."

"I'm coming." The woman made a step toward the door, then she turned back to Mary. "I'm not prejudice'." Her face was contorted. The moan came again, with a resonating bass. "Baby," the woman said to the figure behind the door, and then to Mary, "eat here, then. Eat all you want. I don't care."

Mary stood stiffly, smiled. There was a small silence. "Serve me," she demanded.

"Serve your goddamn self," the older woman said, her voice rising to a screech.

Annie heard the argument, and glanced now and again at Mary and the woman, but now the door was slowly swinging open, and she could see the thick fingers of a man holding onto the edge of it. He was a big man. Big and fat like the sheriff. Annie looked at the woman. She felt her lips part. The moan, almost a groan, vibrated in her chest. The man was like an animal, a hurt animal, calling for his mother, Annie thought. Now she was afraid in a different way. She remembered what her father had told her about hurt animals, how they turned on people who tried to help them, how their mothers attacked ferociously to save them.

"Serve yourself." The woman had turned toward Mary. Her entire body trembled, her hands, now unclasped, fanned the air. She pushed a loaf of sandwich bread across the counter toward Mary. She slapped a package of hamburger buns, causing it to sail and hit Mary on the shoulder. She threw Dixie cups, plastic forks and paper napkins. Mary ducked below the countertop. "Serve yourself," the woman screamed. "Eat all the goddamn food you want."

"Maaahhma."

Stepping cautiously as if walking up to a lame wild dog, Annie slipped through the counter gate. The door pulled all the way open and the man stood there. Annie's heart skipped a beat; she reached back for the counter so she wouldn't fall. First she saw his barrel chest, bulging out in odd places under a pinned-together plaid flannel shirt; then his thick neck, stiffly twisted so that one ear nearly lay against his hulking shoulder. His lips were thick and flat. One side of his face was higher than the other, like a clay face misshapen by a child's hand. His eyebrows were thick ridges that ran together at the top of his wide flat nose.

"Maaaaahhmmaaa."

"He's just a baby," the woman came to the door and took the man's hand. She pulled him into the open, behind the counter, and rubbed the back of his hand furiously. His presence seemed to calm her. She glanced toward Mary and then to Annie. "It's the new place." She smiled as if inviting a stranger to look at an infant, then shot a look at Mary. "He's not used to being over here." She patted the hand and the big man smiled deep dimples. She pinched his cheeks. "Just a baby."

"What's wrong with him?" Annie asked, recovering from the sight of him.

The mother sighed. "Just born thatta way, child. Just born like that." She looked back at Mary who was straightening her clothes and wig. "Maybe we'll all sit and have a piece of pie."

The man smiled at Annie, and Annie managed to smile back. She reached behind her for the counter gate.

"Don't worry," the woman said. "He is as gentle as a fly. He likes to be around people." She changed to baby talk. "Don't you, Willie?" Then she held out the man's hand to Annie. "Here. Pat the back of his hand. That's what he likes."

Annie looked at his face, drool in the corners of his mouth. He had gray eyes that swam lazily in their sockets. Now she looked at the offered hand. It was the whitest hand she had ever seen, with thick, hairy knuckles and nubbed nails.

"Go on and pat him," the woman said. "He's just a boy—your age. Go on, he likes it."

She had never touched a white boy. She reached out for the hand hesitantly. The woman encouraged. Annie wanted to look at Mary, to see what she thought, but she could not break her focus on the man's hand. She saw her hand, so obviously brown, move into her focus, and then move closer and closer to the pale hand until her fingertips touched it.

"Go ahead and give him a pat."

The man's hand was soft and damp, unlike any hand Annie had ever touched. She lifted her hand and patted the big hand twice, and then twice again. The man moaned, not any word but like a dog enjoying a bellyrub.

"See," the woman said. She looked at Mary. "See. We are just people like you are. We don't want to hurt nobody. Not a soul." She took back the man's hand and smiled at Annie. "Tell you what. I'll cut us all a piece of pie."

"Can we have it at the counter?" Mary glared at the woman, her lips poked out.

The woman sighed loudly. "Won't you understand?"

"Then eat it by yo'self."

The woman turned to Annie and touched her hand, "Won't *you* understand?"

Annie hesitated. The doorbell jingled and Mr. May carne in. He was wiping under his straw fedora with a handkerchief. "I'll be glad if that old witch did die," he was saying as he made his way to the back.

Mary spun around and pretended to be interested in the bath soaps. "You being he'ped?" he asked gruffly as he approached her.

"Yes, suh," Mary said.

The woman was trying to push the man back into the storage room. Mr. May stopped and put his hands on his hips. "Damn, Sally, what is he doing out in the store? He's liable to scare somebody to death . . .and what! . . .in the hell is that gal doing *behind* the counter?"

"It's all right." The woman turned and waved Annie through the counter gate. "She was just helping me with him."

"Look at this place? What the hell happened here? Goddamnit, can't you control that freak?

"It's all right," the woman said from inside the room where she was pushing the man. "Y'all run along now."

"That wasn't fair," Mary said as they walked back to the Fairlane. "How come that stupid gorilla had to be there? How come *she* had to be there in the first place? Ole lady May the one I wanted to be there. I could have said something if it hada been her." Annie said nothing.

They passed the monument to the Confederate dead, standing in the courthouse yard.

"I don't know," Annie said. She was beginning to tremble on the inside. The world seemed complex and uncertain. She remembered touching the man, her brown hand against his white one. He was like a baby, soft and damp, and yet something about him, not just his size and his twisted face, frightened her. But she had been charmed by him for a moment, charmed by his softness and his dimples. She remembered the look on the woman's face when she had patted the man's hand. She thought the woman had loved her for a moment.

"We never gone get our rights." Mary clenched her teeth. "Especially with you around pattin' that goddamn monster on the hand."

"What was wrong with that?" Annie said. She knew there was nothing wrong with it. He couldn't help the way he was born.

"If you don't know. . . !" Mary reached out quickly and pinched Annie on the arm just above the elbow. She squeezed her nails into the pinch and twisted it before she let go. "Some civil rights marcher you is. Bill Green will be 'shame' to know you."

Annie whimpered and put her hand over the pinched spot. "No!" she blurted, "I *want* my rights."

"Shit." Mary took Annie by the elbow and led her to the car. "I know you was tryin'. . . . I know . . . it's just that we won't ever get nothing, nothing—unless we, we . . . uggghhh!"—she grimaced—"*kill* them, or something."

They reached the car and got in, then Annie began to cry. Mary touched her hand to comfort her, but Annie pushed her away. Mary sped the car out of town on a road that cut through fields turning brown in the hot autumn sun. Annie put her head on the dash. Things were very complicated, far more complicated than she had ever thought.

1995

The Foundations of the Earth

Randall Kenan

I

Of course they didn't pay it any mind at first: just a tractor—one of the most natural things in the world to see in a field—kicking dust up into the afternoon sky and slowly toddling off the road into a soybean field. And fields surrounded Mrs. Maggie MacGowan Williams's house, giving the impression that her lawn stretched on and on until it dropped off into the woods far by the way. Sometimes she was certain she could actually see the earth's curve—not merely the bend of the small hill on which her house sat but the great slope of the sphere, the way scientists explained it in books, a monstrous globe floating in a cold nothingness. She would sometimes sit by herself on the patio late of an evening, in the same chair she was sitting in now, sip from her Coca-Cola, and think about how big the earth must be to seem flat to the eye.

She wished she were alone now. It was Sunday.

"Now I wonder what that man is doing with a tractor out there today?"

They sat on Maggie's patio, reclined in that after-Sunday-dinner way—Maggie; the Right Reverend Hezekiah Barden, round and pompous as ever; Henrietta Fuchee, the prim and priggish music teacher and president of the First Baptist Church Auxiliary Council; Emma Lewis, Maggie's sometimes housekeeper; and Gabriel, Mrs. Maggie Williams's young, white, special guest—all looking out lazily into the early summer, watching the sun begin its slow downward arc, feeling the baked ham and the candied sweet potatoes and the fried chicken with the collard greens and green beans and beets settle in their bellies, talking shallow and pleasant talk, and sipping their Coca-Colas and bitter lemonade.

"Don't they realize it's Sunday?" Reverend Barden leaned back in his chair and tugged at his suspenders thoughtfully, eyeing the tractor as it turned into another row. He reached for a sweating glass of lemonade, his red bow tie afire in the penultimate beams of the day.

"I . . . I don't understand. What's wrong?" Maggie could see her other guests watching Gabriel intently, trying to discern why on earth he was present at Maggie MacGowan Williams's table.

"What you mean, what's wrong?" The Reverend Barden leaned forward and narrowed his eyes at the young man. "What's wrong is: it's Sunday."

"So? I don't . . ." Gabriel himself now looked embarrassed, glancing to Maggie, who wanted to save him but could not.

" 'So?' 'So?' " Leaning toward Gabriel and narrowing his eyes, Barden asked: "You're not from a churchgoing family, are you?"

"Well, no. Today was my first time in . . . Oh, probably ten years."

"Uh-huh." Barden corrected his posture, as if to say he pitied Gabriel's being an infidel but had the patience to instruct him. "Now you see, the Lord has declared Sunday as His day. It's holy. 'Six days shall thou labor and do all thy work: but the seventh day is the Sabbath of the Lord thy God: in it thou shall not do any work, thou, nor thy son, nor thy daughter, thy manservant, nor thy maidservant, nor thy cattle, nor thy stranger that is within thy gates: for in six days the Lord made heaven and earth, the sea, and all that in them is, and rested the seventh day: wherefore, the Lord blessed the Sabbath day, and hallowed it.' Exodus. Chapter twenty, verses nine and ten."

"Amen." Henrietta closed her eyes and rocked.

"Hez." Maggie inclined her head a bit to entreat the good Reverend to desist. He gave her an understanding smile, which made her cringe slightly, fearing her gesture might have been mistaken for a sign of intimacy.

"But, Miss Henrietta—" Emilia Lewis tapped the tabletop, like a judge in court, changing the subject. "Like I was saying, I believe that Rick on *The Winds of Hope* is going to marry that gal before she gets too big with child, don't you?" Though Emma kept house for Maggie Williams, to Maggie she seemed more like a sister who came three days a week, more to visit than to clean.

"Now go on away from here, Emma." Henrietta did not look up from her empty cake plate, her glasses hanging on top of her sagging breasts from a silver chain. "Talking about that worldly foolishness on TV. You know I don't pay that mess any attention." She did not want the Reverend to know that she secretly watched afternoon soap operas, just like Emma and all the other women in the congregation. Usually she gossiped to beat the band about this rich heifer and that handsome hunk whenever she found a fellow TV-gazer. Buck-toothed hypocrite, Maggie thought. She knew the truth: Henrietta, herself a widow now on ten years, was sweet on the widower minister, who in turn, alas, had his eye on Maggie.

"Now, Miss Henrietta, we was talking about it t'other day. Don't you think he's apt to marry her soon?" Emma's tone was insistent.

"I *don't know*, Emma." Visibly agitated, Henrietta donned her glasses and looked into the fields. "I wonder who that is anyhow?"

Annoyed by Henrietta's rebuff, Emma stood and began to collect the few remaining dishes. Her purple-and-yellow floral print dress hugged her ample hips. "It's that ole Morton Henry that Miss Maggie leases that piece of land to." She walked toward the door, into the house. "He ain't no God-fearing man."

"Well, that's plain to see." The Reverend glanced over to Maggie. She shrugged.

They are ignoring Gabriel, Maggie thought. She had invited them to dinner after church services thinking it would be pleasant for Gabriel to meet other people in Tims Creek. But generally they chose not to see him, and when they did it was with ill-concealed scorn or petty curiosity or annoyance. At first the conversation seemed civil enough. But the ice was never truly broken, questions still buzzed around the talk like horseflies, Maggie could tell. "Where you from?" Henrietta had asked. "What's your line of work?" Barden had asked. While Gabriel sat there with a look on his face somewhere between peace and pain. But Maggie refused to believe she had made a mistake. At this stage of her life she depended on no one for anything, and she was certainly not dependent on the approval of these self-important fools.

She had been steeled by anxiety when she picked Gabriel up at the airport that Friday night. But as she caught sight of him stepping from the jet and greeted him, asking about the weather in Boston; and after she had ushered him to her car and watched him slide in, seeming quite at home; though it still felt awkward, she thought: I'm doing the right thing.

II

"Well, thank you for inviting me, Mrs. Williams. But I don't understand . . . Is something wrong?"

"*Wrong?* No, nothing's wrong, Gabriel. I just thought it'd be good to see you. Sit and talk to you. We didn't have much time at the funeral."

"Gee . . . I—"

"You don't want to make an old woman sad, now do you?"

"Well, Mrs. Williams, if you put it like that, how can I refuse?"

"Weekend after next then?"

There was a pause in which she heard muted voices in the wire.

"Okay."

After she hung up the phone and sat down in her favorite chair in the den, she heaved a momentous sigh. Well, she had done it. At last. The weight of uncertainty would be lifted. She could confront him face to face. She wanted to know about her grandboy, and Gabriel was the only one who could tell her what she wanted to know. It was that simple. Surely, he realized what this invitation meant. She leaned back looking out the big picture window onto the tops of the brilliantly blooming crepe myrtle trees in the yard, listening to the grandfather clock mark the time.

III

Her grandson's funeral had been six months ago, but it seemed much longer. Perhaps the fact that Edward had been gone away from home so long without seeing her, combined with the weeks and days and hours and minutes she had spent trying not to think about him and all the craziness that had surrounded his death, somehow lengthened the time.

At first she chose to ignore it, the strange and bitter sadness that seemed to have overtaken her every waking moment. She went about her daily life as she had done for thirty-odd years, overseeing her stores, her land, her money; buying groceries, paying bills, shopping, shopping; going to church and talking to her few good living friends and the few silly fools she was obliged to suffer. But all day, dusk to dawn, and especially at night, she had what the field-workers called "a monkey on your back," when the sun beats down so hot it makes you delirious; but her monkey chilled and angered her, born not of the sun but of a profound loneliness, an oppressive emptiness, a stabbing guilt. Sometimes she even wished she were a drinking woman.

The depression had come with the death of Edward, though its roots reached farther back, to the time he seemed to have vanished. There had been so many years of asking other members of the family: Have you heard from him? Have you seen him? So many years of only a Christmas card or birthday card a few days early, or a cryptic, taciturn phone call on Sunday mornings, and then no calls at all. At some point she realized she had no idea where he was or how to get in touch with him. Mysteriously, he would drop a line to his half-sister, Clarissa, or drop a card without a return address. He was gone. Inevitably, she had to ask: Had she done something evil to the boy to drive him away? Had she tried too hard to make sure he became nothing like his father and grandfather? I was as good a mother as a woman can claim to be, she thought: from the cradle on he had all the material things he needed, and he certainly didn't want for attention, for care; and I trained him proper, he was a well-mannered and upright young fellow when he left here for college. Oh, I was proud of that boy, winning a scholarship to Boston University. Tall, handsome like his granddad. He'd make somebody a good . . .

So she continued picking out culprits: school, the cold North, strange people, strange ideas. But now in her crystalline hindsight she could lay no blame on anyone but Edward. And the more she remembered battles with the mumps and the measles and long division and taunts from his schoolmates, the more she became aware of her true anger. He owes me respect, damn it. The least he can do is keep in touch. Is that so much to ask?

But before she could make up her mind to find him and confront him with her fury, before she could cuss him out good and call him an ungrateful, no-account bastard just like his father, a truck would have the heartless audacity to skid into her grandchild's car one rainy night in Springfield and end his life at twenty-seven, taking that opportunity away from her forever. When they told her of his death she cursed her weakness. Begging God for another chance. But instead He gave her something she had never imagined.

Clarissa was the one to finally tell her. "Grandma," she had said, "Edward's been living with another man all these years."

"So?"

"No, Grandma. Like man and wife."

Maggie had never before been so paralyzed by news. One question answered, only to be replaced by a multitude. Gabriel had come with the body, like an interpreter for the dead. They had been living together in Boston, where Edward worked in a bookstore. He came, head bowed, rheumy-eyed, exhausted. He gave her no explanation; nor had she asked him for any, for he displayed the truth in his vacant and humble glare and had nothing to offer but the penurious tribute of his trembling hands. Which was more than she wanted.

In her world she had been expected to be tearless, patient, comforting to other members of the family; folk were meant to sit back and say, "Lord, ain't she taking it well. I don't think I could be so calm if my grandboy had've died so young." Magisterially she had done her duty; she had taken it all in stride. But her world began to hopelessly unravel that summer night at the wake in the Raymond Brown Funeral Home, among the many somber-bright flower arrangements, the fluorescent lights, and the gleaming bronze casket, when Gabriel tried to tell her how sorry he was . . . How dare he? This pathetic, stumbling, poor trashy white boy, to throw his sinful lust for her grandbaby in her face, as if to bury a grandchild weren't bad enough. Now this abomination had to be flaunted. —Sorry, indeed! The nerve! Who the hell did he think he was to parade their shame about?

Her anger was burning so intensely that she knew if she didn't get out she would tear his heart from his chest, his eyes from their sockets, his testicles from their sac. With great haste she took her leave, brushing off the funeral director and her brother's wives and husband's brothers—they all probably thinking her overcome with grief rather than anger—and had Clarissa drive her home. When she got to the house she filled a tub with water as hot as she could stand it and a handful of bath oil beads, and slipped in, praying her hatred would mingle with the mist and evaporate, leaving her at least sane.

Next, sleep. Healing sleep, soothing sleep, sleep to make the world go away, sleep like death. Her mama had told her that sleep was the best medicine God made. When things get too rough—go to bed. Her family had been known as the family that retreated to bed. Ruined crop? No money? Get some shut-eye. Maybe it'll be better in the morning. Can't be worse. Maggie didn't give a damn where Gabriel was to sleep that night; someone else would deal with it. She didn't care about all the people who would come to the house after the wake to the Sitting Up, talking, eating, drinking, watching over the still body till sunrise; they could take care of themselves. The people came; but Maggie slept. From deeps under deeps of slumber she sensed her granddaughter stick her head in the door and whisper, asking Maggie if she wanted something to eat. Maggie didn't stir. She slept. And in her sleep she dreamed.

She dreamed she was Job sitting on his dung heap, dressed in sackcloth and ashes, her body covered with boils, scratching with a stick, sending away Eliphaz and Bildad and Zophar and Elihu, who came to counsel her, and above her the sky boiled and churned and the air roared, and she matched it, railing against God, against her life—*Why? Why? Why did you kill him, you heartless old fiend? Why make me live to see him die? What earthly purpose could you have in such a wicked deed? You are God, but you are not good. Speak to me, damn it. Why? Why? Why?* Hurricanes whipped and thunder ripped through a sky streaked by lightning, and she was lifted up, spinning, spinning, and Edward floated before her in the rushing air and quickly turned around into the comforting arms of Gabriel, winged, who clutched her grandboy to his bosom and soared away, out of the storm. Maggie screamed and the winds grew stronger, and a voice, gentle and sweet, not thunderous as she expected, spoke to her from the whirlwind: *Who is this that darkeneth counsel by words without knowledge? Gird up now thy loins like a man; for I will demand of thee, and answer thou me. Where wast thou when I laid the foundations of the earth? Declare if thou hast understanding . . .* The voice spoke of the myriad creations of the universe, the stupendous glory of the Earth and its inhabitants. But Maggie was not deterred in the face of the maelstrom, saying: *Answer me, damn you: Why?,* and the winds began to taper off and finally halted, and Maggie was alone, standing on water. A fish, what appeared to be a mackerel, stuck its head through the surface and said: *Kind woman, be not aggrieved and put your anger away. Your arrogance has clouded your good mind. Who asked you to love? Who asked you to hate?* The fish dipped down with a plip and gradually Maggie too began to slip down into the water, down, down, down, sinking, below depths of reason and love, down into the dark unknown of her own mind, down, down, down.

Maggie MacGowan Williams woke the next morning to the harsh chatter of a bluejay chasing a mockingbird just outside her window, a racket that caused her to open her eyes quickly to blinding sunlight. Squinting, she looked about the room, seeing the chest of drawers that had once belonged to her mother and her mother's mother before that, the chairs, the photographs on the wall, the television, the rug thickly soft, the closet door slightly ajar, the bureau, the mirror atop the bureau, and herself in the mirror, all of it bright in the crisp morning light. She saw herself looking, if not refreshed, calmed, and within her the rage had gone, replaced by a numb humility and a plethora of questions. Questions. Questions. Questions.

Inwardly she had felt beatific that day of the funeral, ashamed at her anger of the day before. She greeted folk gently, softly, with a smile, her tones honey-flavored but solemn, and she reassumed the mantle of one-who-comforts-more-than-needing-comfort.

The immediate family had gathered at Maggie's house—Edward's father,

Tom, Jr.; Tom, Jr.'s wife, Lucille; the grandbaby, Paul (Edward's brother); Clarissa. Raymond Brown's long black limousine took them from the front door of Maggie's house to the church, where the yard was crammed with people in their greys and navy blues, dark browns, and deep, deep burgundies. In her new humility she mused: When, oh when will we learn that death is not so somber, not something to mourn so much as celebrate? We should wear fire reds, sun oranges, hello greens, ocean-deep blues, and dazzling, welcome-home whites. She herself wore a bright dress of saffron and a blue scarf. She thought Edward would have liked it.

The family lined up and Gabriel approached her. As he stood before her—raven-haired, pink-skinned, abject, eyes bloodshot—she experienced a bevy of conflicting emotions: disgust, grief, anger, tenderness, fear, weariness, pity. Nevertheless she *had* to be civil, *had* to make a leap of faith and of understanding. Somehow she felt it had been asked of her. And though there were still so many questions, so much to sort out, for now she would mime patience, pretend to be accepting, feign peace. Time would unravel the rest.

She reached out, taking both his hands into her own, and said, the way she would to an old friend: "How have you been?"

IV

"But now, Miss Maggie . . ."

She sometimes imagined the good Reverend Barden as a toad-frog or an impotent bull. His rantings and ravings bored her, and his clumsy advances repelled her; and when he tried to impress her with his holiness and his goodness, well . . .

". . . that man should know better than to be plowing on a Sunday. Sunday! Why, the Lord said . . ."

"Reverend, I know what the Lord said. And I'm sure Morton Henry knows what the Lord said. But I am not the Lord, Reverend, and if Morton Henry wants to plow the west field on Sunday afternoon, well, it's his soul, not mine."

"But, Maggie. Miss Maggie. It's—"

"Well,"—Henrietta Fuchee sat perched to interject her five cents into the debate—"but, Maggie. It's your land! Now, Reverend, doesn't it say somewhere in Exodus that a man, or a woman in this case, a woman is responsible for the deeds or misdeeds of someone in his or her employ, especially on her property?"

"But he's not an emplo—"

"Well,"—Barden scratched his head—"I think I know what you're talking about, Henrietta. It may be in Deuteronomy . . . or Leviticus . . . part of the Mosaic Law, which . . ."

Maggie cast a quick glance at Gabriel. He seemed to be interested in and entertained by this contest of moral superiority. There was certainly something about his face . . . but she could not stare. He looked so *normal* . . .

"Well, I don't think you should stand for it, Maggie."

"Henrietta? What do you . . . ? Look, if you want him to stop, *you* go tell him what the Lord said. I—"

The Right Reverend Hezekiah Barden stood, hiking his pants up to his belly. "Well, *I* will. A man's soul is a valuable thing. And I can't risk your own soul being tainted by the actions of one of your sharecroppers."

"My soul? Sharecropper—he's not a sharecropper. He leases that land. I—wait! . . . Hezekiah! . . . This doesn't . . ."

But Barden had stepped off the patio onto the lawn and was headed toward the field, marching forth like old Nathan on his way to confront King David.

"Wait, Reverend." Henrietta hopped up, slinging her black pocketbook over her left shoulder. "Well, Maggie?" She peered at Maggie defiantly, as if to ask: *Where do you stand?*

"Now, Henrietta, I—"

Henrietta pivoted, her moral righteousness jagged and sharp as a shard of glass. "Somebody has to stand up for right!" She tromped off after Barden.

Giggling, Emma picked up the empty glasses. "I don't think ole Morton Henry gone be too happy to be preached at this afternoon."

Maggie looked from Emma to Gabriel in bewilderment, at once annoyed and amused. All three began to laugh out loud. As Emma got to the door she turned to Maggie. "Hon, you better go see that they don't get into no fistfight, don't you think? You know that Reverend don't know when to be quiet." She looked to Gabriel and nodded knowingly. "You better go with her, son," and was gone into the house; her molasses-thick laughter sweetening the air.

Reluctantly Maggie stood, looking at the two figures—Henrietta had caught up with Barden—a tiny cloud of dust rising from their feet. "Come on, Gabe. Looks like we have to go referee."

Gabriel walked beside her, a broad smile on his face. Maggie thought of her grandson being attracted to this tall white man. She tried to see them together and couldn't. At that moment she understood that she was being called on to realign her thinking about men and women, and men and men, and even women and women. Together . . . the way Adam and Eve were meant to be together.

V

Initially she found it difficult to ask the questions she wanted to ask. Almost impossible.

They got along well on Saturday. She took him out to dinner; they went shopping. All the while she tried with all her might to convince herself that she felt comfortable with this white man, with this homosexual, with this man who had slept with her grandboy. Yet he managed to impress her with his easygoing manner and openness and humor.

"Mrs. W." He had given her a *nickname*, of all things. No one had given her a nickname since . . . "Mrs. W., you sure you don't want to try on some swimsuits?"

She laughed at his kind-hearted jokes, seeing, oddly enough, something about him very like Edward; but then that thought would make her sad and confused.

Finally that night over coffee at the kitchen table she began to ask what they had both gingerly avoided.

"Why didn't he just tell me?"

"He was afraid, Mrs. W. It's just that simple."

"Of what?"

"That you might disown him. That you might stop . . . well, you know, loving him, I guess."

"Does your family know?"

"Yes."

"How do they take it?"

"My mom's fine. She's great. Really. She and Edward got along swell. My dad. Well, he'll be okay for a while, but every now and again we'll have these talks, you know, about cures and stuff and sometimes it just gets heated. I guess it'll just take a little more time with him."

"But don't you *want* to be normal?"

"Mrs. W., I *am*. Normal."

"I see."

They went to bed at one-thirty that morning. As Maggie buttoned up her nightgown, Gabriel's answers whizzed about her brain; but they brought along more damnable questions and Maggie went to bed feeling betrayal and disbelief and revulsion and anger.

In church that next morning with Gabriel, she began to doubt the wisdom of having asked him to come. As he sat beside her in the pew, as the Reverend Barden sermonized on Jezebel and Ahab, as the congregation unsuccessfully tried to disguise their curiosity—("What is that white boy doing here with Maggie Williams? Who is he? Where he come from?")—she wanted Gabriel to go ahead and tell her what to think: *We're perverts* or *You're wrong-headed, your church has poisoned your mind against your own grandson; if he had come out to you, you would have rejected him. Wouldn't you?* Would she have?

Barden's sermon droned on and on that morning; the choir sang; after the service people politely and gently shook Gabriel and Maggie's hands and then stood off to the side, whispering, clearly perplexed.

On the drive back home, as if out of the blue, she asked him: "Is it hard?"

"Ma'am?"

"Being who you are? What you are?"

He looked over at her, and she could not meet his gaze with the same intensity that had gone into her question. "Being gay?"

"Yes."

"Well, I have no choice."

"So I understand. But is it hard?"

"Edward and I used to get into arguments about that, Mrs. W." His tone altered a bit. He spoke more softly, gently, the way a widow speaks of her dead husband. Or, indeed, the way a widower speaks of his dead husband. "He used to say it was harder being black in this country than gay. Gays can always pass for straight; but blacks can't always pass for white. And most can never pass."

"And what do you think now?"

"Mrs. W., I think *life* is hard, you know?"

"Yes. I know."

VI

Death had first introduced itself to Maggie when she was a child. Her grandfather and grandmother both died before she was five; her father died when she was nine; her mother when she was twenty-five; over the years all her brothers except one. Her husband ten years ago. Her first memories of death: watching the women wash a cold body: the look of brown skin darkening, hardening: the corpse laid out on a cooling board, wrapped in a winding-cloth, before interment: fear of ghosts, bodyless souls: troubled sleep. So much had changed in seventy years; now there were embalming, funeral homes, morticians, insurance policies, bronze caskets, a bureaucratic wall between deceased and bereaved. Among the many things she regretted about Edward's death was not being able to touch his body. It made his death less real. But so much about the world seemed unreal to her these dark, dismal, and gloomy days. Now the flat earth was said to be round and bumblebees were not supposed to fly.

What was supposed to be and what truly was. Maggie learned these things from magazines and television and books; she loved to read. From her first week in that small schoolhouse with Miss Clara Oxendine, she had wanted to be a teacher. School: the scratchy chalkboard, the dusty-smelling textbooks, labyrinthine grammar and spelling and arithmetic, geography, reading out loud, giving confidence to the boy who would never learn to read well, correcting addition and subtraction problems, the taste and the scent of the schoolroom, the heat of the potbellied stove in January. She liked that small world; for her it was large. Yet how could she pay for enough education to become a teacher? Her mother would smile, encouragingly, when young Maggie would ask her, not looking up from her sewing, and merely say: "We'll find a way."

However, when she was fourteen she met a man named Thomas Williams, he sixteen going on thirty-nine. Infatuation replaced her dreams and murmured to her in languages she had never heard before, whispered to her another tale: *You will be a merchant's wife.*

Thomas Williams would come a-courting on Sunday evenings for two years, come driving his father's red Ford truck, stepping out with his biscuit-shined shoes, his one good Sunday suit, his hat cocked at an impertinent angle, and a smile that would make cold butter drip. But his true power lay in his tongue. He would spin yarns and tell tales that would make the oldest storyteller slap his knee and declare: "Hot damn! Can't that boy lie!" He could talk a possum out of a tree. He spoke to Maggie about his dream of opening his own store, a dry-goods store, and then maybe two or three or four. An audacious dream for a seventeen-year-old black boy, son of a farmer in 1936—and he promised, oh, how he promised, to keep Maggie by his side through it all.

Thinking back, on the other side of time and dreams, where fantasies and wishing had been realized, where she sat rich and alone, Maggie wondered what Thomas Williams could possibly have seen in that plain brown girl. Himself the son of a farmer with his own land, ten sons and two daughters, all married and doing well. There she was, poorer than a skinned rabbit, and not that pretty. Was he looking for a woman who would not flinch at hard work?

Somehow, borrowing from his father, from his brothers, working two, three jobs at the shipyards, in the fields, with Maggie taking in sewing and laundry, cleaning houses, saving, saving, saving, they opened their store; and were married. Days, weeks, years of days, weeks of days, weeks of inventory and cleaning and waiting on people and watching over the dry-goods store, which became a hardware store in the sixties while the one store became two. They were prosperous; they were respected; they owned property. At seventy she now wanted for nothing. Long gone was the dream of a schoolhouse and little children who skinned their knees and the teaching of the ABCs. Some days she imagined she had two lives and she preferred the original dream to the flesh-and-blood reality.

Now, at least, she no longer had to fight bitterly with her pompous, self-satisfied, driven, blaspheming husband, who worked seven days a week, sixteen hours a day, money-grubbing and mean though—outwardly—flamboyantly generous; a man who lost interest in her bed after her first and only son, Thomas, Jr., arrived broken in heart, spirit, and brain upon delivery; a son whose only true achievement in life was to illegitimately produce Edward by some equally brainless waif of a girl, now long vanished; a son who practically thrust the few-week-old infant into Maggie's arms, then flew off to a life of waste, sloth, petty crime, and finally a menial job in one of her stores and an ignoble marriage to a woman who could not conceal her greedy wish for Maggie to die.

Her life now was life that no longer had bite or spit or fire. She no longer worked. She no longer had to worry about Thomas's philandering and what pretty young thing he was messing with now. She no longer had the little boy whom Providence seemed to have sent her to maintain her sanity, to moor her to the Earth, and to give her vast energies focus.

In a world not real, is there truly guilt in willing reality to cohere through the life of another? Is that such a great sin? Maggie had turned to the boy—young, brown, handsome—to hold on to the world itself. She now saw that clearly. How did it happen? The mental slipping and sliding that allowed her to meld and mess and confuse her life with his, his rights with her wants, his life with her wish? He would not be like his father or his grandfather; he would rise up, go to school, be strong, be honest, upright. He would be; she would be . . . a feat of legerdemain; a sorcery of vicariousness in which his victory was her victory. He was her champion. Her hope.

Now he was gone. And now she had to come to terms with this news of his being "gay," as the world called what she had been taught was an unholy abomination. Slowly it all came together in her mind's eye: Edward.

He should have known better. I should have known better. I must learn better.

VII

They stood there at the end of the row, all of them waiting for the tractor to arrive and for the Reverend Hezekiah Barden to save the soul of Morton Henry.

Morton saw them standing there from his mount atop the green John Deere as it bounced across the broken soil. Maggie could make out the expression on his face: confusion. Three blacks and a white man out in the fields to see him. Did his house burn down? His wife die? The President declare war on Russia?

A big, red-haired, red-faced man, his face had so many freckles he appeared splotched. He had a big chew of tobacco in his left jaw and he spat out the brown juice as he came up the edge of the row and put the clutch in neutral.

"How you all today? Miss Maggie?"

"Hey, Morton."

Barden started right up, thumbs in his suspenders, and reared back on his heels. "Now I spect you're a God-fearing man?"

"Beg pardon?"

"I even spect you go to church from time to time?"

"Church? Miss Maggie, I—"

The Reverend held up his hand. "And I warrant you that your preacher—where *do* you go to church, son?"

"I go to—wait a minute. What's going on here? Miss Maggie—"

Henrietta piped up. "It's Sunday! You ain't supposed to be working and plowing fields on a Sunday!"

Morton Henry looked over to Maggie, who stood there in the bright sun, then to Gabriel, as if to beg him to speak, make some sense of this curious event. He scratched his head. "You mean to tell me you all come out here to tell me I ain't suppose to plow this here field?"

"Not on Sunday you ain't. It's the Lord's Day."

" 'The Lord's Day'?" Morton Henry was visibly amused. He tongued at the wad of tobacco in his jaw. "The Lord's Day." He chuckled out loud.

"Now it ain't no laughing matter, young man." The Reverend's voice took on a dark tone.

Morton seemed to be trying to figure out who Gabriel was. He spat. "Well, I tell you, Reverend. If the Lord wants to come plow these fields I'd be happy to let him."

"You . . ." Henrietta stomped her foot, causing dust to rise. "You can't talk about the Lord like that. You're using His name in vain."

"I'll talk about Him any way I please to." Morton Henry's face became redder by the minute. "I got two jobs, five head of children, and a sick wife, and the Lord don't seem too worried about that. I spect I ain't gone worry too much about plowing this here field on His day none neither."

"Young man, you can't—"

Morton Henry looked to Maggie. "Now, Miss Maggie, this is your land, and if you don't want me to plow it, I'll give you back your lease and you can pay me my money and find somebody else to tend this here field!"

Everybody looked at Maggie. How does this look, she couldn't help thinking, a black woman defending a white man against a black minister? Why the *hell* am I here having to do this? she fumed. Childish, hypocritical idiots and fools. Time is just slipping, slipping away and all they have to do is fuss and bother about other folk's business while their own houses are burning down. God save their souls. She wanted to yell this, to cuss them out and stomp away and leave them to their ignorance. But in the end, what good would it do?

She took a deep breath. "Morton Henry. You do what you got to do. Just like the rest of us."

Morton Henry bowed his head to Maggie, "Ma'am," turned to the others with a gloating grin, "Scuse me," put his gear in first, and turned down the next row.

"Well—"

Barden began to speak but Maggie just turned, not listening, not wanting to hear, thinking: When, Lord, oh when will we learn? Will we ever? *Respect,* she thought. Oh how complicated.

They followed Maggie, heading back to the house, Gabriel beside her, tall and silent, the afternoon sunrays romping in his black hair. How curious the world had become that she would be asking a white man to exonerate her in the eyes of her own grandson; how strange that at seventy, when she had all the laws and rules down pat, she would have to begin again, to learn. But all this stuff and bother would have to come later, for now she felt so, so tired, what with the weekend's activities weighing on her three-score-and-ten-year-old bones and joints; and she wished it were sunset, and she alone on her patio, contemplating the roundness and flatness of the earth, and slipping softly and safely into sleep.

1992

Recitatif

Toni Morrison

My mother danced all night and Roberta's was sick. That's why we were taken to St. Bonny's. People want to put their arms around you when you tell them you were in a shelter, but it really wasn't bad. No big long room with one hundred beds like Bellevue. There were four to a room, and when Roberta and me came, there was a shortage of state kids, so we were the only ones assigned to 406 and could go from bed to bed if we wanted to. And we wanted to, too. We changed beds every night and for the whole four months we were there we never picked one out as our own permanent bed.

It didn't start out that way. The minute I walked in and the Big Bozo introduced us, I got sick to my stomach. It was one thing to be taken out of your own bed early in the morning—it was something else to be stuck in a strange place with a girl from a whole other race. And Mary, that's my mother, she was right. Every now and then she would stop dancing long enough to tell me something important and one of the things she said was that they never washed their hair and they smelled funny. Roberta sure did. Smell funny, I mean. So when the Big Bozo (nobody ever called her Mrs. Itkin, just like nobody ever said St. Bonaventure)—when she said, "Twyla, this is Roberta. Roberta, this is Twyla. Make each other welcome." I said, "My mother won't like you putting me in here."

"Good," said Bozo. "Maybe then she'll come and take you home."

How's that for mean? If Roberta had laughed I would have killed her, but she didn't. She just walked over to the window and stood with her back to us.

"Turn around," said the Bozo. "Don't be rude. Now Twyla. Roberta. When you hear a loud buzzer, that's the call for dinner. Come down to the first floor. Any fights and no movie." And then, just to make sure we knew what we would be missing, *"The Wizard of Oz."*

Roberta must have thought I meant that my mother would be mad about my being put in the shelter. Not about rooming with her, because as soon as Bozo left she came over to me and said, "Is your mother sick too?"

"No," I said. "She just likes to dance all night."

"Oh," she nodded her head and I liked the way she understood things so fast. So for the moment it didn't matter that we looked like salt and pepper standing there and that's what the other kids called us sometimes. We were eight years old and got F's all the time. Me because I couldn't remember what I read or what the teacher said. And Roberta because she couldn't read at all and didn't even listen to the teacher. She wasn't good at anything except jacks, at which she was a killer: pow scoop pow scoop pow scoop.

We didn't like each other all that much at first, but nobody wanted to play with us because we weren't real orphans with beautiful dead parents in the sky. We were dumped. Even the New York City Puerto Ricans and the upstate Indians ignored us. All kinds of kids were in there, black ones, white ones, even two Koreans. The food was good, though. At least I thought so. Roberta hated it and left whole pieces of things on her plate: Spam, Salisbury steak—even jello with fruit cocktail in it, and she didn't care if I ate what she wouldn't. Mary's idea of supper was popcorn and a can of Yoo-Hoo. Hot mashed potatoes and two weenies was like Thanksgiving for me.

It really wasn't bad, St. Bonny's. The big girls on the second floor pushed us around now and then. But that was all. They wore lipstick and eyebrow pencil and wobbled their knees while they watched TV. Fifteen, sixteen, even, some of them were. They were put-out girls, scared runaways most of them. Poor little girls who fought their uncles off but looked tough to us, and mean. God did they look mean. The staff tried to keep them separate from the younger children, but sometimes they caught us watching them in the orchard where they played radios and danced with each other. They'd light out after us and pull our hair or twist our arms. We were scared of them, Roberta and me, but neither of us wanted the other one to know it. So we got a good list of dirty names we could shout back when we ran from them through the orchard. I used to dream a lot and almost always the orchard was there. Two acres, four maybe, of these little apple trees. Hundreds of them. Empty and crooked like beggar women when I first came to St. Bonny's but fat with flowers when I left. I don't know why I dreamt about that orchard so much. Nothing really happened there. Nothing all that important, I mean. Just the big girls dancing and playing the radio. Roberta and me watching. Maggie fell down there once. The kitchen woman with legs like parentheses. And the big girls laughed at her. We should have helped her up, I know, but we were scared of those girls with lipstick and eyebrow pencil. Maggie couldn't talk. The kids said she had her tongue cut out, but I think she was just born that way: mute. She was old and sandy-colored and she worked in the kitchen. I don't know if she was nice or not. I just remember her legs like parentheses and how she rocked when she walked. She worked from early in the morning till two o'clock, and if she was late, if she had too much cleaning and didn't get out till two-fifteen or so, she' d cut through the orchard so she wouldn't miss her bus and have to wait another hour. She wore this really stupid little hat—a kid's hat with ear flaps—and she wasn't much taller than we were. A really awful little hat. Even for a mute, it was dumb—dressing like a kid and never saying anything at all.

"But what if somebody tries to kill her?" I used to wonder about that. "Or what if she wants to cry? Can she cry?"

"Sure," Roberta said. "But just tears. No sounds come out."

"She can't scream?"

"Nope. Nothing."

"Can she hear?"

"I guess."

"Let's call her," I said. And we did.

"Dummy! Dummy!" She never turned her head.

"Bow legs! Bow legs!" Nothing. She just rocked on, the chin straps of her baby-boy hat swaying from side to side. I think we were wrong. I think she could hear and didn't let on. And it shames me even now to think there was somebody in there after all who heard us call her those names and couldn't tell on us.

We got along all right, Roberta and me. Changed beds every night, got F's in civics and communication skills and gym. The Bozo was disappointed in us, she said. Out of 130 of us state cases, 90 were under twelve. Almost all were real orphans with beautiful dead parents in the sky. We were the only ones dumped and the only ones with F's in three classes including gym. So we got along—what with her leaving whole pieces of things on her plate and being nice about not asking questions.

I think it was the day before Maggie fell down that we found out our mothers were coming to visit us on the same Sunday. We had been at the shelter twenty-eight days (Roberta twenty-eight and a half) and this was their first visit with us. Our mothers would come at ten o'clock in time for chapel, then lunch with us in the teachers' lounge. I thought if my dancing mother met her sick mother it might be good for her. And Roberta thought her sick mother would get a big bang out of a dancing one. We got excited about it and curled each other's hair. After breakfast we sat on the bed watching the road from the window. Roberta's socks were still wet. She washed them the night before and put them on the radiator to dry. They hadn't, but she put them on anyway because their tops were so pretty—scalloped in pink. Each of us had a purple construction-paper basket that we had made in craft class. Mine had a yellow crayon rabbit on it. Roberta's had eggs with wiggly lines of color. Inside were cellophane grass and just the jelly beans because I'd eaten the two marshmallow eggs they gave us. The Big Bozo came herself to get us. Smiling she told us we looked very nice and to come downstairs. We were so surprised by the smile we'd never seen before, neither of us moved.

"Don't you want to see your mommies?"

I stood up first and spilled the jelly beans all over the floor. Bozo's smile disappeared while we scrambled to get the candy up off the floor and put it back in the grass.

She escorted us downstairs to the first floor, where the other girls were lining up to file into the chapel. A bunch of grown-ups stood to one side. Viewers mostly. The old biddies who wanted servants and the fags who wanted company looking for children they might want to adopt. Once in a while a grandmother. Almost never anybody young or anybody whose face wouldn't scare you in the night. Because if any of the real orphans had young relatives they wouldn't be real orphans. I saw Mary right away. She had on those green slacks I hated and hated even more now because didn't she know we were going to chapel? And that fur jacket with the pocket linings so ripped she had to pull to get her hands out of them. But her face was pretty—like always, and she smiled and waved like she was the little girl looking for her mother—not me.

I walked slowly, trying not to drop the jelly beans and hoping the paper handle would hold. I had to use my last Chiclet because by the time I finished cutting everything out, all the Elmer's was gone. I am left-handed and the scissors never worked for me. It didn't matter, though; I might just as well have chewed the gum. Mary dropped to her knees and grabbed me, mashing the basket, the jelly beans, and the grass into her ratty fur jacket.

"Twyla, baby. Twyla, baby!"

I could have killed her. Already I heard the big girls in the orchard the next time saying, "Twyyyyyla, baby!" But I couldn't stay mad at Mary while she was smiling and hugging me and smelling of Lady Esther dusting powder. I wanted to stay buried in her fur all day.

To tell the truth I forgot about Roberta. Mary and I got in line for the traipse into chapel and I was feeling proud because she looked so beautiful even in those ugly green slacks that made her behind stick out. A pretty mother on earth is better than a beautiful dead one in the sky even if she did leave you all alone to go dancing.

I felt a tap on my shoulder, turned, and saw Roberta smiling. I smiled back, but not too much lest somebody think this visit was the biggest thing that ever happened in my life. Then Roberta said, "Mother, I want you to meet my roommate, Twyla. And that's Twyla's mother."

I looked up it seemed for miles. She was big. Bigger than any man and on her chest was the biggest cross I'd ever seen. I swear it was six inches long each way. And in the crook of her arm was the biggest Bible ever made.

Mary, simple-minded as ever, grinned and tried to yank her hand out of the pocket with the raggedy lining—to shake hands, I guess. Roberta's mother looked down at me and then looked down at Mary too. She didn't say anything, just grabbed Roberta with her Bible-free hand and stepped out of line, walking quickly to the rear of it. Mary was still grinning because she's not too swift when it comes to what's really going on. Then this light bulb goes off in her head and she says "That bitch!" really loud and us almost in the chapel now. Organ music whining; the Bonny Angels singing sweetly. Everybody in the world turned around to look. And Mary would have kept it up—kept calling names if I hadn't squeezed her hand as hard as I could. That helped a little, but she still twitched and crossed and uncrossed her legs all through service. Even groaned a couple of times. Why did I think she would come there and act right? Slacks. No hat like the grandmothers and viewers, and groaning all the while. When we stood for hymns she kept her mouth shut. Wouldn't even look at the words on the page. She actually reached in her purse for a mirror to check her lipstick. All I could think of was that she really needed to be killed. The sermon lasted a year, and I knew the real orphans were looking smug again.

We were supposed to have lunch in the teachers' lounge, but Mary didn't bring anything, so we picked fur and cellophane grass off the mashed jelly beans and ate them. I could have killed her. I sneaked a look at Roberta. Her mother had brought chicken legs and ham sandwiches and oranges and a whole box of chocolate-covered grahams. Roberta drank milk from a thermos while her mother read the Bible to her.

Things are not right. The wrong food is always with the wrong people. Maybe that's why I got into waitress work later—to match up the right people with the right food. Roberta just let those chicken legs sit there, but she did bring a stack of grahams up to me later when the visit was over. I think she was sorry that her mother would not shake my mother's hand. And I liked that and I liked the fact that she didn't say a word about Mary groaning all the way through the service and not bringing any lunch.

Roberta left in May when the apple trees were heavy and white. On her last day we went to the orchard to watch the big girls smoke and dance by the radio. It didn't matter they said, "Twyyyyyla, baby." We sat on the ground and breathed. Lady Esther. Apple blossoms. I still go soft when I smell one or the other. Roberta was going home. The big cross and the big Bible was coming to get her and she seemed sort of glad and sort of not. I thought I would die in that room of four beds without her and I knew Bozo had plans to move some other dumped kid in there with me. Roberta promised to write every day, which was really sweet of her because she couldn't read a lick so how could she write anybody? I would have drawn pictures and sent them to her but she never gave me her address. Little by little she faded. Her wet socks with the pink scalloped tops and her big serious-looking eyes—that's all I could catch when I tried to bring her to mind.

I was working behind the counter at the Howard Johnson's on the Thruway just before the Kingston exit. Not a bad job. Kind of a long ride from Newburgh, but okay once I got there. Mine was the second night shift—eleven to seven. Very light until a Greyhound checked in for breakfast around six-thirty. At that hour the sun was all the way clear of the hills behind the restaurant. The place looked better at night—more like shelter—but I loved it when the sun broke in, even if it did show all the cracks in the vinyl and the speckled floor looked dirty no matter what the mop boy did.

It was August and a bus crowd was just unloading. They would stand around a long while: going to the john, and looking at gifts and junk-for-sale machines, reluctant to sit down so soon. Even to eat. I was trying to fill the coffee pots and get them all situated on the electric burners when I saw her. She was sitting in a booth smoking a cigarette with two guys smothered in head and facial hair. Her own hair was so big and wild I could hardly see her face. But the eyes. I would know them anywhere. She had on a powder-blue halter and shorts outfit and earrings the size of bracelets. Talk about lipstick and eyebrow pencil. She made the big girls look like nuns. I couldn't get off the counter until seven o'clock, but I kept watching the booth in case they got up to leave before that. My replacement was on time for a change, so I counted and stacked my receipts as fast as I could and signed off. I walked over to the booth, smiling and wondering if she would remember me. Or even if she wanted to remember me. Maybe she didn't want to be reminded of St. Bonny's or to have anybody know she was ever there. I know I never talked about it to anybody.

I put my hands in my apron pockets and leaned against the back of the booth facing them.

"Roberta? Roberta Fisk?"

She looked up. "Yeah?"

"Twyla."

She squinted for a second and then said, "Wow."

"Remember me?"

"Sure. Hey. Wow."

"It's been a while," I said, and gave a smile to the two hairy guys.

"Yeah. Wow. You work here?"

"Yeah," I said. "I live in Newburgh."

"Newburgh? No kidding?" She laughed then a private laugh that included the guys but only the guys, and they laughed with her. What could I do but laugh too and wonder why I was standing there with my knees showing out from under that uniform. Without looking I could see the blue and white triangle on my head, my hair shapeless in a net, my ankles thick in white oxfords. Nothing could have been less sheer than my stockings. There was this silence that came down right after I laughed. A silence it was her turn to fill up. With introductions, maybe, to her boyfriends or an invitation to sit down and have a Coke. Instead she lit a cigarette off the one she'd just finished and said, "We're on our way to the Coast. He's got an appointment with Hendrix." She gestured casually toward the boy next to her.

"Hendrix? Fantastic," I said. "Really fantastic. What's she doing now?"

Roberta coughed on her cigarette and the two guys rolled their eyes up at the ceiling.

"Hendrix. Jimi Hendrix, asshole. He's only the biggest—Oh, wow. Forget it."

I was dismissed without anyone saying goodbye, so I thought I would do it for her.

"How's your mother?" I asked. Her grin cracked her whole face. She swallowed. "Fine," she said. "How's yours?"

"Pretty as a picture," I said and turned away. The backs of my knees were damp. Howard Johnson's really was a dump in the sunlight.

James is a comfortable as a house slipper. He liked my cooking and I liked his big loud family. They have lived in Newburgh all of their lives and talk about it the way people do who have always known a home. His grandmother has a porch swing older than his father and when they talk about streets and avenues and buildings they call them names they no longer have. They still call the A & P Rico's because it stands on property once a mom and pop store owned by Mr. Rico. And they call the new community college Town Hall because it once was. My mother-in-law puts up jelly and cucumbers and buys butter wrapped in cloth from a dairy. James and his father talk about fishing and baseball and I can see them all together on the Hudson in a raggedy skiff. Half the population of Newburgh is on welfare now, but to my husband's family it was still some upstate paradise of a time long past. A time of ice houses and vegetable wagons, coal furnaces and children weeding gardens. When our son was born my mother-in-law gave me the crib blanket that had been hers.

But the town they remembered had changed. Something quick was in the air. Magnificent old houses, so ruined they had become shelter for squatters and rent risks, were bought and renovated. Smart IBM people moved out of their suburbs back into the city and put shutters up and herb gardens in their backyards. A brochure came in the mail announcing the opening of a Food Emporium. Gourmet food it said—and listed items the rich IBM crowd would want. It was located in a new mall at the edge of town and I drove out to shop there one day—just to see. It was late in June. After the tulips were gone and the Queen Elizabeth roses were open everywhere. I trailed my cart along the aisle tossing in smoked oysters and Robert's sauce and things I knew would sit in my cupboard for years. Only when I found some Klondike ice cream bars did I feel less guilty about spending James's fireman's salary so foolishly. My father-in-law ate them with the same gusto little Joseph did.

Waiting in the check-out line I heard a voice say, "Twyla!"

The classical music piped over the aisle had affected me and the woman leaning toward me was dressed to kill. Diamonds on her hand, a smart white summer dress. "I'm Mrs. Benson," I said.

"Ho. Ho. The Big Bozo," she sang.

For a split second I didn't know what she was talking about. She had a bunch of asparagus and two cartons of fancy water.

"Roberta!"

"Right."

"For heaven's sake. Roberta."

"You look great," she said.

"So do you. Where are you? Here? In Newburgh?"

"Yes. Over in Annandale."

I was opening my mouth to say more when the cashier called my attention to her empty counter.

"Meet you outside." Roberta pointed her finger and went into the express line.

I placed the groceries and kept myself from glancing around to check Roberta's progress. I remembered Howard Johnson's and looking for a chance to speak only to be greeted with a stingy "wow." But she was waiting for me and her huge hair was sleek now, smooth around a small, nicely shaped head. Shoes, dress, everything lovely and summery and rich. I was dying to know what happened to her, how she got from Jimi Hendrix to Annandale, a neighborhood full of doctors and IBM executives. Easy, I thought. Everything is so easy for them. The think they own the world.

"How long," I asked her. "How long have you been here?"

"A year. I got married to a man who lives here. And you, you're married too, right? Benson, you said."

"Yeah. James Benson."

"And is he nice?"

"Oh, is he nice?"

"Well is he?" Roberta's eyes were steady as though she really meant the question and wanted an answer.

"He's wonderful, Roberta. Wonderful."

"So you're happy."

"Very."

"That's good," she said and nodded her head. "I always hoped you'd be happy. Any kids? I know you have kids."

"One. A boy. How about you?"

"Four."

"Four?"

She laughed. "Step kids. He's a widower."

"Oh."

"Got a minute? Let's have coffee."

I thought about the Klondikes melting and the inconvenience of going all the way to my car and putting the bags in the trunk. Served me right for buying all that stuff I didn't need. Roberta was ahead of me.

"Put them in my car. It's right here."

And then I saw the dark blue limousine.

"You married a Chinaman?"

"No," she laughed. "He's the driver."

"Oh, my. If the Big Bozo could see you now."

We both giggled. Really giggled. Suddenly, in just a pulse beat, twenty years disappeared and all of it came rushing back. The big girls (whom we called gar girls—Robert's misheard word for the evil stone faces described in a civics class) there dancing in the orchard, the ploppy mashed potatoes, the double weenies, the Spam with pineapple. We went into the coffee shop holding on to one another and I tried to think why we were so glad to see each other this time and not before. Once, twelve years ago, we passed like strangers. A black girl and a white girl meeting in a Howard Johnson's on the road and having nothing to say. One in a blue and white triangle waitress hat—the other on her way to see Hendrix. Now we were behaving like sisters separated for much too long. Those four short months were nothing in time. Maybe it was the thing itself. Just being there, together. Two little girls who knew what nobody else in the world knew—how not to ask questions. How to believe what had to be believed. There was politeness in that reluctance and generosity as well. Is your mother sick too? No, she dances all night. Oh—and an understanding nod.

We sat in a booth by the window and fell into recollection like veterans.

"Did you ever learn to read?"

"Watch." She picked up the menu. "Special of the day. Cream of corn soup. Entrées. Two dots and a wriggly line. Quiche. Chef salad, scallops . . ."

I was laughing and applauding when the waitress came up.

"Remember the Easter baskets?"

"And how we tried to *introduce* them?"

"Your mother with that cross like two telephone poles."

"And yours with those tight slacks."

We laughed so loudly heads turned and made the laughter harder to suppress.

"What happened to the Jimi Hendrix date?"

Roberta made a blow-out sound with her lips.

"When he died I thought about you."

"Oh, you heard about him finally?"

"Finally. Come on, I was a small-town country waitress."

"And I was a small-town country dropout. God, were we wild. I still don't know how I got out of there alive."

"But you did."

"I did. I really did. Now I'm Mrs. Kenneth Norton."

"Sounds like a mouthful."

"It is."

"Servants and all?"

Roberta held up two fingers.

"Ow! What does he do?"

"Computers and stuff. What do I know?"

"I don't remember a hell of a lot from those days, but Lord, St. Bonny's is as clear as daylight. Remember Maggie? The day she fell down and those gar girls laughed at her?

Roberta looked up from her salad and stared at me. "Maggie didn't fall," she said.

"Yes, she did. You remember."

"No, Twyla. They knocked her down. Those girls pushed her down and tore her clothes. In the orchard."

"I don't—that's not what happened."

"Sure it is. In the orchard. Remember how scared we were?"

"Wait a minute. I don't remember any of that."

"And Bozo was fired."

"You're crazy. She was there when I left. You left before me."

"I went back. You weren't there when they fired Bozo."

"What?"

"Twice. Once for a year when I was about ten, another for two months when I was fourteen. That's when I ran away."

"You ran away from St. Bonny's?"

"I had to. What do you want? Me dancing in that orchard?"

"Are you sure about Maggie?"

"Of course I'm sure. You've blocked it, Twyla. It happened. Those girls had behavior problems, you know."

"Didn't they, though. But why can't I remember the Maggie thing?"

"Believe me. It happened. And we were there."

"Who did you room with when you went back?" I asked her as if I would know her. The Maggie thing was troubling me.

"Creeps. They tickled themselves in the night."

My ears were itching and I wanted to go home suddenly. This was all very well but she couldn't just comb her hair, wash her face and pretend everything was hunky-dory. After the Howard Johnson's snub. And no apology. Nothing.

"Were you on dope or what that time at Howard Johnson's?" I tried to make my voice sound friendlier than I felt.

"Maybe, a little. I never did drugs much. Why?"

"I don't know; you acted sort of like you didn't want to know me then."

"Oh, Twyla, you know how it was in those days: black—white. You know how everything was."

But I didn't know. I thought it was just the opposite. Busloads of blacks and whites came into Howard Johnson's together. They roamed together then: students, musicians, lovers, protestors. You got to see everything at Howard Johnson's and blacks were very friendly with whites in those days. But sitting there with nothing on my plate but two hard tomato wedges wondering about the melting Klondikes it seemed childish remembering the slight. We went to her car, and with the help of the driver, got my stuff into my station wagon.

"We'll keep in touch this time," she said.

"Sure," I said. "Sure. Give me a call."

"I will," she said, and then just as I was sliding behind the wheel, she leaned into the window. "By the way. Your mother. Did she ever stop dancing?"

I shook my head. "No. Never."

Roberta nodded.

"And yours? Did she ever get well?"

She smiled a tiny sad smile. "No. She never did. Look, call me, okay?"

"Okay," I said, but I knew I wouldn't. Roberta had messed up my past somehow with that business about Maggie. I wouldn't forget a thing like that. Would I?

Strife came to us that fall. At least that's what the paper called it. Strife. Racial strife. The word made me think of a bird—a big shrieking bird out of 1,000,000,000 B.C. Flapping its wings and cawing. Its eye with no lid always bearing down on you. All day it screeched and at night it slept on the rooftops. It woke you in the morning and from the *Today* show to the eleven o'clock news it kept you an awful company. I couldn't figure it out from one day to the next. I knew I was supposed to feel something strong, but I didn't know what, and James wasn't any help. Joseph was on the list of kids to be transferred form the junior high school to another one at some far-out-of-the-way place and I thought it was a good thing until I heard it was a bad thing. I mean I didn't know. All the schools seemed dumps to me, and the fact that one was nicer looking didn't hold much weight. But the papers were full of it and then the kids began to get jumpy. In August, mind you. Schools weren't even open yet. I thought Joseph might be frightened to go over there, but he didn't seem scared so I forgot about it, until I found myself driving along Hudson Street out there by the school they were trying to integrate and saw a line of women marching. And who do you suppose was in line, big as life, holding a sign in front of her bigger than her mother's cross? MOTHERS HAVE RIGHTS TOO! it said.

I drove on, and then changed my mind. I circled the block, slowed down, and honked my horn.

Roberta looked over and when she saw me she waved. I didn't wave

back, but I didn't move either. She handed her sign to another woman and
came over to me where I was parked.

"Hi."

"What are you doing?"

"Picketing. What's it look like?"

"What for?"

"What do you mean, 'What for?' They want to take my kids and send
them out of the neighborhood. They don't want to go."

"So what if they go to another school? My boy's being bussed too, and I
don't mind. Why should you?"

"It's not about us, Twyla. Me and you. It's about our kids."

"What's more *us* than that?"

"Well, it is a free country."

"Not yet, but it will be."

"What the hell does that mean? I'm not doing anything to you."

"You really think that?"

"I know it."

"I wonder what made me think you were different."

"I wonder what made me think you were different."

"Look at them," I said. "Just look. Who do they think they are? Swarm-
ing all over the place like they own it. And now they think they can decide
where my child goes to school. Look at them, Roberta. They're Bozos."

Roberta turned around and looked at the women. Almost all of them
were standing still now, waiting. Some were even edging toward us. Roberta
looked at me out of some refrigerator behind her eyes. "No, they're not.
They're just mothers."

"And what am I? Swiss cheese."

"I used to curl your hair."

"I hated your hands in my hair."

The women were moving. Our faces looked mean to them of course and
they looked as though they could not wait to throw themselves in front of a
police car, or better yet, into my car and drag me away by my ankles. Now
they surrounded my car and gently, gently began to rock it. I swayed back
and forth like a sideways yo-yo. Automatically I reached for Roberta, like the
old days in the orchard, when they saw us watching them and we had to get
out of there, and if one of us fell the other pulled her up and if one of us was
caught the other stayed to kick and scratch, and neither would leave the
other behind. My arm shot out of the car window but no receiving hand was
there. Roberta was looking at me sway from side to side in the car and her
face was still. My purse slid from the car seat down under the dashboard. The
four policemen who had been drinking Tab in their car finally got the message and strolled over, forcing their way through the women. Quietly, firmly
they spoke. "Okay, ladies. Back in line or off the streets."

Some of them went away willingly; others had to be urged away from the car doors and the hood. Roberta didn't move. She was looking steadily at me. I was fumbling to turn on the ignition, which wouldn't catch because the gearshift was still in drive. The seats of the car were a mess because the swaying had thrown my grocery coupons all over it and my purse was sprawled on the floor.

"Maybe I am different now, Twyla. But you're not. You're the same little state kid who kicked a poor old black lady when she was down on the ground. You kicked a black lady and you have the nerve to call me a bigot."

The coupons were everywhere and the guts of my purse were bunched under the dashboard. What was she saying? Black? Maggie wasn't black.

"She wasn't black," I said.

"Like hell she wasn't, and you kicked her. We both did. You kicked a black lady who couldn't even scream."

"Liar!"

"You're the liar! Why don't you just go on home and leave us alone, huh?"

She turned away and I skidded away from the curb.

The next morning I went into the garage and cut the side out of the carton our portable TV had come in. It wasn't nearly big enough, but after a while I had a decent sign: red spray-painted letters on a white background— AND SO DO CHILDREN****. I meant just to go down to the school and tack it up somewhere so those cows on the picket line across the street could see it, but when I got there, some ten or so others had already assembled— protesting the cows across the street. Police permits and everything. I got in line and we strutted in time on our side while Roberta's group strutted on theirs. That first day we were all dignified, pretending the other side didn't exist. The second day there was name calling and finger gestures. But that was about all. People changed signs from time to time, but Roberta never did and neither did I. Actually my sign didn't make sense without Roberta's. "And so do children what?" one of the women on my side asked me. Have rights, I said, as though it was obvious.

Roberta didn't acknowledge my presence in any way and I got to thinking maybe she didn't know I was there. I began to pace myself in the line, jostling people one minute and lagging behind the next, so Roberta and I could reach the end of our respective lines at the same time and there would be a moment in our turn when we would face each other. Still, I couldn't tell whether she saw me and knew my sign was for her. The next day I went early before we were scheduled to assemble. I waited until she got there before I exposed my new creation. As soon as she hoisted her MOTHERS HAVE RIGHTS TOO I began to wave my new one, which said, HOW WOULD YOU KNOW? I know she saw that one, but I had gotten addicted now. My signs got crazier each day, and the women on my side decided that I as a kook. They couldn't make heads or tails out of my brilliant screaming posters.

I brought a painted sign in queenly red with huge black letters that said, IS YOUR MOTHER WELL? Roberta took her lunch break and didn't come back for the rest of the day or any day after. Two days later I stopped going too and couldn't have been missed because nobody understood my signs anyway.

It was a nasty six weeks. Classes were suspended and Joseph didn't go to anybody's school until October. The children—everybody's children— soon got bored with that extended vacation they thought was going to be so great. They looked at TV until their eyes flattened. I spent a couple of mornings tutoring my son, as the other mothers said we should. Twice I opened a text from last year that he had never turned in. Twice he yawned in my face. Other mothers organized living room sessions so the kids would keep up. None of the kids could concentrate so they drifted back to *The Price is Right* and *The Brady Bunch*. When the school finally opened there were fights once or twice and some sirens roared through the streets every once in a while. There were a lot of photographers from Albany. And just when ABC was about to send a news crew, the kids settled down like nothing in the world had happened. Joseph hung my HOW WOULD YOU KNOW? sign in his bedroom. I don't know what became of AND SO DO CHILDREN****. I think my father-in-law cleaned some fish on it. He was always puttering around in our garage. Each of his five children lived in Newburgh and he acted as though he had five extra homes.

I couldn't help looking for Roberta when Joseph graduated from high school, but I didn't see her. It didn't trouble me much what she had said to me in the car. I mean the kicking part. I know I didn't do that, I couldn't do that. But I was puzzled by her telling me Maggie was black. When I thought about it I actually couldn't be certain. She wasn't pitch-black, I knew, or I would have remembered that. What I remember was the kiddie hat, and the semicircle legs. I tried to reassure myself about the race thing for a long time until it dawned on me that the truth was already there, and Roberta knew it. I didn't kick her; I didn't join in with the gar girls and kick that lady, but I sure did want to. We watched and never tried to help her and never called for help. Maggie was my dancing mother. Deaf, I thought, and dumb. Nobody inside. Nobody who would hear you if you cried in the night. Nobody who could tell you anything important that you could use. Rocking, dancing, swaying as she walked. And when the gar girls pushed her down, and started roughhousing, I knew she wouldn't scream, couldn't—just like me—and I was glad about that.

We decided not to have a tree, because Christmas would be at my mother-in-law's house, so why have a tree at both places? Joseph was at SUNY New Paltz and we had to economize, we said. But at the last minute,

I changed my mind. Nothing could be that bad. So I rushed around town looking for a tree, something small but wide. By the time I found a place, it was snowing and very late. I dawdled like it was the most important purchase in the world and the tree man was fed up with me. Finally I chose one and had it tied onto the trunk of the car. I drove away slowly because the sand trucks were not out yet and the streets could be murder at the beginning of a snowfall. Downtown the streets were wide and rather empty except for a cluster of people coming out of the Newburgh Hotel. The one hotel in town that wasn't built out of cardboard and Plexiglass. A party, probably. The men huddled in the snow were dressed in tails and the women had on furs. Shiny things glittered from underneath their coats. It made me tired to look at them. Tired, tired, tired. On the next corner was a small diner with loops and loops of paper bells in the window. I stopped the car and went in. Just for a cup of coffee and twenty minutes of peace before I went home and tried to finish everything before Christmas Eve.

"Twyla?"

There she was. In a silvery evening gown and dark fur coat. A man and another woman were with her, the man fumbling for change to put in the cigarette machine. The woman was humming and tapping on the counter with her fingernails. They all looked a little bit drunk.

"Well. It's you."

"How are you."

I shrugged. "Pretty good. Frazzled. Christmas and all."

"Regular?" called the woman from the counter.

"Fine," Roberta called back and then, "Wait for me in the car."

She slipped into the booth beside me. "I have to tell you something, Twyla. I made up my mind if I ever saw you again, I'd tell you."

"I'd just as soon not hear anything, Roberta. It doesn't matter now, anyway."

"No," she said. "Not about that."

"Don't be long," said the woman. She carried two regulars to go and the man peeled his cigarette pack as they left.

"It's about St. Bonny's and Maggie."

"Oh, please."

"Listen to me. I really did think she was black. I didn't make that up. I really thought so. But now I can't be sure. I just remember her as old, so old. And because she couldn't talk—well, you know, I thought she was crazy. She'd been brought up in an institution like my mother was and like I thought I would be too. And you were right. We didn't kick her. It was the gar girls. Only them. But, well I wanted to. I really wanted them to hurt her. I said we did it, too. You and me, but that's not true. And I don't want you to carry that around. It was just that I wanted to do it so bad that day—wanting to is doing it."

Her eyes were watery from the drinks she'd had, I guess. I know it's that way with me. One glass of wine and I start bawling over the littlest thing.

"We were kids, Roberta."

"Yeah. Yeah. I know, just kids."

"Eight."

"Eight."

"And lonely."

"Scared, too."

She wiped her cheeks with the heel of her hand and smiled. "Well, that's all I wanted to say."

I nodded and couldn't think of any way to fill the silence that went from the diner past the paper bells on out into the snow. It was heavy now. I thought I'd better wait for the sand trucks before starting home.

"Thanks, Roberta."

"Sure."

"Did I tell you? My mother, she never did stop dancing."

"Yes. You told me. And mine, she never got well." Roberta lifted her hands from that tabletop and covered her face with her palms. When she took them away she really was crying. "Oh, shit, Twyla. Shit, shit, shit. What the hell happened to Maggie?"

1983

New Readings

Off-Season Travel

Alyce Miller

A few weeks after Ellen won the contest that had something to do with peanut butter, the supermarket arranged to fly her and Glenn to the small resort town of Puerto Cobre, on the west coast of Mexico across from La Paz. Even as they bounced along in the dilapidated taxi on the dirt road from the airport into town, Ellen thought how impossible it seemed that they'd actually disentangled themselves from the multiple complications that shaped their collective life in San Francisco: the children, the fixer-upper house, the asthmatic dog, the stack of bills, the unfolded laundry, the un-defrosted refrigerator, Glenn's job, her job, the firecracker-like gunshots at night from the projects over the hill, the surreptitious drug-dealing of hooded silhouettes on their corner, and their own mutual complaints swirling together and lost in the fog of what could never be fixed. Long ago, specifics were forgotten. All the two of them could remember was that at one time there had been something good, and that what was left was very, very wrong.

In the taxi Ellen was thinking how Glenn, so familiar he'd gone strange, seemed no longer to belong to her. She watched him stare out the window at the brown, barefoot children playing outside their tarpaper shacks alongside the road fifteen hundred miles south of San Francisco. He was mur-muring, "They're so poor," while Ellen considered how she felt nothing, nothing at all.

The supermarket paid for all ground transportation and put them up at La Gran Duchesa, a small, elegant hotel with a narrow stretch of private beach. The imported white sand was dotted with palm-frond cabañas. Inside the flag-stone courtyard was an oblong swimming pool, complete with a full-service bar and submerged stools. A bartender in a red tuxedo jacket was briskly pol-ishing glasses to the rhythm of piped-in Muzak. He barely glanced up as Ellen and Glenn made their way up the outside stairs to the third floor. Their room was small, with two double beds separated by a nightstand, but beyond the slid-ing glass door to the balcony was a wide view of the ocean.

While Glenn showered, Ellen pushed the door open and stepped out onto the balcony into the warm evening air. She wore cut-offs and her oldest son's Little League T-shirt, and carried a bottle of beer in her hand. At home she never drank, but now she took a long swig of beer and considered how, at forty, she still had time to try out a different sort of life.

That was when she noticed a woman to the right at the wrought-iron railing, her back to Ellen, studying the fiery halo of sinking sun that scorched the surface of the ocean. Ellen thought she should announce herself. "It's beautiful, isn't it?" The woman turned around, startled. "The sunset." Ellen gestured toward it.

The woman was tall, striking, and black. She wore a foundation a couple of shades too light so that her skin bore an eerie pallor. Her eyebrows had been plucked until there was only a thin arched line above each eye. Her full mouth was lipsticked pale orange, a color Ellen wouldn't have dared to wear at the risk of looking jaundiced. But on the woman it looked elegant. She wore white pedal pushers and orange sandals. Ellen couldn't help noting with a small pang of envy the long, elegant brown hands, neatly manicured, resting lightly, one on each slim hip.

"Looks like we're neighbors. We just got here."

The woman stared at her, like someone expecting an apology. After a moment she said, "I didn't realize they'd put anyone right next door. After all, it's off-season. The hotel's practically empty." She paused. "I'm Marjorie Pierce."

"Ellen Fitzgerald." Ellen held out her hand and Marjorie leaned forward perfunctorily to accept it. Her fingers were cool, her palm warm. She pulled away as soon as they'd clasped hands.

"Well then . . ." She straightened herself up, raising one slender hand to wave away a small insect. "I better go get dressed."

"Marjorie?" It was a man's voice, half-plaintive, half-annoyed, coming from the open door of her room. A white flash of curtain stirred in the breeze. "Marjorie?" There was a sense of urgency in his tone. "Where the hell . . .?"

He stepped onto the balcony, a tall brown man dressed in one of those awful flowered shirt-and-short sets American tourists wear when they travel to warm climates. When he saw Ellen, he looked as if he thought maybe she'd scaled the side of the hotel on a rope. "Oh, *buenos días*, or is it *noches* already?"

Marjorie introduced them. "Lafayette, this is Ellen. Ellen, my husband Lafayette."

They shook hands. His hand was huge and warm. He peered beyond her to the yellow rectangle of her open door. "We didn't expect neighbors," he said. "You here alone?"

"No, my husband's inside." The shower had stopped. She could hear Glenn moving around inside the room. "Glenn?"

The sunset behind Marjorie and Lafayette lit up their bodies like burning effigies. From behind the hotel the faraway evening sounds of the town, faint traffic and chatter, wafted up.

Glenn padded out on the balcony in bare feet and shorts. He was a tall man, instantly dwarfed by Lafayette. Ellen introduced him. More handshaking between Glenn and Lafayette. Comments on the sunset, the warm night, the fragrant air.

Marjorie tried again to excuse herself.

"Hold on there!" Lafayette plunked one heavy arm down on her shoulders. His eyes were slightly slanted, his eyebrows thick, his forehead broad. He was handsome in a comical sort of way.

"We're having dinner at the El Toro. Why don't y'all join us?"

Ellen looked at Marjorie. She stood slightly behind Lafayette, her neck caught in the hook of his arm. Her orange mouth twisted, then tightened.

"Oh, I don't think so," Ellen was saying at the same time Glenn was accepting.

"Sure, sure, it'll take us a few minutes to get cleaned up . . ." Glenn looked smugly over at Ellen.

Lafayette's big face lit up like a jack-o'-lantern. He released Marjorie and clapped his hands together.

"Okay then! Half an hour? Downstairs in the lobby?"

Marjorie, without a word, pushed past him and went back inside. Ellen had the grim sense she wasn't interested in having dinner with a strange white couple.

"See you soon," grinned Lafayette, backing toward the door. "Glenn and Ellen, right?" He clicked his fingers as if fixing their names in his mind.

"Like the wine," said Glenn. It was one of his favorite jokes. Ellen had heard it a hundred times, exactly ninety-nine more than she cared to.

"Hey, now, *there* you go!" said Lafayette, catching on. He jabbed his finger at Glenn. "That's funny, man. Very funny." And he kept the grin on his face as he backed through the door to his room.

Glenn whistled as he lathered his face, Ellen spoke from the shower. With water coursing over her, she generally found it easier to say what was on her mind. "I think it's weird to go off and eat dinner with total strangers."

The whistling stopped. "What the hell are you talking about?" Ellen knew from the tightness in his voice that he'd pulled one cheek taut to accommodate the razor. "They're nice people." He said enthusiastically, in the hopeful voice he used to disguise disappointment.

"*Nice?* How can you tell?"

Glenn poked his head up against the shower curtain. Half of his jaw was coated with white shaving foam. "I think it's important to find opportunities to mix with people of other races."

Ellen opened the shower curtain. "Are you kidding? That's how you think of them? *People of other races?*"

"You know what I mean," he said. "We don't have any black friends and now there's a chance to mingle. It's a good opportunity."

"Oh God, Glenn."

He turned around and picked up his razor. "Now you're going to tell me I'm a racist. Well, I think when people make an effort, you need to respond."

"I only wish you'd asked me if *I* wanted to go."

"What do you want me to do, go over there and tell them we're not coming?" He used his accusing voice, the "it's all your fault" voice.

"Yes, actually, I do." The shower water rained down on her. Ellen felt the familiar tightening of contrariness inside her, her final defense against anger.

Glenn shook his razor at her. "Why the fuck do you do this? We're on *vacation*, for Christ's sake."

"Not for *Christ's* sake." Ellen plunged her face into the powerful stream of water. "We won a supermarket contest because after I get off work I spend half my life at the supermarket. That's why we're here, Glenn."

Glenn's voice vibrated through the shower curtain. "You really expect me to go say we're not meeting them for dinner?"

"You mean these nice *black* people, don't you?" Ellen said. "You know we're not doing them any favors, don't you? You accepted. Now you can un-accept."

"You're out of your mind. They'll think we're . . ."

Ellen popped her head through the curtain again. "If you'd paid any attention, you'd realize that the wife, what's her name, Marjorie, didn't want to go out with us either."

Glenn was trimming carefully around his mustache. "Ellen, shut up. Can't we just go out and have a good time for once?"

They never fought with conviction anymore. They lacked the energy for it. As usual, Ellen thought, Glenn had missed her point and continued on, confident in his.

The El Toro was a big pink mission-style stucco five blocks down from the hotel. Glenn, dressed in a white shirt and black linen pants, fell into step with Lafayette. He and Ellen had not spoken the whole time they were getting ready. Ellen, in her loose cotton dress, watched his back with a mixture of annoyance and lost affection. The familiar hunch of his shoulders. The awkward launch of one slightly bowed leg stepping in front of the other. These things had once inspired tenderness. Now they conjured up, at best, indifference and, at worst, irritation. Over the last few years her heart had hardened and shrunk into a tight kernel of ill will. Ellen no longer loved Glenn. He knew it too, but they hadn't spoken about it. Now he was pointing toward the sea and Lafayette nodded furiously. Ellen's eyes followed the direction of Glenn's finger. In the twilight a surfer was cresting a wave.

Lafayette's voice drifted back to her. "I'll take you out there tomorrow, buddy. We can rent boards."

Ellen turned to Marjorie, who had been silent. "Is your husband having a midlife crisis too?" She meant it as a joke, an offhand way of connecting with Marjorie and trying to stave off her own rising despair.

But Marjorie kept her head averted, showing no sign of having heard. Ellen thought how beautiful Marjorie looked in her red linen shift and black T-strap sandals. Beside her, she felt matronly and clumsy, as if the extra ten pounds she carried had just announced themselves in some audible way.

Ellen fought the urge to turn around and head back to the hotel when Marjorie said, with precise enunciation, "What do you mean, a *midlife crisis?*"

Ellen tried to capture the levity in her straining voice. "They're talking about surfing tomorrow. Two grown men. Isn't that *crazy?*"

Marjorie seemed not to comprehend. They were now passing three cabbies lounging around a taxi stop. Marjorie ignored the "*Sssst, morena!*" from the shortest of the group, a man with his shirt unbuttoned and a gold cross on his chest, who had fixed his liquid-eyes on her legs. "Surfing?" she said vaguely, and looked out at the dark water without further comment.

They were given a table on the patio, just a few feet from where the band was setting up. Ellen listened to the rhythm of the incoming tide wash over Glenn's and Lafayette's voices, smoothing them out until they were indistinguishable from each other. In San Francisco it was usually much too cold to ever really enjoy the beach. Only crazy people went into the water there, and then not for long. Now Ellen had a sudden desire to abandon her dress and go fling herself into the water. It had been a long time since she'd been swimming and the thought of gliding through water appealed to her.

"Nice night for a swim," she murmured to Marjorie, who was busy studying the pink, portfolio-sized menu.

"I never learned to. I've always been afraid of water."

"We're in the minority in our neighborhood," Glenn was saying congenially, as if testing this fact out for Lafayette's approval. "Mostly Mexican and Asian, I'd say. A few blacks."

"Yeah, well, tell me about being in the minority," Lafayette said. "We're over in the Oakland Hills. We lived in San Francisco when we were first married, but the weather didn't suit us. Don't you know about the radio towers on the top of Twin Peaks, the ones that send out subliminal messages that say, 'Black people, move to Oakland'?"

Glenn looked startled. Lafayette burst out laughing. "It's a joke, man, though not far from the truth. For a major city, San Francisco's got a tiny black population, you know." The waiter interrupted for their orders, and

Lafayette ordered two bottles of wine. "This is your first time here?" he asked after everyone's wine glass had been filled.

Glenn was eager to tell exactly how their trip had come about. He had told their neighbors and relatives, and even now, as the words spilled from his mouth, his syntax never varied. It was as if he were reciting a speech. Ellen couldn't get over how small he looked across from Lafayette. Glenn, who at times had loomed larger than life, whose presence had taken up all the space in her life, now seemed to all but disappear in the candlelight, and if she squinted her eyes ever so slightly she could cause everything about him except for the white shirt to fade into shadow.

"We came here years ago for our honeymoon," Lafayette said. "Just after I got out of med school."

Glenn leaped on this. "Med school," he said. "So you practice medicine." He was obviously impressed. And pleased. A black doctor, Ellen could read his mind. She downed her glass of wine and poured herself a second. The wine went right to her head, bringing up a roar of unrecognizable voices, all clamoring to be heard.

"A cardiologist." Lafayette grinned and reached out to squeeze one of Marjorie's hands. "I take care of other people's hearts and she takes care of mine."

It was obvious, from the weary expression on Marjorie's face, that this was an old joke. "No, I don't," she said flatly. "You're quite capable of caring for your own heart."

Touché! the voices in Ellen's head cried in unison. The woman has got some spark! Before she realized it, she was giggling aloud. Marjorie glanced up sharply. Ellen imagined what Marjorie was thinking: giddy white woman, no common sense. She recovered herself just as Glenn kicked her under the table. He quickly launched into one of his favorite stories about a client of his who was suing a drugstore over a folding lawn chair that unfolded and fell on her head. He had moved to rescue mode, diverting the attention from Ellen.

"Ellen doesn't usually drink so much," he remarked as Lafayette poured her a third glass. He had shifted into paternal mode, the one which guided him to apologize for her behavior.

"Yes, I do," Ellen lied and smiled broadly. She raised her glass and perversely proposed a toast. "To four days of rest and relaxation, to travel." She looked deliberately at Marjorie. "To new friends." It was the voices in her head talking. Strained, self-conscious. Ellen had never said anything so foolish in her life. She was sure Marjorie winced.

Everyone obediently raised a glass, then self-consciously clinked rims and stems together in the center of the table over a bowl of pink flowers floating in water.

Ellen leaned across to Marjorie. Maybe the woman was shy. "Do you two have children?"

There was a quick flicker in Marjorie's dark eyes. "No." She shook her head. "You?"

Ellen held up three fingers. "Three. Three boys. Bad, terrible boys. Three, six, and ten." She clicked them off her fingers. "I haven't had a vacation since the little one was born. Between working and raising three boys . . ." Ellen stopped. She realized she was "going on," as Glenn would say.

Marjorie's eyes rested on her unwaveringly from across the table. In the candlelight Marjorie's skin glowed like bronze. "Boys can be a handful," she said carefully.

"Mine are monsters. They keep me in a constant state of uproar. I needed this break, let me tell you. Just the other day they had me so frazzled I wore two different colored shoes to work. I didn't even notice until one of the secretaries pointed it out in the afternoon."

Marjorie never changed expression. Ellen was sorry she'd made the effort. It's not shyness, she decided. Probably if I were black, I wouldn't want to feel obligated to sit and entertain some white woman.

Marjorie readjusted herself in her seat, then unexpectedly she leaned forward. "I can beat that, girl," she said. She spoke under the voices of the two men. "Last week I mailed our bills in a public trash can."

"You what?"

There was the merest hint of a smile on Marjorie's mouth. Lafayette glanced over at her. Marjorie, unaware, went on. "That's right, girlfriend. Walked right past the mailbox up to a public trash can and tossed my letters in. Bills mostly, if you can believe that. They just kind of floated around down at the bottom in a sea of Coca-Cola."

Lafayette laid a heavy hand on Marjorie's arm. "You don't need to be telling everyone about that."

Marjorie ignored him. "I had to reach down inside that can, just like a bag lady, and fish out my stuff." Her mouth twisted ever so slightly. Ellen couldn't tell if she was smiling or getting ready to cry.

Lafayette frowned, removed his hand, and turned back to Glenn. He went back to explaining the difference between good and bad cholesterol.

Marjorie continued. "Sometimes," she said, her voice barely audible, "I think I'm losing my mind."

She pierced a prawn with the tines of her fork. And then, as if she had been asked, she leaned over and offered Ellen a taste of the broiled scampi. Very delicately, her bracelet jangling on her thin wrist, she lifted her fork to Ellen's lips and deposited one large prawn in her mouth. "They make outrageous garlic sauce," she said. "You'll love it."

Lafayette had launched into a repertoire of uneasy racial jokes. Ellen heard him say, "And then the rabbi said to the black guy . . ." He finished up with the punch line "But the doctor told me I was impo'tant!"

She thought Glenn laughed too hard. He told a "There was a black guy and an Italian guy" joke, which came out badly for the Italian guy (though if told to an Italian, the black guy got the raw deal), and then launched into his "special pig" joke which could be adapted from the old black man to the "redneck farmer" version. Lafayette tipped way back in his chair and hooted.

Marjorie and Ellen managed to insert small bits of polite talk into the conversation. Marjorie was a registered nurse. She worked in pediatrics, but had taken a leave of absence from the clinic. She didn't say why. Ellen managed to find out she was originally from North Carolina, and that she and Lafayette had bought their house in Oakland almost ten years before.

Later, when the band, a group of four young men, struck up a Spanish rendition of "Feelings," Lafayette dragged Marjorie up from the table to dance, and Glenn followed suit with Ellen.

For the next song, a fast salsa number, Ellen danced with Lafayette. She stepped all over his toes while he chuckled and skillfully maneuvered himself around and beside her. Marjorie danced distractedly by herself, with Glenn next to her rocking back and forth on his heels and clicking his fingers. Ellen thought how much of what Marjorie did seemed like a duty. The couples traded back and forth for several more numbers. Ellen felt embarrassed by Glenn, his awkward, jerky motions and the earnest working of his mouth in concentration. Then she felt ashamed of herself for her lack of charity. She saw herself and Glenn as she was sure Marjorie saw them: strangers straining too hard toward friendship.

When the wine wore off, Ellen pleaded weariness. She was surprised when Marjorie suggested that the two of them walk back to the hotel so the men could stay longer.

"Absolutely not!" protested Lafayette, though Ellen could tell Glenn thought it was an excellent idea.

Glenn asked for the bill, and it turned out Lafayette had already slipped the waiter his credit card. Glenn began objecting—Ellen thought, ah, methinks he protests too much!—and yanked out his own wallet, displaying an array of credit cards, most of which should have been buried in their back yard and put out of their misery.

"Put your money away, man," said Lafayette, "this is *my* treat. You can get it next time."

Ellen thought she understood what was happening, as she and Marjorie picked their way silently, even gratefully, over the darkened sidewalks—that Glenn and Lafayette, just a few feet behind, were taking odd solace in each other's anonymity. In the darkness she was filled with longing, but it had nothing to do with Glenn. Ellen knew she was mostly at fault with Glenn, that what she'd known for a long time he was now only beginning to realize. Cowards that they were, neither of them had the guts to bring it up. What

Ellen couldn't figure out was why Marjorie didn't love Lafayette and which one of them, Marjorie or Lafayette, was at fault.

Before she fell asleep that night, she rolled over in the dark, confused by and drawn to the heat of Glenn's body. She began to kiss his chest, pretending he was a stranger, imagining a different face, maybe even Lafayette, dancing inches from her. Glenn exhaled sharply into the air, then pushed himself suddenly inside her. Afterwards, Ellen felt ashamed of herself. Glenn held on to her tightly and whispered, "I told you all we needed was some time away." Ellen closed her eyes and imagined she had dived into the ocean and was riding the crest of a wave just before it crashed and spilled her onto sand with the consistency of angel hair. She pushed away from Glenn and turned over on her side. She lay there for a long time pretending to be asleep. She knew from the way Glenn shifted around and behind her that he knew it too.

The next morning, just as Ellen was rousting herself out of bed, Lafayette knocked on the door to invite Glenn to play golf, something Glenn had never done in his life, but which he eagerly agreed to without consulting her. Apparently the surfing idea had been abandoned. Ellen sagged back against the pillows and realized she was paying for last night's wine. Glenn brought her two aspirin and a glass of water before he left. She rested another half hour or so, with the drapes drawn, then got up and went downstairs, forcing herself to eat some of the continental breakfast offered in the hotel lounge. The lounge was empty, except for a small Mexican woman in white who was reading a magazine and sipping coffee.

A few minutes later, Marjorie appeared. She was wearing white shorts and a red halter top. She looked rested. Ellen felt self-conscious about the whiteness of her own legs compared to Marjorie's smooth brown calves. She tucked her legs under her, tried to make herself seem even smaller.

"Good morning," said Marjorie coolly. "I see Lafayette talked Glenn into golf." She studied the tray of breakfast rolls a moment, examined a piece of fruit which she rejected, then poured herself half a cup of coffee.

"Glenn's thrilled. I woke up with a hangover."

"They're kind of two peas in a pod," Marjorie observed. "I don't play golf."

Ellen had finished her second pastry and stood up. "I think I'm going down to the beach to get some sun," she said, by way of invitation. "What are you planning to do?"

"I have a massage appointment," said Marjorie. Before Ellen could ask her more about this, she had turned, coffee cup in hand, and headed back upstairs. Ellen watched her go, started to call out, then thought better of it.

Ellen strolled out on the empty beach and took a short swim. The water was warm. It was like taking a bath. She found herself staring occasionally up at the hotel for some sign of Marjorie on the balcony. No one else was on the beach. She tried pretending she missed Glenn, but she didn't. She floated on her back in the water and let the sunlight burn through her eyelids. She imagined herself being carried out to sea. She imagined washing up on shore on the other side of the world, dressed only in her swimsuit, without wallet or money, and no way to prove who she was.

On her way back to the room, she stopped at the desk and asked if there had been any phone calls. Nothing. She asked about going into town and the desk clerk told her to walk out front when she was ready and take a taxi.

Aside from the open-air market, downtown Puerto Cobre was mostly made up of stores with overpriced souvenirs. She stopped in front of a window displaying an orchestra of stuffed frogs dressed to look like mariachis. She bought postcards for the boys, though she'd see them before the postcards got to them, and she bought her mother-in-law a shawl that was exactly like something she could buy at home in the Mission District. Then she strolled out along the seawall and watched a group of teenage boys and girls flirt and tease one another.

The heat was overpowering. This time of year in San Francisco the fog was clearing late, if at all, and Ellen imagined the general dreariness of gray skies. She bought an *horchata* from a street vendor and drank it slowly, savoring the sweetness. Then she climbed in a taxi and headed back to the hotel. It was still early.

Glenn wasn't back yet, and the air in their closed-up room was suffocating. The maid had come and straightened, and left a card on the pillow which said, "Your room was cleaned by Rosa." Ellen opened the sliding glass door to let in the air, found a *People* magazine, and went down into the courtyard of the hotel. She longed for a breeze, but the air around her was still. The wind chimes overhead hung silent. An American couple sat waist deep in water at the pool bar, laughing and drinking, and getting drunker by the minute. Ellen guessed they were in their sixties. The woman was dressed in an awful ruffly, skirted pink one-piece, her fat white thighs floating in the water. The man wore turquoise swimming trunks that came up to his armpits, and wrap-around sunglasses. Ellen heard the man say to the bartender in badly accented Spanish, "*Una otra bebida par la mujer!*" and then he yelled over to Ellen, "How do you say 'bride' in Spanish?" Ellen shrugged. Newlyweds.

She tried to imagine what it would be like to get married at their age. Twelve years she had been married to Glenn, plus the three years that they lived together while he finished law school. Her mother had warned her. "If you live together first, chances are it won't work out." Ellen had laughed, called her provincial, myopic, old-fashioned. Last year her mother died very quickly of cancer. She had been married exactly fifty-three years, something which she saw as a triumph.

The woman in the pink bathing suit began to sing "Well, I'm always true to you darlin' in my fashion . . ." The man leaned over and kissed her on the forehead. The top of his bald head was freckled from the sun. They both looked as if the reddened skin on their shoulders were made of leather.

Feeling weak from the sun, Ellen got up and went back upstairs. She was halfway curious to see if Glenn had returned, knowing he wouldn't have, and he hadn't. She rinsed out her bathing suit in the bathroom sink and hung it on the balcony railing to dry. The sliding glass door to Marjorie's room was closed, the curtain drawn.

Ellen wandered down the hall. It was dead silent. She paused in front of Marjorie's door and listened. She wondered in Marjorie were in there and if she would mind if Ellen knocked. Ellen raised her hand and tapped lightly on the door with three fingers. She waited. The hallway carpet smelled faintly of insecticide. She tapped again.

Just as she was about to give up and turn away, the door was cracked open just a couple of inches. Ellen could make out only the tips of Marjorie's fingers, and a crescent of light from one of her eyes.

"Yes?" she said coldly, as if they were strangers.

"Oh, sorry, did I wake you?"

"Do you need something?"

"Just wondered if you'd heard from Glenn and Lafayette."

"No, and I don't expect to."

"They've been gone a long time. How long does golf take?'

Marjorie shrugged.

Ellen couldn't make herself leave. "How was your massage?" she persisted. "I was thinking of getting one myself." This was a lie. Ellen disliked massages.

Marjorie widened the door slightly. She was wearing a robe that she held together with one hand. Ellen could see the white lace of a brassiere through her fingers. "Massage is relaxing," said Marjorie. Ellen couldn't decide whether Marjorie was making fun of her or not.

"Did you go to a man or a woman?"

"It's a woman, but she leaves at noon," Marjorie said. "You have to check with the desk clerk for her schedule." For a moment Ellen thought she was going to shut the door. Instead, she said, "Come on in," and stepped back to let Ellen by.

The room was dark and claustrophobic, the curtains pulled shut. There was a stale, tight odor Ellen associated with sleep. A man's wet swimsuit dried over the bathroom doorknob. There were two open suitcases overflowing with clothes. Right off the bat, Ellen noticed the twin beds, like out of a fifties movie. Both had been slept in. Otherwise, the room was like Ellen and Glenn's room, just turned around.

"Lafayette thrashes," Marjorie remarked, though Ellen hadn't asked. Her robe fell open partially and Ellen saw the flatness of her brown stomach. Marjorie's hair stood stiffly off her head.

The twin bed nearest the door was rumpled.

"What time is it?" Marjorie yawned.

"Three. Four. It's really hot outside. I'm bored to death. I guess I don't know what to do if there aren't kids jumping all over me."

Marjorie sat on the edge of the unmade bed and scratched her scalp.

"Look," Ellen said, "Maybe I should go . . ."

Marjorie looked up. In the semidarkness the blue-white globes of her eyes stood out against her dark face. "It's up to you."

But Ellen didn't go. Instead she took a chance. "You want to go down in the courtyard and sit in the pool and have a drink? They have a bar right in the pool. I never drink at home, but you're supposed to drink on vacation." She meant this as a joke, but Marjorie didn't respond. She looked at Ellen as if expecting her to make the decision for her. "Of course if you don't want to . . ."

"Okay," said Marjorie. She got up and went into the bathroom to shower. Ellen took a seat in the vinyl chair in the corner. It took Marjorie almost half an hour to get ready. Ellen stared at the chaos of the darkened room and thought about what it might be that makes people fall out of love with each other.

They waded waist-deep to the bar and sat on the submerged stools.

"This is nice," said Marjorie. She looked down at her legs floating weightlessly. "I don't usually like the water."

Ellen smiled. She felt she had accomplished something, that Marjorie was beginning to trust her. "These places always seem so artificial to me," she remarked.

"How do you mean?"

"You know, fake sand, a pool, when you could swim in the ocean . . ."

Marjorie shrugged. "I like it. It's not meant to be like real life. That's the whole point."

Ellen's piña colada was too sweet, almost syrupy, but she sipped at it anyway.

Marjorie surveyed the courtyard with its large pots of colorful flowers. "I'm leaving Lafayette," she said matter-of-factly and toyed with the umbrella in her drink.

Ellen wondered if she'd heard right.

"We don't even live together anymore as it is. I've been staying with a girlfriend in East Oakland. And I've just rented an apartment down by the lake. When we get back, I'm moving there."

Ellen curled her toes over the rungs of the underwater bar stool. "I don't understand."

"Lafayette begged me to take this trip with him. I told him there was no point, but you can see how Lafayette doesn't take no for an answer. It's what makes him a good doctor, I guess. That drive he's got. The man never gives up. Nothing's ever finished. Not even us." She took a sudden interest in the gold cross she wore on a chain around her neck.

Marjorie was perfect, thought Ellen, from her earrings to her nails to her long legs shimmering in the water. "You both seem like such nice people." As soon as the words were of her mouth, she knew she'd said something foolish.

"Oh, we are. You know, responsible, respectable, nice people. Lots of friends. Church-going. Very nice. No one nicer than Marjorie and Lafayette." There was an edge to her voice.

"You can't work things out?"

Marjorie shook her head. "Out of the question."

"You're sure?"

Marjorie trailed one of her manicured hands through the water. Without looking up she said, "Three months ago our son died. It was a Saturday. I was at home painting the trim of our new sunroom."

Ellen didn't say anything. She looked at the brilliant blue sky and tried to imagine infinity. She couldn't make sense of what Marjorie was saying. She hadn't even known Marjorie had a son.

Marjorie began to recite. "It was an accident. You know how accidents are. Nobody's fault. Lafayette took Michael—that was our son's name, named for my father—ten years old—for a bicycle trip. An overnighter. Up to the Napa Valley. You know, sleeping bags, the whole bit. They were crossing the highway. I don't even know where exactly. Lafayette said the road was clear. No cars. Michael was right behind on a new mountain bike we'd just bought him. There was a rise to the right. A car was coming fast, but Lafayette didn't see it. Lafayette got to the other side." She paused. "Michael didn't."

Marjorie ordered another drink. "I hate to drink," she said. "I work out too much to handle alcohol."

"When?" Ellen asked softly. "When did you say your son died?"

"Three months ago. Three months ago yesterday actually. He's buried in the cemetery in Piedmont. But you didn't ask me that, did you?"

"How terrible," said Ellen. Her mind jumped to her own sons, fifteen hundred miles away. "Lafayette must feel terrible."

"Lafayette feel terrible? Jolly old good-time, good-natured Lafayette?" Marjorie laughed. "Yeah, he's heartbroken, but you'd never know it, girl. No, he's too busy being the big strong black man, just like he wanted our son to be.

Tough. Better than everyone else. Faster, smarter, sharper, tougher. Better than the white boys is what Lafayette always said you had to be."

Tears appeared from under Marjorie's sunglasses and ran down her cheeks. The bartender looked away. Ellen wanted to reach over and touch Marjorie's hand, but she didn't.

"The thing is," said Marjorie. "I can't stand to look at him. I can't tell you just how much I can't stand to look at him."

Ellen ordered them each another piña colada. She took several long sips. The combination of the alcohol and the sun made her feel fuzzy, forgetful, almost relieved. Ellen imagined losing her boys. She imagined losing Glenn. In the crossfire from the gun battles in their neighborhood, to a falling tree, to a reckless car, to one of those rare lightning bolts that could mean the demise of an entire family. It was a terrible thought and Ellen knew it, but she had run it sometimes like a dare through her mind. And now here was Marjorie, a lightning rod for Ellen's own fears. It had actually happened. The worst had actually happened.

Ellen said to Marjorie. "What a terrible loss for you."

"You have no idea," said Marjorie and she took a long sip through her straw.

"No," said Ellen. "You're right, I don't." Her legs were suddenly chilled in the water. "Is there anything I can do?"

Marjorie turned and looked at Ellen as if she were a crazy woman. "Anything you can do? Don't you think if there was, I'd ask?"

Glenn was exhausted and sunburned when he returned at seven from scuba diving. Ellen had fallen asleep on their bed and awakened to the sound of the key turning in the lock.

"Scuba diving?" she said drowsily, wondering if she'd somehow gotten the day wrong. "Scuba diving?"

Glenn scratched his head sheepishly. "Golf didn't exactly work out." He explained that he and Lafayette had decided instead to rent equipment from someone named Hector who took them out in a leaky boat. "Lafayette's a maniac," he told her proudly, as if this signaled some accomplishment of his own. "The guy is fearless, utterly fearless. Doesn't let anything stop him."

"And you?" Ellen said. "You've never scuba-dived in your life, so tell me who's the maniac?"

"It was incredible, Ellen. You should see the stuff that's down there."

"I think it was a very dangerous thing you two did."

"The man's a barracuda," said Glenn. "You know where he grew up?" He paused for emphasis. "South side of Chicago. You know, poor. Serious poor. Typical story. No dad. Just a grandmother. He told me it was sheer stubbornness that got him to college and into med school. I believe it. The man is a barracuda."

"I thought you had to have a license or something for scuba diving."

"This is *Mexico*," said Glenn. "I wish I'd had the boys with me."

Ellen's mouth felt dry and thick. "I hope you don't really mean you wished you'd had the boys with you. It's bad enough you'd risk your own neck."

Glenn peeled his clothes off. His skin had a sheen, as if it were still coated with water. "What did *you* do, sleep the day away?" He meant this as a joke, but Ellen sensed he might have also considered it a possibility.

"No. I sat in the pool bar and got drunk with Marjorie."

She flung herself back on the bed and let the ceiling whirl. Four piña coladas and a bowl of pretzels for dinner. Ellen was in love with Marjorie, the mystery of Marjorie, all the pain inside her. That Marjorie had made her her secret sharer, something that Glenn had no idea about, gave Ellen a sense of sudden purpose.

"Marjorie's some woman," Glenn said, standing naked before Ellen. "Lafayette's a lucky man. He's so in love with her. Just like me with you." He bent down and rubbed his face against hers. Ellen pulled away from the sandpaper roughness of his cheek. He kept on. "You were so sweet last night!"

Ellen sat up and pulled even farther away. "They're getting divorced," she said fiercely.

Glenn laughed. "Yeah, right." He poked her playfully in the crotch.

"I'm serious. They're getting divorced. Marjorie told me this afternoon." Glenn didn't buy it. "Nah, she's just pissed we went off today."

"I don't think so," Ellen said. "I think that's Lafayette's version." She wanted to hurt Glenn. "You know he's just using you to avoid being around Marjorie. You're a distraction."

She was saving the best for last.

"JE-sus," said Glenn. "Am I in the right room?" He looked around with an exaggerated gesture.

Ellen pulled on her cutoffs and the Little League T-shirt. "I want to do something interesting tomorrow, Glenn. I want to rent a car and go see some sights. We only have a couple days here and I'm bored out of my mind."

Glenn looked uncomfortable. "Well, maybe in the afternoon. I promised Lafayette I'd do this fishing thing with him tomorrow."

"Fishing thing?"

"Yeah, fishing thing. You know, a couple of hours out in a boat. I'll be back before you know it."

"But you hate boats. You get seasick."

"Lafayette does too. But he's got these patches . . ."

Ellen managed to stand up. "I don't fucking believe you!" she said and went into the bathroom and started the shower full blast. "You don't know the first thing about your friend Lafayette!"

When she came out, Glenn was gone. She went downstairs and ate a bowl of lousy American soup by herself in the empty hotel snack bar. Disgusted, she went out for a walk on the beach to clear her head. The sun was setting. She left the pristine strip of white sand and wandered down a beach littered with beer bottles and scraps of paper. Several Mexican families were grouped along the sand staring out at the glowing horizon. A woman with a baby squatted by the edge of the water. As Ellen passed, the woman smiled up at her. Ellen smiled back, enjoying the thought that what had just passed between them, two strangers in a lightning-quick exchange, went deeper. She considered then how easy it would be to keep walking, never looking back until La Gran Duchesa was a speck in the background. She wondered where she might spend the night and what Glenn would do if she didn't return. She tried to imagine what he would tell the children when he returned home without her.

On her way back, the wet sand cooled the soles of her feet. A half dozen young men sat on a rock in the shallows drinking beer. One of them waved and Ellen waved back. She could hear Glenn telling her she was too careless, but she was beyond caring. La Gran Duchesa loomed ahead, turned a rosy pink in the sun's last light. Ellen ducked under the rope that separated the two beaches. She considered her return a defeat. She glanced up toward the shared balcony. It was empty. Her own door appeared to be shut, but the door to Marjorie and Lafayette's room was wide open. From where she stood, Ellen could see the sail of white drapes luffing in the breeze. She stopped and listened. Drifting downward was the muted sound of crying. Immediately she thought of Marjorie, so tightly contained, finally giving in to grief. Then she got a pang thinking it might be Glenn, but she was sure it wasn't. A moment later she caught sight of Marjorie exiting the hotel and briskly retreating down the beach. The thin, disturbing sobs continued from above. Ellen tried to imagine the person who could make such sounds; she was both fascinated and saddened.

Lafayette and Glenn left mid-morning. They'd invited her, but she'd said no. It was just as well, Ellen thought, she would go to the beach and read. She had no idea what kind of fishing they could do at that time of day, but she put on a cheerful front as the two of them trooped off together toward Lafayette's rental car, Glenn with his long pale legs in a pair of shorts and Lafayette sauntering in his flowered shirt and shorts.

Ellen stopped by the desk and picked up a beach chair. She spent the next few hours on the sand, with a book she'd brought along. The sun burned her flesh, and she imagined all the dangers away as watched her thighs darken. Mexican peddlers appeared now and then on the opposite side of the rope and called out to sell their wares. This time of year there weren't many, but occasionally she was interrupted by an insistent "Psst, señorita!"

and someone holding a scarf, a shawl, a dress, a hat and motioning for her to come take a closer look. She shook her head no, then discovered that any acknowledgment was interpreted as encouragement. She turned her chair and pretended not to hear them.

An older Mexican man in a white shirt and loose dark pants came along the beach sweeping the sand smooth with a broom. He passed close by, and Ellen observed him peripherally, but he never looked her way. Besides her, there was only a middle-aged gay couple in matching blue briefs, each with a pair of blue eyecups, spread-eagled on mats. Shortly after, the elderly newlyweds she had seen the day before in the pool spread out an oversized Mickey Mouse towel and played cards. They got redder and redder in the sun.

So this is vacation? Ellen thought. To hell with vacation. Vacations are for people who have good lives they can return to. She closed her book and gave in to the dizzying heat.

It was mid-afternoon when Ellen woke up, hungry and dazed. The sand was too hot to walk on. She slipped on her sandals, wrapped a towel around her waist, and went inside to order a sandwich and a soda from the hotel snack bar. As she passed through the lounge area, she caught sight of Marjorie sitting by the window overlooking the pool bar. She was holding an ashtray in one hand and smoking a cigarette.

Ellen started to walk the other way, but Marjorie glanced up calmly. "Hey." She blew out a stream of smoke.

Ellen tightened her towel around her self-consciously. Now that she was inside, she became aware that her oiled skin was not browning, but reddening. She made a joke about how vacations encouraged unhealthy lifestyles: drinking, smoking, tanning. "I'm out working on a case of skin cancer. Want to come out and sit in the shade with me? We could grab a cabaña."

Marjorie stubbed out the cigarette. Her expression was blank. "Okay," she said. She seemed relieved, as if she were being rescued. "I have to get my suit."

A few minutes later Marjorie joined Ellen in the cabaña. She was wearing a black two-piece bathing suit and a pair of sunglasses. She tied a red scarf over her hair and draped a white towel over her legs. Neither of the two women spoke. Though she had hoped Marjorie would talk, Ellen said nothing. Instead, she read her book and Marjorie slept. Or at least Ellen thought she slept. It was hard to tell whether her eyes were closed behind the dark glasses. Her body remained perfectly still.

At last, when Ellen reached for a bottle of water, Marjorie said, "I could lie here forever. This is almost as good as massage."

Ellen took a long swallow of water. The sun blazed against her exposed feet in the sand. "I have no desire to go back to San Francisco," she remarked. She wanted Marjorie to ask why, to recognize their common bond.

What Marjorie said was "You have good reason to go back. Your children are there." She was reminding Ellen of the gulf between them.

Ellen carved a little hole in the sand with her big toe. She watched it fill itself, grain by grain, in a miniature avalanche. "If I didn't have them, I wouldn't go back."

"But you do," Marjorie said. "You're blessed."

"I don't believe in God," said Ellen. "Not the way you do."

"I don't believe anymore," said Marjorie from behind dark glasses. "It's easy to believe in God when you have everything you want." She placed one hand on her forehead, as if checking her temperature. "Lafayette says what happened is God's will. I say any God who would want my son to be dead isn't the God I want to worship."

She said nothing else after that, but lay absolutely still. Ellen studied her periodically from over the top of her book; the narrow waist, the slight pucker of her navel, the muscled brown legs, and the gold cross glinting on the chain between her breasts. She felt a deep protectiveness toward Marjorie, infused with a longing and envy that extended beyond the boundaries of the roped-off beach.

When Glenn returned, Ellen resigned herself to temporary forgiveness and agreed to wander with him through the streets. They bought tacos at a small stand several blocks away and sat on the brown sand of the Mexican side of the beach. Glenn chatted about inconsequential things: his plan for cementing over the garage floor, which flooded during the rainy season; his thought that he would circulate a neighborhood petition to get rid of the bus shelter on the corner where kids dealt drugs. Because she thought it was deceptive of her to talk about their life together, Ellen changed the subject and ended up telling him about Marjorie and Lafayette's son.

It came as no surprise that Glenn knew nothing about it. He was silent for some time afterwards, staring out over the water, holding his half-eaten taco as if it were something he'd just found on the beach.

"Are you sure?"

"That's what Marjorie told me."

Glenn looked as if Ellen had somehow betrayed him. "He never mentioned it."

"He probably won't."

"I don't get it. He said nothing!"

"He's putting on an act."

"Jesus," said Glenn. "Marjorie really told you this?"

Ellen almost felt sorry for him.

"Yes."

"I didn't realize you and Marjorie covered so much territory." She could tell by his expression that his mind was working quickly, running over the events of the last two days, trying to put the pieces into place.

"We haven't really," Ellen tried to explain. "Marjorie keeps a lot to herself."

"And you?" asked Glenn, turning to her sharply. "What do you keep to yourself?"

"Oh, Glenn . . ." She scrunched her napkin into a tight ball in her fist. "I'm going to call the boys."

"You don't need to . . ."

Glenn got up and began walking swiftly back toward the hotel. He never looked behind. Ellen followed, but didn't catch up. When she got back to the room, Glenn was already on the phone.

Ellen went out on the balcony. She stood against the railing and looked out at the ocean, now dark and turbulent. She could hear Glenn's voice, full of fake cheer. "Hey, *amigo*, this is your old *padre* calling you from Mexico!" From the tone of his voice she knew he was talking to their oldest, Mark. He was telling him about the scuba trip, the fish, the plants, the coral. "Let me speak to John for a minute . . . Well, get him and tell him to hurry . . . Hey, Ben . . ." His voice rose. Ellen imagined Little Ben at the other end with his funny, crooked smile. "I went fishing, Ben, and scuba diving . . . your mom's fine, want to talk to her?" At the reference to herself, she stood poised to go back inside. But Glenn rattled on, excited. He talked on, faster and faster, as if time were getting away from him. "We'll be home day after tomorrow. You boys behaving? Let me speak to Grandma . . . Hi, Mom . . . yeah, yeah, I know I said that, but I thought we should just check in . . . they haven't burned the house down? . . . oh, she's fine . . . we're having a blast. Couldn't be more beautiful."

What? thought Ellen. This place isn't beautiful, it's hideous. There's not one pretty thing here, except the sunsets. There was a chill to the air. She wrapped her arms around herself and stood shivering against the railing. In a moment she would have her turn with the boys. But for now she was content to stand at a distance and simply imagine their voices.

It didn't bother Ellen one bit that Glenn and Lafayette set off to rent horses the next day. She had made it clear, hadn't she, that she preferred to be left alone? Yet as soon as Glenn was gone, she had regrets for the way she was going about all this. Marjorie had left for her masseuse and then was scheduled over at another hotel to have her nails manicured. Ellen learned this from Lafayette, who let it be known that he had arranged in advance for all sorts of appointments for Marjorie and that so far she'd had her hair done and legs waxed. "I promised her the works!" he said cheerfully. He winked at Glenn. "You know how women are, they love to be pampered." For the first time Ellen noticed the thick gold band with a row of diamonds on Lafayette's ring finger. It was an ugly ring, expensive and gaudy.

"Not all women like to be pampered," she said.

Glenn shot her a warning look, but she pretended not to see and gathered up a string bag with her suit and towel, and fastened her money belt around her waist under her T-shirt.

Outside the hotel she caught a cab into the center of town again and bought serapes for the boys. She bought more postcards and sat in a café and addressed them to a long list of people, some of whom she only vaguely knew. "What heaven! Puerto Cobre sunsets are the most beautiful in the world," she wrote. It took her over two hours to finish all the postcards. Then she went for stamps and mailed them. Duty accomplished. She'd told everyone what they would want to hear. Then she counted her traveler's checks, wondering how far they would get her.

She imagined herself traveling around the world. She would write to the boys every day. She thought of Ben's small hard body in her arms and his sour baby breath on her face. Ellen began to cry. She left the café and walked along the seawall. She wept loudly, knowing that it was safe because she was anonymous, and because no one would really care about an unhappy *gringa*.

"Our last night!" said Glenn, with intended irony, when they'd both gotten back to the room. He was making an effort to keep things light. "Are we speaking? You want to go out to dinner, or are we still mad?"

Ellen started to say, "Mad?" but didn't. Instead she said, "No Lafayette?" as a joke, to ease the tension.

"No Lafayette," he said. There was a rueful edge to his voice. "We're stuck with each other tonight." He added with hope. "Lafayette and I've got plans to get together back home. Know what he wants to learn to do? Hang gliding. Over there south of the Cliff House. Is this guy a nut, or what?"

"He's a nut all right," Ellen said. "A real nut with a death wish." She added, "Dinner sounds fine, your choice," because she didn't have the courage to disappoint him. She felt almost friendly toward him, but that was only because she knew that soon she would have to tell him. "I'm going down on the beach for an hour or so, before all the sun is gone."

"Take your sun protection," Glenn warned. "You're starting to burn." He reached out and caught her in his arms. "Ellen, do you even love me anymore?"

She stared into the face she knew so well it struck her as comical. His anxiety pulled on her like a weight. "Of course I do," she lied, wresting herself free. "Don't be silly."

"I tried to give you time to miss me over the last couple days . . ." He slowly released her. There was no anger when he turned away, only a tired sadness. "I think I'll call the boys while you're gone," he said. "Make sure they're okay."

"They're okay." Ellen started out the door. She paused and said with emphasis, "They're *okay*, Glenn." She felt bad for them both. "Tell the boys I love them. Tell them I've got presents. Tell them I'll see them very soon."

It was sunset. The sky was lit up as if it were on fire. Along the horizon the light was so blinding Ellen was forced to avert her eyes and focus on the dark waves lapping at the edge of the beach. Tomorrow they would go home. Tomorrow she would tell Glenn.

She found a spot on the sand and sat down. Instantly her chest expanded and she filled her lungs with air. She stretched her arms up over her head and let the last warm rays of sun play over her face. When she turned to lie down, she caught sight of a figure running down the beach toward her. She made out pink shorts and the flash of white T-shirt. As the figure got closer, Ellen recognized Marjorie, barefoot, pounding along the shore. She was coming fast and hard, her arms pumping at her sides.

Ellen put on her sunglasses to block out the glare of the setting sun and watched as Marjorie picked up speed. She was pounding harder and harder on the packed sand. Her head was thrown back, she was gulping in air. Ellen had no idea Marjorie was a runner. But then she thought how little she really knew about Marjorie at all. As she got closer, Ellen could hear the faint smack, smack of her bare feet striking the wet sand. She ran past Ellen, never noticing her. Ellen had a sudden urge to leap up and try to follow. There was an intensity in Marjorie's stride that dissuaded her. Without warning, Marjorie made a ninety-degree turn and plunged headlong into the surf. She completely disappeared. For a moment Ellen thought she was witnessing a suicide. Marjorie, who had made such a point of telling her she couldn't swim. But Ellen found herself rooted to the spot, unable to make a move to stop her. Her eyes focused on the spot in the water where Marjorie had disappeared, now streaked by orange light. Ellen had a vague thought that if she had to go for help she needed to know exactly where it was Marjorie had gone in. The waves rolled in and curled onto the beach. Ellen sat transfixed.

A moment later Marjorie resurfaced, and Ellen saw her dark arms pulling water and the flash of pink shorts above the waves. Now she swam as hard as she had run, her arms punching at the water. White foam followed in her wake. Her body bobbed up and down on the waves. Behind her, a large wave broke and rolled in. Marjorie came with it. She landed on the beach, coughing, her legs spread out behind her. When she stood, her hair hung ruined, dripping wet and sparkling with sand. She let the water run off her legs and onto the sand. She was out of breath, and her chest heaved. She placed her hands on her hips and sucked in air.

Ellen got up and moved cautiously toward her, beach towel in hand. When Marjorie saw her, she turned her head fast and looked back out over the ocean, her chest still heaving.

"Take the towel," said Ellen.

"I want to stay wet," Marjorie said. Droplets of water glistened on her eyelashes. Without makeup, she was beautiful, young. Three Mexican boys in blue jeans stood on the other side of the rope, idly watching the water. Marjorie observed them. "You know, this place makes me really sick. They aren't even allowed on the hotel beach."

Ellen didn't say anything.

"I guess it's the same the world over," Marjorie remarked matter-of-factly. "Black and brown people are usually on the other side of the fence."

"I thought you said you don't swim," Ellen said.

"I don't, I almost drowned out there." She cleared her throat several times.

"That was stupid," Ellen said, but Marjorie didn't answer.

Ellen turned and walked toward the hotel. She glanced back twice. Marjorie stood motionless in the same spot, her back to Ellen. Dwarfed by the ocean and backlit by the lowering sun, hers was a childlike silhouette. A breeze came over the water. Ellen thought about how she would explain it all to Glenn. She'd try first getting an apartment. Just during the weekdays. She'd come back on the weekends, help out, take the boys places. She'd still be involved, she'd still be a mother, but she wouldn't be a wife. And during the week she'd work longer hours. She might even exchange numbers with Marjorie. They'd get together and have coffee in the afternoons. Or lunch. They'd get massages, have their nails done together. Ellen would buy better clothes.

She passed through the courtyard. The pool was empty. She took the stairs fast and easily. The door to their room was partially open. On her approach, she heard the sound of voices. Then falsetto male laughter, followed by a deep voice. Ellen paused just outside the door and peeked in. Glenn and Lafayette were sitting, one on either side of the double bed by the window, drinking beer. Glenn was in his boxer shorts and Lafayette had on the ridiculous flowered shirt and shorts. Glenn said something Ellen couldn't quite catch and Lafayette threw his head back and howled too hard, like a wolf. Then Glenn burst out laughing and rolled back on the bed, clutching the beer bottle to his chest. They were playing at being great big ignorant boys getting away with something.

Ellen backed away a couple of inches so they wouldn't see her. She stood shivering in the hallway and listened to her husband laugh in a voice that could have been Lafayette's. Then she realized it was Lafayette's voice, full of exaggerated heartiness. Why was it, she thought, she was no longer able to distinguish the joyful sounds her own husband was capable of?

1994

McGregor's Day On

David Means

McGregor walked to work each day pondering the high psychic cost of his own success. He considered himself more a philosopher than a businessman; more a thinker than a doer. But despite his philosophical bent, he still wore a suit to work each day.

It was late October. The dank stench of summer air had been shoved aside by a succession of Canadian cold fronts. The air was clear. McGregor drew deep breaths with each few steps. It felt good to take in as much air as possible. On the West Side, where he lived with his wife, the trees in Riverside Park had exploded into color one weekend, and then, just as quickly, dropped their leaves. Now the scrawny elms in front of the brownstones were whisked clean. Although the world was dying, McGregor felt a brisk, invigorating sense of transformation, which seemed for the good.

Inside the elevator he wedged himself between two men from the real estate firm on the fourteenth floor. He knew their faces from previous trips. Behind him, there was the brooding silence of people on their way to work. He faced his own fuzzy reflection in the silver doors. Even in the scratched metal, his sharp chin showed; his thick black eyebrows; the scoop of his receding hair. When the elevator jerked to the first stop and the doors slid open, he was startled. His body split in two. As he stepped aside to let the men through, one tossed him a nervous glance. The doors slid shut again. He ignored his own reflection, or tried to, looking at the numbers light up.

He was startled again when he reached his floor. The doors opened and Harrison Blake was standing outside facing him. He wore a white shirt, the collar of which pressed into his neck. His dark black skin was almost purple in the dim light and against the white walls of the lobby.

"Oh," Blake said when their eyes met. "Oh, I'm going up."

McGregor held the door open. It jerked against his hand, pulled back, then tried to shut again. Someone in the elevator said, "Come on, let it go or get on."

But Blake's voice had made McGregor pause. He waited for Blake to say more.

"I'm going up to personnel to see Jacobson," he said.

McGregor got out and let the door slide shut.

"Sorry," he said, "but I couldn't hold it any longer."

"That's all right," Blake said, his voice even softer. It seemed to fade into the noise of the building, the clicking of elevator cables behind the doors. "I'm in no hurry, actually."

"You're either getting fired or going over the new dental plan," McGregor said. "Or both."

"Right," Blake said and punched the up button. "I'm getting fired account of deese teeth," he said parting his lips into a mock smile. "They're too white. Too white for the likes of you."

They were bright, perfect teeth, McGregor noticed; it felt strange to look at his teeth that way, to really look closely at them.

Blake closed his lips and didn't smile.

"You're a wit on wheels," McGregor said, smiling hard at Blake. "The funny man." His jaw ached. It had been a long time since they had laughed together at anything.

"Lighten up McGregor," Blake said. Then he let a genuine smile break over his face. "God knows I can't lighten up." He held up the back of his arm to the light and examined it closely.

"Blake," McGregor said. "Seriously, Blake. Maybe it's time we sat down and talked this out a bit. I mean, I don't know what Jacobson's deal is. I hear things. But maybe I can help out in some way. And anyway, it's been a long time since—well, since you know. Okay?"

"I'll let you know."

When the elevator doors closed on Blake, the cables clanked and sang in the long shafts, running all the way up to the thirtieth floor and down into the deep recesses of the basement. In his mind, McGregor saw Blake being hauled up through space and time by the big drum-wrapped cables, away and outward.

"I've got to get to work," he said in the building's stuffy air.

By ten o'clock, McGregor was engulfed by several projects: a contract for a Japanese edition of an American children's book on barn owls, an easy sale of a German title to an American publisher, a fax sent to a subagent in Spain, a friend who wanted McGregor to represent his book of stories, a first serial deal to a magazine, and another friend who wanted to plan a weekend ski trip to Vermont. Under this load, he became so involved that he took no notice when Blake returned to his office.

McGregor continued to work, typing and sending more faxes to England, Japan, and West Germany, feeding the sheets one at a time into the machine and listening to it beep and dial: A green light spread across the paper as it fed, seeping out from the underside of the machine—a magic luminous fluid that picked the print from the page and piped it a few thousand miles away. Speed and magic, McGregor thought, typing a Telex to a Madrid newspaper.

At lunchtime, Blake appeared in McGregor's doorway with his arms up on the doorjambs and his overcoat on.

"You've been busting your chops today," Blake said. He looked behind McGregor out the window where the sky was gray, mottled and dirty; and the wind was blowing so hard the glass flexed and shook.

"Too many deals," McGregor said, immediately wanting to take it back. "How was it with Jacobson?"

"It was," he answered. "Jacobson has his job; I have mine." Then he shrugged and let go of the door frame.

"Anything I should know about?"

"I'm not sure," Blake said. "To be perfectly honest—well, not perfectly, but at least a little bit honest, I'm not sure if it's something anybody should know about or not."

Blake went to the window and put his palms to the cold glass. "Questions," he said, his lips close to the glass, whitening it with his air.

McGregor turned in his chair to face him and said, "Let's simplify this thing."

"What thing?"

"Everything, today, right now. I don't know what's bothering you, exactly, but maybe at least I can show you how to prioritize them."

"You would," Blake said as he sunk and squeaked back into the director's chair.

"What'dy mean by that?"

"You know sometimes you sound like one of those horrible self-help manuals you try to sell," Blake said. "You could prioritize your life into the ground if you had time. Lucky for you, you don't have the time—'cause you've got a whole load of priorities to prioritize, if you know what I mean."

"And not a lot of ground to prioritize them into," McGregor added.

Blake sat again, hanging his long leg over the wooden arm of the chair. It sagged under the weight. His pant cuffs slid up past his socks.

Then McGregor said, suddenly, "Let's take the rest of the day off and get out of this place."

"You mean shirk our responsibilities to the job at hand?" Blake put both legs over the arm of the chair. "Personnel would not like that."

"Maybe not," McGregor said. "But I wanted to prioritize; and, well, taking the afternoon off seems to be the first on the list—at least the first that is applicable to the two of us, equally."

The lobby floor was dark and glossy, freshly waxed. A delivery man stood by the check-in desk, leaning against his dolly. He eyed their silk ties;

the almost-matching knee-length mohair coats, cuffed trousers breaking slightly over spit-polished oxfords, and watched them as they went through the revolving door, rubber seals gulping air.

On the street, afternoon shadows, big and blocky, fell across the sidewalks.

"We're free," McGregor said and spun around in two complete circles, his coat splaying out like a ballerina's tutu.

He faced Blake, whose expression revealed only annoyance at his friend's overdramatic gesture.

"Do you feel guilty—taking time away from the job?" McGregor said.

"No, not really," Blake said. But his voice sounded tight. He was lying. They were the pained words of a lie, McGregor thought.

Where did that pain come from? He knew so little about his friend. He had guessed that Blake was ashamed of his background, imagining some Deep South childhood of poverty, skimped meals, and the desertion of a father.

"Personnel might be down on me for taking off an afternoon, but I'm certainly not down on it," Blake said, stepping off. "Come on."

They took McGregor's usual route to the subway, down Twelfth Street, past Sixth to the Seventh Avenue entrance near St. Vincent's Hospital, where cars double-parked to pick up or drop off patients.

"Just as many people are coming out as going in," McGregor pointed out. "I notice that every day. The great equalizer, hospitals."

"If you're lucky they are. If you're not, you die."

"I'll think about that," McGregor said.

They sat silently on the train. They had failed to achieve the proper words, the necessary chitchat. McGregor did want to say something right, something that would get to the heart of the matter—if he knew what that matter really was. He wanted to ask Blake, 'Is silence the great equalizer? Did I break us apart?' He could barely recall the night their friendship had ended, when Blake had become unwilling to let the walls down. McGregor could only understand his own bitterness. It grew from his own opinion of himself as a compassionate man. I am a compassionate man, he told himself repeatedly. I am. It is the one thing about myself of which I am totally sure.

But with Blake he came up against something hard and unmoving.

It had happened one night, the previous spring, when a freak blizzard struck and the railroads were shut down because of the snow. Blake could not get north to his home in Westchester and his wife, Malona. The streets were clogged with the heavy flakes. When McGregor invited him to stay the night at his apartment, Blake hesitated and called the train station several times before saying yes. Even then he did not sound enthusiastic about the idea. He said yes with a sigh, as if giving in.

That night, with the snow falling gently outside, they got drunk together in the jazz room at the West End bar, a gritty, beer-stained place on Broadway near Columbia. With the heat, the noise, and the music, they did little talking at first. But soon the ritual of drinking together, of lifting glasses in unison to their lips, matching vodka tonics one on one, made them want to talk.

"Blake, now that we're drunk, can I be honest with you?"

"You mean you aren't, usually?"

"That's funny. But what I mean is, can I be really honest with you?"

"I certainly hope so."

McGregor drank and wiped his mouth. "Blake, this is the Eighties, right? And my parents raised me to be open-minded about Blacks and to always respect them—but I never had any black friends, really. You're the first. So whatever I can know about black people, I'll know from you, to be honest. But you don't say much about who you are. Not really."

Blake pointed his finger to get the bartender's attention and ordered a whiskey straight up.

"To be blunt, fuck your parents, McGregor," he said, coughing after a swallow of his drink. "I don't want to shock you, but that's old ditty shit. My parents raised me to respect white people. What does that mean? You pull that one out of your vest pocket like a magic scarf, when the fact of the matter is you're scared of me the way I am. Why you want to know so much is because you're scared."

"I'm not scared to share with you, Blake. My life's an open book. My head's swimming I'm so drunk."

"Your life has been an open book since Plymouth fuckin' Rock." Blake held his glass near his chin and looked into the lineup of bottles behind the bar, backlit, glimmering.

"White people been shoving that open book in our faces since God knows when. And I'm not bitter. Don't get me wrong, McGregor. You wanted honesty, but don't get it wrong when you get it. This is the Eighties and you're getting the end-of-the-decade truth from me is all. And the truth is that nothing is as simple as digging up a few of a person's past facts and then thinking that fills out the whole story."

He swirled the ice in his drink. When they'd first arrived, the musicians had been working over a few sentimental, overblown pieces. The quartet had seemed so bored with the music that they were ready to fall off the rickety platform. As the night got deeper, though, the sets began to build. Now the men seemed uncontrolled, flaying away at the instruments.

"What do you want to know about me McGregor?" Blake said.

"What do I want to know?"

"Yes. What is it that I can tell you that would really make a difference between you and me?"

After he finished off the bottom of his drink, McGregor said, "I don't know. Let me think."

"How much time you need? You already had a couple of centuries. Down deep, you just know that any question you come up with will be an answer."

"You're drunk Blake."

The trumpet player was working his solo, drawing out the notes long and sorrowfully, as if pulling them out from the bell of his horn with a long rope. When he changed notes it was by pushing the keys down so slowly that they melded into each other.

"Does Jacobson treat you like the rest of us?"

"Who, him? In his fucking handmade shirt collars and deluxe wide striped seersucker with the French fly. No kidding. We were in the john pissing together and he tells me his tailor gives him a wide selection of zippers or whatnot for his flies. There he is giving me a history of his pants in earnest detail. Next thing, he calls me into his office to wonder why I'm not earning out this year's advance, and all I can do is try not to look at his crotch, wondering what kind of latch he's got between the world and his underwear."

"Don't make me laugh. That man has our lives in his hands."

"Ain't that the truth."

The crowd was getting silent. The trumpet player persisted taking all the air from the room.

"I don't know what to say," McGregor whispered.

"That's the point," Blake whispered back.

As the audience began to applaud McGregor saw his friend's lips set firmly together in an embouchure, as if he were finishing the trumpet solo.

The music ended. "Let's go," Blake said. "It ain't gonna get better or worse than that solo."

They went out onto snow-covered Broadway, staggering drunk. So clear and fresh, it wasn't any city they knew; it was like Bedford Falls in *It's a Wonderful Life*. Cars were stopped dead in the street, abandoned and left on their own. In the wedge of gray sky between the buildings, McGregor could trace the paths of flakes high into the sky.

"God am I drunk," he said.

"I'm not too bad."

"You're as drunk as I am, at least."

"How the hell do you know that?"

McGregor put his arm around Blake's shoulder, "Because we matched each other glass for glass and you can hardly walk now—and don't blame the snow for the way you walk. You're as good as drunk and you know it." He squeezed Blake against him.

Blake twisted out from under his arm. "Get the fuck off me," his voice cracked, arms up slightly, as if to fend off a blow.

McGregor clamped his arm tight around Blake's back. They stumbled under each other, down on the snowy sidewalk. Before he knew what hit him, he felt a fist sink into his gut. At that moment, Blake's face was right up close to his, sparkling with melted snow, balled up with fury.

He pushed back, but again he felt a fist dipping into his stomach. Then they rolled. He tossed his clenched hands into space, catching the bulk of a body at times. People gathered around them to watch.

McGregor began choking. He spit yellow bile into the snow. Sobbing, Blake rolled away, against the iron grating of a closed-up supermarket. McGregor let himself go faceup.

The bystanders, mostly students from the university, walked away shaking their heads.

Blake struggled to his feet and went over to help McGregor, reaching down with both hands and leaning back to pull him up. On the ground was the messy record of their fight, an imprint of McGregor's back and wide swoops from their boot toes.

Both still drunk, they walked to McGregor's apartment. At the apartment they drank hot herbal tea that Joanna made—and the fight became a distant action in another world.

Before he fell asleep that night, McGregor thought he would never forget the dull pain of Blake's eyes as the sky dumped into them.

The train squeezed into the curve of the South Ferry station, the end of the line, a tight fit.

"I knew we were going to end up here," Blake said, getting up. "At the end of the island."

Blake led the way up the stairs. Cavernous and smelly, the ferry terminal echoed violently with the din of the only people who traveled on a weekday midafternoon—the poor and destitute. Bag people loaded down with junk. The homeless. Tight-jeaned kids wandering, killing time.

They sat on a wooden bench in the middle of the room, facing the wide sliding doors above which a sign would light up announcing the ferry's arrival.

A flock of pigeons gathered high in the rafters, waiting for the slightest indication of food below. An old lady leaned down to toss bits of popcorn to the smooth floor, and the birds swooped down to fight over the bounty.

"My God," McGregor said, "I feel like I've been thrown back into nineteen-thirty or something."

"The whole room looks like it's coated in something sticky," Blake said. "It's a long road from Wall Street."

"Uum hum." McGregor nodded. A crowd gravitated knowingly to the doors. A shudder had triggered the migration as the boat lazily thudded into the berth at an angle askew to the rotting pylons.

Two workers shoved open the doors, and the crowd of standing people were vaporized by the bright light coming in through the windows outside the doors. Blake and McGregor joined in the mass movement to the boat, following directly behind the last straggler, an old woman, off-balance with a load of crinkly shopping bags. They went down the creaking floorboards, which seemed tacked together, then up the lowered ramp, covered with rubberized slipproof sheets, onto the boat—neither bow nor stern, just the side that happened to jam into the creosote-covered pylons.

The engine rattled and drummed the metal deck.

"Let's stay out here," McGregor said as he sat down on the bench between the entrance doors to the main cabin. All the other passengers were inside.

Blake stood with his coat pulled tight around him, shifting from foot to foot. The air smelled of dead seaweed, exhaust fumes that wafted up from the tailpipes, and rotting wood. The terminal was only half used. The other berth, next door, had been allowed to decay beyond repair, a pile of broken timbers and pigeon nests.

"Half of New York is dead and unused," Blake said as he studied the wound in the building.

McGregor said, "Do you remember the guy who went wild with the ax on the ferry and chopped up a bunch of people? I can't remember, but I think he killed someone. A cop tried to stop him, or shot him—an off-duty cop I'm sure, they're always off-duty when they get into situations like that."

A man came down and put up the chains. The entry ramps were raised and with a slight rumble of the engines the wide boat squeezed and bumped out from between the pylons, into open water, moving swiftly away from lower Manhattan.

The wind intensified as they left the terminal behind and a wide expanse of water, dark and chopping, opened up.

Blake stood looking very much, to McGregor, like he was poised for a movie scene—a lonesome, morose black man at odds with the city shrinking before him. He was the odd man out, job falling away from him—a round of cocktail parties, poetry readings, contract negotiations.

As they passed the Statue of Liberty, as close to open sea as they would get, Blake sat down.

"Do you want to go in?" McGregor gently asked.

"No, let's stay out here in the fresh air," Blake said. "It feels good to be out here and away from that place, doesn't it?"

"It does," McGregor answered. "The boat moves so fast. You're halfway out before you know it."

McGregor put his hands on his knees.

"I don't know what's happened to us, since the fight I mean. And this thing with personnel, I mean you're not connecting with anyone in the office. Well—you know. I don't have to tell you what's been going on with Jacobson; if anything, you should probably fill me in."

Consciously, he met Blake's eyes: "I want to be a good friend to you. And since that night, you've been lost to me."

Blake stood up and walked over to the railing, tilting his head up at the sky. Manhattan looked far away. Gulls still followed the boat wistfully, anticipating food.

"You know I've been trying to sell this Hanson novel, right?" Blake said, raising his voice over the wind. "And you know I think it's damn good. It's the one you always knew you'd get—the classic. And you knew it was going to be a hard sell, because it was a classic. But how hard should it be, actually? I don't know if it's being rejected because it's about a black man or black experience, or because it's just too goddamn good."

"Maybe it's time to let go of it," McGregor said. "That's the painful part of the job."

"Let go. Let go. Maybe you're right. That's exactly what Jacobson said—let go of it Blake. Now. Maybe we should all just let go of these things. Let the rejection letters bow us down: 'We did a black novel recently,' or, 'We found this to be a moving portrait of the black experience'—never a moving novel of human experience—'but it just isn't right for our list.' "

"I still don't know what happened with us, Blake."

Blake turned to look at McGregor.

"I know you don't McGregor."

"If it was that fight we had. Then I apologize, again. If that's what it is, I'll be glad to say I'm sorry. I didn't mean to pry into your life."

"McGregor," he said, pulling his body up a bit, "both of us were drunk. Both of us happened to allow ourselves to punch our true feelings out. But the truth be known, it was more than that, of course."

"Well, tell me."

"I can't. Part of it has to do with you wanting to know things in the first place, wanting to walk in my shoes, my muddy, shucked-up boots. You wanted to know just so you could know."

"There's nothing wrong with wanting to know someone."

"Let me put it this way, maybe my history is the key to friendship with you. Maybe. Maybe not. But who do you want to know? And why? What makes you want to know me, and not some other Joe on the street—now I know what you're going to say. Don't say it. You're gonna say I'm being ridiculous. Maybe I am. Maybe that's why I can't explain it, because it comes out ridiculous, it's based on the ridiculous, on those boots I keep seeing, on where I'm from."

McGregor shifted his feet. "But it's more than that. Isn't it? A lot more. I mean with personnel and everything."

"That's just it. You want it to be more. But my situation," he said flatly, "is no different and has all the difference from yours."

"What do you mean?"

"Face it, McGregor," he said, sadly, "basically, we're all in the same boat."

McGregor said, "Well, at least we're on the same boat."

They laughed.

"No, I mean we all are—very basically—we work, earn money, survive, or we don't. Maybe I'm closer to the don't."

Blake let out a long breath. The boat was closing quickly on Staten Island.

Blake continued, speaking in a low voice. "What's in it for you, McGregor?"

"What's in it for me?"

"Knowing these things, anyway. I mean what's in it for you?"

"I really don't know what you're talking about," McGregor said, a little angry. "It would make me feel good. All right? Just make me feel good."

"I don't mean to put you on the spot or to be facetious, but it's something I've been asking myself, around the office mostly; why someone wants to know the nitty-gritty stuff, when you shop, where you buy gas for the car."

"So there isn't anything we can do about it now," McGregor said in a way that wasn't angry, or judgmental. It was just a statement of fact.

"No," Blake said in the softest voice McGregor had ever heard from a man. It was a light brush of air against the vocal cords. "No, I'm afraid—and really, I do mean afraid—not."

When the walkways were lowered back in Manhattan, McGregor and Blake joined the rush up and into the terminal, then down the stairs to the subway platform where the number 1 train stood waiting with its doors open, ready to make its rush hour run into the heart of Manhattan and back out the other side.

When they reached 42nd Street, Blake said, softly, "Nobody owns nothing."

"Is that a question or an answer?"

"Both."

Then, upon the electronic ding-dong and the closing of the doors, he turned around on his way out of the station and gave McGregor, who was looking out the window, a slow, understanding nod of his head, and lifted his hand to wave good-bye.

1991

The Business Venture

Elizabeth Spencer

We were down at the river that night. Pete Owens was there with his young wife, Hope (his name for her was Jezzie, after Jezebel in the Bible), and Charlie and me, and both the Houston boys, one with his wife and the other with the latest in a string of new girlfriends. But Nelle Townshend, his steady girl, wasn't there.

We talked and watched the water flow. It was different from those nights we used to go up to the club and dance, because we were older and hadn't bothered to dress, just wore slacks and shorts. It was a clear night but no moon.

Even five years married to him, I was in love with Charlie more than ever, and took his hand to rub the reddish hairs around his wrist. I held his hand under water and watched the flow around it, and later when the others went up to the highway for more whiskey, we kissed like two high school kids and then waded out laughing and splashed water on each other.

The next day Pete Owens looked me up at the office when my boss, Mr. McGinnis, was gone to lunch. "Charlie's never quit, you know, Eileen. He's still passing favors out."

My heart dropped. I could guess it, but wasn't letting myself know I really knew it. I put my hard mask on. "What's the matter? Isn't Hope getting enough from you?"

"Oh, I'm the one for Jezzie. You're the main one for Charlie. I just mean, don't kid yourself he's ever stopped."

"When did any of us ever stop?"

"You have. You like him that much. But don't think you're home free. The funny thing is, nobody's ever took a shotgun to Charlie. So far's I know, nobody's ever even punched him in the jaw."

"It is odd," I said, sarcastic, but he didn't notice.

"It's downright peculiar," said Pete. "But then I guess we're a special sort of bunch, Eileen."

I went back to typing and wished he'd go. He'd be asking me next. We'd dated and done a few things, but that was so long ago, it didn't count now. It never really mattered. I never thought much about it.

"What I wonder is, Eileen. Is everybody else like us, or so different from us they don't know what we're like at all?"

"The world's changing," I said. "They're all getting like us."

"You mean it?"

I nodded. "The word got out," I said. "You told somebody, and they told somebody else, and now everybody is like us."

"Or soon will be," he said.

"That's right," I said.

I kept on typing letters, reeling them on and off the platen and working on my electric machine the whole time he was talking, turning his hat over and picking at a straw or two off the synthetic weave. I had a headache that got worse after he was gone.

Also at the picnic that night was Grey Houston, one of the Houston brothers, who was always with a different girl. His former steady girlfriend, Nelle Townshend, kept a cleaning and pressing shop on her own premises. Her mother had been a stay-at-home lady for years. They had one of those beautiful old Victorian-type houses—it just missed being a photographer's and tourist attraction, being about twenty years too late and having the wooden trim too ornate for the connoisseurs to call it the real classical style. Nelle had been enterprising enough to turn one wing of the house where nobody went anymore into a cleaning shop, because she needed to make some money and felt she had to be near her mother. She had working for them off and on a Negro back from the Vietnam war who had used his veterans' educational benefits to train as a dry cleaner. She picked up the idea when her mother happened to remark one night after she had paid him for some carpenter work, "Ain't that a dumb nigger, learning dry cleaning with nothing to dry-clean."

Now, when Mrs. Townshend said "nigger," it wasn't as if one of us had said it. She went back through the centuries for her words, back to when "ain't" was good grammar. "Nigger" for her just meant "black." But it was assuming Robin had done something dumb that was the mistake. Because he wasn't dumb, and Nelle knew it. He told her he'd applied for jobs all around, but they didn't offer much and he might have to go to Biloxi or Hattiesburg or Gulfport to get one. The trouble was, he owned a house here. Nelle said, "Maybe you could work for me."

He told her about a whole dry cleaning plant up in Magee that had folded up recently due to the old man who ran it dying on his feet one day. They drove up there together and she bought it. Her mother didn't like it much when she moved the equipment in, but Nelle did it anyway. "I never get the smell out of my hair," she would say, "but if it can just make money I'll get used to it." She was dating Grey at the time, and I thought that's what gave her that much nerve.

Grey was a darling man. He was divorced from a New Orleans woman, somebody with a lot of class and money. She'd been crazy about Grey, as who wouldn't be, but he didn't "fit in," was her complaint. "Why do I have to fit in with her?" he kept asking. "Why shouldn't she fit in with us?" "She was O.K. with us," I said. "Not quite," he said. "Y'all never did relax. You never felt easy. That's why Charlie kept working at her, flirting and all. She maybe ought to have gone ahead with Charlie. Then she'd have been one of us. But she acted serious about it. I said, 'Whatever you decide about Charlie, just don't tell me.' She was too serious."

"Anybody takes it seriously ought to be me," I said.

"Oh-oh," said Grey, breaking out with fun, the way he could do—in the depths one minute, up and laughing the next. "You can't afford that, Eileen."

That time I raised a storm at Charlie. "What did you want to get married for? You're nothing but a goddamn stud!"

"What's news about it?" Charlie wanted to know. "You're just getting worked up over nothing."

"Nothing! Is what we do just nothing?"

"That's right. When it's done with, it's nothing. What I think of you—now, that's something." He had had some problem with a new car at the garage—he had had the GM agency then—and he smelled of clean lubricating products and new upholstery and the rough soap where the mechanics cleaned up. He was big and gleaming, the all-over male. Oh, hell, I thought, what can I do? Then, suddenly curious, I asked: "*Did* you make out with Grey's wife?"

He laughed out loud and gave me a sidelong kiss. "Now that's more like it."

Because he'd never tell me. He'd never tell me who he made out with. "Honey," he'd say, late at night in the dark, lying straight out beside me, occasionally tangling his toes in mine or reaching for his cigarettes, "if I'd say I never had another woman outside you, would you believe it?"

I couldn't say No from sheer astonishment.

"Because it just might be true," he went on in the dark, serious as a judge. Then I would start laughing, couldn't help it. Because there are few things in the world which you know are true. You don't know (not anymore: our mamas knew) if there's a God or not, much less if He so loved the world. You don't know what your own native land is up to, or the true meaning of freedom, or the real cost of gasoline and cigarettes, or whether your insurance company will pay up. But one thing I personally know that is *not* true is that Charlie Waybridge has had only one woman. Looked at that way, it can be a comfort, one thing to be sure of.

It was soon after the picnic on the river that Grey Houston came by to see me at the office. You'd think I had nothing to do but stop and talk. What he came about was Nelle.

"She won't date me anymore," he complained. "I thought we were doing fine, but she quit me just like that. Hell, I can't tell what's the trouble with her. I want to call up and say 'Just tell me, Nelle. What's going on?'"

"Why don't you?" I asked.

Grey is always a little worried about things to do with people, especially since his divorce. We were glad when he started dating Nelle. She was hovering around thirty and didn't have anybody, and Grey was only a year or two younger.

"If I come right out and ask her, then she might just say, 'Let's decide to be good friends,' or something like that. Hell, I got enough friends."

"It's to be thought of," I agreed.

"What would you do?" he persisted.

"I'd rather know where I stand," I said, "but in this case I think I'd wait awhile. Nelle's worrying over that business. Maybe she doesn't know herself."

"I might push her too soon. I thought that, too."

"I ought to go around and see old Mrs. Townshend," I said. "She hardly gets out at all anymore. I mean to stop in and say hello."

"You're not going to repeat anything?"

See how he is? Skittery. "Of course not," I said. "But there's such a thing as keeping my eyes and ears open."

I went over to call on old Mrs. Townshend one Thursday afternoon when Mr. McGinnis's law office was closed anyway. The Townshend house is on a big lawn, a brick walk running up from the street to the front step and a large round plot of elephant ears in the front yard. When away and thinking of home, I see right off the Townshend yard and the elephant ears.

I wasn't even to the steps before I smelled clothes just dry-cleaned. I don't guess it's so bad, though hardly what you'd think of living with. Nor would you particularly like to see the sign outside the porte-cochere, though way to the left of the walk and not visible from the front porch. Still, it was out there clearly, saying "Townshend Dry Cleaning: Rapid Service." Better than a funeral parlor, but not much.

The Townshend house is stuffed with things. All these little Victorian tables on tall legs bowed outward, a small lower shelf, and the top covered katy-corner with a clean starched linen doily, tatting around the edge. All these chairs of various shapes, especially one that rocked squeaking on a walnut stand, and for every chair a doily at the head. Mrs. Townshend kept two birdcages, but no birds were in them. There never had been any so far as I knew. It wasn't a dark house, though. Nelle had taken out the stained glass way back when she graduated from college. That was soon after her older sister married, and her mama needed her. "If I'm going to live here," she had said, "that's got to go." So it went.

Mrs. Townshend never raised much of a fuss at Nelle. She was low to the ground because of a humpback, a rather placid old lady. The Townshends were the sort to keep everything just the way it was. Mrs. Townshend was a

LeMoyne from over toward Natchez. She was an Episcopalian and had brought her daughters up in that church.

"I'm sorry about this smell," she said in her forthright way, coming in and offering me a Coke on a little tray with a folded linen napkin beside it. "Nelle told me I'd get used to it and she was right: I have. But at first I had headaches all the time. If you get one I'll get some aspirin for you."

"How's the business going?" I asked.

"Nelle will be in in a minute. She knows you're here. You can ask her." She never raised her voice. She had a soft little face and gray eyes back of her little gold-rimmed glasses. She hadn't got to the hearing-aid stage yet, but you had to speak up. We went through the whole rigmarole of mine and Charlie's families. I had a feeling she was never much interested in all that, but around home you have to it. Then I asked her what she was reading and she woke up. We got off the ground right away, and went strong about the President and foreign affairs, the picture not being so bright but of great interest, and about her books from the library always running out, and all the things she had against book clubs—then Nelle walked in.

Nelle Townshend doesn't look like anybody else but herself. Her face is like something done on purpose to use up all the fine skin, drawing it evenly over the bones beneath, so that no matter at what age, she always would look the same. But that day she had this pinched look I'd never seen before, and her arms were splotched with what must have been a reaction to the cleaning fluids. She rolled down the sleeves of her blouse and sat in an old wicker rocker.

"I saw Grey the other day, Nelle," I said. "I think he misses you."

She didn't say anything outside of remarking she hadn't much time to go out. Then she mentioned some sort of decorating at the church she wanted to borrow some ferns for, from the florist. He's got some he rents, in washtubs. "You can't get all those ferns in our little church," Mrs. Townshend said, and Nelle said she thought two would do. She'd send Robin, she said. Then the bell rang to announce another customer. Nelle had to go because Robin was at the "plant"—actually the old cook's house in back of the property where they'd set the machinery up.

I hadn't said all I had to say to Nelle, so when I got up to go, I said to Mrs. Townshend that I'd go in the office a minute on the way out. But Mrs. Townshend got to her feet, a surprise in itself. Her usual words were, You'll excuse me if I don't get up. Of course, you would excuse her and be too polite to ask why. Like a lot of old ladies, she might have arthritis. But this time she stood.

"I wish you'd let Nelle alone. Nelle is all right now. She's the way she wants to be. She's not the way you people are. She's just not a bit that way!"

It may have been sheer surprise that kept me from telling Charlie all this till the weekend. We were hurrying to get to Pete and Hope Owens's place for a dinner they were having for some people down from the Delta, visitors.

"What did you say to that?" Charlie asked me.

"I was too surprised to open my mouth. I wouldn't have thought Mrs. Townshend would express such a low opinion as that. And why does she have it in the first place? Nelle's always been part of our crowd. She grew up with us. I thought they liked us."

"Old ladies get notions. They talk on the phone too much."

To our surprise, Nelle was at the Owenses' dinner, too. Hope told me in the kitchen that she'd asked her, and then asked Grey. But Grey had a date with the little Springer girl he'd brought to the picnic, Carole Springer. "If this keeps up," Hope said to me while I was helping her with a dip, "we're going to have a Springer in our crowd. I'm just not right ready for that." "Me either," I said. The Springers were from McComb, in lumber. They had money but they never were much fun.

"Did Nelle accept knowing you were going to ask Grey?" I asked.

"I couldn't tell that. She just said she'd love to and would come about seven."

It must have been seven, because Nelle walked in. "Can I help?"

"Your mama," I said, when Hope went out with the tray, "she sort of got upset with me the other day. I don't know why. If I said anything wrong, just tell her I'm sorry."

Nelle looked at her fresh nail polish. "Mama's a little peculiar now and then. Like everybody." So she wasn't about to open up.

"I've been feeling bad about Grey is all," I said. "You can think I'm meddling if you want to."

"Grey's all right," she said. "He's been going around with Carole Springer from McComb."

"All the more reason for feeling bad. Did you know they're coming tonight?"

She smiled a little distantly, and we went out to join the party. Charlie was already sitting up too close to the wife of the guest couple. I'd met them before. They have an antique shop. He is tall and nice, and she is short (wears spike heels) and nice. They are the sort you can't ever remember what their names are. If you get the first names right you're doing well. Shirley and Bob.

"Honey, you're just a doll," Charlie was saying (if he couldn't think of Shirley, Honey would do), and Pete said, "Watch out, Shirley, the next thing you know you'll be sitting on his lap."

"I almost went in for antiques myself," Nelle was saying to Bob, the husband. "I would have liked that better, of course, than a cleaning business, but I thought the turnover here would be too small. I do need to feel like I'm making money if I'm going to work at it. For a while, though, it was fun to go wandering around New Orleans and pick up good things cheap."

"I'd say they'd all been combed over down there," Bob objected.

"It's true about the best things," Nelle said. "I could hardly afford those anyway. But sometimes you see some pieces with really good design and you can see you might realize something on them. Real appreciation goes a long way."

"Bob has a jobber up in St. Louis," Shirley said. "We had enough of all this going around shaking the bushes. A few lucky finds was what got us started."

Nelle said, "I started thinking about it because I went in the living room a year or so back and there were some ladies I never saw before. They'd found the door open and walked in. They wanted to know the price of Mama's furniture. I said it wasn't for sale, but Mama was just coming in from the kitchen and heard them. You wouldn't believe how mad she got. 'I'm going straight and get out my pistol,' she said."

"You ought to just see her mama," said Hope. "This tiny little old lady."

"So what happened?" Shirley asked when she got through laughing.

"Nothing real bad," said Nelle. "They just got out the door as quick as they could."

"Yo' mama got a pistol?" Charlie asked, after a silence. We started to laugh again, the implication being plain that a Charlie Waybridge *needs* to know if a woman's mother has a pistol in the house.

"She does have one," said Nelle.

"So watch out, Charlie," said Pete.

Bob remarked, "Y'all certainly don't change much over here."

"Crazy as ever," Hope said proudly. It crossed my mind that Hope was always protecting herself, one way or the other.

Shirley said she thought it was just grand to be back, she wouldn't take anything for it, and after that Grey and Carole arrived. We had another drink and then went in to dinner. Everybody acted like everything was okay. After dinner, I went back in the kitchen for some water, and there was Charlie, kissing Shirley. She was so strained up on tiptoe, Charlie being over six feet, that I thought, in addition to being embarrassed, mad, and backing out before they saw me, What they need is a stepladder to do it right.

On the way home, I told Charlie about catching them. "I didn't know she was within a country mile," he said, ready with excuses. "She just plain grabbed me."

"I've been disgusted once too often," I said. "Tell it to Bob."

"If she wanted to do it right," he said, "she ought to get a stepladder." So then I had to laugh. Even if our marriage wasn't ideal, we still had the same thoughts.

It sometimes seemed to me, in considering the crowd we were always part of, from even before we went to school, straight on through, that we were all like one person, walking around different ways, but in some permanent way breathing together, feeling the same reactions, thinking each other's thoughts. What do you call that if not love? If asked, we'd all cry Yes! with one voice, but then it's not our habit to ask anything serious. We're close to religious about keeping everything light and gay. Nelle Townshend knew that, all the above, but she was drawing back. A betrayer was what she was turning into. We felt weakened because of her. What did she think she was doing?

I had to drive Mr. McGinnis way back in the woods one day to serve a subpoena on a witness. He hadn't liked to drive since his heart attack, and his usual colored man was busy with Mrs. McGinnis's garden. In the course of that little trip, coming back into town, I saw Nelle Townshend's station wagon turn off onto a side road. I couldn't see who was with her, but somebody was, definitely.

I must add that this was spring and there were drifts of dogwood all mingled in the woods at different levels. Through those same woods, along the winding roads, the redbud, simultaneous, was spreading its wonderful pink haze. Mr. McGinnis sat beside me without saying much, his old knobby hands folded over a briefcase he held upright on his lap. "A trip like this just makes me think, Eileen, that everybody owes it to himself to get out in the woods this time of year. It's just God's own garden," he said. We had just crossed a wooden bridge over a pretty little creek about a mile back. That same creek, shallower, was crossed by a ford along the road that Nelle's car had taken. I know that little road, too, maybe the prettiest one of all.

Serpents have a taste for Eden, and in a small town, if they are busy elsewhere, lots of people are glad to fill in for them. It still upsets me to think of all the gossip that went on that year, and at the same time I have to blame Nelle Townshend for it, not so much for starting it, but for being so unconscious about it. She had stepped out of line and she didn't even bother to notice.

Once the business got going, the next thing she did was enroll in a class—a "seminar," she said—over at the university at Hattiesburg. It was something to do with art theory, she said, and she was thinking of going on from there to a degree, eventually, and get hold of a subject she could teach at the junior college right up the road. So settling in to be an old maid.

I said this last rather gloomily to Pete's wife, Hope, and Pete overheard and said, "There's all kinds of those." "You stop that," said Hope. "What's supposed to be going on?" I asked. (Some say don't ask, it's better not to, but I think you have to know if only to keep on guard.)

"Just that they're saying things about Nelle and that black Robin works for her."

"Well, they're in the same business," I said.

"Whatever it is, people don't like it. They say she goes out to his house after dark. That they spend too much time over the books."

"Somebody ought to warn her," I said. "If Robin gets into trouble she won't find anybody to do that kind of work. He's the only one."

"Nelle's gotten too independent is the thing," said Pete. "She thinks she can live her own life."

"Maybe she can," said Hope.

Charlie was away that week. He had gone over to the Delta on business, and Hope and Pete had dropped in to keep me company. Hope is ten years younger than Pete. (Pete used to date her sister, Mary Ruth, one of these beauty-queen types, who had gone up to the Miss America pageant to represent Mississippi and come back first runner-up. For the talent contest part of it, she had recited passages from the Bible, and Pete always said her trouble was she was too religious but he hoped to get her over it. She used to try in a nice way to get him into church work, and that embarrassed him. It's our common habit, as Mary Ruth well knew, to go to morning service, but anything outside that is out. Anyway, around Mary Ruth's he used to keep seeing the little sister Hope, and he'd say, "Mary Ruth, you better start on that girl about church, she's growing up dynamite." Mary Ruth got involved in a promotion trip, something about getting right with America, and met a man on a plane trip to Dallas, and before the seat-belt sign went off they were in love. For Mary Ruth that meant marriage. She was strict, a woman of faith, and I don't think Pete would have been happy with her. But he had got the habit of the house by then, and Mary Ruth's parents had got fond of him and didn't want him drinking too much: they made him welcome. So one day Hope turned seventeen and came out in a new flouncy dress with heels on, and Pete saw the light.)

We had a saying by now that Pete had always been younger than Hope, that she was older than any of us. Only twenty, she worked at making their house look good and won gardening prizes. She gave grand parties, with attention to details.

"I stuck my neck out," I told Hope, "to keep Nelle dating Grey. You remember her mama took a set at me like I never dreamed possible. Nelle's been doing us all funny, but she may have to come back someday. We can't stop caring for her."

Hope thought it over. "Robin knows what it's like here, even if Nelle may have temporarily forgotten. He's not going to tempt fate. Anyway, somebody already spoke to Nelle."

"Who?"

"Grey, of course. He'll use any excuse to speak to her. She got mad as a firecracker. She said, 'Don't you know this is nineteen seventy-six? I've got a business to run. I've got a living to make!' But she quit going out to his house at night. And Robin quit so much as answering the phone, up at her office."

"You mean he's keeping one of those low profiles?" said Pete.

Soon after, I ran into Robin uptown in the grocery, and he said, "How do you do, Mrs. Waybridge," like a schoolteacher or a foreigner, and I figured just from that, that he was on to everything and taking no chances. Nelle must have told him. I personally knew what not many people did, that he was a real partner with Nelle, not just her hired help. They had got Mr. McGinnis to draw up the papers. And they had plans for moving the plant uptown, to an empty store building, with some investment in more equipment. So maybe they'd get by till then. I felt a mellowness in my heart about Nelle's effort and all—a Townshend (LeMoyne on her mother's side) opening a dry cleaning business. I thought of Robin's effort, too—he had a sincere, intelligent look, reserved. What I hoped for them was something like a prayer.

Busying my thoughts about all this, I had been forgetting Charlie. That will never do.

For one thing, leaving aside women, Charlie's present way of life was very nearly wild. He'd got into oil leases two years before, and when something was going on, he'd drive like a demon over to East Texas by way of Shreveport and back through Pike and Amite counties. At one time he had to sit over Mr. McGinnis for a month getting him to study up on laws governing oil rights. In the end, Charlie got to know as much or more than Mr. McGinnis. He's in and out. The in-between times are when he gets restless. Drinks too much and starts simmering up about some new woman. One thing (except for me), with Charlie it's always a new woman. Once tried, soon dropped. Or so I like to believe. Then, truth to tell, there is really part of me that not only wants to believe but at unstated times does believe that I've been the only one for Charlie Waybridge. Not that I'd begrudge him a few times of having it off down in the hollow back of the gym with some girl who came in from the country, nor would I think anything about flings in New Orleans while he was in Tulane. But as for the outlandish reputation he's acquired now, sometimes I just want to say out loud to all and sundry, "There's not a word of truth in it. He's a big, attractive, friendly guy, O.K.! But he's not the town stud. He belongs to *me*."

All this before the evening along about first dark when Charlie was seen on the Townshend property by Nelle's mother, who went and got the pistol and shot at him.

"Christ, she could have killed me," Charlie said. He was too surprised about it even to shake. He was just dazed. Fixed a stiff drink and didn't want any supper. "She's gone off her rocker," he said. "That's all I could think."

I knew I had to ask it, sooner or later. "What were you doing up there, Charlie?"

"Nothing," he said. "I'd left the car at Wharton's garage to check why I'm burning too much oil. He's getting to it in the morning. It was a nice evening and I cut through the back alley and that led to a stroll through the

Townshend pasture. That's all. I saw the little lady out on the back porch. I was too far off to holler at her. She scuttled off into the house and I was going past, when here she came out again with something black weighting her hand. You know what I thought? I thought she had a kitten by the neck. Next thing I knew there was a bullet smashing through the leaves not that far off." He put his hand out.

"Wonder if Nelle was home."

I was nervous as a monkey after I heard this, and nothing would do me but to call up Nelle.

She answered right away. "Nelle," I said, "is your little mama going in for target practice these days?"

She started laughing. "Did you hear that all the way to your place? She's mad 'cause the Johnsons' old cow keeps breaking down our fence. She took a shot in the air because she's tired complaining."

"Since when was Charlie Waybridge a cow?" I asked.

"Mercy, Eileen. You don't mean Charlie was back there?"

"You better load that thing with blanks," I said, "or hide it."

"Blanks is all it's got in it," said Nelle. "Mama doesn't tell that because she feels more protected not to."

"You certainly better check it out," I said. "Charlie says it was a bullet."

There was a pause. "You're not mad or anything, are you, Eileen?"

"Oh, no," I warbled. "We've been friends too long for that."

"Come over and see us," said Nelle. "Real soon."

I don't know who told it, but knowing this town like the back of my hand, I know how they told it. Charlie Waybridge was up at Nelle Townshend's and old Mrs. Townshend shot at him. Enough said. At the Garden Club Auxiliary tea, I came in and heard them giggling, and how they got quiet when I passed a plate of sandwiches. I went straight to the subject, which is the way I do. "Y'all off on Mrs. Townshend?" I asked. There was a silence, and then some little cross-eyed bride, new in town, piped up that there was just always something funny going on here, and Maud Varner, an old friend, said she thought Nelle ought to watch out for Mrs. Townshend, she was showing her age. "It's not such a funny goings-on when it almost kills somebody," I said. "Charlie came straight home and told me. He was glad to be alive, but I went and called Nelle. So she does know." There was another silence during which I could tell what everybody thought. The thing is not to get too distant or above it all. If you do, your friends will pull back, too, and you won't know anything. Gradually, you'll just turn into, Poor Eileen, what does she think of all Charlie's carryings-on?

Next, the injunction. Who brought it and why? I got the answer to the first before I guessed the second.

It was against the Townshend Cleaners because the chemicals used were a hazard to health and the smell they exuded a public nuisance. But the real reason wasn't this at all.

In order to speed up the deliveries, Nelle had taken to driving the station wagon herself, so that Robin could run in with the cleaning. Some people had begun to remark on this. Would it have been different if Nelle was married or had a brother, a father, a steady boyfriend? I don't know. I used to hold my breath when they went by in the late afternoon together. Because sometimes when the back of the station wagon was full, Robin would be up on the front seat with her, and she with her head stuck in the air, driving carefully, her mind on nothing at all to do with other people. Once the cleaning load got lighter, Robin would usually sit on the back seat, as expected to do. But sometimes, busy talking to her, he wouldn't. He'd be up beside her, discussing business.

Then, suddenly, the business closed.

Nelle was beside herself. She came running to Mr. McGinnis. Her hair was every which way around her head and she was wearing an old checked shirt and no makeup.

She could hardly make herself sit still and visit with me while Mr. McGinnis got through with a client. "Now, Miss Nelle," he said, steering her through the door.

"Just when we were making a go of it!" I heard her say; then he closed the door.

I heard by way of the grapevine that very night that the person who had done it was John Houston, Grey's brother, whose wife's family lived on a property just below the Townshends. They claimed they couldn't sleep for the dry-cleaning fumes and were getting violent attacks of nausea.

"Aren't they supposed to give warnings?" I asked.

We were all at John and Rose Houston's home, a real gathering of the bunch, only Nelle being absent, though she was the most present one of all. There was a silence after every statement, in itself unusual. Finally John Houston said, "Not in cases of extreme health hazard."

"That's a lot of you-know-what," I said. "Rose, your family's not dying."

Rose said: "They never claimed to be dying." And Pete said: "Eileen, can't you sit right quiet and try to use your head?"

"In preference to running off at the mouth," said Charlie, which made me mad. I was refusing, I well knew, to see the point they all had in mind. But it seemed to me that was my privilege.

The thing to know about our crowd is that we never did go in for talking about the "Negro question." We talked about Negroes the way we always had, like people, one at a time. They were all around us, had always been, living around us, waiting on us, sharing our lives, brought up with us, nursing us, cooking for us, mourning and rejoicing with us, making us laugh, stealing from us, digging our graves. But when all the troubles started coming in on us after the Freedom Riders and the Ole Miss riots, we decided not to talk about it. I don't know but what we weren't afraid of getting nervous. We couldn't jump out of our own skins, or those of our parents, grandparents, and those before them. "Nothing you can do about it" was Charlie's view. "Whatever you decide, you're going to act the same way tomorrow as you did today. Hoping you can get Alma to cook for you, and Peabody to clean the windows, and Bayman to cut the grass." "I'm not keeping anybody from voting—yellow, blue, or pink," said Hope, who had got her "ideas" straight from the first, she said. "I don't guess any of us is," said Pete, "them days is gone forever." "But wouldn't it just be wonderful," said Rose Houston, "to have a little colored gal to pick up your handkerchief and sew on your buttons and bring you cold lemonade and fan you when you're hot, and just love you to death?"

Rose was joking, of course, the way we all liked to do. But there are always one or two of them that we seriously insist we know—really *know*—that they love us. Would do anything for us, as we would for them. Otherwise, without that feeling, I guess we couldn't rest easy. You never can really know what they think, what they feel, so there's always the one chance it might be love.

So we—the we I'm always speaking of—decided not to talk about race relations because it spoiled things too much. We didn't like to consider anyone of us really involved in some part of it. Then, in my mind's eye, I saw Nelle's car, that dogwood-laden day in the woods, headed off the road with somebody inside. Or such was my impression. I'd never mentioned it to anybody, and Mr. McGinnis hadn't, I think, seen. Was it Robin? Or maybe, I suddenly asked myself, Charlie? Mysteries multiplied.

"Nelle's got to make a living is the whole thing," said Pete, getting practical. "We can't not let her do that,"

"Why doesn't somebody find her a job she'd like?" asked Grey.

"Why the hell," Charlie burst out, "don't you marry her, Grey? Women ought to get married," he announced in general. "You see what happens when they don't."

"Hell, I can't get near her," said Grey. "We dated for six months. I guess I wasn't the one," he added.

"She ought to relocate the plant uptown, then she could run the office in her house, one remove from it, acting like a lady."

"What about Robin?" said Hope.

"He could run back and forth," I said. "They do want to do that," I added, "but can't afford it yet."

"You'd think old Mrs. Townshend would have stopped it all."

"That lady's a mystery."

"If Nelle just had a brother."

"Or even an uncle."

Then the talk dwindled down to silence.

"John," said Pete, after a time, turning around to face him, "we all know it was you—not Rose's folks. Did you have to?"

John Houston was sitting quietly in his chair. He was a little older than the rest of us, turning gray, a little more settled and methodical, more like our uncle than an equal and friend. (Or was it just that he and Rose were the only ones so far to have children—what all our parents said we all ought to do, but couldn't quit having our good times.) He was sipping bourbon. He nodded slowly. "I had to." We didn't ask any more.

"Let's just go quiet," John finally added. "Wait and see."

Now, all my life I'd been hearing first one person then another (and these, it would seem, appointed by silent consensus) say that things were to be taken care of in a certain way and no other. The person in this case who had this kind of appointment was evidently John Houston, from in our midst. But when did he get it? How did he get it? Where did it come from? There seemed to be no need to discuss it.

Rose Houston, who wore her long light hair in a sort of loose bun at the nape and who sat straight up in her chair, adjusted a fallen strand, and Grey went off to fix another drink for himself and Pete and Hope. He sang on the way out, more or less to himself, "For the times they are a-changing. . ." and that, too, found reference in all our minds. Except I couldn't help but wonder whether anything had changed at all.

The hearing on the dry cleaning injunction was due to be held in two weeks. Nelle went off to the coast. She couldn't stand the tension, she told me, having come over to Mr. McGinnis's office to see him alone. "Thinking how we've worked and all," she said, "and how just before this came up the auditor was in and told us what good shape we were in. We were just about to buy a new condenser."

"What's that?" I asked.

"Takes the smell out of the fumes," she said. "The very thing they're mad about. I could kill John Houston. Why couldn't he have come to me?"

I decided to be forthright. "Nelle, there's something you ought to evaluate . . . consider, I mean. Whatever word you want." I was shaking, surprising myself.

Nobody was around. Mr. McGinnis was in the next county.

Once when I was visiting a school friend up north, out from Philadelphia, a man at a party asked me if I would have sexual relations with a black. He wasn't black himself, so why was he curious? I said I'd never even thought about it. "It's a taboo, I think you call it," I said. "Girls like me get brainwashed early on. It's not that I'm against them," I added, feeling awkward. "Contrary to what you may think or may even believe," he told me, "you've

probably thought a lot about it. You've suppressed your impulses, that's all."
"Nobody can prove that," I said, "not even you," I added, thinking I was
being amusing. But he only looked superior and walked away.

"It's you and Robin," I said. I could hear myself explaining to Charlie,
Somebody had to, sooner or later. "You won't find anybody really believing
anything, I don't guess, but it's making people speculate."

Nelle Townshend never reacted the way you'd think she would. She did-
n't even get annoyed, much less hit the ceiling. She just gave a little sigh.
"You start a business, you'll see. I've got no time for anything but worrying
about customers and money."

I was wondering whether to tell her the latest. A woman named
McCorkle from out in the country, who resembled Nelle so much from the
back you'd think they were the same, got pushed off the sidewalk last Saturday and fell in the concrete gutter up near the drugstore. The person who
did it, somebody from outside town, must have said something nobody heard
but Mrs. McCorkle, because she jumped up with her skirt muddy and stockings torn and yelled out, "I ain't no nigger lover!"

But I didn't tell her. If she was anybody but a Townshend, I might have.
Odd to think that, when the only Townshends left there were Nelle and her
mother. In cases such as this, the absent are present and the dead are, too.
Mr. Townshend had died so long ago you had to ask your parents what he
was like. The answer was always the same. "Sid Townshend was a mighty
good man." Nelle had had two sisters: one died in her twenties, the victim of
a rare disease, and the other got married and went to live on a place out from
Helena, Arkansas. She had about six children and could be of no real help to
the home branch.

"Come over to dinner," I coaxed. "You want me to ask Grey, I will. If
you don't, I won't."

"Grey," she said, just blank, like that. He might have been somebody she
met once a long time back. "She's a perpetual virgin," I heard Charlie say
once. "Just because she won't cotton up to you," I said. But maybe he was
right. Nelle and her mother lived up near the Episcopal church. Since our
little town could not support a full-time rector, it was they who kept the
church linens and the chalice and saw that the robes were always cleaned and
hung in their proper place in the little room off the chancel. Come to think
of it, keeping those robes and surplices in order may have been one thing that
started Nelle into dry cleaning.

Nelle got up suddenly, her face catching the light from our old window
with the wobbly glass in the panes, and I thought, She's a grand-looking
woman, sort of girlish and womanish both.

"I'm going to the coast," she said. "I'm taking some books and a sketch
pad. I may look into some art courses. You have to have training to teach anything, that's the trouble."

"Look, Nelle, if it's money— Well, you do have friends, you know."

"Friends," she said, just the way she had said "Grey." I wondered just what Nelle was really like. None of us seemed to know.

"Have a good time," I said. After she left, I thought I heard the echo of that blank, soft voice saying, "Good time."

It was a week after Nelle had gone that old Mrs. Townshend rang up Mr. McGinnis at the office. Mr. McGinnis came out to tell me what it was all about.

"Mrs. Townshend says that last night somebody tore down the dry cleaning sign Nelle had put up out at the side. Some colored woman is staying with her at night, but neither one of them saw anybody. Now she can't find Robin to put it back. She's called his house but he's not there."

"Do they say he'll be back soon?"

"They say he's out of town."

"I'd get Charlie to go up and fix it, but you know what happened."

"I heard about it. Maybe in daylight the old lady won't shoot. I'll go around with our yardman after dinner." What we still mean by dinner is lunch. So they put the sign up and I sat in the empty office wondering about this and that, but mainly, Where was Robin Byers?

It's time to say that Robin Byers was not any Harry Belafonte calypso-singing sex symbol of a "black." He was strong and thoughtful-looking, not very tall, definitely chocolate, but not ebony. He wore his hair cropped short in an almost military fashion so that, being thick, it stuck straight up more often than not. From one side he could look positively frightening, as he had a long white scar running down the side of his cheek. It was said that he got it in the army, in Vietnam, but the story of just how was not known. So maybe he had not gotten it in the war, but somewhere else. His folks had been in the county forever, his own house being not far out from town. He had a wife, two teenaged children, a telephone, and a TV set. The other side of Robin Byers's face was regular, smooth, and while not especially handsome it was good-humored and likable. All in all, he looked intelligent and conscientious, and that must have been how Nelle Townshend saw him, as he was.

I went to the hearing. I'd have had to, to keep Mr. McGinnis's notes straight, but I would have anyway, as all our crowd showed up, except Rose and John Houston. Rose's parents were there, having brought the complaint, and Rose's mama's doctor from over at Hattiesburg, to swear she'd had no end of allergies and migraines, and attacks of nausea, all brought on by the cleaning fumes. Sitting way in the back was Robin Byers, in a suit (a really nice suit) with a blue-and-white-striped "city" shirt and a knit tie. He looked like an assistant university dean, except for the white scar. He also had the look of a spectator, very calm, I thought, not wanting to keep turning around and staring at him, but keeping the image in my mind like an all-day sucker, letting it slowly melt out its meaning. He was holding a certain surface. But he was scared. Half across the courtroom you could see his temple throbbing, and the sweat beads. He was that tense. The whole effect was amazing.

The complaint was read out and Mrs. Hammond, Rose's mother, testified and the doctor testified, and Mr. Hammond said they were both right. The way the Hammonds talk—big Presbyterians—you would think they had the Bible on their side every minute, so naturally everybody else had to be mistaken. Friends and neighbors of the Townshends all these years, they now seemed to be speaking of people they knew only slightly. That is until Mrs. Hammond, a sort of dumpling-like woman with a practiced way of sounding accurate about whatever she said (she was a good gossip because she got all the details of everything), suddenly came down to a personal level and said, "Nelle, I just don't see why if you want to run that thing you don't move it into town," and Nelle said back right away just like they were in a living room instead of a courtroom, "Well, that's because of Mama, Miss Addie. This way I'm in and out with her." At that, everybody laughed, couldn't help it.

Then Mr. McGinnis got up and challenged that very much about Mrs. Hammond's headaches and allergies (he established her age, fifty-two, which she didn't want to tell) had to do with the cleaning plant. If they had, somebody else would have such complaints, but in case we needed to go further into it, he would ask Miss Nelle to explain what he meant.

Nelle got up front and went about as far as she could concerning the type of equipment she used and how it was guaranteed against the very thing now being complained of, that it let very few vapors escape, but then she said she would rather call on Robin Byers to come and explain because he had had special training in the chemical processes and knew all their possible negative effects.

And he came. He walked down the aisle and sat in the chair and nobody had ever seen such composure. I think he was petrified, but so might an actor be who was doing a role to high perfection. And when he started to talk you'd think that dry cleaning was a text and that his God-appointed task was to preach a sermon on it. But it wasn't quite like that, either. More modern. A professor giving a lecture to extremely ignorant students, with a good professor's accuracy, to the last degree. In the first place, he said, the cleaning fluid used was not varsol or carbon tetrachloride, which were known not only to give off harmful fumes but to damage fabrics, but something called "Perluxe" or perchlorethylene (he paused to give the chemical composition), which was approved for commercial cleaning purposes in such and such a solution by federal and state bylaws, of certain numbers and codes, which Mr. McGinnis had listed in his records and would be glad to read aloud upon request. If an operator worked closely with Perluxe for a certain number of hours a day, he might have headaches, it was true, but escaping vapor could scarcely be smelled at all more than a few feet from the exhaust pipes, and caused no harmful effects whatsoever, even to shrubs or "the leaves upon the trees." He said this last in such a lofty, rhythmic way that somebody giggled (I think it was Hope), and he stopped talking altogether.

"There might be smells down in those hollows back there," Nelle filled in from where she was sitting, "but it's not from my one little exhaust pipe."

"Then why," asked Mrs. Hammond right out, "do you keep on saying you need new equipment so you won't have any exhaust? Just answer me that."

"I'll let Robin explain," said Nelle.

"The fact is that Perluxe is an expensive product," Robin said. "At four dollars and twenty-five cents a gallon, using nearly thirty gallons each time the accumulation of the garments is put through the process, she can count on it that the overheads with two cleanings a week will run in the neighborhood of between two and three hundred dollars. So having the condenser machine would mean that the exhaust runs into it, and so converts the vapors back to the liquid, in order to use it once again."

"It's not for the neighbors," Nelle put in. "It's for us."

Everybody had spoken out of order by then, but what with the atmosphere having either declined or improved (depending on how you looked at it) to one of friendly inquiry among neighbors rather than a squabble in a court of law, the silence that finally descended was more meditative than not, having as its most impressive features, like high points in a landscape, Nelle, at some little distance down a front bench, but turned around so as to take everything in, her back straight and her Townshend head both superior and interested; and Robin Byers, who still had the chair by Judge Purvis's desk, collected and severe (he had forgotten the giggle), with testimony faultlessly delivered and nothing more he needed to say. (Would things have been any different if Charlie had been there? He was out of town.)

The judge cleared his throat and said he guessed the smells in the gullies around Tyler might be a nuisance, sure enough, but couldn't be said to be caused by dry cleaning, and he thought Miss Townshend could go on with her business. For a while, the white face and the black one seemed just the same, to be rising up quiet and superior above us all.

The judge asked, just out of curiosity, when Nelle planned to buy the condenser that was mentioned. She said whenever she could find one secondhand in good condition—they cost nearly two thousand dollars new—and Robin Byers put in that he had just been looking into one down in Biloxi, so it might not be too long. Biloxi is on the coast.

Judge Purvis said we'd adjourn now, and everybody stood up of one accord, except Mr. McGinnis, who had dozed off and was almost snoring.

Nelle, who was feeling friendly to the world, or seeming to (we all had clothes that got dirty, after all), said to all and sundry not to worry, "we plan to move the plant uptown one of these days before too long," and it was the "we" that came through again, a slip: she usually referred to the business as hers. It was just a reminder of what everybody wanted not to have to think about, and she probably hadn't intended to speak of it that way.

As if to smooth it well into the past, Judge Purvis remarked that these little towns ought to have zoning laws, but I sat there thinking there would-n't be much support for that, not with the Gulf Oil station and garage right up on South Street between the Whitmans' and the Binghams', and the small appliance shop on the vacant lot where the old Marshall mansion had stood, and the Tackett house, still elegant as you please, doing steady busi-ness as a funeral home. You can separate black from white but not business from nonbusiness. Not in our town.

Nelle came down and shook hands with Mr. McGinnis. "I don't know when I can afford to pay you." "Court costs go to them," he said. "Don't worry about the rest."

Back at the office, Mr. McGinnis closed the street door and said to me, "The fumes in this case have got nothing to do with dry cleaning. Has any-body talked to Miss Nelle?"

"They have," I said, "but she doesn't seem to pay any attention."

He said I could go home for the day and much obliged for my help at the courthouse. I powdered my nose and went out into the street. It wasn't but eleven-thirty.

Everything was still, and nobody around. The blue jays were having a good time on the courthouse yard, squalling and swooping from the lowest oak limbs, close to the ground, then mounting back up. There were some sparrows out near the old horse trough, which still ran water. They were splashing around. But except for somebody driving up for the mail at the post office, then driving off, there wasn't a soul around. I started walking, and just automatically I went by for the mail because as a rule Charlie didn't stop in for it till noon, even when in town. On the way I was mulling over the hear-ing and how Mrs. Hammond had said at the door of the courtroom to Nelle, "Aw right, Miss Nellie, you just wait." It wasn't said in any unpleasant way; in fact, it sounded right friendly. Except that she wasn't looking at Nelle, but past her, and except that being older, it wasn't the ordinary thing to call her "Miss," and except that Nelle is a pretty name but Nellie isn't. But Nelle in reply had suddenly laughed in that unexpected but delightful way she has, because something has struck her as really funny. "What am I supposed to wait *for*, Miss Addie?" Whatever else, Nelle wasn't scared. I looked for Robin Byers, but he had got sensible and gone off in that old little blue German car he drives. I saw Nelle drive home alone.

Then, because the lay of my home direction was a shortcut from the post office, and because the spring had been dry and the back lanes nice to walk in, I went through the same way Charlie had that time Mrs. Townshend had about killed him, and enjoyed, the way I had from childhood on, the soft fragrances of springtime, the brown wisps of spent jonquils withered on their stalks, the forsythia turned from yellow to green fronds, but the spires still white as a bride's veil worked in blossoms, and the climbing roses, mainly wild, just opening a delicate, simple pink bloom all along the back fences. I was crossing down that way when what I saw was a blue car.

It was stopped way back down the Townshend property on a little connecting road that made an entrance through to a lower town road, one that nobody used anymore. I stopped in the clump of bowdarc trees on the next property from the Townshends'. Then I saw Nelle, running down the hill. She still had that same laugh, honest and joyous, that she had shown the first of to Mrs. Hammond. And there coming to meet her was Robin, his teeth white as his scar. They grabbed each other's hands, black on white and white on black. They started whirling each other around, like two schoolchildren in a game, and I saw Nelle's mouth forming the words I could scarcely hear: "We won! We won!" And his, the same, a baritone underneath. It was pure joy. Washing the color out, saying that the dye didn't, this time, hold, they could have been brother and sister, happy at some good family news, or old lovers (Charlie and I sometimes meet like that, too, happy at some piece of luck to really stop to talk about it, just dancing out our joy). But, my God, I thought, don't they know they're black and white and this is Tyler, Mississippi? Well, of course they do, I thought next—that's more than half the joy—getting away with it! Dare and double-dare! Dumbfounded, I just stood, hidden, never seen by them at all, and let the image of black on white and white on black—those pale, aristocratic Townshend hands and his strong, square-cut black ones—linked perpetually now in my mind's eyes— soak in.

It's going to stay with me forever, I thought, but what does it mean? I never told. I didn't think they were lovers. But they were into a triumph of the sort that lovers feel. They had acted as they pleased. They were above everything. They lived in another world because of a dry cleaning business. They had proved it when they had to. They knew it.

But nobody could be counted on to see it the way I did. It was too complicated for any two people to know about it.

Soon after this we got a call from Hope, Pete's wife. "I've got tired of all this foolishness," she said. "How did we ever get hung up on dry cleaning, of all things? Can you feature it? I'm going to give a party. Mary Foote Williams is coming home to see her folks and bringing Keith, so that's good enough for me. And don't kid yourself. I'm personally going to get Nelle Townshend to come, and Grey Houston is going to bring her. I'm getting good and ready for everybody to start acting normal again. I don't know what's been the matter with everybody, and furthermore I don't want to know."

Well, this is a kettle of fish, I thought: Hope, the youngest, taking us over. Of course, she did have the perspective to see everything whole.

I no sooner put down the phone than Pete called up from his office. "Jezzie's on the warpath," he said. (He calls her Jezzie because she used to tell all kinds of lies to some little high school boy she had crazy about her—her own age—just so she could go out with Pete and the older crowd. It was easy to see through that. She thought she might just be getting a short run with us and would have to fall back on her own bunch when we shoved her out, so she was keeping a foothold. Pete caught her at it, but all it did was make him like her better. Hope was pert. She had a sharp little chin she liked to stick up in the air, and a turned-up nose. "Both signs of meanness," said Mr. Owens, Pete's father, "especially the nose," and buried his own in the newspaper.)

"Well," I said doubtfully, "if you think it's a good idea. . ."

"No stopping her," said Pete, with the voice of a spectator at the game. "If anybody can swing it, she can."

So we finally said yes.

The morning of Hope's party there was some ugly weather, one nasty little black cloud after another and a lot of restless crosswinds. There was a tornado watch out for our county and two others, making you know it was a widespread weather system. I had promised to bring a platter of shrimp for the buffet table, and that meant a whole morning shucking them after driving out to pick up the order at the Fish Shack. At times the lightning was popping so close I had to get out of the kitchen. I would go sit in the living room with the thunder blamming so hard I couldn't even read the paper. Looking out at my backyard through the picture window, the colors of the marigolds and pansies seemed to be electric bright, blazing, then shuddering in the wind.

I was bound to connect all this with the anxiety that had got into things about that party. Charlie's being over in Louisiana didn't help. Maybe all was calm and bright over there, but I doubted it.

However, along about two the sky did clear, and the sun came out. When I drove out to Hope and Pete's place with the shrimp—it's a little way north of town, reached by its own side road, on a hill—everything was wonderful. There was a warm buoyancy in the air that made you feel young and remember what it was like to skip home from school.

"It's cleared off," said Hope, as though in personal triumph over Nature.

Pete was behind her at the door, enveloped in a huge apron. "I feel like playing softball," he said.

"Me, too," I agreed. "If I could just hear from Charlie."

"Oh, he'll be back," said Pete. "Charlie miss a party? Never!"

Well, it was quite an affair. The effort was to get us all launched in a new and happy period and the method was the tried and true one of drinking and feasting, dancing, pranking, laughing, flirting, and having fun. I had a new knife-pleated silk skirt, ankle length, dark blue shot with green and cyclamen, and a new off-the-shoulder blouse, and Mary Foote Williams, the visitor, wore a slit skirt, but Hope took the cake in her hoop skirts from her senior-high-school days, and her hair in a coarse gold net.

"The shrimp are gorgeous," she said. "Come look. I called Mama and requested prayer for good weather. It never fails."

"Charlie called," I said. "He said he'd be maybe thirty minutes late and would come on his own."

A car pulled up in the drive and there was Grey circling around and holding the door for Nelle herself. She had on a simple silk dress with her fine hair brushed loose and a pair of sexy new high-heeled sandals. It looked natural to see them together and I breathed easier without knowing I had been doing it for quite a while. Hope was right, we'd had enough of all this foolishness.

"That just leaves John and Rose," said Hope, "and I have my own ideas about them."

"What?" I asked.

"Well, I shouldn't say. It's y'all's crowd." She was quick in her kitchen, clicking around with her skirts swaying. She had got a nice little colored girl, Perline, dressed up in black with a white ruffled apron. "I just think John's halfway to a stuffed shirt and Rose is going to get him all the way there."

So, our crowd or not, she was going right ahead.

"I think this has to do with you-know-what," I said.

"We aren't going to mention you-know-what," said Hope. "From now on, honey, my only four-letter words are 'dry' and 'cleaning.'"

John and Rose didn't show up, but two new couples did, a pair from Hattiesburg and the Kellmans, new in town but promising. Hope had let them in. Pete exercised himself at the bar and there was a strong punch as well. We strolled out to the pool and sat on white-painted iron chairs with cushions in green flowered plastic. Nelle sat with her pretty legs crossed, talking to Mary Foote. Grey was at her elbow. The little maid passed out canapés and shrimp. Light was still lingering in a clear sky barely pink at the edges. Pete skimmed leaves from the pool surface with a long-handled net. Lightning bugs winked and drifted, and the new little wife from Hattiesburg caught one or two in her palm and watched them crawl away, then take wing. "I used to do that," said Nelle. Then she shivered and Grey went for a shawl. It grew suddenly darker and one or two pale stars could be seen, then dozens. Pete, vanished inside, had started some records. Some people began to trail back in. And with another drink (the third, maybe?), it wasn't clear how much time had passed, when there came the harsh roar of a motor from the private road, growing stronger the nearer it got, a slashing of gravel in the drive out front, and a door slamming. And the first thing you knew there was

Charlie Waybridge, filling the whole doorframe before Pete or Hope could even go to open it. He put his arms out to everybody. "Well, whaddaya know!" he said.

His tie was loose two buttons down and his light seersucker dress coat was crumpled and open but at least he had it on. I went right to him. He'd been drinking, of course, I'd known it from the first sound of the car—but who wasn't drinking? "Hi ya, baby!" he said, and grabbed me.

Then Pete and Hope were getting their greetings and were leading him up to meet the new people, till he got to the bar, where he dropped off to help himself.

It was that minute that Perline, the little maid, came in with a plate in her hand. Charlie swaggered up to her and said, "Well, if it ain't Mayola's daughter." He caught her chin in his hand. "Ain't that so?" "Yes, sir," said Perline. "I am." "Used to know yo' mama," said Charlie. Perline looked confused for a minute; then she lowered her eyes and giggled like she knew she was supposed to. "Gosh sake, Charlie," I said, "quit horsing around and let's dance." It was hard to get him out of these moods. But I'd managed it more than once, dancing.

Charlie was a good strong leader and the way he danced, one hand firm to my waist, he would take my free hand in his and knuckle it tight against his chest. I could follow him better than I could anybody. Sometimes everybody would stop just to watch us, but the prize that night was going to Pete and Hope, they were shining around with some new steps that made the hoop skirts jounce. Charlie was half drunk, too, and bad on the turns.

"Try to remember what's important about this evening," I said. "You know what Hope and Pete are trying for, don't you?"

"I know I'm always coming home to a lecture," said Charlie and swung me out, spinning. "What a woman for sounding like a wife." He got me back and I couldn't tell if he was mad or not, I guess it was half and half; but right then he almost knocked over one of Hope's floral arrangements, so I said, "Why don't you go upstairs and catch your forty winks? Then you can come down fresh and start over." The music stopped. He blinked, looked tired all of a sudden, and, for a miracle, like a dog that never once chose to hear you, he minded.

I breathed a sigh when I saw him going up the stairs. But now I know I never once mentioned Nelle to him or reminded him right out, him with his head full of oil leases, bourbon, and the road, that she was the real cause of the party. Nelle was somewhere else, off in the back sitting room on a couch, to be exact, swapping family news with Mary Foote, who was her cousin.

Dancing with Charlie like that had put me in a romantic mood, and I fell to remembering the time we had first got serious, down on the coast where one summer we had all rented a fishing schooner. We had come into port at Mobile for more provisions and I had showered and dressed and was standing on deck in some leather sandals that tied around the ankle, a fresh white T-shirt, and some clean navy shorts. I had washed my hair, which was short then, and clustered in dark damp curls at the forehead. I say this about myself because when Charlie was coming on board with a six-pack in either hand, he stopped dead still. It was like it was the first time he'd ever seen me. He actually said that very thing later on after we'd finished with the boat and stayed on an extra day or so with all the crowd, to eat shrimp and gumbo and dance every night. We'd had our flare-ups before, but nothing had ever caught like that one. "I can't forget seeing you on the boat that day," he would say. "Don't be crazy, you'd seen me on that boat every day for a week." "Not like that," he'd rave, "like something fresh from the sea." "A catfish," I said. "Stop it, Eileen," he'd say, and dance me off the floor to the dark outside, and kiss me. "I can't get enough of you," he'd say, and take me in so close I'd get dizzy.

I kept thinking through all this in a warm frame of mind while making the rounds and talking to everybody, and maybe an hour, more or less, passed that way, when I heard a voice from the stairwell (Charlie) say: "God Almighty, if it isn't Nelle," and I turned around and saw all there was to see.

Charlie was fresh from his nap, the red faded from his face and his tie in place (he'd even buzzed off his five-o'clock shadow with Pete's electric razor). He was about five steps up from the bottom of the stairs. And Nelle, just coming back into the living room to join everybody, had on a Chinese-red silk shawl with a fringe. Her hair, so simple and shining, wasn't dark or blond either, just the color of hair, and she had on the plain dove-gray silk dress and the elegant sandals. She was framed in the door. Then I saw Charlie's face, how he was drinking her in, and I remembered the day on the boat.

"God damn, Nelle," said Charlie. He came down the steps and straight to her. "Where you been?"

"Oh, hello, Charlie," said Nelle in her friendly way. "Where have *you* been?"

"Honey, that's not even a question," said Charlie. "The point is, I'm *here*."

Then he fixed them both a drink and led her over to a couch in the far corner of the room. There was a side porch at the Owenses', spacious, with a tile floor—that's where we'd all been dancing. The living room was a little off center to the party. I kept on with my partying, but I had eyes in the back of my head where Charlie was concerned. I knew they were there on the couch and that he was crowding her toward one end. I hoped he was talking to her about Grey. I danced with Grey.

"Why don't you go and break that up?" I said.

"Why don't you?" said Grey.

"Marriage is different," I said.

"She can break it up herself if she wants to," he said.

I'd made a blunder and knew it was too late. Charlie was holding both

Nelle's hands, talking over something. I fixed myself a stiff drink. It had begun to rain, quietly, with no advance warning. The couple from Hattiesburg had started doing some kind of talking blues number on the piano. Then we were singing. The couch was empty. Nelle and Charlie weren't there . . .

It was Grey who came to see me the next afternoon. I was hung over but working anyway. Mr. McGinnis didn't recognize hangovers.

"I'm not asking her anywhere again," said Grey. "I'm through and she's through. I've had it. She kept saying in the car, 'Sure, I did like Charlie Waybridge, we all liked Charlie Waybridge. Maybe I was in love with Charlie Waybridge. But why start it up all over again? Why?' 'Why did you?' I said. 'That's more the question.' 'I never meant to, just there he was, making me feel that way.' 'You won't let me make you feel any way,' I said. 'My foot hurts,' she said, like a little girl. She looked a mess. Mud all over her dress and her hair gone to pieces. She had sprained her ankle. It had swelled up. That big."

"Oh, Lord," I said. "All Pete and Hope wanted was for you all—Look, can't you see Nelle was just drunk? Maybe somebody slugged her drink."

"She didn't have to drink it."

I was hearing Charlie: "All she did was get too much. Hadn't partied anywhere in months. Said she wanted some fresh air. First thing I knew she goes tearing out in the rain and whoops! in those high-heeled shoes—sprawling."

"Charlie and her," Grey went on. Okay, so he was hurt. Was that any reason to hurt me? But on he went. "Her and Charlie, that summer you went away up north, they were dating every night. Then her sister got sick, the one that died? She couldn't go on the coast trip with us."

"You think I don't know all that?" Then I said: "Oh, Grey!" and he left.

Yes, I sat thinking, unable to type anything: it was the summer her sister died and she'd had to stay home. I was facing up to Charlie Waybridge. I didn't want to, but there it was. If Nelle had been standing that day where I had stood, if Nelle had been wearing those sandals, that shirt, those shorts—Why pretend not to know Charlie Waybridge, through and through? What was he really doing on the Townshend property that night?

Pete, led by Hope, refused to believe anything but that the party had been a big success. "Like old times," said Pete. "What's wrong with new times?" said Hope. In our weakness and disarray, she was moving on in. (Damn Nelle Townshend.) Hope loved the new people; she was working everybody in together. "The thing for you to do about *that*. . ." she was now fond of saying on the phone, taking on problems of every sort.

When Hope heard that Nelle had sprained her ankle and hadn't been seen out in a day or so, she even got Pete one afternoon and went to call. She had telephoned but nobody answered. They walked up the long front walk between the elephant ears and up the front porch steps and rang the old turning bell half a dozen times. Hope had a plate of cake and Pete was carrying a bunch of flowers.

Finally Mrs. Townshend came shuffling to the door. Humpbacked, she had to look way up to see them, at a mole's angle. "Oh, it's you," she said.

"We just came to see Nelle," Hope chirped. "I understand she hurt her ankle at our party. We'd just like to commiserate."

"She's in bed," said Mrs. Townshend; and made no further move, either to open the door or take the flowers. Then she said, "I just wish you all would leave Nelle alone. You're no good for her. You're no good I know of for anybody. She went through all those years with you. She doesn't want you anymore. I'm of the same opinion." Then she leaned over and from an old-fashioned umbrella stand she drew up and out what could only be called a shotgun. "I keep myself prepared," she said. She cautiously lowered the gun into the umbrella stand. Then she looked up once again at them, touching the rims of her little oval glasses. "When I say you all, I mean all of you. You're drinking and you're doing all sorts of things that waste time, and you call that having fun. It's not my business unless you come here and make me say so, but Nelle's too nice to say so. Nelle never would—" She paused a long time, considering in the mildest sort of way. "Nelle can't shoot," she concluded, like this fact had for the first time occurred to her. She closed the door, softly and firmly.

I heard all this from Hope a few days later. Charlie was off again and I was feeling lower than low. This time we hadn't even quarreled. It seemed more serious than that. A total reevaluation. All I could come to was a question: Why doesn't he reassure me? All I could answer was that he must be in love with Nelle. He tried to call her when I wasn't near. He sneaked off to do it, time and again.

Alone, I tried getting drunk to drown out my thoughts, but couldn't, and alone for a day too long, I called up Grey. Grey and I used to date, pretty heavy. "Hell," said Grey, "I'm fed up to here and so are you. Let's blow it." I was tight enough to say yes and we met out at the intersection. I left my car at the shopping-center parking lot. I remember the sway of his Buick Century, turning onto the Interstate. We went up to Jackson.

The world is spinning now and I am spinning along with it. It doesn't stand still anymore to the stillness inside that murmurs to me, I know my love and I belong to my love when all is said and done, down through foreverness and into eternity. No, when I got back I was just part of it all, ordinary, a twenty-eight-year-old attractive married woman with family and friends and a nice house in Tyler, Mississippi. But with nothing absolute.

When I had a drink too many now, I would drive out to the woods and stop the car and walk around among places always known. One day, not even thinking about them, I saw Nelle drive by and this time there was no doubt who was with her—Robin Byers. They were talking. Well, Robin's wife mended the clothes when they were ripped or torn, and she sewed buttons on. Maybe they were going there. I went home.

At some point the phone rang. I had seen to it that it was "out of order" when I went up to Jackson with Grey, but now it was "repaired," so I answered it. It was Nelle.

"Eileen, I guess you heard Mama turned Pete and Hope out the other day. She was just in the mood for telling everybody off." Nelle laughed her clear, pure laugh. You can't have a laugh like that unless you've got a right to it, I thought.

"How's your ankle?" I asked.

"I'm still hobbling around. What I called for, Mama wanted me to tell you something. She said, 'I didn't mean quite everybody. Eileen can still come. You tell her that.'"

Singled out. If she only knew, I thought. I shook when I put down the phone.

But I did go. I climbed up to Nelle's bedroom with Mrs. Townshend toiling behind me, and sat in one of those old rocking chairs near a bay window with oak paneling and cane plant, green and purple, in a window box. I stayed quite a while. Nelle kept her ankle propped up and Mrs. Townshend sat in a tiny chair about the size of a twelve-year-old's, which was about the size she was. They told stories and laughed with that innocence that seemed like all clear things—a spring in the wood, a dogwood bloom, a carpet of pine needles along a sun-dappled road. Like Nelle's ankle, I felt myself getting well. It was a new kind of wellness, hard to describe. It didn't have much to do with Charlie and me.

"Niggers used to come to our church," Mrs. Townshend recalled. "They had benches in the back. I don't know why they quit. Maybe they all died out—the ones we had, I mean."

"Maybe they didn't like the back," said Nelle.

"It was better than nothing at all. The other churches didn't even have that. There was one girl going to have a baby. I was scared she would have it right in the church. Your father said, 'What's wrong with that? Dr. Erskine could deliver it, and we could baptize it on the spot.'"

I saw a picture on one of those little tables they had by the dozen, with the starched linen doilies and the bowed-out legs. It was of two gentlemen, one taller than the other, standing side by side in shirtsleeves and bow ties and each with elastic bands around their upper arms, the kind that used to hold the sleeves to a correct length of cuff. They were smiling in a fine natural way, out of friendship. One must have been Nelle's father, dead so long ago. I asked about the other. "Child," said Mrs. Townshend, "don't you know your own grandfather? He and Sid thought the world of one another." I had a better feeling when I left. Would it last? Could I get it past the elephant ears?

I didn't tell Charlie about going there. Charlie got it from some horse's mouth that Grey and I were up in Jackson that time, and he pushed me off the back steps. An accident, he said; he didn't see me when he came whamming out the door. For a minute I thought I, too, had sprained or broken something, but a skinned knee was all it was. He watched me clean the knee, watched the bandage go on. He wouldn't go out—not to Pete and Hope's, not to Rose and John's, not to anywhere—and the whiskey went down in the bottle.

I dreamed one night of Robin Byers, that I ran into him uptown but didn't see a scar on his face. I followed him, asking, Where is it? What happened? Where's it gone? But he walked straight on, not seeming to hear. But it was no dream that his house caught fire, soon after the cleaning shop opened again. Both Robin and Nelle said it was only lightning struck the back wing and burned out a shed room before Robin could stop the blaze. Robin's daughter got jumped on at school by some other black children who yelled about her daddy being a "Tom." They kept her at home for a while to do her schoolwork there. What's next?

Next for me was going to an old lady's apartment for Mr. McGinnis, so she could sign her will, and on the long steps to her door, running into Robin Byers, fresh from one of his deliveries.

"Robin," I said, at once, out of nowhere, surprising myself, "you got to leave here, Robin. You're tempting fate, every day."

And he, just as quick, replied: "I got to stay here. I got to help Miss Nelle."

Where had it come from, what we said? Mine wasn't a bit like me; I might have been my mother or grandmother talking. Certainly not the fun girl who danced on piers in whirling miniskirts and dove off a fishing boat to reach a beach, swimming, they said, between the fishhooks and the sharks. And Robin's? From a thousand years back, maybe, superior and firm, speaking out of sworn duty, his honored trust. He was standing above me on the steps. It was just at dark, and in the first streetlight I could see the white scar, running riverlike down the flesh, like the mark lightning leaves on a smooth tree. When we passed each other, it was like erasing what we'd said and that we'd ever met.

But one day I am walking in the house and picking up the telephone, only to find Charlie talking on the extension. "Nelle . . ." I hear. "Listen, Nelle. If you really are foolin' around with that black bastard, he's answering to *me*." And *blam!* goes the phone from her end, loud as any gun of her mother's.

I think we are all hanging on a golden thread, but who has got the other end? Dreaming or awake, I'm praying it will hold us all suspended.

Yes, praying—for the first time in years.

1987

Quitting Smoking

Reginald McKnight

Jan. 16, 1978
Manitou Spgs., CO

Dear B——,

Happy New Year and all that. Man, are you ever hard to get a hold of. I wrote your ex–ol' lady first, and she said, and I quote, "As to his whereabouts, well, your guess is as good as mine. The last I heard he was still with TWA, but based in London. I do know that he was suspended for six weeks for giving free tickets to London to that girlfriend of his. I'm surprised they didn't flat out fire him." She mainly ranted about how you only write and send money on your boy's birthday. She's still pretty pissed off at you, my man. Anyway, she said that your folks might know and she gave me their new address and phone # in Texas. I didn't even know they moved. Anyway, money's been a little tight lately, and I don't even have a phone at the moment, so I wrote a card. Didn't here anything for a long time, but then your kid sister, Mayra, wrote me, and this is what she said, "We got your letter a long time ago, but we don't know excatly where B—— is My brother has moved a lot in the last couple of years because of his job. The reason I'm writing you instead of my mother is because my mother is discusted with B——. But she won't tel any-body why. And she says she doesn't know his address. I know she does but can't find it any where. But I will look for it and if I find it I will send it to you. My big sister Letonya said if she gets the address she will send the let-ter to B—— but I don't think so because she is getting married and is always forgetting to do things. Mamma is discusted with Letonya because she says shes too young to get married. right now your letter is on the fridge with a magnit on it."
    I thought you'd like that, B——.
    Then I called TWA. They were kind of nasty, and no help at all. They did tell me you were on leave, though, but wouldn't say where. So, how did I get your address? Letonya came through. She said you were living it up in Madrid for six months, and then you'd be going back to London. I guess she'd be married by now.

I guess you're probably surprised to hear from me after all these years, homes, and I bet you're surprised at how long this letter is, or for me right at this second, how long it's gonna be. This'll be the longest thing I'll ever have written by the time I'm done. I know that already, B——, 'cause the stuff I got on my mind is complicated and confusing. I've been sleeping pretty bad lately, cause I've been thinking about that thing that happened when you, me, Stick, and Camel saw that guy snatch that woman into his car in front of Griff's, just after hoops practice. I'm sure you remember. It bothered me a lot back then, of course, but you know it's been nine years now and you get over things like that after awhile. And for a long time I didn't really think about it all that much. But something happened a few weeks ago between me and my girl friend, Anna, that brought all that stuff up again and has pretty much messed up things between me and her. The stuff I'm gonna tell you, speaking of "between," is just between you and me. Period. OK? but I've gotta tell you the whole thing so you'll understand where I'm coming from and understand why I've done what I've done. I feel bad that I've gotta talk about Anna behind her back like this, but goddamnit, you're the only guy who'd understand what I'm trying to work out in my mind. You and me are pretty much cut from the same tree, you could say. We both grew up in this town, well, I'm in Manitou, now and not Colo. Spgs, but I'll get to that later. We both hung around maybe too many white people growing up. We're both tall and black, but can't play hoops worth a damn. We both have had very weird relationships with redheaded, greeneyed women, only you actually married yours. Anna and I just lived together. Yeah, "live" in the past tense. Looks like it might be over between me and Anna. Over, unless, after you've read all this you think what I've done is wrong, and you say that I should give Anna another chance, or she should give me one. You know, I was gonna try to get in touch with the other "fellas" about this, too. I know where the Stick is. I think I do, anyway. I ran into Coach Ortiz at José Muldoon's and he told me the Stick is teaching Poli Sci at some college in Athens, Georgia. I'd tried his folks' place first, but the old phone number don't work and they're not in the book. The last I heard about Camel is that he joined the service. The army or the airforce, I'm not sure. Can you imagine that big buck-tooth hippie in the service? But anyway, I decided not to write or call those guys 'cause, to be honest, they're white and I don't think they'd understand.

Right now, I'm living in Manitou Springs, like I said, in a place called Banana Manor. A big stone monster painted bright yellow and trimmed in brown. It used to be a hotel, I guess. It's kind of a hippie flop house. Lot's of drugs, sex, rock n' roll, long hair and cheap rent. I got a room here and pay only $65 a month for it. Most of my stuff's still at the place me and Anna shared, and I still go by there and pick up my mail and stuff, but I only go there when she's not around, mainly cause it'd hurt too much to see her. I leave her notes and still pay my share of the rent. Don't know how long I'll do that though.

Before I get to my point (sorry it's taking me so long) I guess I oughta catch you up on me. After all, B——, we ain't seen each other in about six years, or written or called since you split with Kari. How's your boy, by the way? Good, I hope. Well now, I finally got my certificate in cabinetry at Pikes Peak Comm. Col. Actually, I copped an A.A. in general studies, too. I had the money and the time, so I figured, what the fuck. Besides, Anna kept ragging on me till I did. Graduated third in my cabinetry class, quit this stock-BOY gig I'd had at Alco's and got a part timer at Chess King. I sold shake yo' booty clothes to mostly army clowns from Fort Cartoon. (That's what my Anna calls Fort Carson.) Well, I got fired for "studying at work" and "ignoring customers," which all I have to say about is if you remember my study habits in high school, you'll know it was all bullshit. They fired me 'cause I wouldn't wear their silly-ass clothes on the job. My mom always used to tell me, "You ain't got to dress like a nigro to look like a nigro, boy."

So I was out of work for about two months and moved in with Anna, which had its ups and downs (no pun). Anna's got a couple of years on me. Actually five, but she looks about 20. She has a kid, though, and to tell you the truth, I could do without the instant family stuff. But Max, her kid is alright for a rug rat. I mean, he wets the bed sometimes, and he's about as interested in sports as I'm interested in Sesame Street, but he's smart, funny, and likes me, so I could hang with it. To tell you the truth, I miss him a lot.

But like I'm saying, there were some good things about living with Anna, and some things that weren't so good. Good and not so good. The usual. She's divorced, and 31, like I said. We met at the community college about a year and a half ago. It was in the Spring Quarter, and the weather was perfect, in the 80's, sky like a blank blue page. I was sitting on a bench outside the cafeteria, talking to this friend of mine when she walked by in a pink Danskin top and a pink and white flowered skirt. My asshole friend yells out, "Hey! You got the most beautiful breasts I've ever seen." And she blushed and kept walking. I told Steve that was no way to talk to a woman and he told me that broads like that kind of talk, and besides, he didn't say "tits." I told him to screw off and ran after her. I apologized to her and told her I had nothing to do with what Steve'd said. She kind of nodded real quick, mumbled something and kept walking. Then I walked away, and didn't figure I'd ever see her again. I felt like an idiot. Didn't even wanna think about it.

Well, about two weeks later I was in the parking lot and just about to my car when I hear this little voice say, "You have the most beautiful ass I've ever seen." It was Anna, and as they say, da rest is history. She's 5'2" and has a body that would make your teeth sweat. Steve was right about her bust, but he missed the rest. Like I say, she's got red hair, green eyes, but the weird thing is she tans real good. Not like most redheads who sit out in the sun for two seconds and end up looking like blisters with feet, or get so many freckles that you wanna hand em a brown magic marker and go tell em to finish the job. So anyway, she's also about a hundred times smarter than I am, which is no big deal, cause she never jams it down my throat. Besides since I started at the cabinet mill I make more scratch than she does. (She's on welfare.) Anna's a sociology major at Colorado College, now, and she'd been trying to talk me into going there to get a degree in something, but for one thing I don't have the money, and for another thing, you don't exactly see legions of folks our color over there so I doubt they'd want me. Anyhow, I'm not exactly a genius. I might have done good in cabinet school, but I couldn't pull higher than six or seven B's in general studies. Screw em. Plus, I know the kind of bullshit you had to put up with at Graceland College, amongst all that wheat and corn and cow squat. I still have that letter where you told me about the "joke" (ha ha) Klan party your friends threw for you on your birthday. That kind of thing ain't for the kid here.

Anyway, let me get to my point before I bore you to death. OK, so like one night, about a month ago, Anna and I were in the sack and she wouldn't even kiss me good night. This is strange, I was thinking, cause usually she's more interested in sex than I am, which means she likes it more than a woodpecker likes balsa. So I asked her what the hell was wrong. (Actually, I said, "Hey, babes, you OK?") And she started crying, real slow and silent. So I got up and burned a doobie. (Yes. I smoke now. Actually, I smoke cigarettes, too, but I'd pretty much quit while I was with Anna. More about that later.) I passed it to her and she took a couple hits. So like I asked her again what was up and she said she got upset cause that day in class they were talking about social deviants (sp?) and her prof said that all of society makes it easy for men to commit rape and that there was no real way to completely eradicate it. So Anna said back to the guy that castration would sure the hell stop it. And then nobody said much of anything for like a minute. Then the prof came back with all that talk show crap that rape isn't sexual, but violent, etc., etc. And Anna just sat there for a while, while the guy kept talking, and she told me that she'd made up her mind not to say anything else. But then, before she knew what hit her, she just sort of blared out, "Then give them the fucking death penalty!" That's exactly what she said. And that started a huge argument in the class.

Well, Anna crushed out the joint in the ashtray. She did it real hard and all I could think about was somebody crushing out a smoking hard-on, which I'm sure she wanted me to think. She's really into symbols and shit. In fact, I think she wanted me to get my A.A. just so I'd get all the symbols she dumps on me. Alright, so I was kind of surprised, cause even though Anna's kind of a women's libber, she's always been pretty mellow about things, and she's always been real anti-death penalty. So I asked her why she'd said that stuff in class. She didn't say anything for about a minute. She was just staring up at the passion plant that we have hanging over our bed. So I asked her if she was ever raped. I asked her flat out, and I was sorry I had. She still didn't say anything. And then she just sort of curled up on the bed. She curled up as tight as a fist and goddamn did she ever cry. Jesus, Jesus, Jesus, B——, I was scared, kind of. I've never seen nothing like that. She didn't make any kind of sound hardly. It was like she was pulling up a rope that was tied to something heavy as the moon. Goddamn, those tears were coming from way, way down. I touched her and every muscle in her was like bowed oak. She was just kind of going uh, uh, uh, her whole body jerking like a heart. Then she threw her arms around me so fast, I thought for a second she wanted to slug me. I couldn't swallow, and I could feel my veins pounding where the inner part of my arm touched her back and shoulders. We held each other so tight, we were like socks rolled up and tucked away in a drawer. I guess I never loved or cared so much about anybody as then.

About, I don't know how long later, she told me about it. We'd went into the kitchen cause I was hungry, and she wanted some wine. Her eyes were all puffy and red. Her voice croaked. And every once in a while she'd shiver, and get this scared look in her eye and look all around the room. She was whispering cause she didn't want to wake up Max, who's room is right next to the kitchen. But the whispering sort of made it weirder or scarier or something. I kept gulping like some cartoon character, and my feet and hands were like ice. I couldn't look at her.

It was this friend of her ex's who'd did it. She says they were sitting in her and her old man's living room. Her old man was at work. He was a medic at Ft. Cartoon. I met him once when he came from Texas, where he lives now, to see Max. Guy's an extreme red neck. So anyway, she says she and this guy were getting high on hash, and just talking about stuff. Anyway, they were just sitting there, getting high, when just like that, this guy pulls a knife and tells her to strip and he rapes her. It made me kind of nervous and sick to hear all that. She told me she'd never told anyone else. I guess it sounds kind of dumb, but I felt honored that I was the only person she'd ever told that to. It sort of made me love her even more. Then just like on some cop show or something, she started telling me that she felt all dirty because of what that guy did. It kind of surprised me that a real woman would talk that way. I pretty much thought that kind of stuff was just made up. But she doesn't even watch TV, except for the news and tennis matches, so I'm sure she wasn't saying it because she'd heard someone else say it. But I hugged her real tight, after she said that, and I told her that she was the sweetest, most beautiful woman I'd ever known. I meant it too. I didn't stop telling her till she smiled a little.

We went back to the bedroom and got back in bed. I never did get anything to eat. Pretty soon she was asleep, but I couldn't sleep at all. It was partly because of what she'd told me, and partly because of what she'd made me remember. That's why I'm writing you, B——. I couldn't and I still can't sleep because of what you and me and Stick and Camel saw that one night when we were standing outside the gym. It was the only time the four of us ever just hung out together like that. I don't even know why we were all there together. Do you? I mean, the Stickmeister never hung with the three of us, cause we weren't real popular. And Camel could have walked home. Usually it was just you and me who'd be out there, waiting for the activity bus. It was colder than Jennifer Lash's underdrawers out there. Remember? You didn't have a jacket, and you offered five bucks to Camel if he'd let you wear his. I remember we all cracked up when you did that.

So, laying there next to Anna it's like I was reliving that night. I kept seeing the blue car, and how the woman kept saying, please, please, please, please, and how she tried to crawl under the car, and how you and me were starting across the street, but Stick grabbed your arm and said, He might have a gun, He might kill her—and then how you just stood there saying, Hey! Hey! Hey! And then they were gone. Everything was just taillights all of a sudden. I can't believe we just stood there. And I was so goddamn embarrased when the cop asked what year the car was, and we didn't know, what the license plate read, and we didn't know. And I think we were all embarrased when we told the cop our stories. I remember you said she was dressed like a nurse and you saw her on the sidewalk, just walking and then the car pulled up and the guy pulled her in. Then I told them that, no, no, no, first she tried to crawl under the car, then he pulled her in. Then Camel said, no, no, no, there were two guys, and the guy in the passenger seat had a gun. Then Stick said no, no, no, no, I think she was in the car first and tried to get out, and the guy pulled her back in. Come on guys, Stick said, don't you remember when the guy kept asking her for the keys? and, no Camel, there wasn't a gun I just thought the guy might have a gun. And I remember, you said, B——, God! What's wrong with you, Stick, that was the woman saying, *please, please, please*; nobody said a damn thing about no keys! She was crawling under the car and screaming please!

Jesus. Please, keys, tease, ease, bees, knees, cheese. Jeez, what a buncha idiots we must've looked like. But the thing that got me the most, the thing that fucked me up the most that night was when the cop asked the big money, bonus question, What color was the guy? You and me said, Couldn't tell. Too dark, Camel and Stick said, at the same time, Black. Then we started arguing. No, no, no, too dark to tell. No, no, no, Afro, he had an Afro. No, butthole, how could you tell? Do you remember if the woman was black? No? Then what makes you think the guy was black? The woman was white, you chump. Yeah? Well what color was her hair? How long was it? How tall was she? Heavy-set, was she, or thin? Old or young? too dark to tell. Too dark to tell. And what makes you think she was in the car first, Stick?

God, what idiots we were. And I sat up in bed that night, after Anna'd told me what she told me and I couldn't get it out of my head. But I thought about other things, too, B——. I thought about how I used to fantasize when I was a kid, after I'd seen "To Kill a Mockingbird." I used to fantasize about how I was on trial for raping a white woman, and how I knew I was innocent, and I'd be up on the witness stand with the prosecuting attorney's hot, tomato-faced mug right up in mine. He'd be spitting crap like, Didn'cha, boy? Didn'cha? You lusted afta those white arms, and those pink lips and those pale blue, innocent eyes, didn'cha, nigger boy?

Objection!

Sustained. Mr. Hendershot, I have warned you about—

Forgive me yo honor—and then he dabs his tomato face down with a crumpled hanky—but when ah think of the way these . . . these animals lust afta our sweet belles, why, sir, it makes mah blood boil. No more questions. Yo witness, Mistah Wimply.

And my defender would get up there and sputter and mumble. The prosecutor'd be laughing into his cuffs, dabbing his face, winking and blinking at the jury. Wimply'd look like a fool, but somehow I'd be able to say the right things, and I'd speak as powerfully as Martin Luther King Jr. himself. And while I talked I'd be looking at my accuser with my big puppy eyes and I'd talk about love and justice and peace, equality, never taking my eyes off her beautiful face. She'd start to sweat and tremble, then she'd pass out. The crowd'd go huzzah, hummah, huzzah. The judge would bang away with his gavel. But soon enough the testimony would end, the jury would come back and basically say, Hang the black bastud. Then we'd come back the next day, and the judge would say, Scott Winters, you have been found guilty by a jury of your peers. You have committed a vile and foul crime, my boy, and this court has decided to make you pay the ultimate penalty . . . But all of a sudden, B——, my accuser would pop up from her seat and say, No! He's innocent! Innocent, I tell you. I accused him of the crime because I love him, but all he did was ignore me every time I tried to talk to him or smile at him. He ignored me. Then she'd cry like a son of a bitch, and the crowd'd start up with the Huzzah, hummah, huzzah. And the judge would be hammering away with his gavel, the prosecutor'd be patting his fat face with his hanky, and the woman would run into my arms. And that'd be that.

Don't ask me why I'd fantasize about that, and I'm not sure if "fantasy" is even the right word. I just played that, whatever it is, in my head, night after night, and I don't know why, exactly, but I think it's because when somebody says rapist, what picture comes to mind? I know I don't have to tell you, B——, it's me and you and your brother and your dad, and my dad, and all our uncles and cousins, and so on. It's like how Anna said at breakfast last year when she was preaching to me like she always does about women's lib stuff. She said, "Scott, if I were to come back from the doctor's today, came home with tears in my eyes because of what the doctor had told me, what would you say?" Well, I didn't know what she was driving at, and I shrugged and said, "Well, first thing I'd ask is, What'd he tell you?" And she jumped up from her chair and spilled her coffee and mine in the process and said, "Bingo! See! See! 'What did He say' that's my point. Do you understand me now? We've got these images imbeded in our heads and they're based on stereotypes!" I'll tell you what, man, I did get her point, but if I hadn't I woulda said I'd got it just the same. Cripes.

Anyway, there I was in bed with her, listening to her breathing, thinking about those old fantasies, and about that day we saw the woman being snatched off the street, and how this beautiful woman laying next to me had to suffer so hard over something she could never, ever forget. I couldn't sleep. I wanted a cigarette bad, the first time I'd really even thought about squares since her and I moved in together. I slipped out of bed and dressed. I was gonna walk up to the 7–Eleven and buy a pack of Winstons, my old brand. I was gonna walk back home, smoking one after another and think about things like why guys are such dogs, and how in hell Anna could love or trust any guy after what'd happened to her. It was cold that night, and snow was falling, but not too hard or thick. They were big flakes, and the sky was pinkish gray. You could see as far as a block or two. Real beautiful. It was dead quiet, no traffic, no voices, no dogs barking. You know how Colorado Springs can be on a winter night at two in the morning. It's funny, but I kept expecting the night to be split in two by screams, and I imagined myself running to wherever the screams'd come from, and I'd find some bastard pinning a woman down on the sidewalk, holding a blade to her throat and hissing, Shut the fuck up you goddamn cunt. And I'd see his big red balls hanging over her. I'd plow my ol' two-ton mountain boots so hard into them sacks it'd take a team of surgeons to pull em out his stomach. I could see myself taking the knife out his weak hands, and making one clean, quiet slice on his throat, and that'd be that. I'd walk the woman home and call the cops, and split before they got there. I was thinking so deep about this stuff, B——, it took me awhile to notice that my fists were clenched, and so were my teeth. And it took me just as long to notice that I was walking, then, in the same goddamn neighborhood where the four of us had seen the woman, the guy, and the blue car.

It really kind of freaked me out. I didn't recognize it right away, because in '69, of course, there'd been a Griff's Burger Bar(f) on that lot. Then they made it into a Taco John's. Now it's some kind of church, but there I was— probably standing exactly on the spot where nine years ago that woman'd stood. Man, I just stood there for maybe five minutes. And then I went and sat on the steps of the church. All them things were going through my mind, all the stuff I was fantasizing about, all the stuff I could and couldn't quite remember. Then I started feeling guilty about being there, on my way to get a pack of squares. I hadn't had a cigarette in eight months. Like I said, it was Anna who'd help me quit them things. It was, in a way, the basis of our relationship. Anna's into health like you wouldn't believe. She used to smoke cigarettes, but quit them, and coffee, when Max was born. She took up swimming and running to get back in shape after he was six months or so. Then when he was like two or three, she quit eating meat. The first couple times we went out we ate at a pizza place, and it was the first time in my life I'd ever had a pizza with no meat on it. It wasn't bad, but I was still hungry. I told her too, but she said, "It's psychological. You're meat-hungry." I paused for a minute and grinned real big. Then she laughed and said, "God, you've got a dirty mind." Well, we went to her place. I'd never even been inside before. It was different, really hippyish. There were plants at every window, and it smelled like incense. There was all this beautiful art on the walls, paintings and prints and lithos. Her bedroom was a loft. It sure didn't look like a welfare house, not what I thought one would look like, anyway. Well, I paid the babysitter, even though she didn't want me to. Then we got high. Then we made love.

I'd never felt so good with a woman. It was all so quiet and natural, but still intense. But when I say quiet, I don't mean she was silent. She made so much noise I thought she'd wake her kid. When I say quiet, though, I mean peaceful, sort of spiritual. She went to sleep, but I stayed awake, and then I went outside and lit up a square. When I went back inside, I noticed how bad I stunk. Tobacco'd never smelled so strong or so bad to me. I went to the bathroom and washed my hands and face, tried to brush my teeth with toothpaste and my finger. Next morning, we got up and she fixed me a fritata. (Don't know if I spelled that right or not). It's this thing with eggs and vegies. We had apple juice and Morning Thunder tea. At first I thought something was wrong with the juice because it was brown, but Anna told me it was natural, and was supposed to look like that. It tasted great. And after breakfast I didn't have a cigarette, which is what I usually do. It wasn't hard. I just didn't want one. We went to school, and met each other during the day as much as we could. I didn't have a cigarette all day. After classes, I picked her up and then we got Max from school, and I took them home. Anna wanted me to stay for dinner, but I was dying for a smoke. When I got home I smoked like a fiend. But the more time I spent with her, the less I cared about cigarettes. It was easy. I quit eating meat, too. I wasn't whipped man. It just didn't feel right anymore.

So, anyway, B——, there I was on the steps of the church feeling guilty about getting cigarettes. I sat there for a long time, but then got up and walked back home. When I got back into bed with Anna, she woke up, and told me how cold I was. "I went for a walk," I said, which was true, but it felt like a lie. I felt guilty about a whole lot of things that night—for wanting a cigarette, for being a man, and for not telling her about that night and what we saw. It was work night, too, even though it felt like a Friday. I knew there'd be hell to pay if I showed up late for work. Old man Van Vordt is a prick-and-a-1/2. You show up more than thirty seconds late and he fires you. You cut a piece of lumber as much as 1/16 of an inch too short and he fires you. You take more than the twenty minutes he gives us for lunch and you might as well pack your trash and ride out of Dodge. In the six months I've worked with him, he's fired about thirty guys. He only wants to tell you something once. Fuck it up, and you die. He pays good money, though, and that's why I keep going back to that freckle-headed ol' fart. Besides, I love the smell of wood, and the precision and beauty of what we do. He's the best cabinet maker I've ever run into, and for some reason, he likes me. I'm the only black guy he's ever had working for him. Maybe he believes in affirmative action. But anyway, my point is that I decided to stay up that night, cause I couldn't sleep, and I didn't want to be late to work. That made me want a cigarette all the more.

I started smoking about five years ago. To tell you the truth I like smoking a lot. Cigarettes, I mean. Pot's ok, but I like a cigarette buzz more, for some reason. And I like the way my lungs fill up. It makes me feel warm inside, makes me dreamy, sort of. I like making smoke rings, french inhaling, shot guns. And even though it stinks like hell, I like it when my room fills up with smoke. It's like having indoor clouds. I do go through about a can of air freshener a week, and I gotta run fans and keep windows open to kill the smell, but when the sun's shining through my windows in the afternoons, I'll shut em, fire up square after square, lay in my bed and blow cloud after cloud of blue and yellow smoke. And I hate it when a friend busts into my room on those days and says, "Jeezuz, it stinks in here." Hell, I know it stinks, but you can't smell worth a damn if you're inhaling and blowing. And it's my room.

I started smoking in '73, like I say, when I was still living at my folks' place and you were in college at Graceland. I'd went down to Alamosa to visit with Gary T— and Dale P—. They were juniors, I think, and were living off campus. Let me tell you, if you think those guys were partiers in high school, you shoulda seen em then. There whole place was set up for partying. No rugs, black lights, strobe lights, lava lamps. They had a refrigerator in the basement that was filled with beer, maybe twelve cases. They had a wet bar upstairs, and this big ass cabinet filled with every type of booze you could name. Then there was this fishbowl in the kitchen that was full of joints, pills, and blotter acid. It was unreal. Serious to God, I wasn't into any of that stuff at the time, and most of it I'm still not. I've never done acid, speed, coke, downers, dust, and I can't stand most booze. I might have a beer every so often, but I just nurse the hell out of em. Man, I can make a can of beer last for a whole party. I did speed once in high school, and once again a couple months ago when I was working twelve-hour days at the mill. Anyway, I went up to check out Gary and Dale cause I hadn't seen them in a year, or more. I was really surprised at what they looked like. Both of em had hair down to the middle of their backs. Dale was wearing this big honkin fu manchu and

Gary had a full beard. It was incredible. Neither of them was playing hoop anymore. Gary'd quit and Dale'd wrecked his knees.

So, anyway, they weren't having any party that night, but people kept coming by all afternoon and all night to buy drugs. They had quite a nice business. They were each pulling down about 20 thou a year. It's how they paid their tuition. Far as I know they're still dealing.

So like, we shake hands and bullshit, etc, etc, and they show me around their place, etc, etc, and then Gary's fiance comes by, and we go down to the basement and sit on bean bags and then Gary brings out a gas mask and a bag of Panama Red. Oh, Lord, I started thinking. What if the cops bust down the door and start blazing away? What if it's bad stuff and we OD or something? (Yeah, I was pretty naive.) Then Dale said, "You get high, Scott?" And I said, "Oh sure." So when the mask came my way, I huffed and pulled and sucked, but didn't feel a thing. I took about fifteen hits in all, but still didn't feel a thing. Except I did feel paranoid (or as Gary would say, "noid"). I told em I still lived with my folks and they'd kill me if I came home reeking. So Dale reached into his T-shirt pocket and took out a pack of Marlboros, and said, "Smoke these on the way back. You'll smell like cigarettes, and that might make em mad, but you won't smell like weed, which'll make em toss you out." I put em in my pocket, and we hung out for a while longer and talked, etc, etc. Then we ordered a couple pizzas, ate, and then I split back home.

I got back to the Springs about one in the morning and I'd forgot all about the cigarettes till I was almost home, so I pulled off at this junior high parking lot, lit one up. After about five minutes I felt like I was floating. I felt calm. It was weird. I mean, I'd spent the entire evening smoking dope and hadn't felt a thing, but I was getting ripped on a damn cigarette. Well, that was it, man, I was hooked. Into it big time. My mom was pissed off at me when she found out I was smoking, but what could she say really? I mean both my folks'd started smoking when they were in their teens, and they smoke maybe a pack a day a piece. Things got a little tense around the house, though, so I moved out.

Like I say, I wanted a cigarette, but I didn't smoke. Anna went to school and I went to work. Things seemed pretty normal. I was dragging ass at work, though, and ol' Van de Man was a demon. "Scott! Where's those rabbit cuts I asked you for? Scott! I thought I asked you to clean that planer. Scott! You building a goddamn ark or what? Thought I asked you for them chester drawer legs a half hour ago!" I saw my career flash before my eyes a half dozen times. It wasn't only cause I was tired, and it wasn't only cause I would have given my left nut for a cigarette, and it wasn't just that I walked around all day with my guts feeling like Jello cause I was afraid every second of what might happen to Anna when I wasn't home. It was because I thought that since she'd told me about the worst thing that'd ever happened to her, that I should tell her about the worst thing that I ever let happen to someone else. But when I got home that afternoon, I made dinner, we ate, she did the dishes, we went to bed and made love for a long, long time. And that was it. It took me four hours to get to sleep that night.

Days went by and days went by and still I didn't say anything. But all I could think about was how that woman was trying to dig her nails into the pavement while she was under that car. And all I could think about was some bastard holding a knife to my woman's throat and breaking into her like a bullet. And I started getting weird and jealous in funny ways, like once when I drove by campus to pick her up from the library, and she was out front talking to this dude. She was standing out on the lawn, holding her books up over her breasts, and this tall blond bearded dude was craning over her, smiling, talking, moving his hands like he was conducting a goddamn band. I could tell they were looking deep in each other's eyes. I thought I could tell she was into this dude. B——, I know this'll sound stupid, but I was sitting there in my car, thinking, You idiot, don't you know what he's got on his mind? Don't you know what he could do to you? I acted like a prick all night long. To her anyway. With Max, I was like Santa Claus. I rode him on my back like a horse, I played checkers with him, I read him a couple stories. Then after everybody was in bed, I slipped out the house, walked to the 7–Eleven and bought a pack of cigarettes, and a bottle of mouthwash. I went to Monument Valley Park and smoked half a pack, washed my mouth over and over till the bottle was empty, and then I split back home. Soon as I got back I smoked a joint to mask the smell.

I thought we should be getting closer. I thought she should mistrust every man, but me. But then I got to thinking that maybe she could sense something about me, knew I was holding something back, which I was. I was holding two things back. I thought she was sensing something, 'cause her attitude was changing at home. She'd gotten pretty rough with Max. Didn't hit him or anything, but she'd go pyro on him if he spilled milk or messed up his clothes. And she only seemed interested in talking to me about stuff she was doing at school. And when all I could say back was something like, " . . . . . . ?" she started giving me all this women's lib stuff to read. Gyno-this and eco-gyno-poly-that. And when I still didn't get it, she'd just click her tongue at me and roll her eyes, sigh real loud and stomp off. She started correcting my English, which is something she'd never done, she started having long phone conversations with people and she'd never tell me who she was calling. And every time I thought maybe I'd better tell her about what you and me and the fellas saw, that night she'd do something else to piss me off, and I'd keep my mouth shut. I think from the time I lit that first square, the base of our relationship started to crumble. But then she was keeping something from me, too. I didn't know for sure, but I could feel it. I couldn't keep my mind off that tall blond son of a bitch.

I started picking up a pack of smokes on the way to work every day. And I started keeping mouthwash, gum, soap, air freshener, a toothbrush, and deodorant in a day sack in my trunk. Sometimes she'd say to me, "Geez, have you been at work or at a disco?" I'd tell her I just thought she'd like it if I didn't come home smelling like a bear. "You smelled like sawdust," she said, "and I like sawdust." But I couldn't stop smoking. And I started up eating meat again, too. On the way to work, I'd toss my cheese and sprout sandwiches and grab a hoagie, a chillie dog, didn't matter. So I'd play Mr. Tofu Head at home and go to work and let myself get scuzzy as hell. It never occurred to me once to look into other women, but I felt just as guilty. I couldn't sleep for shit, and I was getting kinda soft in bed, if you know what I mean. I couldn't stand myself. And I couldn't stand her. After we'd screw—and it was screwing by then, not love—I couldn't stand the touch of her. It was like every damn day I felt like I was gonna explode. I could see myself dropping to the floor at Anna's feet and begging her to forgive me for all the stuff I was doing, and all the stuff I'd failed to do. I'd beg her to forget that tall motherfucker and come back to me.

B——, I tried and tried and tried to tell her, but I couldn't, and I knew I was smoking a wall between us. I knew that, man, so I'd try every day to quit. I'd crush my cigarettes before leaving work and flush em down the toilet. I'd spray, wash, brush, rinse my ass till I was clean as a pimp. I'd do this every day, and every day I saw them squares, spinning round and round that white water, and going down, I thought that'd be it, that I wouldn't smoke any more. I bought a book on self-hypnosis, and a self-hypnosis tape at this health food place where we used to shop. I tried herbal teas, and hot showers, gum, candy, jogging, prayer. And I'd go home every day with a new idea, or a new way of picking up the subject of rape. I figured that of all the reasons I'd gone back to smoking, that was it. One day, I said, "Hey, babe, why don't we start giving money to one of them women's shelter things?" She was cooking dinner at the time. It was her day to do it. I was kicking back at the kitchen table, drinking some juice. She didn't say anything for like 30 seconds, enough time for me to get nervous, and start looking around. I watched Max tumbling around in the back yard. He looked cute as hell, his hair looked like pure white light the way the sun hit it. Then I looked back at Anna. She just picked up a handful of vegie peelings and flung em in the trash. "I think that'd be a good idea," she said, but she was looking really tight, really serious when she said it. I knew something wasn't "organic" as she would say, so I asked her what was up. Well, she flung that red hair out of her face, wiped away some sweat from her forehead with the back of her hand, dried her hands on a towel, and left the room. She came back in a minute with a little stash box, and I was relieved for a second cause I thought she was gonna twist up a joint and haul me off to bed. I was smiling, I think. She opened the box, reached in and tossed a cigarette, my brand, on the table. "I found it in your pocket when I did laundry yesterday," she said. She just stood there. I just sat there. "Busted," I said.

Yeah, we fought about it, but I didn't have too much fight in me, really. What could I say? It was mine. "I trusted you," she said. "You told me that when you met me, quitting smoking was the easiest thing in the world," she said. Scott Winters, I was thinking, a jury of your peers has found you guilty . . . It really surprised me when she started crying. I didn't think she'd took it that serious. I mean, she never'd asked me to quit smoking. Never said a word about it. And it was easy. When we moved in together, I just didn't buy any more squares. That was it.

From that day on, the day I was busted, is when I started thinking about getting in touch with you, B——. I wanted to ask you how you felt when Kari found out about you and that chick you were seeing. How you felt when you got busted. Kari called me up one day, after you and she'd split, and she was so angry I could hear the phone lines sizzling. She said, "I just wanna ask you one thing, Scott. Will you be honest with me?" And I said sure I would. And she asked me, "Did B—— really tell you he'd dreamt about me six weeks before he and I actually met? Was that true, Scott?" Well, B——, I'm sorry, bud, but I felt bad for her, and I figured that it wouldn't make any difference since you two'd already split. I told her the truth. I told her no, you hadn't told me that. Then she asked me if it was true what your girlfriend had told her, that you'd been picked up for flashing back in '72 when you lived in San Francisco, and I told Kari that's what you told me. Then—and her voice got higher and I could tell she was gonna cry—she said, "And then that bitch told me that B—— had gotten a woman pregnant when he was in college. Do you know if that's true?" I told her that I'd heard about it from a very unreliable source. That's all I knew. But it was good enough for her. She started crying, and God did I feel bad. She kept saying, "Thank you, Scott, thank you, thank you. I'm sorry to bother you, but I just wanted the truth for once. All of it. I just wanted to hear someone tell me the truth." She hung up without even saying goodbye.

That's why you haven't heard from me, B——. I was confused and felt ashamed. In fact, that last letter I got from you a few years back is still unopened. I just figured that Kari had called you up to bust your chops, 'cause of what I'd told her, and you were writing to bust mine. I couldn't take that. And if you don't write back now, I'll understand. Anyway, that time, there at the kitchen table, staring at the cigarette, is when I started thinking about you.

I tried to quit, but I couldn't. Sure, I told her I'd quit again, but I never did. I just got smarter about hiding things. I'd quit smoking so close to the end of the work day, always kept my squares in my locker at work. That kind of thing. On weekends, I never even thought about cigarettes. I'd take Max to the playground. I'd go grocery shopping. I'd go down to Pueblo to fish with my folks, with Anna & Max, or by myself, and I'd never even think about them. But I just couldn't do it this time. Anna was ok after a few days, but I could tell things were kind of slipping. And I got to feeling that she didn't care about whether I smoked or not. I knew I had to tell her about that night. I just never could. It's like she could sense what I was gonna say, and she'd say something, or give me a look, and I'd freeze up. Like this one time when she and I took Max to the "Y" for a swim. She and I got out after a few laps and I asked her what that guy might have done if she cried out for help. I just kind of blurted it out. I don't think she was ready to talk about this thing at a place like that, at a time like that. She just hugged Max's towel to her chest, and looked at the water. She was quiet so long I didn't think she was gonna say anything. "Well," she said, finally, and her answer was pretty much what I thought it'd be except she didn't say, *you stupid asshole idiot fuck*, but I could feel it—"Scott, he said he would kill me. He probably would have." Then she was quiet for awhile, and just slicked her hair back with her hand. Then she said, "There're times I wish he would have." She walked away from me and dove back into the water. That was it. Right then, I knew I was losing her, and I had to tell her. But you know, sometimes I think if I hadn't tried, I wouldn't be sitting up here on the third floor of Banana Manor, listening to the people next door screw their insides out, and hearing some butthead teenager slamming Fleetwood Mac out his speakers for the world to hear. I wouldn't be sitting inside this stinking little cloud of mine at two, now three, now four in the morning, with a terminal case of writer's cramp, trying to lay down something I wish never'd happened.

I was gonna tell her, B——, about everything, the way we all just stood there, and watched a huge piece of that woman's life get sucked away into a car, the make, model, and year of which I guess we'll never know. Man, we watched that piece of her life shrink down to a pair of taillights, and we went on with our own. Yeah, I was gonna tell Anna. I was finally gonna do it, and I was hoping both that she would and wouldn't tell me about that tall blond dude.

I called in sick to work, and ol' Van de Man was pissed because we were behind schedule on a contract we'd had with Pueblo 1st Federal. I'd never took a day off before, though, and I told him that. He pretty much let me slide then, but he did it in Van Vordt style. "You screw me one more time, like this, Winters and ya might as well not come back! Just might as well not come back!" I'm sure that freckled head was hot enough to cook rice. So, anyway, I picked out a great recepie from Diet for a Small Planet, and whipped that up. I ran to Weber Street Liquors and bought her a bottle of Mateus rosé. It's her favorite. I was nervous as hell, and couldn't sit down all day. I went to the Safeway twice and bought a pack of Winstons both times. The first one, I opened the pack, drew one and lit up, but put it out. The next one I opened as soon as I got home, but I crushed em into the toilet and flushed. I cleaned up the house and bought flowers. I was so nervous, I was twitching. I paced around the house all afternoon, trying to think up ways I could tell her, but it all sounded so stupid—*More wine, dear? Oh, by the way, I witnessed an abduction of a woman when I was a sophomore in high school, didn't do a damned thing about it, though. It probably lead to her rape. Maybe even a murder. Just say when!* I was thinking, Scott, you dork. What good is a clean house and rosé wine gonna do? I felt like a bozo.

So, I went to pick up Max from school, since I knew it was Anna's day to do the laundry. I took the kid into the back yard and I threw him the football for awhile, but I was throwing so hard I just about cracked his ribs. He was ok, though. Didn't even cry all that much, but I hugged him and took him inside, fixed him a snack and let him watch the tube. I really love that kid, I guess. In a way, I guess. At first I was embarrased at all the stares him and I used to get when I'd take him places. I'm sure some people thought I'd kidnapped him or something, but after awhile I didn't even think about it. I think I know how you must feel about being away from your boy.

Anna came home about a quarter to five. Her eyes were all big and she kept asking what the occasion was, and I kept saying, "Cause I love you, that's all." We had dinner, put Max to bed, and broke out the wine. Anna didn't know what was bugging me, but she knew I wasn't very together for some reason or another, and it was like she got nervous, too. She got up after awhile and started putting laundry away. I looked at her—from her little pink feet to her bush of red hair—and I was thinking, "Cause I love you, that's all." She looked gorgeous, and I just knew that what I was gonna tell her'd bring us closer, even if it started off with some hurt. She started to change the sheets on the bed, but I'd already handled that. I swear, the house never looked cleaner, and she kept asking me why this, and why that, but there wasn't, like, excitement in her voice, but it was like kind of an almost irritated tone, like she felt bad that she hadn't helped, or that I was trying to tell her how to *Really* clean house. She kept getting more and more nervous. I think she was figuring I was gonna propose to her, and she's real nervous about marriage. She says she doesn't even wanna think about marriage till she graduates, and gets financially together. You know, just in case the next guy dumps her like the first one did.

So she went back to putting laundry away, and I was following her around the house, just yacking about nothing. Then I just sort of started talking real casual about this essay she'd asked me to read. It was by this woman named Sue Brownmiller. I can't remember the title, and it was pretty tough reading, but it's about how women are better at cooperation and being sensitive than guys, and that's what we need in this world. Maybe that's not all she was saying, but that's basically what I got out of it. Took me forever to read it.

Anyway, I started talking to Anna about the article and she started talking about something we argue about all the time—that if women ran the world, it might be a little bit less organized than it is now, but it would definitely be more peaceful. Instead of saying what I usually say, which is, Look, as long as there're men on the planet, there'd still be violence, etc., etc., I figured that here was my chance to get to my point. So I just kind of blurted out, "You know, babe, considering all that's happened to you, I wouldn't be surprised if you hated men." And at first I didn't think she knew what I meant, 'cause she just kept opening up drawers and putting stuff away and closing them back up. I figured she'd just click her tongue at me, and roll her eyes and say, "You missed the point, Scott." But then she kind of turned in my direction, but didn't look at me. She pulled her hair away from her face and flung it back. Then she said, "I'm surprised I don't hate black men. The guy who raped me was black." Then she walked out the room with a stack of laundry in her arms. Then she closed the goddamn door. She closed it soft.

I just stood there, staring at the door, B——. It was like she'd stabbed me in the chest and kicked me in the balls at the same time. I'm not exaggerating, man, my nuts were hurting so bad I had to squat for a minute and take some deep breaths. That ever happen to you, where your blood and adrenelin get pumping so bad it hurts your nuts? It took the wind out of me. It was unreal. I never, ever thought she'd say anything like that to me. It was from Mars, man. Why didn't she tell me that night? I was thinking. Why now? This way. Like a weapon. What the fuck did I do to deserve that? I just sat there, and my hands were shaking and I thought for sure I was gonna throw up. I felt sick and dead and I couldn't breathe right. It was like my veins'd been tapped and were leaking out all over the floor.

Then, after my blood slowed a bit, I opened up the drawers she'd just shut and I grabbed 3 or 4 of everything, plus a bunch of shit from the closet. Shoes and things. I packed a couple of bags, and I walked into the living room, and to the front door. I looked around the place. It was damned clean, that's for sure. She saw me from the kitchen and she said, "Where do you think you're going?" I just looked at her and shook my head. I wanted to tell her to stick it, but I just shook my head and stepped out. She was on my heels, though, right dead on my heels. She kept pulling on my shoulder and arm, trying to get me to turn around. She kept saying, "What are you doing? Where are you going? What's going on?" Shit like that. I could see her long blue skirt sweeping around and I could see her pink feet. It was cold out there. I felt bad, B——, bad for all kinds of reasons, but I kept moving, jerking my arm or shoulder away from her, you know? My throat was all clutched up tight, and even if I'd wanted to say something to her I couldn't have. I couldn't look at her either. I stuck my car key into the lock, but before I could twist the lock open she grabbed the key ring, and she was flipping by now, practically screaming, ripping at my wrists and hands with her fingernails, "What's going on? What're you doing? Talk to me, Scott, please," and all that. I grabbed her wrist, forced open her hand, took the keys, got in, cranked it up. I never looked back at her face. If I had, I probably wouldn't've split. I mean she was acting completely innocent, like she didn't have any idea of what she'd said. And for a second there, I wasn't sure I was doing the right thing, or if she'd even understood what she'd said or the way she'd said it. By then I was goddamn crying, too. And as I was backing out, she kept saying, "Please, please, please, Scott, please." That's basically why I'm writing you, brother. Do you think she knew what she'd done? I mean, here's kind of the reason why, what I'm gonna tell you now.

I tried not to listen, ok, and I was pulling away. I couldn't see good, because of the tears, but I could see her in the rearview mirror. She was standing in the street with her hands in her hair, pulling it back like she does when it's wet. She kept saying, "Please, please, please, Scott, please," but the farther away I got, it started sounding more like, keys, keys, keys, Scott, keys.

Right now I don't know, B——. Sometimes you just don't know. Sometimes you just can't tell what you see or hear or feel. Or remember.

Take care, man,
Love, Scott.

1991

A Cold Winter Light

Alyce Miller

The winter Olivia turned sixteen she discovered her father had taken up with a black woman, someone unknown to her, but someone possibly connected with her father's old high school counseling job in Elyria, eight miles north by the edge of Lake Erie.

Olivia came across the snapshot stuffed in the back of a dark drawer of her father's basement work table. It lay imprisoned under a screwdriver and a crushed nail box half full of old rubber bands. Olivia had been deliberately snooping again, as was her habit of late. She considered it her duty to periodically patrol the cabinets and closets and drawers of her house. On the days she got home from school before everyone else, she held unopened mail up to the light. It seemed to be the only way she found things out in this house, now that her parents no longer spoke to each other.

The snapshot, a Polaroid, was stuck to the bottom of the work table drawer. Olivia carefully pried it out with the tips of her fingernails and held it up to the rectangle of winter sunlight framed by the high basement windows: a tall, dark black woman stared back coyly, the way subjects do when the photographer knows them intimately. Along the bent edges of the snapshot, spots of color and paper were missing. But the woman herself was intact.

Olivia stared hard. The woman was beautiful. She was what her father's mother would call "*too* black" in that half-deprecating, half-sympathetic way some light-skinned people had, even though her own husband, Olivia's grandfather, was the color of black walnut shells.

The woman wore a medium-sized natural; her features were broad, perfect, her eyes shaped like almonds. She was long and leggy, about the same age as Olivia's mother. She wore a short red leather skirt that hugged her hips and a see-through black blouse with lace on the wide collar. From her earlobes dangled large silver hoops that reflected light from a source Olivia couldn't see. The woman had posed herself familiarly in the doorway of a kitchen Olivia didn't recognize. The bottom right-hand corner of the photo was feathered by the decorated lower branches of someone else's Christmas tree.

Down to the last detail, this woman was the exact opposite of Olivia's small, white, red-haired mother.

Olivia turned the photo over. On the back in lazy, loopy handwriting was written: "Merry Christmas to my Chocolate Santa. Love, Wilma."

Olivia suddenly understood what she'd suspected all along. Christmas Eve, two months earlier, she and her mother and Pam and the boys lounged around the living room idly stuffing themselves on tangerines and nuts and chocolate while the open boxes of Christmas tree ornaments sat untouched. A space had been cleared over by the picture window for the Christmas tree. Hours before, Olivia's father had slammed off in a huff to search for one, irritated that her mother had waited until the last minute. No one else had wanted to ride along with him, preferring the warmth of the house to the freezing night. The red and green metal tree stand stood empty under the mantel.

Waiting for him, they'd all pretended not to, as Olivia's mother played a Nat King Cole recording of "Winter Wonderland" over and over, and flipped through magazines. Around ten or so she brought out eggnog from the fridge. She seemed about to burst from some unnamed emotion and turned giggly and reckless, mischievously pouring a shot of rum in everyone's eggnog glasses. She could be capricious, a bad child, when Olivia's father wasn't around. In his absence, she often resorted to small, harmless indulgences, treating her children as if they were all just friends.

Then, much to Olivia's annoyance, her younger sister Pam had started acting drunk and talking crazy. Leave it to Pam to spoil things! Olivia's mother sighed and put the rum away and told Pam she'd better straighten up fast before her father returned.

The hour had grown late. The fire in the fireplace burned down to embers, and a chill spread inward from the walls. Olivia glanced at the ticking clock with growing agitation. Her mother fell asleep curled up on the sofa and the boys sprawled in the middle of the floor and played with their Lego set. Pam slipped off to the kitchen and whispered to someone on the phone behind the closed door.

Chilled, Olivia pulled on her robe and sat in the overstuffed chair, staring out the broad picture window at the snow falling, cold and white. She pretended to be watching her brothers, but she was waiting. Each time a car passed on the snowy road, she felt herself stiffen. When at last the headlights of the red station wagon turned into their driveway, Olivia leaned over and poked her mother awake. Just in time, too. Her father crossed the threshold, irritable and flustered, dragging in a short-needled, scrawny tree. "Well," he said, "what do you expect when we wait until Christmas Eve? All the lots were empty and I wasn't about to go tromping off through the woods at one of those cut-your-own places." He fussed on and on and stamped his snowy boots in the front hallway. Then he argued with the boys about the mess of Legos on the floor while the tree lay on its side, forgotten.

That was when Olivia first noticed that her father had skipped several shaves and his hair was lengthening into a natural. It had been a while since she'd looked directly at him, but while he and the boys screwed the tree upright into the stand she sat in the overstuffed chair, warm inside her robe, studying his gestures and expressions, and drawing her own conclusions.

Olivia considered stealing the snapshot, but then decided against it. She pushed the picture to the back of the drawer and placed the screwdriver on top. She kept thinking of the woman's wide, pouty smile, intended (and this was the unthinkable part!) for Olivia's father.

Bastard, Olivia thought. She thought of her mother upstairs in the den, obliviously glued to the Merv Griffin show and waiting for the children to get home from school. It was like a quadruple deception somehow: her father's infidelity, the woman's beauty, the woman's blackness, and now, Olivia's discovery.

Olivia stood a moment longer under the bare beams, her sock feet soaking up the cold from the cement floor. Her father had promised last year to finish off the basement and turn it into a family room, but he'd gotten busy with his new job at the college and never found time. The room remained rough and approximate, the ceiling pipes exposed.

Olivia turned and walked back up the basement steps to the kitchen, closed the door softly behind her, and took the wide-mouthed jar of cold water out of the refrigerator. She poured a drink. Outside the kitchen window the yard lay blanketed in snow, and the pond beyond was frozen solid. Grim February, what Olivia's mother jokingly called "the longest short month."

The front door banged shut and Olivia knew Pam had finally dragged herself in from school, a good hour late. Pam was only thirteen, but she tried to act grown, wearing her skirts so short there wasn't much left to the imagination. Now she was going with a twenty-year-old hoodlum named Reggie who wore a dew rag and washed dishes for a living over at the college cafeteria. Reggie drove a beat-up Ford around town and called Pam "sweet thang."

Imagine, in the eighth grade, with a grown-up boyfriend! Old fast yellow Pam, calling herself slick, walking downtown and swinging her hips with her big chest poked out.

Sometimes, at night when everyone was asleep, Pam would go out. Last summer Olivia had caught her at it. She awakened to muffled clunks and bangs in the next room, Pam's room. There were voices whispering. She sat up in bed and looked out the window. Once her eyes adjusted, she made out two silhouettes of neighborhood boys over by the pond. A moment later the soft swift shadow of Pam in her bathrobe and bare feet made its way across the grass in the moonlight. Olivia watched Pam and one of the boys disappear across the field and past the line of trees that marked the edge of their property. The second boy paced along the edge of the pond, staring into the dark water.

Olivia crept quietly out of her room to Pam's. The high aluminum-framed window had been pulled to one side. She had a clear view of the pond straight ahead. She knelt on Pam's bed and leaned her elbows on the windowsill. The air smelled of moist, freshly cut grass. Olivia thought of closing the window and locking Pam out, but she didn't have the courage to hurt her mother. Instead, she did nothing, just watched with a mixture of envy and disgust. Sometime later Pam traipsed back across the damp lawn, her hair askew. She wore a smug, elfish grin. Olivia ducked down and scurried back to her own room. She heard Pam's feet scrape heavily over the windowsill, then the thunk! of her body hitting the bed. A few moments later a car engine revved from the road.

The next morning Olivia eyed Pam hard until Pam put her hand on her hip and said, "What are *you* looking at?"

Olivia hissed, "You better not get pregnant, girl," and Pam rolled her eyes.

"I'm *serious!*" Olivia warned.

Pam snaked her neck several times and glared. "You don't even know what you're talking about, Miss Whitegirl."

Now, Pam strolled into the kitchen with the one book she'd bothered to carry home from school. She was lighter than Olivia, with skin the color of shredded wheat, but her features were broader and her hair was naturally nappier though, like Olivia, she had a perm and wore her hair in a shoulder-length page-boy. She clunked across the floor in her black snow boots.

"Anybody call for me?" she asked in her deep raspy voice.

"I don't know, stupid, I just got here myself." Olivia sipped her water. She considered telling Pam about the snapshot, just to shock her into getting all big-eyed. But the timing was wrong.

Pam leaned back against the kitchen counter. "Reggie said he saw you today."

"Big deal," said Olivia. "I wouldn't know him if I saw him." She walked out of the kitchen.

"That you, Olivia?" her mother called out from the den.

Olivia poked her head in. The drapes were drawn and the room was dark and overcrowded. Over in the corner her mother's sewing machine was set up with a long piece of brown wool fabric spread out under the needle. Olivia's mother made almost all of the girls' clothes. She saw to it they were two of the best-dressed girls at school. New clothes every week when she could. She spent a lot of time poring through catalogs and choosing patterns and calling the girls into the den to be measured.

"Have a seat." Olivia's mother patted the empty space on the sofa next to her. She'd pulled her bathrobe on over her nurse's uniform and propped up her small white feet on the coffee table.

"You sub at the hospital today?" Olivia asked. She sat gingerly on the edge of the sofa.

"Just this morning. Pam home yet?"

Olivia nodded. The den struck her as depressing. Her mother spent too much time there. Beyond the heavy drapes spread the cloudless blue sky, and in the over-bright, frozen air the winter sun sparkled on the snow banked along the sidewalks.

"Can you pick up the boys from Boy Scouts at five? Gina and Jerry are coming by tonight for ribs and I've got to make potato salad."

"I thought Daddy picked up the boys on Wednesdays."

Olivia's mother never took her eyes from the TV screen. "Well, he can't tonight," she said sharply.

Olivia pulled herself up off the sofa. She towered over her mother. "Is he going to be here when Gina and Jerry come?"

Her mother shrugged. "I don't know and I really don't care. You know how he is." She reached up and ran one small white hand over Olivia's brown arm. "You look so pretty today. I'm glad the new skirt fit."

"I don't understand why Daddy can't pick up the boys." It was the closest Olivia had gotten to outright accusing her father of what she now knew to be true.

Her mother sighed. "Don't pay any attention to your father these days. What matters to me now is you and the other kids."

Gina and Jerry Woods were Olivia's parents' longtime best friends. They lived on the other side of town by the golf course with their six teenage children. Gina wasn't American, she was actually from some war-torn Eastern European country, and she had an unpronounceable name, so everyone just called her Gina. She was heavyset, blonde, and pale, and spoke rapidly in a heavy accent, a mixture of black and Eastern Europe. She did hair for a living. Jerry was quiet, a mail carrier with light skin the color of wheat and eyes with a greenish cast. All the Woods kids had the same wheat-colored skin and green eyes and sandy hair. They were notoriously wild kids, rowdy and undisciplined, and the boys were as handsome as the devil himself. You could spot a Woods boy a mile away. It irritated Olivia when people mixed her up with them and asked her if she was a Woods.

Gina and Olivia's mother were drinking beers together in the kitchen while Gina stuffed herself on barbecue. "Earl don't know what he's missin'," she said of Olivia's father.

Olivia's mother shrugged and said, "Maybe he does."

Over ribs and potato salad Olivia listened to her mother and Gina Woods talk, as they had for years. Their words were familiar, even predictable, but the meanings shifted with kaleidoscopic quickness into new patterns Olivia could now comprehend. She knew that by listening, without appearing to, she would find out the things no one told her directly. Jerry Woods and Olivia's brothers were huddled on the sofa in the den watching the game on TV, and Pam was in her bedroom, tying up the phone. The two women seemed to have forgotten that Olivia was even in the same room.

Olivia's mother's voice was tired, uncertain. "I don't know what I'm going to do with Pam. She acts just like her father. Doesn't tell me a thing." And Gina, through a mouthful of barbecue, spat back advice and gestured emphatically. "Don't let her throw you off balance. I've got *two* of 'em at home don't act right. Just last week I caught Rita and Lizzie smoking, and then turns out they been cutting school together. Jerry don't know. He'd kill 'em."

Olivia picked a piece of white bread apart and rolled the sections into little hard balls between her thumb and index finger. Her mother let out a sigh of sympathy. "It's hard nowadays," she said. "I try to give both my girls a certain amount of freedom. I don't want them to feel . . . you know, any more different than they already do."

Gina licked barbecue from her fingers. "Thaz why I let my girls do like they want. I can't keep 'em under lock and key. I hear the talk. But you got to go easy with mixed kids. They got it rough."

Olivia pushed herself forcefully away from the table. "Excuse me," she said stiffly, "I have homework."

Her mother and Gina smiled up at her in unison. Their faces were bright and approving. "You're a good girl," said Gina, patting Olivia's behind. "And getting so grown-up too!"

Olivia was halfway down the hall when she heard her mother say with conviction, "Olivia's my dependable one. I don't know what I'd do without her."

By Saturday another big snowstorm was predicted, and Olivia's mother left early with Pam for Fisher-Fazio to stock up on groceries. The boys played whiffle ball in the cold basement with their jackets and gloves on. Olivia could hear the smack-smack of the bat hitting the plastic ball. She turned on the vacuum in the living room and cranked up Aretha Franklin as high as she could on the stereo console. "Ain't no way / for me to lo-o-ove you-ou / if you won't-a let me . . ." Sister Caroline's background vocals soared on top at ear-splitting levels. Olivia sang along, squatting down to get under the sofa with the vacuum wand.

Out of the corner of her eye, she caught a movement in the doorway. She glanced over to see her father opening the front hall closet door. He pulled on his heavy winter coat and pressed onto his rising natural the Russian hat with ear flaps that so embarrassed her. At Christmas she had given him a black beret and he rejected it, saying he'd look like a Black Nationalist. He had treated the hat as an insult from her, uncomfortable with the implications.

"They wear berets in *France*," Olivia had said sarcastically, and her father snapped back, "I'm not French." What she felt like saying now was "And you aren't Russian either," but she didn't.

Her father gestured impatiently for her to turn down the music. She pretended at first not to understand, then shut off the vacuum and stood up stiffly, arms folded across her chest. "What?" she mouthed.

"You're going to blow my damn speakers!" He'd taken to referring to their collective family belongings in the first-person possessive: my sofa, my refrigerator, my car.

Olivia leaned over and lowered the volume to a whisper.

"Where's your mother?"

"Grocery."

Olivia stabbed at the living room carpet with the long wand of the vacuum.

"I have a committee meeting this afternoon. I'll be home late."

"On a Saturday, Daddy?" She had the snapshot on her side. She could afford to be impulsive.

"I have no idea what you mean." He took up his briefcase in one hand and an umbrella in the other.

"When will you be home?" Olivia pushed, hand on her hip.

He frowned. "Did she take your car or mine?"

"I thought it was her car too."

"Don't be smart-assed, girl, and you know what I mean." He cleared his throat several times. "I'm asking you in a nice way, am I stuck with the Corvair?"

"No, she took the Corvair. She wouldn't think of taking *your* precious station wagon."

Olivia's father pulled open the front door. A blast of cold wind gusted through. He paused. "By the way, I read in the paper that your boyfriend what's-his-name Michael Blakely got a speeding ticket. I don't want you driving around with him anymore."

Olivia laughed. "If you paid attention to what goes on around here, you'd know that Michael and I broke up over two months ago."

Her father slammed out the door. Through the picture window she watched him scuttle like a beetle down the icy driveway to the station wagon. Big white flakes floated down and settled on the shoulders of his heavy dark coat and on the crown of his Russian hat.

Olivia held up the vacuum wand and shook it at his receding back, as though marking him with a curse. He climbed into the station wagon and sat behind the frosty windshield, warming the engine. "You know how I hate your lyin' ass," she yelled after him. "It's a little late to try to get black on us now!" She switched the vacuum back on, and cranked the stereo volume up so loud the walls vibrated. "This is the house that Jack built, y'all!" Olivia sang. "Remember this house. This is the land that he worked by hand / This is the dream of an upright man . . ."

All that Olivia told Tonya when she drove over through the thickening snow in the Corvair was that they were going for a drive. Tonya's mother was perturbed about the weather. "I'd like to know where you two are off to, just in case," she said in her polite white way. "The roads could get really bad."

Olivia smiled broadly. "I'm running an errand for my mother at the mall."

"Just the two of you?" Tonya's mother had never come right out and said it, but Olivia knew she was growing more and more worried about "certain influences."

Tonya got busy with her mittens and boots.

"Just the two of us," Olivia confirmed.

"This doesn't involve boys?"

Olivia knew exactly what kind of boys Tonya's mother meant. Black boys. She felt irritation rising in her chest. Her friendship with Tonya had been so much simpler when they were younger. Now sometimes Olivia wondered why she bothered with it at all.

"No boys," said Tonya. "I told you, Olivia and I are going alone!"

"When can I expect you home?"

"How about six?" said Olivia. She had learned that by phrasing her responses as questions she got a lot further with Tonya's mother.

Tonya's mother was not pleased. "Tonya will miss dinner."

Olivia knew dinner was not the issue at all.

"Tonya can eat at my house."

"Well-l-l . . ." Tonya's mother couldn't look Olivia straight in the face anymore.

"My mom's making spaghetti, Tonya's favorite."

"I wish you'd asked in advance."

This was how it always was with Tonya's mother—Olivia negotiating and reassuring, Tonya remaining silent and depressed.

"We'll call you from my house, okay?" said Olivia brightly.

Tonya's mother looked at Tonya. "Seven o'clock," she said sharply. "I want a call from you by seven o'clock."

Inside the Corvair, Tonya let out several groans. "I *really* want to run away. I can't stand it anymore." She said this at least three times a week. "Let me come live with you, Olivia."

"Why? You think I have it any easier?"

Tonya smiled ruefully. "At least your father's gone all the time. My mother is *always* there."

Olivia started up the clanking car heater.

"Quick, get out of here before she changes her mind." Tonya sank low into her seat. "She's in there thinking up some excuse to call me back in." There was a slight movement of the curtain at the living room window.

"Your mother's changed" was all Olivia said bitterly as she backed the Corvair down the drive.

Snow fell steadily in big, wet flakes. The houses and bushes looked like pieces of furniture covered in protective white sheets. Olivia made a left at the corner and drove slowly over sludge and ice to the edge of the college campus. She peered out the fogged-up window. "Look and see if my dad's station wagon is in that parking lot over there."

Both girls craned their necks. The lot was empty.

"I knew he was lying," Olivia muttered to herself.

"What are you talking about?"

"You'll see." Olivia stopped at the red light marking the main intersection downtown. She turned on the radio and sang along to "Ooh, Ooh, Child" by the Five Stairsteps. She felt bored by Tonya, irritated with her presence. She was sorry now she'd brought her along, but she had, and now she was stuck.

Turning onto Route 58, they found themselves on the tail of a large truck. The snow was so thick now that all they could make out were red taillights and an occasional glimpse of revolving rubber tires spitting snow. Oncoming traffic was dense and slow, a succession of blurred headlights on the two-lane highway.

"Maybe we shouldn't go," said Tonya, nervously wiping at the windshield with a mittened hand.

Olivia boosted the volume on the car radio. When she didn't know the words to songs, she substituted nonsense syllables. It didn't really matter, you could sing whatever you wanted, it was all the same.

"What are we doing, Olivia?"

Olivia clicked her forgers and hummed. The song ended. "What are we doing? Looking for my father, that's what we're doing." She dug down in her coat pocket and pulled out the snapshot of the black woman. She handed it to Tonya, without explanation.

Tonya held the snapshot in her mittened hands and stared. "I don't get it." Recognition slowly dawned. "Your father? Does your mother know?" Olivia could see that Tonya was intrigued.

Olivia shrugged. "My mother needs to dump his ass. She sacrificed everything to marry him and now look at how he's acting." She said it as if the events signaled some fault of Tonya's.

Tonya was poring over the snapshot carefully. "She sure is pretty. God, what I'd give to have skin like that. I get so white in the winter."

Olivia snatched the snapshot back and stuffed it in her coat pocket. "She's not that pretty. My father's rebelling, that's all," she said sarcastically. "My father's decided to try being black after years of being an Uncle Tom."

"Why do you hate him so much?" asked Tonya.

"You don't know him." Olivia felt the car tires spin briefly on a slick patch in the road. "You don't have a clue."

Tonya asked Olivia to stop at Lawson's. She returned with bubble gum, a sack of chives and sour cream chips, two blisteringly cold red cream sodas, and two sticks of beef jerky.

"Why do you wanna buy that old nasty stuff?" remarked Olivia grouchily, but she ate anyway, sitting there in the Lawson's lot, staring out at the bleak intersection and watching the snow pile up on the sidewalks, the bushes, even the telephone wires overhead.

A low-slung black Olds pulled into the lot and honked. One of the windows was covered over with a piece of tattered plastic attached by long strips of masking tape. There were three boys inside, two up front, one in back. The driver pulled up next to the Corvair and motioned for Olivia to roll down her window.

"Say, mama," he called cheerfully, leaning out of the car so that his thick hair caught the falling white snow like a net. "I couldn't help noticing you and your friend over here by yourselves.

"I'm not your mama," Olivia responded, but she kept her window down just the same.

"And just where might you two lovely young ladies be going on a cold, wintry afternoon like this?" the boy asked. He was brown-skinned with wide eyes and long lashes. Pam's type, thought Olivia. Fast. Nothing but trouble.

"We're visiting a friend," she said, keeping her jaw tight. She felt the pressure of his eyes. Let him look all he wants, she thought.

"We'd sure like to hook up with you two and your *friend*," said the boy. "I'm Freddie and this here's my partner Bobby and that's my play cousin Louis. Where y'all from?"

Tonya was trying to peer past Olivia. "The driver's so cute," she squealed. Olivia silenced her with a look.

"I'm Rhonda, and this is my friend Regina," said Olivia. "We're stewardesses from Cleveland."

"Stewardesses!" the boy guffawed. "Stewardesses! You two?" He consulted with the two passengers in the Olds and turned back to Olivia. "Where y'all from in Cleveland?" he asked, amused.

"East 98th," Olivia said coolly. It was the first thing that came to mind.

"Both y'all?" Freddie began to laugh. He gestured toward Tonya. "Her too? You're pulling my leg. I know *she* ain't from there."

Olivia poked out her lip and raised her eyebrows. "She's my cousin," she said meaningfully.

"I don't mean no disrespect," Freddie chuckled, "but I'd like to catch *her* down on East 98th." He turned back to his companions and said something. The sound of laughter spilled from their open window. He looked back over at Olivia. "Y'all like to skate? We're going to the roller rink."

Olivia let out a world-weary sigh. "I told you, we're on our way to our friend's house."

She rolled up her window and started the engine. The boy tooted his horn in a fast staccato, but Olivia concentrated on shifting the Corvair in reverse.

"Why can't we go to the skating rink?" asked Tonya. "Just for a half hour. Come on, they were *cute*."

Olivia resisted the urge to slap her. "You sound just like Pam," she said. "Besides, your mother would kill me."

"My mother's not here. Why do you always have to be such a goody-goody, Olivia?"

"Why do you want to go off with some hoodlums?" said Olivia. "That driver was a white-girl lover, couldn't you tell? He figured you'd be easy. Don't you know anything, girl? I was just saving you a lot of trouble."

"I really hate it when you play me off," Tonya sulked.

"I *said* you were my cousin." Olivia's patience had worn thin.

"You played me off," Tonya insisted. "Why don't you make up your mind whether you're my best friend or not?"

Olivia clicked on the wipers to clear the windshield. She kept her voice steady, purposeful. "I can't get you in with black kids, Tonya. I have my own troubles. You're on your own."

They both fell silent as Olivia made a right turn toward the lake and the north end of town where the high school was. She didn't care that she'd hurt Tonya, her words had come as a relief. She was worn out trying to keep people around her happy.

They sat in the empty high school parking lot and watched the snow fall. Every few minutes Olivia started up the engine and ran the heater. Snow covered the hood of the Corvair.

"This school looks like a prison," remarked Tonya.

"This is where my father used to work."

Olivia's father had counseled dropouts and taught driver's ed in the red brick building for almost fifteen years before he was hired last year to teach sociology at the college. He had been asked as a response to increasing pressure from black students who demanded more black faculty. Olivia had been present at several of the student demonstrations. She remembered the night her father had gotten the phone call.

"They never wanted me before," he told Olivia's mother bitterly. "Suddenly I'm in high demand when it's convenient for them."

"It's only right," she said. "You deserve this."

"They don't believe that. I'm just a quick fix. And these young black students . . ." He'd paused. "They think I can work miracles."

"Maybe you can," Olivia's mother had said. Because, Olivia thought bitterly, it would take a miracle.

It was only weeks later that D.T., one of the campus radicals, stood in the band shell of the square and announced through a bullhorn to a crowd of college and high school students that Olivia's father was "an Uncle Tom, the white administration's puppet, married to the oppressor, hired to appease, and an enemy to the struggle." Olivia had been standing right there, after school, on the edges of the swelling crowd with three black schoolmates, and she'd heard it with her own ears, the truth that she had never dared put into words. She found herself caught up in the words themselves, felt the crowd's anger and frustration, and found resonating deep within her the chant that grew with the crowd's increasing enthusiasm, "Power to the people!" She never mentioned it to her mother, but when she looked at her father from then on, she felt wave after wave of pity and contempt.

Inside the idling Corvair, Tonya began to complain. "I'm so sick of cold and snow. When I go to college, I'm going to move some place warm. I want to have a tan and feel warm all the time."

"I like the snow," said Olivia, feeling ornery, "even if it is white."

She was considering the one lone car parked in a far corner of the lot. It was a blue Buick LeSabre with a solid layer of snow on the hood and roof. Ice covered the windows.

"How long do we have to sit here?" Tonya asked.

"You didn't have to come," Olivia reminded her. She put the car in gear and, as a concession, slowly circled the lot. She drove past the LeSabre. There were no tire tracks anywhere near it, just a smooth layer of snow.

"What are we doing here?" Tonya asked.

Olivia didn't answer.

"Let's go to the mall. I never get out of the house."

"Just cool your jets," said Olivia in her mother's voice.

Tonya slumped in the seat and pulled her coat more closely around her.

"Okay, Miss Impatient, we'll go to the mall."

Olivia turned the Corvair in the direction of the street. Out of the corner of her eye she saw the flash of headlights. Through the falling snow a car approached, turning slowly into the wide white parking lot from the other side. The shape of the front of the car registered as vaguely familiar, though Olivia's thoughts didn't acknowledge this. The car plowed through the curtain of white, a slow, heavy creature, headlights glowing, windshield wipers slapping against the glass. And then, without warning, Olivia was seized by recognition.

"Oh, my God!" she exclaimed. "Oh, my God!" She hadn't really believed, had she? She hadn't bargained for the sudden wave of panic that swept over her. She slammed on the brakes and ducked her head below the windshield. Her right foot trembled on the brake.

Tonya was a second behind her, sliding out of the seat onto the floor. "Did he see us?" she whispered from under the dashboard.

"Shshshsh!" Olivia raised her head slowly. She heard the rumble of the other engine beside them, and the smack of wheels on wet snow.

"Oh, my God, he's seen us."

"What should we do?" asked Tonya, still crouched on the floor. She was furiously twisting the ends of her scarf.

Olivia gave a backwards glance, but the rear window was a blur of white. She cracked her window and peered over the top into the frosty air. The red station wagon had pulled up next to the blue LeSabre, where it sat, exhaust smoking in the air. Now the passenger door was opening. Out of the car stepped a tall dark-skinned woman in a long navy-blue maxi coat and black boots. She was drawing up the hood of the coat over her head with red-gloved hands. She leaned down into the car, and at that moment Olivia felt every muscle in her body constrict. Then the driver got out. He came around to the passenger side, and the two figures stood there in the snow, apart and talking. Gone was the mystery of the woman in a red leather skirt posed in the kitchen doorway. The very ordinariness of the two figures, man and woman, struck Olivia with a note of sadness. They were trapped like figures in a paperweight, snow whirling around and containing them.

Tonya dragged herself halfway up to the passenger seat. "Are you going to talk to him?"

"Hell no, I'm not going to talk to him!" said Olivia fiercely. She watched her father lean forward and plant a kiss on the side of the woman's face. She realized then that he was wearing, not the Russian hat he'd left the house with that morning, but the black beret she'd given him on Christmas. Flat like a saucer, it caught the snow, turning the top of his head white.

Olivia's foot slipped off the clutch. The car jerked forward, then died.

The woman turned ever so briefly in their direction, but her face was hidden by the wide hood of her coat. She looked back at Olivia's father for a moment before walking quickly toward the LeSabre, her shoulders drawn up in the cold. Olivia's father, head down, trudged back around to the driver's side of the station wagon and climbed inside. Olivia heard the dull thud of his car door closing.

"Here he comes," warned Tonya, her face stricken.

Olivia turned the key several times in the ignition and pressed the accelerator. The engine wouldn't turn over. She began to curse, her exhalations making soft, smoky circles in the air.

The red station wagon backed up slowly, exhaust curling up over it like smoke from a chimney. It turned and crossed the lot. The LeSabre's headlights flashed several times. The station wagon honked twice. Now head-lights flooded Olivia's rear mirror. The station wagon was behind them, then swerving, and now the red hood of the car was abreast. It slid past, slowly, and made a sharp turn back into the snowy street.

"He looked right at you," said Tonya. "I saw him."

Olivia rammed the accelerator again with her foot. The engine roared, and the car lurched forward.

Now the LeSabre was alongside. Tonya twisted around in her seat. "Can you see her?" she asked.

"Shut up" was all Olivia could say. The LeSabre passed and turned in the same direction the station wagon had.

Olivia braked softly on the ice, felt the slight skid of tires, and then because the LeSabre had turned right, made a left. She roared up to the stop-light and made another fast left.

"That light was red!"

"I don't care." Olivia sped up and shot over the icy railroad tracks that separated one side of town from the other.

"Slow down!" said Tonya.

The Corvair's wheels spun on a hidden patch of icy railroad tie, the back end of the car swung unexpectedly halfway around to where the front had been, and Olivia found herself completely turned around on the snowy road staring into oncoming headlights from the other side of the tracks.

"You're going to kill us!" Tonya slapped the dashboard with her mit-tened hand. "Olivia, stop it!"

Olivia backed up against the curb and turned the steering wheel. Two cars swerved around them with a blare of horns. Between the falling snow and the tears she couldn't be sure which way the road went, but she made no apologies to Tonya, just buried her chin in her coat collar and counted in her mind the number of times the sticky wipers clicked across the windshield.

Tonya ate at Olivia's. She phoned her mother to weasel permission to spend the night, citing bad weather and snowy roads as good reason. Olivia, the only one still at the dinner table, heard the painful struggle on Tonya's end. No, she didn't need to come back home and pick up her nightgown, she could wear one of Olivia's. Her voice was feeble and discouraged. Yes, Olivia's mother was home, and no, there wouldn't be boys there. Finally, Olivia's mother intervened.

Olivia busied herself with twirling strands of overcooked spaghetti onto her fork with the help of a soup spoon.

"Hi, it's Lois," her mother said reassuringly into the phone. "How are you, Sue? Can you believe this weather? I didn't think the girls should try to go back out in it."

Olivia chewed, and concentrated on her mother's negotiations. She wished Tonya would go home.

When Olivia's mother hung up, she winked and said triumphantly to Tonya, "It's all set."

"I hate my mother," said Tonya.

Olivia's mother squeezed herself back down at the table between the two girls. There was a weariness about her that made Olivia feel protective. "Your mother means well."

"But you don't track down Olivia every step she makes," Tonya said. In the harsh kitchen light her features seemed all squeezed together and pasty. "You let your kids have *freedom*."

Olivia's mother sighed. "I don't know if it's so much freedom . . ." She paused. "I guess I just try to take into consideration that my children are, well, half black, and these are difficult times." Dead silence followed.

Olivia thought how those were Gina's words coming out of her mother's mouth. *Half black. Difficult times.* She hated her mother's small, thin mouth, so smugly set in the shape of those words. Olivia began to imagine the snow falling on them there in the kitchen, forcing its way through the roof and the ceiling and piling up on the table. She saw her mother and Tonya, two strangers suddenly lit up in the cold winter light. Slowly they disappeared into the whiteness, indistinguishable from all the other white people she knew.

"If my children were white," Olivia's mother went on matter-of-factly in this new voice of betrayal, "I would probably be inclined to be more like your mother—stricter. . ." She glanced over at Olivia. "I believe in speaking frankly about these things. It's so much better when things are out in the open, don't you agree, honey?"

The front door opened, then slammed shut. Heavy footsteps announced Olivia's father's return. Olivia heard him bang the hall closet door and bark something at the boys.

Olivia's mother sighed. "Oh, well, just when we were having a *real* conversation." She got up with her plate in hand.

Footsteps thudded toward them in the hallway. A moment later Olivia's father filled up the frame of the kitchen doorway. He was only a medium-sized man, unremarkable in most respects, but he suddenly seemed bigger. His hair, Olivia noticed, was mashed flat on his head from the beret.

"What's for dinner?" he asked without looking at any of them. He took the lid off a pot on the stove and stared down inside.

"I didn't realize you'd be home for dinner," said Olivia's mother. "It's all gone."

His expression tightened, but he made no comment. Instead, he went to the refrigerator and caused a big commotion going through its contents.

While he searched, Olivia's mother brushed past him on her way out of the kitchen. Olivia heard the den door close and, a moment later, the muted sounds of canned television laughter.

Without looking at the girls, Olivia's father began to speak. His face was as blank and remote as the empty parking lot earlier. "I'm going to need to use the Corvair tomorrow morning." He cleared his throat and leveled the words in a careful monotone just above Olivia's head. "So don't plan anything. I'm taking your grandmother to church."

He seemed to notice Tonya for the first time. "Well, hello there, Tonya. How are you?" Without waiting for her answer, he turned and walked out of the room.

Olivia let herself collapse back in her chair. "God, I hate him," she muttered. She slouched lower, kicking her legs out. "And I can't believe what my mother just said to you. I can't believe either of them anymore."

Tonya sat wordlessly. She poked indifferently at the food on her plate.

Olivia straightened herself. "Hey, you want my family so bad? You want my mother? You can have her. But, remember, then you get *him* too." She stood up and pushed her chair in hard under the table. "You can have them both!"

She strode down the hall to the coat closet where she found her winter coat and boots. The Corvair keys jingled in her pocket. The snapshot was still stuffed deep inside her coat pocket. She fished around and pulled it out. On a whim she held it up, exposed, where anyone could walk in and see her with it. Excitement surged through her as she waited to see who might happen in. Pam? Her father? The boys? Her mother? She could imagine the expressions of shock on their faces.

It was Tonya, though, who appeared in the doorway. Her cheeks were streaked with red. "Your father went down to the basement," she whispered. "He looked mad." Then she saw the snapshot. "What are you doing, Olivia?"

Olivia smiled and gently waved the snapshot to the empty living room. "I think I should go home," said Tonya. "I better call my mother."

"Do what you want." Olivia walked around Tonya and headed back into the kitchen. A cold draft blew up from the basement through the open door. Below, she could hear her father pacing and the sound of his radio being tuned. A few seconds of station-searching, then the radio was snapped off. It got very still. Olivia inched herself to the top of the basement stairs. A pool of yellow light marked the center of the basement where her father's work table stood. She was certain he was going through the drawers.

Behind her, Tonya waited pale and uncertain in the kitchen door.

"Watch this," Olivia said, holding up the snapshot by just a corner, between her thumb and forefinger. The black woman twisted back and forth in her fingers. A flash of red leather skirt, the sparkle of silver earrings. It was as if she had come alive.

"Dare me?" said Olivia. She didn't wait for the answer.

She released the snapshot. It hovered for a moment, caught on a current of air, and then the black woman began her looping descent. Slowly, slowly, she fell over the basement stairs, graceful as a falling leaf. Olivia looked down. The picture had landed face up on the bottom step.

With great calm, Olivia carefully closed the basement door, taking comfort in the soft click of the latch.

Her mind leaped forward to the tremendous changes that lay ahead. They began with her descent into the wintry night, leaving Tonya in her place. From now on, regardless of the lateness of the hour, the changing months, the shift of seasons, the occasions that would mark her growing up, she, Olivia, would come and go in the Corvair as she pleased, unhurried and unquestioned. Now it was just a matter of saying, "Excuse me," as she slipped past Tonya and down the hallway to the coat closet. She pretended she didn't hear her mother's voice calling from the den, "That you, Olivia?"

1993

Judgment

Clifford Thompson

"Not too many of *us* here," I said. The two of us stood in the middle of the Bowl, the huge lawn in front of Field College's library.

"You and me, that's about it," she said. This was my first time talking to her, but I'd noticed her before; she was one black student at this tiny school in the middle of Nowhere, Pennsylvania, and I was the other. She was beautiful—her long hair was pulled back, showing off her high, curved forehead and blemishless skin. "Are you a freshman, too?"

"Yeah. My name's Wayne," I said, and we shook hands.

"I'm Roxie. Nice to meet you. Where are you from?"

"D. C."

"*Really?* Me too! I'm from Silver Spring."

I gave her a look of mock disgust, and said, "*That's* not D.C."

"All right, then, Maryland," she said, laughing. "Close enough."

We stood there talking for about twenty minutes. I was surprised by her. Before we met I had mentally assigned her a way of speaking and a set of mannerisms which, it turned out, were all wrong. But I liked the real ones—her easy laughter, and the way she tilted her head when she asked a question. Before we parted we made plans to get together for coffee that evening.

Around eight o'clock I left my dorm and headed for Pete's, a diner on the edge of campus. The shortest distance between these two points took me across the Bowl and past the library and the main lecture hall. It was September of 1980, which made these buildings 155 years old; they didn't seem to have been built so much as just carved out of rock and set among all the trees and grass. In the daytime they looked like a painting of a college campus. Now, silhouetted against the night sky, they looked like medieval castles. They were a little scary, and I thought that a year ago I would've picked up my pace. But *I'm in college*, I thought; *I'm a man now.*

"My father's a lawyer," Roxie said. We were in Pete's, hunched over a table in a tiny booth. "I think that's where I get my argumentativeness from. It used to drive the boys in high school crazy."

"If two people agree on everything all the time, one of them is unnecessary," I said. "I can't remember where I heard that, but I like it." She laughed.

"Well, my father's a cabdriver," I said. "Was before he retired, anyway.

He's argumentative enough, though. Well, no, that's not really right . . . he doesn't argue with you so much as he just—does what he thinks the situation calls for, and if you're with him on it, fine, and if you're not, then it's just too bad."

"Are you like him?"

"Well . . . " I laughed. "Nobody's really *like* my father. I think I take after him in some ways, though."

"I think I'd like him then," she said and smiled. We looked at each other, longer than people usually do without speaking.

I started to think I might just like this college thing.

I liked my roommates, too. Remi and Dave. Coming from D.C., I hadn't spent much time around white people before, and it took some getting used to. They talked differently from the guys I'd grown up with, and about different things—Elvis Costello instead of Chuck Brown and the Soul Searchers, *My Dinner With Andre* instead of *Cooley High*. But the same things made them happy, the same things annoyed them, they had the same moods. Dave had a good, solid relationship that year with a girl named Nancy, and sometimes Remi longed to be Dave. Remi was always going out with somebody new, and once in a while, when Dave commented on it, I could hear the envy in his lazy Southern voice. After a while I stopped thinking of the two of them as my white roommates and thought of them as just my roommates, and then, gradually, as my friends.

The three of us used to triple-date sometimes. I'd bring Roxie, Dave would bring Nancy, and Remi would drag along whoever he was going out with that week. One night we all went to Lorenzo's, a little pizza place; it sort of marked the border between the campus and the town and was one of the few places where both crowds hung out. The night we went it was full of high school kids, so the six of us squeezed around a square table meant for four and ate greasy pepperoni and mushroom pizza.

"It doesn't get any better than this," Remi said, quoting a TV commercial. We all laughed.

Remi's date that night was an extremely thin, red-haired girl named Michele. She said, "I hate to think what all this grease is gonna do inside my stomach."

I smiled and said, "I figure it'll do like that jar of bacon grease my mother keeps beside the stove. Form a nice, thick, white layer on top, and . . ."

Michele looked shocked. I figured she was going to say, "Stop, you're grossing me out," but she said, "Your mother keeps a jar of bacon grease beside the stove?"

"Yeah," I said.

"Mine does, too," Roxie said.

Michele said, "Why?"

"To cook with," I said.

"You're *kidding.*"

"Nope."

Michele sort of shuddered. Roxie and I glanced at each other knowingly.

Remi said, "This some kind of racial thing?" Remi, Dave, and I looked at each other and smiled, because we were used to this kind of talk. Roxie, Nancy, and Michele looked down at the food; they weren't.

After enough time had passed, Nancy asked me, "How's the econ going?" I made a face. It was a class I was struggling with.

Michele said, "You're taking economics?"

"I'm taking it up the butt," I said. Dave almost spit out his pizza. Everybody laughed.

"You're braver than I am," Michele told me.

We stayed a pretty long time, talking and laughing and listening to music on Lorenzo's jukebox. We finished off two pizzas and two pitchers of beer, and the bill, when we finally asked for it, came to around thirty dollars.

"Comes out to six bucks a head, with the tip," Dave said. He, Remi, Michele, and Nancy threw money to the middle of the table. I turned to Roxie and said, "All I have is ten bucks. Do you have anything?"

Roxie reached into her jacket pocket. I noticed Michele looking at Roxie, then at me.

Freshman year seemed to go by very fast. I was on a scholarship then, but I didn't have any other money coming in; sometime around March my savings from the previous summer's job dried up.

"You mind if we go Dutch again tonight?" I asked Roxie. I was in her room, sitting on her bed.

She sat down and sighed. "This is the third Dutch treat this week," she said. "I think you're taking me for granted."

"Look, I'm sorry. My last name's not Rockefeller, okay? It's not that I don't want to take you out, I just can't afford to now."

"Or ever. Why don't you get a campus job, or something?"

"Come on. I'm having a rough enough time with my classes now," I said. "Anyway . . . what's wrong with going Dutch? Remi and Dave do it all the time. *Everybody* does."

"So you're taking your cues from the white boys now?"

I didn't know what to say to that, so I didn't say anything. "Listen," I finally said. "If I have to pay for both of us tonight, we can't go. It's that simple. To tell you the truth, I don't feel much like it now, anyway."

"Fine," she said.

And that was that.

When I left her room I walked around campus for a while because I was too mad to do much else. Soon my anger gave way to hunger. I had missed dinner at the dining hall, so I walked to Lorenzo's, grabbed a small pizza, and took if back to my room.

Remi and Dave were stretched out on their beds listening to The Police when I walked in. I said, "Hello, gentlemen," and fell sideways onto my bed. Remi and Dave sat up and looked at each other, then at me.

Remi said, "That was one fast date."

"Sure nuff," I said, opening my box of pizza.

"What happened?"

"I only had fifteen bucks. I asked if we could go Dutch. She got mad. I got mad. Here I am." I took a bite of pizza.

"You're kidding," Dave said.

"Do you see me sittin' here eating this pepperoni and grease pizza? No, I'm not kidding."

Dave said, "What century was *she* born in?"

"You want *my* advice," Remi said, "I'd let her alone for a while."

"Whatever," I said. "If you don't mind, I'd rather not talk about it right now."

"No prob," Remi said, and he and Dave stood up. "We were leaving anyway. We've declared this 'I'm Sick to Death of Being a Student' night. We're going to the game room now, and then later a bunch of us are gonna meet at the disco. You oughtta come." He smiled. "Only costs seventy-five *cents* to get in the *disco*. Seriously, come. Around ten."

"Yeah, maybe," I said. Remi clapped me on the shoulder, and he and Dave left.

I finished my pizza, then just lay back on my bed with my hands clasped behind my head. I stayed like that for the longest time, thinking about things and looking around the room. I stared at the Rolling Stones poster above Remi's bed; at the maps over Dave's bed, those maps of Spain and France and Australia and Russia he loved so much; at the globe on my desk, the one my father had given me just before I left for school ("Take this with you so you don't forget where D.C. is," he'd told me). When I first arrived on campus and got set up in my room, I could spend a lot of time doing exactly what I was doing now, just sitting and looking around the walls. I would think about how I was on my own, and the feeling that gave me was enough to entertain me for the evening. I would wish some of my high school classmates could see me. But with the passing of the months, my room had lost its power to charm me. All I felt now, lying on my bed and staring at the walls, was boredom.

"What the hell, I'll go to the disco." I said, to no one in particular.

The disco was in a big room in the basement of the student union building. I walked down the hall, toward the pounding, wall-shaking music, and gave my ID to the guy at the door. He stamped my hand, and I went in. It was a good twenty degrees hotter in there. The place was pretty full; I looked out at all the white people—some of them dancing to the rhythm, some of them hopelessly and happily off. I made my way to the edge of the dance floor to look for Remi and Dave. Just about then the strobe light started flashing, and I had to squint and look down to keep my balance.

I felt a hand hit my shoulder. I looked up, and it was Dave. "Hey, guy!" he shouted. "Glad you made it!"

He grabbed my arm and pulled me onto the floor, where Remi and a few other guys and girls were dancing sort of in a circle. I joined in. After a while, I started to really enjoy myself. The D. J. played The Police, The Cars, and The Knack, and also Rick James, songs from Michael Jackson's "Off the Wall" album, and some old Motown. We made periodic trips to the bar, soaked with sweat, and bought cups of beer, which we drank like water. Then we'd head back out to the dance floor.

At one point I felt someone tap me on the back. I turned around, and Dave and Remi were waving good–bye. "I think we've had it," Dave shouted. "You gonna stay a while?"

"I think so," I shouted back.

There was no such thing as partners here; it was a kind of musical free-for-all. I'd dance half a song in front of one person, then she'd wander off, or I'd wander off, and I'd finish the song with someone else—or no one. It didn't seem to matter. That evening, almost nothing did.

I stumbled out of there at about two o'clock. I found myself walking across the Bowl with a blond girl named Joanne, whose dorm was in the same general direction as mine.

"*God*, I needed that," I told Joanne. "I might just make it through the rest of the week now."

"This place getting you down?" she said.

"Ah, this place and a few other things," I said. "My girlfriend's driving me bonkers. She lives to drive me bonkers, I think." All those beers were talking now.

"How does she drive you bonkers?" Joanne asked. We were passing the library, and under its floodlights, which stayed on all night. I got my first good look at her—at her high, sculpted cheekbones, her nearly pointed nose, the tuft of blond hair that hung down in front and met her eyebrows.

"Oh, man," I said, "it'd take me an hour to tell you. The latest thing is, I can't afford to take her out anywhere 'cuz I'm broke, and she's mad about it. I have to pay for everything, even though I don't have a dime to my name."

She said, "Sounds like you need to either win the lottery or get a new girlfriend."

"I think I have equal shots at both."

"I wouldn't say *that*. You've got about a one-in-a-million shot at the lottery. There are six hundred women on campus. If I were you, I'd save my dollar," she said, smiling.

I remember, then, my lips pressing together to form the word "But," and I remember my mouth expelling the necessary amount of air. No word came out, though.

We reached the walkway that led up to her dorm. We stopped and faced each other. She said, "Well, thanks for walking me."

"No problem," I said.

I can describe, but not explain, the moment that followed. It was full of knowledge of what was going to happen, like that half-second between seeing the other car coming and smashing into it. And it was almost that frightening: I was afraid of seeing Roxie after tonight, and afraid, although I wasn't sure why, of crossing this kind of racial line. Afraid—but not ashamed. The certainty that I would go through with it seemed to take it out of my hands, somehow. I stepped toward Joanne feeling scared, excited, and, through it all, blameless.

. . . and after minutes—ten? twenty?—of standing there and exploring each other's mouths with our tongues, after her saying, "I have to get up in the morning," and smiling at me over her shoulder as she went inside, I walked away.

I walked past my own dorm, because I knew I wouldn't be able to sleep, and went several more blocks until I came to the duck pond. I stood at the edge, tossing in pebbles and listening to the ducks quietly talking to each other. Now it started. With Joanne safely back in her room, my cloud of innocence was dissipating; the words *what did I just do?* kept repeating in my mind.

I tossed in a pebble and watched the ripples widen. I watched as they jostled the ducks, and felt bad about disturbing their peace. I wanted to make it up to them, but I didn't have the slightest idea how.

The next morning I woke up and decided that nothing had happened, or at least I would act as if nothing had. As I stood in the shower, hot water cascading over me, it seemed perfectly clear. Nothing had happened. It was that simple.

And it seemed that simple through most of the day. I went to breakfast, and the line servers wore their usual groggy expressions under their white caps. Nothing was different. My classes went as they always did; none of my professors stared at me accusingly. Business as usual.

I got to the dining hall for dinner at six. I got a plate of spinach-something-or-other, then squeezed my way through the mob toward the soda fountain. I was standing in front of it, trying to decide between Coke and Dr Pepper, when someone to my right said, "Hi there." It was Joanne. She looked a little different from the night before; her hair was tied back, and she looked a lot more put-together than you do after thrashing around on a dance floor.

"Uh. Hi," I said.

She smiled and said, "Are you eating with anyone?"

I said, "Um . . ." I looked away, scanning all the faces for Remi or Dave. They weren't anywhere. Joanne didn't know that, though. I turned back to her—looking not in her face, exactly, but toward it—and said, "Yeah. "

Before she could respond I was gone, off to find as remote a table as I could, and feeling for all the world like somebody else.

The next day I was walking across the Bowl when I saw her coming toward me. When we were about ten feet apart, our eyes met for the briefest of moments, and then we each looked away. We walked by each other without a word or a glance—which set the tone of our relationship for the rest of freshman year.

Meanwhile, I kept things hobbling along with Roxie. Gradually, without any spoken agreement, things between the two of us became kind of . . . formal. When we saw each other, it was because we had made plans beforehand; we didn't just drop by each other's rooms anymore. I would call her Thursday night about going out on Friday, and when we'd agreed on a time and place, we'd hang up. And it wouldn't cross my mind—or hers either, I don't think—to talk in between making the date and the date itself.

I remember, for some reason, a conversation we had one Friday night. We had just been to see *To Have and Have Not* (in the theater that doubled as the chemistry lab), and I was walking her back to her dorm.

"I'm starting to see one theme over and over again in Bogie's movies," I said. "He's always the guy who swears he's just going to look out for himself, and then he ends up fighting for truth, justice, the American way, and all that other stuff. It was the same thing in *Casablanca*, *Key Largo*, *The African*—"

"He wouldn't make it as a leading man today, I'll tell you that," Roxie said.

"Huh?"

"You see how skinny he was? I hear he wasn't but five foot seven, too. He couldn't stand up against some of these muscle-bound men we've got in the movies today. "

I was quiet for a second. Then I said, "No. Guess not."

We were passing the rear of the library. Across the street were faculty houses. My English professor, Mr. Graham, lived in one of them. The one with the flag on the outside, I thought. It was a clear night; I could see the moon just over one of the houses. It was full and huge and yellow as mustard.

"You ever see any of those movies?" I said. "*Key Largo*, or *The African Queen?*"

"Which one is *The African Queen?*"

"The one with Katharine Hepburn—"

"I love Katharine Hepburn. I saw her in *The Philadelphia Story.* Her and Cary Grant. I *love* Cary Grant."

"I like him, too," I said, and I went back to looking at the moon.

The last day of freshman year around three in the afternoon I was in my room, alone. That morning Remi and I had hugged Dave good-bye and watched him and his family drive off for North Carolina. Around two o'clock I said good-bye to Remi, who was heading back to Brooklyn for the summer. I was packing the last of my junk into a cardboard box on my bed; my father would be there to pick me up in a couple of hours or so. As I tossed in various things—my globe, my desk lamp, a football—I looked around the room. Remi's posters and Dave's maps were gone; the only traces of them were the marks from the tape that had held them up. I couldn't turn on Dave's stereo because it was in the trunk of his father's car, on its way to North Carolina. I had never, I thought, seen a room look as empty as this.

Right about then there was a tap on the door, and Roxie walked in. I remember what she was wearing: white shorts and sneakers and a sky-blue terry-cloth shirt. She looked like summer itself, I thought. "Hi," I said.

"Hi there," she said. "How's it coming?"

"I've about got it under control," I said. "This is the last of it, really. Everything else can go in the car like it is." I looked around the walls again, and said, "Have you ever seen a room look more deserted than this?"

"Looks pretty bare," she said. She sat down on the edge of the mattress; the box I was loading dipped to one side.

I said, "What time are your folks coming?"

"In about three hours."

"You all packed?"

"Just about. I've got a little more to do. I wanted to come over and see you, though."

I said, "Well . . ." and couldn't think what else to say. I put something else in the box, letting it fall more noisily than it had to so it could fill up some of the silence. I finally said, "Did I give you my number at home?"

"Yeah. You have mine, right?"

"Yeah."

She looked around at all my junk, packed in boxes and bags, sitting in heaps on the floor. "Had some god times this year," she said, nodding, still looking at the junk.

"Yeah," I said. I stepped from behind my box and walked over to where she was sitting. I stood in front of her, looking down, my thumbs hooked into the pockets of my jeans. "Had some good times," I said.

She stood up then and put her arms around me, and we hugged for a while. Then we looked at each other and kissed. It was a little more than friendly, but not really passionate; we seemed almost to be saying something to each other through that kiss, something like, "No hard feelings." When it was over she rubbed my chest, then patted it, then started moving away, toward the door. She whispered " 'Bye," moved her fingers up and down in a kind of wave, and was gone.

I had wondered how Roxie and I were going to see out the year, and now I guessed I knew. There had been no hideous breakup; we'd made no attempt to smooth out the rough areas. In the end the relationship, all by itself, just dwindled down to nothing.

It felt like a week and a half before I was back on campus again. I roomed with Remi again; we had planned on it being the three of us, but sometime in July Dave's father had gotten pretty sick, and he couldn't come back this semester.

The day before classes started, I was walking across the Bowl when I saw Joanne coming toward me. As a reflex I started to go into my "ignore" mode—and just think hard about something else until we had passed each other. But then something occurred to me. I looked back at what happened between us, and now, somehow, I seemed to be looking at it from a great distance. We had necked outside her dorm, once, six months ago. So what? Surely, there must have been some sort of statute of limitations regarding these things, and if there was, it must have been in effect by now. As we got closer, I studied her. She was looking elsewhere, and seemed to be thinking about something I couldn't even guess at (she was in *her* ignore mode now). When we were about four feet apart, I stepped directly in her path. I said, very loudly, "Hi."

She looked startled. But then she saw my expression—my lips were pressed together tightly, in a kind of suppressed smile—and she developed a similar one. With a mock seriousness in my voice, I said, "And where . . . are you going?"

"To . . . the . . . bookstore," she said, imitating me.

"May . . . I . . . accompany you?"

"Why . . . yes . . . you may."

We walked back across the Bowl, around the lecture hall, and through Central Square to the campus bookstore. We talked on the way about our summers. She had spent most of hers in Boston, helping her father add a new room to the house. I had worked delivering packages for an office supply store—which, I told Joanne, was about as exciting as it sounded.

"At least you got to be outside," she said.

"Good point."

In the bookstore she had to get all the books she needed for her classes. The store had carts, miniature versions of grocery store carts, for this purpose. I pulled one out and pushed it behind Joanne while she pulled books from the shelves. "Aagh," I said, after she had pulled out a book on macroeconomics and put it in the cart.

She smiled. "You don't like econ? I think it's fun."

"Fun," I said. "One day when I was six years old, I was running down the street, and I slipped and fell. Landed on my face, and knocked out both my front teeth. *That* was more fun than taking economics."

Joanne made a face and said, "You're weird."

When she paid for the books the cashier put them in a brown grocery store bag, and we left. I tried to carry the bag for her, but she insisted on doing it herself. We crossed the street and walked back through Central Square, past the trees and squirrels and stone benches, without talking much. I was working out in my mind how to apologize for last year. The problem now was that it seemed so long ago and trivial, and by bringing it up I would seem to be making a big deal over nothing, yet it didn't seem quite right to pretend that *nothing* had happened. Finally I compromised with myself.

"You ever—um—ever get off on the wrong foot with somebody and not quite know how to get on the right one again?"

She looked at me and smile, with her lips together. "Yeah," she said. "I think I know what you're talking about."

Later that day I was sitting on my bed, absentmindedly leafing through *The Norton Anthology of English Literature*, when somebody knocked on the door. "It's open," I said, and a second later Roxie walked in.

"Roxie!" I jumped up off the bed.

"Hel*lo*," she said. "How *are* you?"

We met in the middle of the floor and hugged, then sat down on the bed. She said, "How was your summer?" At first I thought she meant this as an accusation. Our parents' houses were forty-five minutes apart, and we hadn't seen each other once all summer. But she was smiling; I decided it was an innocent question.

"It wasn't bad," I said.

"What did you do?"

"I was—uh—I delivered packages for an office supply store."

"Pret-ty exciting," she said sarcastically.

She had spent June, July, and August, she said, working in a movie theater, which we agreed was about half a notch above my job. Then we talked about what classes we were taking. She said she was looking at an even heavier workload than last year, and I said I was, too.

"So," she said. "What are you doing tonight?"

"Well, I'm kind of busy tonight." Truth was, I was going to the movies with Joanne.

"How about tomorrow night? You want to go have some coffee, or something?"

"Um, yeah," I said, nodding. "Let's do that."

"Okay."

To my surprise, she leaned over and kissed me, and to my disbelief, she stuck her tongue approximately halfway down my throat. Then she stood up, giving me a last peck on the lips, and said, "Talk to you tomorrow." And she left.

For a couple of minutes I just walked around the room—from my bed to my desk to Remi's bed to Remi's desk—with my hand on the back of my head. Then I sat down again. And I decided that if I lived a good long time, if I outlived my children and my children's children, there would still be some things I wouldn't understand.

I picked up Joanne at her room at about seven-thirty. When she opened the door, she looked really great. She wasn't made up or particularly dressed up—she wore beige slacks and a light green plaid top. But she was really . . . pretty. "Hi," she said. "Ready?"

The Strand, Field's second-run movie house, was about a block from the campus bookstore. They were showing *The World According to Garp* that night, which neither of us had seen (although we'd both read it). "The writing in that book is so witty," Joanne said, as we walked diagonally through Central Square. "That's most of what I liked about it. I don't know how they're going to capture that on screen."

"Well," I said, "if I know Robin Williams, he can bring it off. As much as it can be brought off, anyway."

"I hope so."

When we were half a block away, I saw someone standing under the marquee. I realized then that the thing I'd been afraid of all day, the thing I'd protected myself against last year, was about to happen.

I don't know why Roxie was standing under the marquee—she was waiting for one of her friends, I guess. "Hi," I said to her, as Joanne and I walked up to the theater; it wasn't quite what I thought I should say, but then I didn't know quite what I thought I should say.

"Hi," she said, looking from one of us to the other.

While Joanne paid for her ticket, Roxie and I just looked at each other. Her expression was flat and almost unreadable, except for a slight narrowing of her eyes, which made all the difference; it seemed to be saying, "Uh-huh. I've got your number now."

I bought my ticket, and Joanne and I walked in.

Roxie and I didn't get together for coffee the next night. I didn't hear from her, and I didn't call. To tell the truth, we hardly ever spoke to each other again. We passed each other on campus, when we couldn't avoid it. Sometimes she looked at me, other times she didn't; but each time, whether we made eye contact or not, her presence made me feel I was being accused of something.

Joanne and I sat on a half-full bus, heading away from the college and into the town of Field itself. We weren't talking, not for the moment, because we'd just reached the point where we were comfortable enough not to talk if we didn't feel like it. We held hands, and she looked out the window, and I looked around the bus. My eyes met the eyes of a white boy, maybe fifteen; he stared at me until he realized I wasn't going to look away, and then *he* looked away. At the front of the bus, two black girls in seats that faced sideways were talking to each other and looking at me. I couldn't hear what they were saying, I could only see their smiles, which weren't really smiles at all.

This wasn't my first trip to town, or Joanne's (we were sophomores now). But it was our first trip together, and our first this school year. We needed a break from campus; we wanted to visit "the real world" for a while, or at least get as close to it as we could. So we rode quietly as the trees and small houses rolled past, and soon there we were in—"Don't blink, or you'll miss it," went the stale joke—downtown Field.

"Where do you want to go first?" Joanne asked me, just as we'd gotten off the bus.

I looked up and down the block. There was a Woolworth's, and beside that a card shop, and beside that a record store, and beside that a pizza joint. Across the street were a post office and a bank.

"Let's go to Woolworth's."

We reached for each other's hand and went down the sidewalk. Now I played a different game from the one on the bus. There I had wanted to see how much direct confrontation I could get away with; here, walking down Main Street, I wanted to see how much I could ignore people. I felt the eyes of the white people, and the few black people, on us; from the corner of my eye I saw their heads turn. But I didn't look at them, and I didn't look at them in a way that must've been obvious.

Looking straight ahead, Joanne said, "I know what *these* people are gonna talk about at dinner tonight." She meant it to sound flip, I could tell. And it did, but only around the edges. Something else was at its center—a kind of little girl's confusion. I squeezed her hand, and she leaned her head toward my shoulder.

We went into Woolworth's. We walked up and down the junk-filled aisles and made fun of everything. I picked up a fake-wood desk lamp; the glue holding the base to the rest of it was showing, and we giggled at that. We giggled at the orange and pea-colored 85 percent polyester clothes that were on sale; at the crushed-velvet paintings of cats and cowboys and Elvis Presley; at everything. The fat white security guard sitting in the corner kept his eyes on us. We giggled at him, too.

When we got tired of that, we went to the pizza joint for lunch. The only person in there, besides us, was the stocky, sweating Italian man behind the counter. He smiled at us when we came in. We smiled back. For a moment I wanted to hug him.

We ate at a table by the window so we could look at the "Pennsylvanians," as Joanne liked to call them. She said, "I talked to my mom last night."

"Oh, yeah?"

"Yeah. I told her I started seeing this great new guy . . ."

"Well, now. Did you tell her what this great new guy looks like?"

"I sure did."

"What did she say?"

"Well, she seemed a little surprised. She said it didn't matter to her, though. She asked me if you were nice, and I said you were. Then she asked me what you were majoring in, and I told her you were undecided, but leaning toward English. She liked that. She was an English major."

"You're quite lucky," I said.

"I know. They're great. So have you told your parents about me yet?"

"Not yet. I think I'm gonna wait until I go home for break."

"Is it gonna be that big a deal?"

"To tell you the truth, I don't know. In nineteen years the topic never came up once."

"So . . . if it matters to them, will it matter to you?"

I made a show out of thinking about this. I looked at the ceiling, my brows knitted; I looked at the floor and scratched my head. Finally I looked her in the eye and said, "Nope."

This delighted her, and she laughed.

After we left the pizza place, Joanne and I messed around in a record store for a while, then went to catch the bus back to campus. We stood under one of those sheltered, Plexiglas bus stops across the street from the Field Savings Bank. Two white people were waiting with us—a middle-aged man in a green polyester leisure suit with white stitches, and a girl who didn't look older than fifteen.

I looked at Joanne. "Quite a town," I said quietly.

"Quite a town," she said.

I felt the urge to kiss her then, but held back. Then I thought about it, and I went ahead and did it.

A group of white boys, five or six of them, about high school age, came down the street. They were talking among themselves, and as they passed the bus stop I heard the words "wrong color." Joanne's eyes met mine for one brief, alarmed moment. Then I just watched, in silence, as the boys continued down the street. Finally I shouted, "What?!"

One of the boys looked back; the group kept walking.

"What? What!" I yelled, until Joanne took hold of my arm.

During the bus ride back to campus, it rained. First there was a drop here and there on the windows, and then the sky opened up completely, suddenly, the way it does on bad TV sitcoms. Soon the black road was shiny, and the tires of the cars and trucks were reflected in its surface like the edges of some adjacent, upside-down universe. I felt like going to that universe. Maybe there, I thought, Joanne and I could walk around together without being stared at or even noticed by anybody. But I knew it wouldn't work. I knew if I tried to go there, tried to dive below the surface, I'd never get past the hard, hard street.

1990

Biographical Notes on Authors

Alice Adams was the author of ten novels, five collections of stories, and a travel book about Mexico. Her novel *Families and Survivors* was nominated for the 1975 National Book Critics Circle Award, and several of her stories have been chosen for *Best American Short Stories* and the *O. Henry Awards* collections. Her work has appeared in the *Atlantic Monthly*, *Mademoiselle*, *McCall's*, the *New Yorker*, *Paris Review*, *Redbook*, *Shenandoah*, the *Virginia Quarterly Review*, and *Vogue*. The recipient of both National Endowment for the Arts and Guggenheim fellowships, she taught at the University of California at Davis, the University of California at Berkeley, and Stanford University. Born in 1926 in Fredericksburg, Virginia, she lived in California until her death in 1999.

Toni Cade Bambara was a civil rights activist, a professor of English and of African American studies, an editor of anthologies of African American literature, and an award-winning writer. She was the author of two collections of stories, *Gorilla, My Love* and *The Sea Birds Are Still Alive*, and nine screenplays, including one based on Toni Morrison's novel *Tar Baby* and one on the life of Zora Neale Hurston. She wrote four novels, *Raymond's Run; If Blessing Comes; The Salt Eaters*, which won the 1981 American Book Award; and *Those Bones Are Not My Child*, which was published posthumously in 1999. Her work appeared in *Audience*, *Black Works*, *Liberator*, the *Massachusetts Review*, *Negro Digest*, *Prairie Schooner*, *Redbook*, *Umbra*, and *Onyx*. Three of her stories, "Gorilla, My Love," "Medley," and "Witchbird," have been adapted for film. Born in 1939 in New York City, she also lived in Atlanta and Philadelphia. She died in 1995.

Ellen Douglas is the pen name of Josephine Haxton. Her first short story, "On the Lake," was included in the 1961 *O. Henry Awards* collection, and her first novel, *A Family's Affairs*, won the 1961 Houghton Mifflin Fellowship. She is the author of five other novels: *Where the Dreams Cross; Apostles of Light*, which was a finalist for the National Book Award; *The Rock Cried Out; A Lifetime Burning;* and *Can't Quit You, Baby*. Her other publications include a collection of short fiction, *Black Cloud, White Cloud;* a collection of classic fairy tales retold, *The Magic Carpet;* and a nonfiction collection, *Truth: Four Stories I Am Finally Old Enough to Tell*. In 1989 she received the fiction award from the Fellowship of Southern Writers. She has written for *Esquire*,

Harper's, the *New Republic*, the *New York Times Book Review*, and the *New Yorker*. She was writer-in-residence at Northeast Louisiana University and the University of Mississippi, and visiting professor at Hollins College and the University of Virginia. Born in 1921 in Natchez, Mississippi, she grew up in small towns in Mississippi, Arkansas, and Louisiana. She now lives in Jackson, where she is Welty Professor at Millsaps College.

Anthony Grooms is a poet, fiction writer, arts administrator, and teacher. He is the author of *Ice Poems* and *Trouble No More*, a collection of stories that won the 1996 Lillian Smith Award for Fiction. His work has appeared in the *African American Review, Callaloo, Catalyst*, and the *George Washington Review*. He has taught creative writing and American literature at Macon College, Clark Atlanta University, the University of Georgia, Spelman College, and Morehouse College. Currently he is a professor at Kennesaw State College. Born in 1955 in Charlottesville, Virginia, he now lives in Atlanta, Georgia.

Randall Kenan began his career as an editor at Knopf. When his novel, *Visitation of Spirits*, was published in 1989, he turned his full attention to writing and the teaching of writing. He has published a biography of James Baldwin; a travel narrative, *Walking on Water: Travels through Black America*; and a collection of short stories, *Let the Dead Bury the Dead*, which was nominated for the 1992 National Book Critics Circle Award. He has taught at Sarah Lawrence College, Vassar College, Columbia University, Duke University, the University of North Carolina at Chapel Hill, the University of Mississippi, and the University of Memphis. Born in 1963 in Brooklyn, New York, he grew up in North Carolina.

Reginald McKnight is the author of a novel, *I Get on the Bus*, and three collections of stories: *The Kind of Light That Shines on Texas; White Boys*; and *Moustapha's Eclipse*, which won the 1989 Ernest Hemingway Foundation Award from PEN. His work has appeared in *Black American Literature Forum*, the *Kenyon Review, Leviathan*, the *Massachusetts Review, Players*, and *Prairie Schooner*, and his story, "The Kind of Light That Shines on Texas," was included in the 1989 *O. Henry Awards* collection. Born in 1956 in Fuerstenteldbruek, Germany, he grew up in California, Colorado, Texas, Alabama, and Louisiana. He now lives in Pittsburgh, Pennsylvania, where he teaches creative writing at the University of Pittsburgh.

James Alan McPherson has won numerous awards and grants for his writing, including a Guggenheim fellowship and a MacArthur fellowship. After the publication of his first story collection, *Hue and Cry*, he received a National Institute of Arts and Letters Award, and his second collection, *Elbow Room*, won the 1978 Pulitzer Prize. A contributor to the *Atlantic Monthly, Esquire, New York Times Magazine, Playboy, Reader's Digest*, and *Callaloo*, his essays have been chosen for several of the *Best American Essays* collections. His most recent works are a memoir, *Crabcakes*, and a collection of essays, *A Region Not Home: Reflections from Exile*. He has taught writing at the University of California at Santa Cruz, Morgan State University, and the University of Virginia. Born in 1943 in Savannah, Georgia, he now lives in Iowa City, where he is a professor of creative writing at the University of Iowa.

David Means is the author of two collections of stories, *A Quick Kiss of Redemption* and *The Gesture Hunter*. His short fiction has appeared in *Harper's*, the *Paris Review*, and *The Pushcart Prize Stories 2000*. Born in Kalamazoo, Michigan, he now lives in Upper Nyack, New York.

Alyce Miller has won awards for both her writing and her teaching. She is the author of *Stopping for Green Lights* and *The Nature of Longing*, a collection of stories that won the Flannery O'Connor Award for Short Fiction. Her stories have appeared in *Glimmer Train*, the *Kenyon Review*, *Los Angeles Times Magazine*, the *New England Review*, *Prairie Schooner*, the *Southern Review*, *Story*, and *Witness*. She has also published poetry and personal essays. Born in Switzerland, she was raised in Michigan and Ohio but spent most of her adult life in San Francisco. She now lives in Sonoma County, California, and in Bloomington, Indiana, where she is a professor of English and creative writing at Indiana University.

Toni Morrison has won most of the major awards for literature, including the 1977 National Book Critics Circle Award and the American Academy and Institute of Arts and Letters Award for her novel *Song of Solomon*, the 1988 Pulitzer Prize for *Beloved*, the 1993 Nobel Prize, and the 1996 National Book Foundation Medal for Distinguished Contribution to American Letters. She is the editor of three books and the author of seven novels as well as numerous essays and reviews. She was a senior editor at Random House for twenty years and a professor at Texas Southern University in Houston, Howard University, the State University of New York at Purchase, and the State University of New York at Albany. Currently she is Robert F. Goheen Professor of the Humanities at Princeton University. Her book of literary criticism, *Playing in the Dark: Whiteness and the Literary Imagination*, came out of her 1990 Massey Lectures at Harvard University. Born in 1931 in Lorain, Ohio, Toni Morrison now lives in New York.

Reynolds Price is a novelist, short story writer, essayist, playwright, poet, songwriter (with James Taylor), and professor. His writing has earned him numerous awards and grants, including a Guggenheim fellowship, a National Endowment for the Arts fellowship, and a National Institute of Arts and Letters Award. His first novel, *A Long and Happy Life*, won the William Faulkner Foundation Award; *The Surface of the Earth* won the 1976 Lillian Smith Award for Fiction; and *Kate Vaiden* won the 1986 National

Book Critics Circle Award for Fiction. In 1994 he was a finalist for the Pulitzer Prize in fiction for his *Collected Stories*, and he published *A Whole New Life*, a narrative detailing the fight for his life against cancer of the spine. Price has been a writer in residence at the University of North Carolina at Chapel Hill, the University of Kansas, the University of North Carolina at Greensboro, and Washington and Lee University. He has contributed poetry, reviews, and articles to numerous magazines and newspapers, including *Harper's*, the *Saturday Review*, *Time*, and the *Washington Post*. Born in 1933 in Macon, North Carolina, he now lives in Durham, North Carolina, where he is James B. Duke Professor of English at Duke University.

Frances Sherwood is the author of a collection of stories, *Everything You've Heard Is True*, and two novels, *Green* and *Vindication*, the latter a fictionalized biography of Mary Wollstonecraft. Her stories have appeared in two O. Henry Awards collections. The recipient of a National Endowment for the Arts fellowship, she has contributed short stories to many periodicals, including *California Quarterly*, the *Cream City Review*, the *Greensboro Review*, *Kansas Quarterly*, *Playgirl*, the *Seattle Review*, *Sequoia*, and the *Sonora Review*. Born in 1940 in Washington, D.C., she now lives in South Bend, Indiana, where she is a professor of creative writing and journalism at Indiana University at South Bend.

Elizabeth Spencer has won several O. Henry awards for her short stories, as well as a medal from the American Academy and Institute for Arts and Letters. Her novel *This Crooked Way* received an award from the National Institute of Arts and Letters, and her novel *The Voice at the Back Door* received an award from the American Academy of Arts and Letters. The recipient of many other awards as well as Guggenheim and National Endowment for the Arts fellowships, she has published stories in the *Atlantic Monthly*, the *New Yorker*, *Redbook*, *Southern Review*, and *Texas Quarterly*. Her novella, *The Light in the Piazza*, was made into a film. She has taught creative writing at Concordia University in Montreal and at the University of North Carolina at Chapel Hill. Born in 1921 in Carrollton, Mississippi, she has lived in Italy and Canada, but she now makes her home in Chapel Hill, North Carolina.

Ekwueme Michael Thelwell was director of the Washington, D.C., office of the Student Nonviolent Coordinating Committee in the early 1960s, and his 1987 collection of essays, *Duties, Pleasures, and Conflicts*, is an overview of the struggle for civil rights. His writing career was launched when he won first prize in a 1967 *Story* magazine contest for his story "The Organizer" and a 1968 National Foundation of the Arts and Humanities award for his essay "Notes from the Delta." He is the author of several film scripts and a novel, *The Harder They Come*, which was inspired by the Jamaican film of the same title. His essays and stories have appeared in numerous anthologies and periodicals, including *Black Scholar*, the *Massachusetts Review*, *Motive*, *Negro Digest*, *Spectrum*, *Short Story International*, and *Story*. Born in 1939 in Ulster Spring, Jamaica, he moved to the United States to attend Howard University. He now lives in Pelham, Massachusetts, where he teaches Afro-American Studies and English at the University of Massachusetts at Amherst.

Clifford Thompson has published essays, reviews, and short stories in the *Iowa Review*, the *Threepenny Review*, *Commonweal*, *Emerge*, *Scholastic Voice*, the *Brownstone Review*, *Cineaste*, and *Hardboiled*. He is the editor of *Current Biography* and other biographical titles published by the H. W. Wilson Company. Born in 1963 in Washington, D.C., he lives in Brooklyn, New York.

Alice Walker is a writer and an activist for both the civil rights movement and the women's movement. She is the author of six novels and numerous collections of poetry, essays, and stories. Her novel *The Color Purple*, which won both the Pulitzer Prize and the American Book Award in 1983, was made into a feature film directed by Steven Spielberg. Her stories have been selected for *Best American Short Stories* and *O. Henry Awards* collections. Her work has been widely anthologized, and she has contributed to numerous periodicals, including *Black World*, *Canadian Dimension*, *Denver Quarterly*, *Essence*, *Freedom Ways*, *Harper's*, *Ms.*, *Negro Digest*, the *New York Times*, and *Southern Voices*. Her concern with the issue of female genital mutilation led to *Warrior Masks*, which is both a documentary film and a book coauthored with film director Pratibha Parmar. She is the recipient of fellowships from the Guggenheim Foundation, the National Endowment for the Humanities, and the MacDowell Colony, and she has won many other awards, including the Lillian Smith Award and the American Academy and Institute of Arts and Letters Award. She has taught at Jackson State College, Wellesley College, the University of Massachusetts at Boston, the University of California at Berkeley, and Brandeis University. Born in 1944 in Eatonton, Georgia, she now lives in San Francisco, California.

Joan Williams coauthored the teleplay *The Graduation Dress* with William Faulkner in 1960. Since then she has published short stories in the *Atlantic Monthly*, *Esquire*, *Mademoiselle*, the *Saturday Evening Post*, and *Virginia Quarterly Review*. She is the author of a collection of stories, *Pariah and Other Stories*, and five novels, *The Morning and the Evening*, *Old Powder Man*, *The Wintering*, *Country Woman*, and *Pay the Piper*. Born in 1928 in Memphis, Tennessee, she lived there until recently moving to Charlottesville, Virginia.

John A. Williams has won awards for both his writing and his teaching. He began his writing career as a journalist, working as European correspondent for *Ebony* and *Jet* and later as African correspondent for *Newsweek*. In 1967 his novel *The Man Who Cried I Am* brought him international attention; in

1983 his novel *!Click Song* earned him the American Book Award from the Before Columbus Foundation. He has written twelve novels, eight books of nonfiction, several scripts for television and film, and a book of poetry, *Safari West*. He has edited anthologies of literature as well as contributed to them. His work has also appeared in *Ebony, Essence, Emerge, Holiday, Negro Digest, New York, Saturday Review,* and *Yardbird*. Born in 1925 in Jackson, Mississippi, he grew up in Syracuse, New York. He is retired Paul Robeson Professor of English at Rutgers University, and he now lives in Teaneck, New Jersey.

Permissions